CRONATION

A NOVEL

BY

PAT B. ALLEN

ISBN

Print: 978-0-9971257-1-9

Ebook: 978-0-9971257-0-2

Excerpt from "Coming In from the Cold" from LIVING BY THE WORD: Selected Writings 1973-1987 by Alice Walker. Copyright © 1986 by Alice Walker. Reprinted by permission of Houghton Mifflin Harcourt Publishing Company. All rights reserved.

Published in the United States by

Blue Jay Ink, 451 A East Ojai Ave. Ojai California 93023

bluejayink.com

Book design by Ojai Digital, David Reeser and Amy Schneider

Cover illustration by Shea Cadrin

Cronation is a work of fiction, and all characters in the story are a product of the author's imagination, any resemblance to actual people, living or dead, is synchronistic. However, many actual historical persons and events are referenced in the work. To learn more about those characters visit http://cronation.org

DEDICATION:

Cronation is dedicated to my mother-in-law, Natalie, a true Crone, who is now assisting the Shift from the Other Side. And to Remez Ner, my grandson, who lights up my life. Together may you help us connect the seen and the unseen realms and complete the circle of transformation to the era of light and joy where all children the world over are sheltered, nurtured and appreciated and allowed to grow up in peace and harmony.

CRONATION

Crone: A woman over forty who seeks to embrace Earth's cycles of life, death, and transformation with the wisdom and compassion of an open heart.

Nation: A group of people united by a common interest.

"And when all of us and all the old ones are hugged up inside this enormous warm room of a world, we must build very quickly, really, or die of a too shallow mutual self-respect, you will see, with me, through the happy spirits of our grandchildren, such joy as the planet has never seen. And until that day, let us grow to understand a paraphrase of another of our brother Marley's songs. Let us understand that to keep alive in us the speech and voices of the ancestors is not only to "lively up" the old spirits through the great gift of memory, but to "lively up" our own selves as well."

-Alice Walker, 1984,

Coming in from the cold: Welcoming the old, funny-talking ancient ones into the warm room of present consciousness, or Natty Dread rides again in LIVING BY THE WORD, Selected Writings, 1973-1987

1

I remember the day like it was yesterday; the lights of Western civilization were flickering wildly, oil was running out, and the USA had entered its "Fall of the Roman Empire" stage. But none of that was real to me as I walked to the train under a Roger Brown sky. I was pumped. Chicago might be cold and clammy gray with cartoon clouds ready to drop the apocalypse on your head at any moment, but I was generating my own sunshine. Maybe my mouth was a little dry and I was wearing glasses instead of contact lenses because my eyes hurt — but, hey, a fiftieth birthday needs a serious celebration — and if your birthday falls on a Wednesday, well, who says the world will still be here on the weekend? Carpe diem and all that.

We celebrated in style: dinner at Spiaggia — the dining room, not the café — with fabulous osso buco, drinks, serious wine. Gina and Marty and Rae, my closest pals since college, went all out. After all, we were celebrating a lot more than my birthday. I was about to crown my stellar rise, the moment of crashing through the glass ceiling of corporate America. I had played the game with the Big Boys and was about to get the brass ring or the gold star or whatever the metaphor of the day was.

Marty had always been skeptical, but she was in the midst of menopause before the rest of us and was wise enough to refuse hormones and that was causing her to wake up a little bit more quickly than the average gal. Rae tried to get Marty to at least use yam cream but no dice. Marty was hard core; she wore overalls. She worked as a video editor for non-profits, still trying to make a difference in old-school, leftist ways after all these years.

Gina ran her family's pizza joint in Elmwood Park and led what seemed to be a normal life with kids and a dog and a husband that ran around with other women once in a while.

Rae was well married and well divorced, as the saying goes. She was on the Board of the Flicker Foundation, a leftover from the days of the first President Winger, "a thousand points of light" and all that. "Flicker you must, but don't combust" was the foundation's message to women. Meaning plan your galas, raise funds for plastic surgery for homely children, or lead the charge for city dog parks with special hours for dogs who weigh less than 15 pounds just, God forbid, don't forget to schedule your facial, and your manicure, and your bikini wax, and don't — under any circumstances, ever — ask menacing questions.

We were unlikely friends in many ways, but since college none of us had missed a birthday, special event, or major personal meltdown of any of our foursome. There was just enough feminist glue to make us stick together without any need to critique each other's choices too harshly. Or at least that's how I saw things that morning.

"Eve, you kick butt, girl!" Rae shouted when I announced how many hours I spent on the Aversmith presentation (270, I kept track). "You show those men what's what."

Marty just rolled her eyes, and Gina pushed the breadbasket in my direction.

"You look too skinny, Eve," she said, a true girlfriend.

So what if I survived on take-out Thai food for a month? I never missed a day at the gym, although the gym wasn't quite the mecca of body restoration it had been in years past when I could stay up all night, eat an execrable pizza and just burn it off on the treadmill the next day. I was retaining water and my knees were acting up but, as soon as I got Aversmith signed, I'd get a week in the Islands and a transfer to L.A. Goodbye, gray skies. I'd give a decent burial to all my houseplants that died of neglect and I'd be off to plan a drought-resistant garden somewhere in the foothills of Santa Monica. I'd trade in the SUV with the snow tires for a teeny little sports car — a hybrid, of course, or maybe all electric. And, point of gender pride, I've done it all without a wife. Once I got to L.A., I'd kick back and lose my pasty complexion. Hey, fifty isn't old — I might even take up surfing, start collecting art. But I'd definitely work from within the company to make things better for women. That was the whole reason we earnest women took these jobs in the 1980s, to make change from within, solidarity with our mothers who'd led the first wave of the women's movement. We learned about the '60s from them. They said the revolution would not be televised, but we knew that if it isn't televised, rolled out on social media platforms, and then dissected there the following day, it didn't really happen. No, we were sensible. Positive change could not come as a riot on the evening news but as a gradual shift of the status quo made by women like us in boardrooms across America, not only not making coffee for the Boss anymore, but being the Boss. A new, enlightened, egalitarian Boss. Something like that.

My mother marched in New York City in the 1969 protest where women allegedly burned their bras. She said it never happened.

"Have you ever set a synthetic fabric on fire? The fumes would have dropped anyone within a hundred feet!"

She named me Eve, after the primordial woman, original Earth Mother, wife of Adam, long before she learned about Lilith. Legend has it that Lilith, Adam's first wife, insisted on equality, wanted to be on top in the bedroom, that sort of thing. Adam couldn't handle it and went whining to God, who obliged with a more cooperative spouse. Some versions of the story have Adam sending back two or three more models until he got a nice little helpmate. Mom was in her sixties and attending a Jewish Renewal conference in the Poconos when she first heard Lilith's tale. She was heartbroken; felt she'd damned me to a life of submission. She even tried to get me to change my name, but, by that time, I was an established professional with printed business cards. She never got over it. On her deathbed a few years ago she was still nagging me about it. After she died, I got a second cat and gave her the name. She's sleek, black, and spooky, a perfect Lilith. In the story, Lilith flees the Garden of Eden in a rage and takes up with a heavy-duty demon named Azazel. I picture him as Eden's own Keith Richards, skull earring and all. They make millions of baby demons that grow up to become stars of reality shows on television. Just kidding. But I had Lilith the cat spayed, just in case.

My father was a good-looking Irishman named O'Malley who left college to work construction. A self-described 'working stiff,' he accused Mom's pals of being Commies.

"These women don't know how great they got it," he used to fume. "If they had more children they wouldn't have time for all the mischief."

I was the apple of O'Malley's eye; he about burst with pride when I graduated from college. He did burst a blood vessel not long after, as a matter of fact, and went to his reward without seeing me join the ranks of the 'new titans of industry,' a phrase he picked up from a Newsweek article on women in business. A life-long union man, he found college classroom discussions less substantial than the ones he'd had growing up at the dining room table and witnessed at his dad's knee in the local tavern. The changes of the '60s and '70s more or less passed O'Malley by. He even served in Vietnam, but he never made a big deal out of it. For all her politics, O'Malley, with his work boots and white tee shirts, his beer belly and Reader's Digest, was the anchor my mother counted on in her forays into higher consciousness and justice for all. She was never the same without him.

But, as I was saying, that was then, at the "End of the World as We Know It," as REM once sang, my last happy moment of delusion, my last second of believing I was in charge of my life, a successful B-school grad (undergrad in Art History, which made me "interesting." Did anyone else in the Chicago office even know who Roger Brown was?). That had come in very handy in the early meetings with Aversmith who fancies himself a contemporary-art connoisseur. By which he means he has a membership to the Museum of Contemporary Art and writes a check when his wife, a board member, twists his arm. I was wishing that morning that my dad was around to see my success, talk about it in the corner bar to his pals. I was still planning to prove to my mother that working within the system was the way to go. They both had agreed (a rare event) that studying Art was a waste of time, hence Art History, where I learned how, in the 1950s, Business became the new engine of the art world. Aversmith's firm socked away a fortune in contemporary art.

"That Warhol in the lobby is better than any blue chip stock, Missy," he'd say every time I met him, as if we were co-conspirators and investing in art was a little bit revolutionary. I asked him once if the firm had any works by women artists.

"For heaven's sake, Eve, women are unreliable. A woman artist decides to have a family, quits painting, becomes a nobody, the investment goes down the drain."

Aversmith was one of the contingent that never did get what all the fuss was about women's rights. The smart ones were just like men in skirts: he respected their abilities, was happy to give them their due. The rest, well, they were another species, the seeing eye dogs of the human race, faithful servants; they did all that important stuff you get your secretary to do, like send flowers and gifts. Women, in the wife, mother, even mistress category, would always be second to a man's first love: work. He firmly believed that wives of wealthy men shouldn't work. They were needed to run the boards of cultural edifices, between manicures and choosing prep schools for the kids, of course. This kind of man, who had briefly seemed challenged by stay-at-home dads and a couple of female Secretaries of State, proved simply to be dormant — like a bad strain of flu growing resistant to antibiotics — until about 2003 or 2004, when he morphed into the CEO from hell, a grandiose, unchecked version that finally confirmed that workaholic and alcoholic were indeed cut from the same cloth. "Just a few bad seeds," that was the party line among the men I worked with. They never imagined that the siren song of greed that so many of their fellow big shots fell for was the last rude gasp of an era staggering to its knees.

In the U.S.A., where (if I rely on my admittedly sketchy recall of my U.S. History course from high school) people fled to escape religious persecution in Europe, the Catholics had by this time allied themselves with the Christian fundamentalists in "focusing on the family" — code for control of the bodies and minds of women — and the Islamic world had decided that choosing the color of her hijab made every day Ladies Day. More freedom than that would be an affront to the Koran. Never mind that the wife of the prophet Mohammed was a successful businesswoman who he regularly consulted on matters of import. Strangely, men of all persuasions banded together across party lines, ideological divides, and even sports team rivalries to reach a critical mass of agreement: Women were the problem. Not the melting polar ice cap, not air pollution or depleted fisheries, not gangs or drugs or guns or corrupt politicians and CEOs. Nope, deep down the whole damn thing went back to women. It was subtle at first. Women like me couldn't really see it. I mean, I worked every day with corporate guys, the old-school, classic enemy of my mother's generation. They respected me. We were on equal terms, no doubt about it.

The masses of women we sat next to on the train, going to and from minimum-wage jobs, many raising kids alone — we respected them in some vague way. We convinced ourselves that our efforts at job parity were part of the tide that would raise their boats. And those slightly whack younger women, with their multiple piercings and full-body, full color tattoos? Their poetry slams and vegan diets, their retro tie-dye that was back around for at least the third time since my mom's friends wore it at Woodstock? Women like me didn't give the whole transgender, transcultural, transparently self-absorbed bunch another thought; they seemed like an alien species out of a post-apocalyptic Road Warrior movie. Who could blame some wholesome family firm or international corporation for not hiring them? Sure, every once in a while you'd hear about some twenty-something named Wren or Chinook who sat in a Redwood tree for fifty-seven months and extracted a promise from the Men in Charge not to chop it down to make dining room furniture. Or the girl in Guatemala who saw litter all over the ground and started a business making fashion items for first-world bistro radical wannabes. But those types were a flash in the pan. We "working women" saw ourselves as the serious ones, solid, Midwestern practical women, like the pioneers who believed in working as hard as the men while bringing change from within. I guess in a way I became my Mom's worst fear. Not a baby machine like the women of my extended family on O'Malley's side — the birth control pill prescription for my thirteenth birthday took care of that. No, I became her Mom, a reactionary stooge of the Establishment, shaky though it was. My grandmother Fay was a supporter of all things American: capitalism, the corporation, assimilating into that was her only goal. Protest? That could get you killed. She had the memories to prove it.

Yes, I guess I must admit, at my age, even growing up around a bit of labor rights and a lot of feminist/shamanic/cultural resistance, I was some kind of lumpen dress-for-success hybrid workaholic sure that, in a rational way, I was contributing to the liberation of all people by "Blazing a Trail of

Fairness in the Workplace" (the title of my MBA thesis).

But I don't mean to obsess on my paltry little worldview in the last months of the mid-decade. No, because I was just another delusional dame, one more crazed careerist, one little domino waiting to fall, one minute fractal about to snap into place, one tiny video signal traveling across the fire wire about to upload the new vision, lead the old guard off center stage and finally, finally, shift the paradigm.

I almost tripped over the cleaning woman. She seemed to blend into the marble floor in the enormous foyer of Wentworth & Wentsouth. I didn't remember having seen a woman scrubbing the floor on her hands and knees before. I made a note to speak to Mr. Wentsouth about this. I hope this building isn't hiring illegals to work and stashing them in a storage room to sleep at night like WalMart did. That's the first thing I'll do when I get to California: check on how the non-professional staff is hired and managed. Maybe start a mentoring program with the young associates to help these women move up in the ranks. I was jacked. Wentsouth himself had called me at home last night and asked me to come in at 7:00 a.m. I knew he was psyched that I was still working when he called at 10:30. The meeting with Aversmith wasn't until noon. Despite the "teamwork," nobody had the grasp of this presentation like I did. I was legendary in the office for my attention to detail. My power points didn't rely on lame clip art and dull graphs. I spent hours at the library at the Art Institute choosing clever historical art references for my slides. Once I used Picasso's Guernica to subtly evoke a theme of war in a hostile takeover we did a few years back. The guys loved it, always talk about it at company parties.

The elevator doors opened and Lydia looked up at me through the glass doors with sorrowful eyes. Does that woman live here? As early as I'd ever arrived at the office, Lydia was the one person I never beat. She was an old-time secretary to the Big Man, a real throw-back, honey-blond hair that must come out of a Revlon bottle from the '50s, hourglass figure, elegant tasteful knit dresses with a brooch pinned on one side, something out of a Donna Reed revue from Provincetown. But the look in her eyes caught me. I made a mental note to ask around the office; maybe her cancer had come back. Lydia was periodically missing from the office and the word was she was having treatment for some kind of cancer, but she always looked great when she returned. Maybe that was a honey-blond wig she was wearing. Lydia got up and sort of leaped in front of me, "Ahem, Sugar, Mr. Wentsouth will be with you in just a minute."

"Yikes! Thanks, Lydia, I almost barged right in there. Is he on the can or something?" Wentsouth had his own bathroom in his office suite. Rumor has it he can't go in a public restroom, something about a trauma at camp as a child.

Just then the frosted glass doors to Wentsouth's office flew open and he and Candace, a young associate I had recruited from Harvard, came out together. Candace grabbed my hand with both of hers and fixed me with a reverential gaze.

"Eve, I'm so glad you could make it in early. I know you've been working on the final details. Your work is incredible. I am so honored to be making the presentation to Aversmith. I've memorized your flow chart; I can run the numbers in my sleep. I Googled every piece of art in case he asks me any questions. I promise I'll totally absorb whatever changes you made, down to the decimal point."

I felt my face contort and get hot. Candace's French manicured handshake was firm and dry; my hand turned to jelly, sweaty jelly, and sweat was running down my armpits like heavy drizzle. I nodded like an idiot as Candace let go of my hand and reached for the binder that held the colorful flow charts and the flash drive of my presentation that I was holding limply in the other hand. She looked into my eyes, hers shining and awestruck, punched me in the shoulder, then turned and strode through the doors, with Wentsouth's arm around her shoulder, out into the hallway. Lydia put a cup of coffee in my hand and pushed me through the door into Wentsouth's office.

I was still in shock as he bounded back into the office and settled himself in his chair as if everything was hunky dory. Whatever Wentsouth said in the next hour I processed as buzzing, like a flyspecked florescent tube about to blow out over a lunch counter in an Edward Hopper painting. I heard the word "trooper," something about being a great team player, setting a high bar for the women to follow, and a mishmash of mixed metaphors from too many motivational speakers — and then I was on my feet and he was slapping me on the back.

"You know those older guys like Aversmith — so blown away by the young cute ones who can talk numbers and art. I should know. That's why we hired you back in the day, Eve, and now look at us, a couple of war-horses, ready for greener pastures."

What the hell was he talking about?

After that I was back in the reception area and Lydia was removing the coffee cup from my clenched fist, which I had drained at some point in Wentsouth's office, and saying, "Don't worry, Honey, don't worry, you just need to take a hot bath and relax. You've worked so hard."

It's 8:30 in the goddamn morning and I was being led off like the rabbit at a dog track to make way for the greyhounds. The Armani suit I bought for the power lunch hanging limply on my deflated frame, armpits sweat stained; Candace charging out with my portfolio of the presentation as if I was Knute Rockne and had just given her an inspirational speech, a few revised plays and sent her back in to run the ball downfield. If I could have, I would have throttled her right there in reception and then poked my sweaty fingers into her eyes till they bled. A bath? Visions of, "The Last Breathe of Jean-Paul Marat," by Jacques Louis David with Marat slumped in his bathtub after being murdered by Charlotte Corday came to mind. Are revolutionaries always fated to be murdered by those we aim to liberate? Et tu, Candace? As I'd eventually learn, all change has unintended consequences.

"Lydia, I think I need a few minutes in my office. There are a few minor corrections I made last night..." Not that I'd have put a bug into the program or anything like that.

I staggered down the hall awash with Lydia's sympathetic murmurings and the lingering scent of her White Gardenia perfume. I closed the door to my office and sat down, opened my briefcase and pulled out the marked-up hard copy of the Aversmith file. It represented my crowning achievement. I had added the last touches and made a clean copy right before dawn, the copy that Candace now had in her dry, well-manicured hands and was on her way to memorizing. I was rendered anonymous, a corporate drone. No evidence of my work, my loyalty, my sacrifice. Would Aversmith even notice that Candace wasn't me? He'd probably just say "Hi there, Missy, new hair-do?" and pat himself on the back for being sensitive.

Hell, this kind of thing happened to men all the time. They expected it, lived with it. They went home to the wife after a day like this and never let on that their hearts and spirits were broken. Okay, maybe they poured themselves three fingers of scotch before dinner instead of two. Maybe they were a bit distant when little Johnny hugged them and asked for help with his math homework that night. Now and again a man might snap after something like this, like Watson in accounting after the leClerc merger tanked last year, start drinking heavily, ask for a divorce out of the blue, leaving the wife confused and blaming her thighs — or go on a shooting rampage before blowing his brains out like those post office guys. Nobody said, "There, there, go home and take a nice bubble bath, that'll set the world to rights." I didn't even have a wife to leave or dump on. Lilith and Butch, my other cat, would be indifferent to my fate, at least until the bag of cat chow ran out. Funny, I always believed I was savvier than the guys. I really thought that understanding the game put me beyond the reach of its uglier consequences.

I swiveled my chair to see my only-slightly-compromised view of Lake Michigan and bent down to pull a flask of Stolichnaya from my desk drawer. Actually the vodka was stored in a hot pink Nalgene bottle from a breast cancer Walk for Life that I'd saved in anticipation of hiking in the Sierras on weekends in California, where, (unlike in Chicago, I imagined) I would achieve, finally, an elegant balance between work and play. All the magazines said that's how it would be: success in your fifties, a new beginning. Not that I had time to read magazines, but who could miss the screaming headlines in the checkout line: "You've Finally Made It, How's the View?" For God's sake, Oprah herself promoted this vision. I took a long, deep swig of vodka. I could almost hear my mother sighing from the grave.

"Go to work in business to save the world, are you meshuganah?" she said when I declared my ambition for graduate school. "Didn't I make you watch Death of a Salesman? I told you: they'll chew you up and spit you out."

And so, except for the shouting — which I couldn't do because I had no one to shout at (cats don't give a shit about human raving) — that is the history of the moment that ended my meteoric rise to the glass ceiling, where like so many before me, I cracked my head but didn't make a dent and was replaced at the last minute by a younger, hipper, hotter but equally delusional version of myself in the dog-eat-dog world of corporate America. That's all there was to it. Or so I believed.

Lydia knocked and let herself into my office without waiting for a response. I spun around, splashing vodka up onto my face.

"How are you, Lydia?" I said a little too brightly, so brightly that she staggered backward a step.

"How many times have you seen it, Lydia? How many idiots have offered up their fertile years only to be treated like overcooked pasta at what should be their moment of triumph?" I slumped in my chair, spent and bewildered, with no idea what to do next.

"Let me call you a cab, Sugar. No sense shuffling home in the rain."

Lydia's big blue eyes were dark. For a moment I thought of resting my head on her ample, perfumed bosom and crying my eyes out. But, of course, that wouldn't do. Before I knew it, I was downstairs on the street climbing into the backseat of a Rainbow cab. Lydia, who had insisted on taking me down to the lobby herself, said something to the cleaning woman who was still scrubbing away. Then we were out in the wet morning and Lydia waved off the cab already at the curb and said something into a walkie-talkie I hadn't noticed her carrying before. When the purple cab with rainbows painted on the sides pulled up she slid my briefcase onto the front seat and gave the driver my address in a too loud, too cheery voice. They seemed to know each other, which seemed odd, as the driver was a young, tough-looking Black gal with an aggressively spiked hairdo and a motorcycle jacket with a patch on the sleeve that said "CIA." I'd never seen this cab company before. Maybe Lydia called this women's cab company in her own little campaign to advance women's rights; I'd have to ask her about that next week. But for now the lack of sleep and the Stoli on an empty stomach had relaxed me enough: I began to snooze just about the time it seemed we'd gone way too far north. When I roused myself to look out the window, the lake was missing on the right and there were way too many trees.

"Driver, this isn't Evanston!"

2 ──────────────

Aurelia Astarte Marx swept into the room in a purple batiked caftan. Her gray-streaked dreadlocks cascaded down her back and formed an aureole around her face, which was round and glowing with high glistening cheekbones and full lips that rested in the perpetually slight smile of a Nubian bodhisattva. She was followed by a pack of dogs of indeterminate mixed breed with many shapes, colors, and sizes. They settled themselves around her feet as she stood before the group like a live oak and spread her arms, radiating energy that crackled through the room. One woman, who had endured a lifetime of permanent wave hairdos and was now nearly bald, swore that what hair she still had curled right back up whenever Aurelia entered a room.

"Sistahs!" she boomed at the assembled faces of women of every color and size but distinctly in the age group catered to by the AARP, which had recently moved its recruiting age up to fifty after a marketing survey showed that every single issue of their magazine sent to forty year olds was thrown out upon receipt without so much as a page being turned. Except for the ones used to scoop up dog poop and line birdcages.

The throng of women answered Aurelia with a cacophony of whistles, shouts, and ululations that lasted for a full minute. A part Blue Tick hound capped off the symphony with an extended soulful howl, and everybody settled down.

"I am here to tell you the latest news on our blessed Goddess awakening, life celebrating, woman-man-and-child-loving movement to welcome the blessed Crone to Her rightful place as Queen Mother, Dark Lover, and Chieftess Command-Dear of this ailing Gaian spaceship called Planet Earth. Each of you has a role to play, a gift to bring, a story to contribute. As She Who Gives Life to All wakens from Her cycle of slumber, Her numinous napping, Her gathering of light, power and hootchie kootchie erotic electric energy, we, Her Crones, stand ready to welcome Her and to serve Her. Yes, we are ready to serve the new world, the new nation — yes, Sistahs, the Crone-Nation: Cronation is about to arrive, unfold and sweep us up — every woman, child, and lost man — into the embrace of the Dear Goddess and Her abundant and everlasting love!"

The cacophony resumed and continued on for another five minutes while Aurelia beamed at the women, her face alight and shining with pure, genuine love. Aurelia's soul was so light-filled that just being within ten feet of her could lower blood pressure, cause endorphins to flood the brain, and cure arthritis. It wasn't always so, however, Aurelia had traveled a hard road to this moment of the arrival of Cronation.

Aurelia Astarte Marx had her awakening at about age sixteen when her mother, a meter reader for Commonwealth Edison, lost her job. The family had resided comfortably, if modestly, for Aurelia's early years in the Astor Village housing project on Chicago's near Westside. Aurelia's parents were labor organizers in the Black community.

Her father, Jerome, was a member of the Black Panther Party, shot in his bed for no good reason except that it could be done: even sleeping-while-Black was a life-threatening experience in those days if a man had exhibited the slightest signs of political activism at any time while awake. Like many Black men, Jerome had become sick at heart at the death of Dr.

King and considered the potential of violence to bring change less remote after that. Such sentiments registered on the radar of those men whose job it was to infiltrate political organizations and keep an eye on men like Jerome and pretty much confirmed the expectations of the Men in Charge. In those days, Black man thinking could easily equal dead man walking, no matter how creative or venal the means needed to accomplish that end.

Shortly after the shooting (for which the city issued neither apology nor compensation, just an "Oops, we thought he was a gang leader"), Phoebe, Aurelia's mother, found that her job, and hence her subsidized housing, had mysteriously disappeared. The Men in Charge took no chances when it came to disrupting all impulses the Movement might have to reorganize itself after Dr. King's death.

Phoebe took Aurelia and went south, back to relatives in Mississippi, to recoup. After depositing Aurelia safely with her own mother, Riva, Phoebe went underground with other women from the Movement to vision a new strategy for the resumption of the revolution, as it seemed the U.S. government had declared war not just on Black Americans but on change and progress itself.

Before leaving, Phoebe imparted several important precepts to Aurelia that stuck with her: The U.S. Government is a rigged game, in favor of the Men in Charge and those like them; and not only will the revolution not be televised, but TVs will help keep any revolutionary impulses at bay by co-opting any daring impulse you might have, adding a punchy tagline, backing it up with the music you first made love to, and using it to convince folks that buying some car, hair product, or sandwich is really a subversive act.

No, if there is to be a revolution, it will have to be run by women in a manner as yet to be invented because men, even wonderful men like her dear, murdered Daddy, were a little bit too much like the Men in Charge — temperamentally that is — to see through the game to how it all worked. They did not understand how to bide their time, work with the cycles of Earth, enlist the powers of Nature, especially when embodied in the form of women of the Movement, and keep their fool mouths shut when necessary. "All men," Phoebe often counseled, "are simply prone to jump the gun." This was one of Phoebe's theories based upon her meditations on the differences in men's and women's sexual anatomy. She felt the short, intense, explosive nature of men's climax was a metaphor for pretty much how they did everything. "Boom" and it's over. Like a gunshot. Mission accomplished. That was why so many of them found modern weapons so compatible. Women, on the other hand: "We work in concentric rings of pleasure and stimulation, coming closer and closer to the target, but not in any hurry to finish the job. We like to prolong the process. This drives some men crazy."

This circling behavior, as opposed to going straight for the center (even if that was an eventual goal), she said, meant that in each circle, a woman saw more, felt more, could understand more about the center, could appreciate nuances and make subtle adjustments if necessary. "Why, a skilled woman can stay in a cycle of arousal in, say, the third or fourth ring from the center for days, in the groove, communing with the Creative Source, intuition broadcasting and receiving, having orgasms by shifting her seat on a chair, vibing like a subtly spinning gyroscope."

Of course, a man who could provide the kind of touch to get that gyroscope in motion in the first place was rare, and one who felt it was his honor and duty to do so on a regular basis was even rarer. The rock bottom basis of white racism is the white man's unconscious fear that every man of color is privy to this secret that will — in his own pale body, goal-driven and results-oriented mind — remain forever a mystery. While it isn't true that men of color have a lock on the secret, Phoebe's husband, Jerome, had been such a man. Consequently she had a personal grudge against the Chicago Police Department and all the Men in Charge. They'd killed the love of her life, her sexual spin-doctor — not just any angry Black man — when they dispatched Jerome. She told Aurelia that had Jerome not been taken from her, "Honey, we might have eventually repaired to the bedroom and never come out, to hell with the revolution." As it was, instead, Phoebe had been left vibrating on that third ring ever since and, from practicing Tantra, had learned how to apply herself to channeling the revolution as well as multiple orgasms.

"Honest pleasure is the true purpose of life," Phoebe said. "That is what delights the Source." Dedicating her erotic energy for the good of humankind, she became a Tantrika for Justice, reviving a little known sect whose origins, though shrouded in mystery, go back to the year 1000 BCE, at least.

"Timing," said Phoebe, "is everything."

Speaking of timing, Phoebe explained, "Our community let our righteous grief over the loss of Dr. King play right into the Man's hands. There was a window of time after Dr. King's murder, that cruel and unforgivable act, when we might have sucked up that rage and horror, that grief and disbelief, and banked it for the future. Pulled in amongst ourselves and done our grief work in private, in honor of Dr. King's teaching of nonviolence. We would have had to let women leaders rise up naturally to carry the next phase of the struggle. We needed to use our dignity to shame the Men in Charge who'd let this ugly thing take place, and to remove an easy and obvious target. But none of us was ready for that and who could blame us? Instead we stormed and grieved, busting up our own communities, handing the Men in Charge a big victory that sealed things, at least for a long stretch. They had mown down John Kennedy and his brother Robert, too — and now Martin. It was a terrible time."

The Men in Charge, believing they were saving the country, could sit back and watch these murders teach white liberals just how fragile their commitment was to "the Movement." Black and White, most of those politicized young people, and many of their elders, pulled away from the struggle for equality to tend to their own lives and resources. They weren't prepared for the long haul. Rainbow visions of food coops and communal housing, peace and love were no match for bullets, explosions, and jail cells. Now that they had silenced Martin, the road seemed unimpeded to the Men in Charge — though it never is to those who rule by fear, their own shadows are always working overtime to manufacture ever-larger enemies to justify their tactics.

Still, although it couldn't have been articulated then, this was the beginning of the end for the male way of doing things: the "Boom, you're dead, problem solved." The stirrings of remembering a female way: Drop a pebble into the water and watch the concentric circles flow out from the smallest possible intervention and before you know it that little pebble begets a tsunami of change. Phoebe was determined to make sure that eventually, as soon as possible, that female way would be strong enough and clear enough for enough women to really take hold. "Make love, not war will be for real," she told Aurelia. Guns will be melted down into jewelry and kitchen utensils and farm implements for community gardens. "That's the love of lending a hand to your neighbor. It is simple things we do that make it work."

Behind the scenes, unnoticed and undaunted, there had always been women, and especially Black women, working for peace and justice.

"As far back as the 1890s Josephine St. Pierre Ruffin knew the importance of women meeting together to share their strength. She published the first newspaper for black women. Ida B. Wells, Mary McLeod Bethune, they worked tirelessly. Change was these women's middle name. They marched, they staged sit-ins, ran newspapers, helped write the U.N. Declaration of Human Rights. Thanks to them, by 1948, Civil Rights had become the dominant issue in national politics. By the 1960s and '70s, feminists within the Civil Rights Movement veered off and became more vocal for women's rights. You come to this work naturally with many righteous foremothers," Phoebe taught Aurelia during her occasional visits to Riva's during the visioning years.

Many of the women of Phoebe's generation weren't as willing as their elders to blend in so seamlessly to the cause as it became clear that their men were just as bent on running their own show as the Men in Charge were in running theirs. That time of foment and social unrest marked one of the Earth's awakening spasms of a new consciousness. There were those who tried to create new institutions. Many other folks were seduced by the lure and excitement of violence, from middle-class college kids to the Black Panthers to the Nation of Islam. Though as it turned out, in the end, no one but the long-standing Men in Charge really had the stomach or the blindness or the bedrock of fear to carry out hard-core violence turned outward toward others as a means of trying to maintain their power and allay their own fear.

Then there were some, mostly Black women from that early '60s time, who heard a crying from Mother Earth, incessant and nagging, grief and loss being one of Her clearest calling cards. Phoebe was one of those who heard. They didn't know exactly what it meant but they knew how to listen. They weren't a full generation away from the land so they knew where to go for their schooling: back to the South, back to the red clay earth and the spreading trees that sighed for them. Back where their ancestors learned the discipline to bide their time, gather their power, and step into freedom when the time was right. Phoebe knew that ultimately the Earth Herself is in charge — that over and above politics, economics, and any other stories humans conjure up to make sense of life, there was the unfolding of a bigger story. People could get with that or not, but sooner or later the Divine She would wake up and shake things up. From Her eye, what humans did could be shaken off like dust from a dog if need be.

And these women knew what was coming up North, too: A shit-storm was coming. Drugs were coming. Under the cover of a "War on Drugs," the Men in Charge would preside over the wholesale incarceration of Black men at unprecedented rates. Those folks that couldn't see past their own grief were left in the burnt-out moonscape of the ghettos of Newark, Oakland, and Chicago's Westside. Another Black Diaspora — this time spiritual and psychological, bitter and fueled by grief, drugs, gangs and self-doubt — dragged them into the aching heart of darkness that followed the demise of the blooming and then withering of the American Civil Rights Movement. The Men in Charge just couldn't seem to stem the tide of weed, heroin, and crack cocaine that flooded poor neighborhoods. Oh well, that was just one of the mysteries of life.

Riva, Phoebe's mother and Aurelia's grandmother, gave Phoebe and the women her blessing and support. She took in a number of their offspring.

"Go into the desert, children," she said to the women. "Stay until you grieve no more, purge your souls of every ounce of hatred and open your selves to the Great Divine Source. And get back here as soon as She gives you your marching orders and whup this place into shape."

So they went to do penance and have visions for a generation that meant well but never knew their ass from their elbow about how to really change the world and never got that it was about studying the natural world for signs and making the changes needed in their own hearts and lives. They went to learn from the Earth Herself how to work with Her and let go of the fools' game of trying to subdue Her.

What Aurelia knew at age sixteen was that she was pissed. Her father gets shot and then her mother drags her to the sticks and walks away? She became belligerent when Phoebe didn't come back, even angrier whenever she did. She raged at Riva and beat some of the other children with her fists and then collapsed sobbing. She resented the other children and, being the oldest, she had to help them in their confusion, parentless, pulled from the cities to a world they knew only as summer vacation, if that. Riva just watched and sent Aurelia into the woods behind her house when it got too much.

"Go sleep under the cottonwood tree and give it all back to the earth," Riva advised. When Aurelia would return the next day or sometimes two or three days later, her grandmother would feed her soup and cornbread and put her to work in the vegetable patch.

"Tending things that grow," said Riva, "teaches you that anger has a place: its energy is good for turning the soil and pulling weeds, good for turning your face back to God, which is the same thing. But when the sprouts show themselves, know they are fragile. Watch them to learn what is likewise fragile in you and tend to that as well."

And so time passed as Aurelia spent her anger tilling the soil and wrangling youngsters. Slowly she began to lead the little ones, cuffing them when they quarreled and sending a particularly angry one to sleep under the cottonwood tree as she had done, to watch the moon and wonder about the meaning of it all while the pain seeped slowly into the red earth that never refused it. Riva schooled Aurelia, and Aurelia taught the others that anger, hate, and despair are forms of energy, knotted up like knitting thread sometimes gets and then of no use to anyone. The patient practice of detangling yarn would often calm Aurelia and give her soul time and space to speak to her from its depths.

For her seventeenth birthday, Riva got Aurelia a set of paints. Now when she couldn't sleep, Aurelia often went to the barn and painted little sketches. Soon she ran out of sketchbook pages and began to use scraps of wrapping paper, paper bags, anything she could find. Peace would overtake her when she became absorbed in making marks on paper. She began to hear the voice of God in the images that arrived. Aurelia would ask a question, and she would feel — almost hear out loud — a reply. A red horse, with a smiling, wizened old woman riding it bareback under a full moon became one of Aurelia's frequent guides. The girl began to haunt the hardware store in town, buying up cans of outdated paint and cheap brushes. She got herself a job there on Saturdays and most of her spending money went for supplies. At first, only Aurelia was allowed in the barn to paint. It was off limits to the other children. So no one, not even Riva, saw the results of Aurelia's work.

Six months passed, and then a year. Aurelia's eighteenth birthday rolled around. At some point Aurelia had run out of paper and had begun painting on the walls of the old barn itself. She brought a few blankets out and began to sleep there in this space, surrounded by all her painted conversations with the Divine Source. Riva just smiled. "If painting up the barn settles Aurelia down, if she misses her momma a little less, well, that was a good thing," she mused. Then one day Riva stood in the barn looking at the walls and sensed there was much more taking place.

Aurelia explained that the images spoke to her, worrying what Riva might say. "Well, if Moses heard prophecy from a scraggly little bush," the old woman said, "there is no reason God can't choose a paintbrush for a microphone." Riva hugged Aurelia hard and blessed her work.

Eventually, Aurelia stopped chasing the younger children away from the barn and let them stay and paint too. She taught them how to ask their hardest questions to the Divine Source — which was also the wisdom inside themselves — and then paint until the answers arrived. She taught them to write about the paintings and converse with the images that showed up. They learned the names of their guiding images from the books on symbols, religion, and mythology that Aurelia brought back from the library. The barn and the surrounding land became their school, their church, and their cherished playground.

One night after dinner Riva looked down the length of the trestle table at the children's faces. To a one they were calm and glowing as they gazed back at her expectantly. Aurelia sat at the opposite end of the table looking into her grandmother's eyes.

"Take hands everybody," she said and the children did as they were told, bowing their heads, expecting grace after the meal, as usual. Until tonight that had been Riva's role, but now Aurelia spoke instead. They hadn't discussed it; it was just time. And Aurelia's words were different: no prayer of thanksgiving to the Eternal Father, who, (no matter who said the prayer), conjured up an old white man with a beard and a cranky attitude.

"Feel the energy passing through your hands around this circle," Aurelia whispered. "Now close your eyes. Picture that energy as light, bright, warm golden light. See it getting stronger, brighter and feel that strength flowing through you and to the next one and the next. Everything that lives, every single thing you see on this earth has that golden light in it. There are no enemies; there are only those whose light is dampened down in fear. You must practice to become completely fearless so that your light calls to theirs, no matter how deeply hidden it is, and wakes it up.

So even when you are out in the world, even when you don't have this table to sit at and these hands to hold, know that you can hold a rose, or an acorn, or an apple, or the hand of a stranger and feel that same light. As long as your light is switched on, it will call forth the light in everything and everyone else. And that is what we are put here for: to keep that light switched on and growing brighter until everyone in every place is illuminated with the shining light of Divine love. Amen."

The children were silent. Some had their eyes closed. As Aurelia spoke, it seemed the whole room was filled with golden light. Riva had tears in her eyes as she nodded slightly and smiled, "Amen."

* * *

Aurelia shook off her reverie and gazed out over the shining, expectant faces of the women now before her. Some of them had been the children with her that night at Riva's when she took the reins of the struggle firmly in her own hands. Aurelia's eyes filled with tears.

"We are ready, Sistahs," she thundered, "We are ready!"

* * *

Checking on the various Cronation initiatives and teleconferencing with Crones worldwide kept Aurelia busy and she was glad to be back at the Farm. Being with the women gave her strength. She had been prepping the advance guard for the triangle plantings and compassionista brigade landings, all the diverse and decentralized actions worldwide that were leading up to and preparing the way for the Great Shift. In spite of the study and planning, there was no way to know when the next steps would unfold. Like birth itself, Aurelia knew, there is a Mystery at the bottom of it all that even the wisest Crone couldn't come close to unraveling, though the Divine Source surely loves it that we try. That, plus the fact that different folks are vibrating at such varied levels of consciousness. Some of the women just loved and believed in Aurelia, what she said just "felt right." These women would go anywhere and do anything for Cronation. It had taken Aurelia years to realize that just because women went along or agreed didn't mean they fully understood what was going on and why. The terrific burden on a leader who aimed to be both wise and inclusive of everyone at the same time was no small matter.

"As you all know," Aurelia continued, "I recently returned from a trip around the country de-briefing with women who'd taken part in the estrogen weather project. After years of studying extreme weather patterns, our Cronation scientists began mapping the estrogen levels of women in affected areas. When the maps of the hormone levels were overlaid with the weather maps it became clear that there was a correlation. It was delicate and top-secret research. We had suspected that the overload of estrogen in the bodies of young girls and women from the consumption of meat and dairy products over the years that had been treated with growth hormones were partly responsible." The women clucked and shook their heads as Aurelia elaborated.

"We didn't want to make it easy for the Men in Charge to scapegoat the girls when it was their own factory farming practices that caused the mess. Especially when we learned that the areas with the highest concentration of human-based estrogen interacted to intensify the storm patterns.

"Our scientists guided a series of experiments where groups of our post-menopausal Crones with low estrogen levels were situated in areas expecting severe weather. While storms did still occur, the damage was lessened, as if the wind and rain didn't have to fight as hard. Or, perhaps, as Phoebe said, 'The Divine She is only slightly less pissed off at what's been done to Her youngsters when Her Crones make their presence known. She's just trying to get our attention and get us to do something!'"

The women cheered and shouted, "Yes, bless our mother Phoebe, may her memory be a blessing!"

"And no offense to Al Gore," Aurelia chuckled, "Bless him, but some part of global warming is the Earth's own menopause. Just as with women, hot flashes can be mitigated by right action."

"We hear you, Aurelia," the women shouted, "We know the blessed heat!"

It wasn't that the Crones were trying to "fix" something; they simply understood the necessity of gathering to support the Divine through Her next change. Working with What-Is serves as a Cronation watchword.

"The women of the estrogen project stayed in the homes of local women who were familiar with the specific terrain of their city or town, and together they staged their actions: either walking a labyrinth or drumming in a circle during the weather event or painting in rooms nearby or chanting and singing in groups. Seeing a whole gang of Crones in those yellow slickers, banging those weatherproof fiberglass drums, why I didn't know whether to laugh or cry," Aurelia declared. "It was a sight to behold!"

The women erupted into a chant, clapping and cheering. As Aurelia bowed slightly, one of the women shouted, "We are glad to have you back here with us, Sister! May the Source bless us in our work!"

3 ———————

I awoke to the sound of tires crunching gravel. My tongue felt like an old sock stuck to the roof of my mouth. I was dreaming about my early years at Wentworth and Wentsouth. The guys were sitting forward in their chairs as I finished a presentation on some company I believed we should acquire. I was passionate, I was eloquent, I was dazzling, if I do say so myself. They were eating glazed donuts, their ties loose and their shirtsleeves rolled up, as I triumphantly finished with a projection of revenues for the first quarter. I asked if there were any questions. In the charged moment of silence, Smithfield asked if he could have the last chocolate donut. Wentsouth chuckled. Then he stood up and said to the shirtsleeves: "If she didn't work twice as hard as you pricks, you'd all be out on the street." The men had a hearty laugh and finished their donuts. I glowed with pride.

"Where the hell are we?" I said to the back of the cab driver's head.

"Oh, you're awake! That's great. You're at the Farm."

"The farm? I don't live on a farm. I live in a nice little three-flat with a yard in Evanston!"

"Don't worry, everything is taken care of. Madge and Elly are going to stay at your place while you're here at Heartscape Farm. They'll take care of your plants, such as they are, and the cats and they'll tell the neighbors that they're your cousins from Philadelphia."

"How do you know about my cats?" My jacket had dried out, and I had stiff white sweat rings under each arm that I noticed as I tried to sit up.

"Lydia has had you under surveillance since you started as an intern at Wentworth and Wentsouth in the early '80s."

"Lydia? Wentsouth's secretary? Are you insane? Who is she doing surveillance for, Mary Kay Cosmetics?"

"I know!" The cabbie went on, "Isn't her cover amazing? She has it so down! She really enjoys that persona and it makes her so effective, I mean, she's been coordinating the Midwest region from her desk there since the 1970s and nobody has ever suspected a thing! You'd never know Lydia was a bomb-building anarchist in 1969, would you?"

I vaguely remembered slugging down some vodka after the shock of Candace snatching the brass ring at the would-be apex of my career, but what the hell was this? If Lydia had ever been a bomb-building anarchist, I'd been....

"A corporate stooge?" the cabbie offered quizzically.

"What, now you're reading my thoughts? Was there something in that vodka?"

The cabbie interrupted, "Oh, and your mother's spirit has been here for awhile. She was filling me in while we drove. She's thrilled for you. That you're here, I mean. She says she doesn't want to say she told you so, but she told you so!"

Things were getting weirder by the minute. I banged my shin on the door handle trying to get out of the car (which was locked) — and it hurt, so I knew I wasn't dreaming. But none of this made sense. My mother speaking to, then through, the cab driver? The driver acting as if that was about as natural as a batch of pancakes? Had I missed some major cultural leap? Did corporations now "disappear" older workers to remote farms like the Maoists during the Cultural Revolution? Maybe I should have paid more attention in those HR benefit sessions.

"Look, you've had a rough day," the driver soothed sympathetically. "Let's just get you inside. A half hour in the whirlpool, a detoxifying massage, maybe a paraffin foot soak and it will all start to make sense."

"Is this some kind of golden parachute from Wentworth and Wentsouth? A stint at a fat farm to take the play out of you before they pension you out, reviewing due diligence documents while your ovaries finally screech to a halt?"

"No, no, Wentsouth thinks you've just taken a few days. He thinks you're thrilled that Candace is taking over, you being such a team player and all. Don't worry. Lydia will handle everything. I'm telling you, she's done this for almost twenty-five years and she has it together. Every detail. She'll be up this weekend; you can thank her then. Come on, let's get you some sweats and a protein drink. You're really looking kinda frazzled."

The cabby's voice had deepened and taken on a shade of East Coast grit — and for a moment she actually sounded like my mother. I burst into tears....

When I was a teenager and would get really worked up about a test I was studying for or a science project that was due, my mother would stand in the doorway of my room and gaze at me, headphones on, listening to one of her Grateful Dead tapes, while I scribbled furiously on notecards or typed away on my computer, surrounded by stacks of books, Xeroxed articles and notes, a project timeline on the bulletin board above my desk.

"Jerry Garcia would cry if he could see the way you work," she'd say. Then she'd disappear and return with a protein drink or a fruit smoothie, "Here, drink this. You look kinda frazzled..."

"Oh, it's okay," the cabbie scrambled over into the back seat and pressed a crumpled tissue into my hand. "I'm a really easy channel. And the vibration of all the women at the Farm is so high it thins the veil between worlds; you can really start to see how simultaneous realities are. You're gonna be fine, really. This is great; the detox is starting all ready. Did you know that tears taste different when you're discharging emotional debris? No shit, there's like a totally different chemical makeup to tears you cry when you're watching a sappy movie than when you're crying about stuff that you truly grieve. Those tears taste real metallic. Go ahead, lick your lips, I bet it will taste like licking a hubcap."

Mom used to distract me with stuff like this when I was little — like telling me arcane facts, half of which were probably made up, the other half from Mother Jones magazine, about the content of fabrics and the working conditions in Malaysia — when we were shopping for school clothes at Kids 'R' Us and I was getting ready for a meltdown.

I just sobbed harder. The cabbie hugged me and rocked me and said: "That's cool, it's great, let it all out."

Suddenly there was a sharp knocking on the side window.

"Hey, Mattie, what the hell is going on in there?" I looked up to see a woman's face, topped by a rather severe steel-gray brush cut, trying to peer into what were now some pretty steamed-up windows.

"Hi, Rochelle. This is Eve, the one we've been waiting for. She just had a little detoxifying cry. She's really ready, aren't you, Sister?"

"Ready for what?" I asked. Had I been kidnapped by lesbian survivalists? I saw a segment about them on a news magazine program a few weeks ago. "Going Off-Grid with Greta and the Girls" or something like that, on the Oxygen network.

A second woman arrived at the car. Mattie disentangled herself, climbed back into the front seat and opened the door. The second woman poked her head in.

"How you doing, Kid?" It was Marty!

"Okay, the only thing that would surprise me now is if Rae and Gina showed up! Can someone please tell me what's going on? If this is an elaborate birthday prank, I'm going to kill all of you."

Marty and Mattie both laughed. "Isn't she a hoot?" Marty said.

"Don't worry, Rae is picking up Lydia and Lorelei at the airport; she'll be here tonight. Gina runs the kitchen; she'll be at dinner. Let's get you out of that Armani schmatte and into something more comfortable. You look like hell."

4 ———————

Aurelia loved the Farm. It combined the best of her childhood at Riva's with the chance to practice the highest values Cronation had evolved with a community of wonderful women. The women at the Farm aimed for what Phoebe described as effortless on the "Other Side": knowledge of Divine love and the ability to see and fully experience it through the inter-connectedness of all of Creation. More than that, a deep knowing that all things, even those that seem debased or evil, are held in love by the Divine Source. The women had many ways of practicing their values and beliefs. Through art, music, writing, playing together and working with the land, they developed and expanded their consciousness. Over the years Aurelia's early days of receiving an art and writing practice in Riva's barn developed into a powerful form of co-creative research that had come to be known as Collaborative Inquiry Through Art: CIA for short. The women loved the playful appropriation of the name of the government spy agency.

As Aurelia said: "Art is a way of knowing; if the Creative Source isn't the real Central Intelligence Agency, well, I don't know what is."

Consulting the Source together through creative engagement, the women received guidance on everything from how best to plant their crops, to how to care for women who came to the Farm after terrible experiences, to how to nurture and revive those who came when their work in the world drained them. Sites like Heartscape Farm, in the guise of spas and retreat centers, served as nodes of energy on a powerful web of light that stretched all over the world, holding the Earth and everything on it in an embrace of support and compassion.

The main buildings were deep in a grove of oak, sumac, and maple trees surrounded by the flat terrain of cornfields broken only by an occasional farmhouse or lone tree. Aurelia found it peaceful to look over the various garden patches of the Farm. Some were orderly furrows of plowed fields, others were spiral gardens of herbs for medicines, and still others were forest gardens that yielded food and forage. Especially as the changes in the world were manifesting such chaos, the joyful order of the Farm soothed her. At the Farm, she always spent some time sitting on the grassy knoll that held Phoebe's remains, now permanently and literally "underground" and, if not in peace, at least where Aurelia could always get ahold of her, a drastic improvement over Aurelia's adolescence when Phoebe was so often absent doing the groundwork for this present time.

After addressing the women, Aurelia always checked in with Phoebe to share what had gone on and get her advice. Stretched out on the grass she waited for Phoebe's directives to begin. Channeling didn't seem so strange in the age of computers: Aurelia's meetings with her mother were just an extended download of sense impressions and ideas Phoebe transmitted from the Other Side, a soulcast, if you will.

As she basked in the unseasonably warm December sun, Aurelia was startled from her musings by the sound of crunching grass and a shadow falling across her. She opened her eyes and shaded her face with her arm.

"Hey, Harvey, what's up, man?"

"Just feeling kind of lonely, and then I saw you up here. I haven't seen you much since you got back from your travels. All the hustle and bustle at the Farm — something big is going on, isn't it?"

Harvey was a big man, six feet tall with curly dark hair and a wide-open face. He sat down next to Aurelia. She propped herself up and tousled his hair.

"Yep," Aurelia smiled.

"That's all? Yep?"

"Yep."

"Come on, Aurelia."

"Ouch!" Aurelia felt a pinch on her shoulder and heard Phoebe say: "Now don't you play with this man like he was your baby brother. Show a little respect!" Nowadays Phoebe never stopped 'cuffing the cub.' She'd missed out on that part of Aurelia's growing up and loved that she could do it invisibly from the Other Side.

Harvey looked quizzically at her, but Aurelia just said, "Mosquito."

"In December? Come on, Aurelia, what's up?"

"Oh, Harvey, I don't know myself. I was waiting for Momma to come in when you arrived. I haven't got all the details yet."

"And I'm here all right! You be kind to this man, you hear me?" Phoebe hectored her daughter, somewhat sad that Harvey couldn't hear her. She had a soft spot for that man.

"Listen, Harvey, a new woman arrived today. By all the signs she might be the one that completes this phase or brings some piece we've needed; it isn't clear yet. We know one person isn't going to lead the next step like in all the old stories, but we've had lots of messages about a convergence of some kind. We just have to follow the signs. We won't know much until we get her in the SAC. She's coming straight out of a corporate job meltdown. Lydia has had her under surveillance for quite a while. Can you help Mattie run her through the Story Alignment Chair a few times?"

Harvey grinned, "You mean it? Sure!"

* * *

Harvey was one of the men responsible for dispatching Phoebe to the Other Side. She'd been crouching down to move a caterpillar off the road to keep it from getting squished. A truck full of hunters hit her. They were on their way north for deer season just a few weeks shy of the winter solstice a few years back.

"I just exchanged my usual form for hers," Phoebe told Aurelia in a dream the night after it happened. "I just fell for an old-paradigm bugaboo: trying to rescue something or someone else." The concept of salvation and the need to work for it for others or ourselves was just "dead wrong," Phoebe quipped.

"Seriously, Aurelia, do you think deciding this little mouse or that big old barn owl has to be protected above all else makes sense? That just opens the way for endless conflict and deception and competition in the Victim Sweepstakes."

Phoebe taught that all beings, from the simplest to the most complex, were part of an exquisite and miraculous scheme that is ever unfolding, each with the choice of its role and how to play it. Invisible to humans, perhaps, but true nonetheless. Even a seemingly badly timed demise had a meaningful effect. The job of humans is to cultivate the belief in meaning and not be too attached to how its pattern unfolds, but rather to hold the meaning that allowed the most compassionate view of all involved, while holding space for Mystery. This was one of the core teachings given to the women of Cronation.

"Every moment holds a decision tree," Phoebe counseled. "Choose for love, curiosity, and joy. Leave yourself eager to know what's next. Humans need story as much as food for the soul to thrive."

Harvey's pelvis was fractured in the accident that ended Phoebe's earthly sojourn. He healed pretty well physically though his spirit remained tormented. He contacted Aurelia from the hospital when he found out about Phoebe's death, wanting to make some kind of restitution. It was such a loving and honest act that Aurelia was deeply moved. She shared his wish with the Crones, and the elder council suggested inviting him to come by the Heartscape Farm and see what moved him. Harvey spent weeks just walking the property, fixing fence posts, trimming trees, until eventually he came to live at the Farm and, without making a big deal of it, dedicated his life to the Cronation Movement.

Phoebe was instantly taken with Harvey.

"You see, Aurelia? That is absolutely all it takes in this world for love to continue to flow! Admit your mistakes, ask for forgiveness, and make amends. This is a good man." The other three men continued hunting that year, seemingly unchanged by the accident.

Harvey wasn't particularly political and had never been a fan of the macho tactics of the Men in Charge; he could see that they were wearing thin everywhere and a change was needed. But like so many men, he was stuck in a mix of guilt and doom fantasies, not seeing any real alternatives. It had been his first time going hunting, on a dare from his brother-in-law. When he woke up after the accident he was overcome with guilt and the horror of having taken a life. He never wanted to hunt again.

"Bad things happen when you go against your own nature," he told Aurelia. "I never wanted to be a hunter."

He accepted Aurelia's offer to work at Heartscape, and after a while, with the blessings of the elders, he built a small cabin at the far edge of the property. He couldn't get over Aurelia not being angry with him for running her mother over. Harvey didn't know exactly what was up with the women on the Farm; he suspected from the start it was more than massages and bubble baths and art workshops advertised in the brochures that described Heartscape as "A peaceful getaway for today's busy woman," but he just felt right helping out there. After a while, Harvey just absorbed the vibe of love at the highest level from Aurelia and the other elders. Harvey was an opportunity, Phoebe said, Aurelia's chance to put the lesson of love and forgiveness to the test. She could still hear Phoebe telling her to just be still as Harvey poured out his soul.

"Aurelia, you don't need to counsel this man, just listen when he wants to talk, accept his labor, and send love his way; that's all there is to it. He's not going to be that hard, he doesn't have a lot of fear blocking his heart. Once he gets used to not being judged he will blossom like a rose. We are all here on earth simply to witness one another unfolding in the miraculous unique way we are meant to be and to help each other over the rough spots."

Aurelia had her moments of anger at her mother; she'd barely had Phoebe back in her life when she was gone again, well, sort of. Mostly, her own heart, too, was melted by Harvey's sincere anguish and remorse.

Aurelia slowly taught him the rules of fair exchange, kind inference, discernment of right action, and service to the higher good for all beings — the core values that made up the Ethic of Care, which guided the Cronation community. "These truths are known deep in every heart," she told him. "We are all here to continually and with love remind one another."

Harvey came eventually to be a trusted member of the Cronation movement, at least by the elders. Some of the women, of course, reacted as if Harvey, simply for being a man, was the devil incarnate, so he generally steered clear of the group meetings, lectures, Collaborative Inquiry Through Art sessions and other events so as not to trigger any women who'd been abused and saw pretty much any man as a threat. As time went on, most of the women accepted Harvey's presence, trusting Aurelia in her judgment to allow him to live at Heartscape. Harvey also helped test out a number of the breakthrough devices the women's inventor cells came up with — like the SAC, the Story Alignment Chair. He didn't know the scale of what was planned, or the exact history of Cronation, but he knew enough to sense that this was transformative and he felt lucky to be a part of it.

A cloud formed a sort of lopsided heart in the sky above Aurelia and Harvey.

"See that, Harvey? That heart-shaped cloud? That's Momma saying it's okay for you to run the SAC."

"Don't patronize that man!" Phoebe scolded. "Where would your Tantra women be without Harvey?"

Harvey recruited many of the young men who served as consorts for the Tantrikas. On the south side of the Cronation property a cadre of women lived with younger men, perfecting a form of balancing the world through the sexual meditation of Tantra. Harvey designed and managed the website that brought young men in for the kind of internship not found in their college career counseling office.

"Speaking of the SAC," Harvey had a serious look in his eyes, "I had a dream last night that a big black raven landed in that field over there and then turned into a woman. She was dark and kind of scary; I thought I should tell you."

Aurelia's eyes narrowed as she searched Harvey's face. To have a dream with collective imagery, that was a big responsibility. She silently blessed Harvey's soul and asked the Divine Source to protect him.

"I told you, Aurelia, don't play with him," Phoebe scolded. "This man is as tuned in as any woman."

"Well then, Harvey, you have your work cut out for you in the SAC," Aurelia said, her eyes betraying concern. "Have you checked it out on the dream monitor?"

"No, my regular session isn't until tomorrow."

All the Heartscape Farm residents learned to monitor their dreams for transmissions from the Other Side, observe the animal kingdom for Earth wisdom and important weather shifts that could signal danger or opportunity. This was the first time Harvey had had a dream that seemed to him important enough to mention.

The sun went behind a dark gray cloud. "Wow, no, it didn't, the cloud moved, not the sun!" Aurelia thought, in startled self-correction. That kind of subtle patro-centric thought distortion was disturbing to her and could only mean one thing — some kind of strong patriarchal thought force was nearby.

"Um, Harvey, I need to get with Momma now and see her angle on what's happening. Why don't you see if you can get in a full scan of that dream today and we'll talk later."

Harvey noticed the chill in the air as he patted Aurelia on the shoulder, got up, and loped off toward the technology center.

It's funny, she thought, how people think of one's spirit being everywhere after death — if they believe in spirit at all. Yet for many, through life events, parts of their spirit get split off and need to be reconnected through soul retrieval and other such methods. Some spirits, due to fear, don't make the transit to the Other Side successfully. They wander lost or sometimes take up residence in those who have weakened auras, causing illness and disease in the unknowing host. Much of the healing at the Farm included sessions to release these spirits attached to troubled women and to allow them to continue their journey to the light or to new incarnations in their soul's evolution. The Cronation women learned a great deal about the meaning of death as simply another transition, yet, one that needed — as all transitions do — careful tending.

Our actual physical matter, decomposing though it may be, continues to give off energetic vibrations as it breaks down. As it turns out, a sudden accidental death, like Phoebe's, allows the soul to linger on in the vicinity of the living, enabling them to keep working on whatever projects they had left undone. Or, in some cases, they stayed to work out their anger towards whatever caused their untimely demise, probably the state that is called purgatory by some religions. The work is accomplished by kickboxing with angels. Not the higher orders, like the Seraphim, but the warrior-in-training kind of adolescent post-Cherubim angels. These antics are one of the Other Side's best-attended sporting events. Phoebe's sparring was legendary; she was the undisputed mortal-side favorite since she'd arrived. All the angels had to say was "You know, Phoebe, Jerome is vibrating at such a high frequency now, you really won't be ready for him until you let go of all this anger." Phoebe, for all her own spiritual advancement, still held plenty of anger at the men who'd killed Jerome, the system that created oppression and carelessness with which so many were blind to the truth. She would be kicking like a mule chasing off a hornet in no time and the hooting and hollering would be on. Those who imagined the life beyond the veil to be a boring round of harp concerts and floating on clouds were "dead" wrong.

Phoebe made sure Aurelia knew that all the pain of life on earth commences in the erroneous belief in the separation of humans from the Source; the difference on the Other Side is that everyone there knows better. Life continues in another quite glorious form. Once that simple lie of estrangement is undone, the love that flows between all beings manifests in ways that are as complex and beautiful as anything else in the universe. Then the true meaning of life can unfold: the co-creative call and response between the Source and Her creation through story, song, dance, invention, and play — and the same unfolding among humans of all kinds, an ever elaborating sharing of ideas, games, and stuff.

As Aurelia watched Harvey disappear down the hill she felt a light buzzing in her hands and feet.

"Momma? You there?"

Even though Phoebe transmitted through thought waves, when Aurelia was alone she liked to speak to her mother out loud. It gave her comfort to hear her own voice and seemed to make Phoebe's replies clearer too.

"Humans have a built-in instinct to create new things," Phoebe was saying. "It works like the hunger that gets us to eat. Unfortunately, this hunger for delight is as crippled in most folks as the healthy desire to eat is in the eating disordered, which is just about everybody these days. It could be getting humans to create art, create new recipes, or come up with ways to get houses built for all those who need them, but it gets yanked off course by loops of T.V. theme songs and commercial nonsense that have made habitual grooves in the neural pathways. Instead of inducing a joyful sense of play, these stolen pathways are given over to fear and dis-comfort — paired with the idea that getting the product being advertised or watching the TV show will fix such feelings. Plain old propaganda, but for commercial ends."

"Momma, I still don't understand," Aurelia mused. "Exactly why you all fought against the movement to ban T.V. commercials."

She had settled herself down on the hill after Harvey left to begin her session with her mother. As usual, she was tuning in to one of Phoebe's lectures already in process for interested beings on the Other Side; she did a lot of continuing education classes for those soon-to-be-returned to earth in embodied form.

"It will take time to get used to creative and loving impulses combin-ing to create sweet pleasure and knowing to call it that. Most people in the twentieth century, since that nephew of Sigmund Freud's invented the field of marketing, have been conditioned to find natural pleasure a waste of time. They mostly only respond to the satisfaction of created needs, the poor dumb things." Phoebe was addressing the assembled beings on the Other Side as well as her perception of Aurelia's concerns.

"All right, you all, go on now," Phoebe shooed off her throng of stu-dents, "that's it for the present; I have to get with my daughter for a while. Meanwhile you all go practice those memory skills. It would be nice if more of you remembered something I said after you get back in a body instead of being all clueless for the first twenty-some years."

Aurelia felt the buzzing in her hands and feet growing stronger, sig-naling Phoebe was finally tuning into her frequency full force.

"How people don't see that it is their own light that they freely spend, one might say squander, on celebrities is the main thing that keeps those folks up there and shining…" Phoebe sighed. Sorting out the pop culture phenomenon was part of the Cronation mission. The women explored such ideas as they shared insights from their SAC and CIA experiences with one another, many waking from the cultural trance for the first time.

"It's as if they think their own light doesn't mean anything because it isn't on T.V.," Aurelia mused. "That's the tragedy of never being properly witnessed, I suppose."

"Mass media is now a playground of the people's creativity, Aurelia, how many times have I said so? Thanks to the Internet, of course." Phoebe didn't miss a beat picking up on her time with her daughter. "Our story-making skills are being kept alive under cover. The Men in Charge can't keep up with monitoring everything that is being put out there. Though the Chinese surely try hard to do so.

If we had gone along with those who wanted to ban T.V., we'd have lost a big asset in this evolution. At this point, there are Crone cells making commercials for love and big-bodied women, for Goddess sake, and the Men in Charge don't even notice. For heaven's sake, beautiful shape-shifting beings like our transgender sisters and brothers are showing us so much joyful possibility. And, they are doing it in primetime! The Men in Charge may change the channel to another political talk show or football game, but all over the world, hidden in cable channels and local T.V. shows, new messages are being broadcast that are adding energy to the shift. Remember, the simple experience of hearing compassionate truth can topple years of cynicism and indifference."

"I know, Momma, I know," Aurelia was anxious to get onto other subjects, like the new woman and Harvey's dream, but Phoebe was still warmed up from her previous lecture.

"What the Divine Source teaches," Phoebe continued, "is that exercising creativity is every person's birthright. There is no absolute moral code except to do what is creative and loving; yet free will is real. Everyone's development is uneven; this causes lots of problems. You are free to be creative and a prick, loving in one place and oppressive in another. Staying in alignment with one's highest self takes practice by the individual and also requires the loving support and thoughtful reflection of a community."

The system of competition based on individual performance was another error that Cronation sought to correct. So many women came to Cronation broken in spirit from being made to feel unworthy in work or relationships.

"It is a choice, of course," Phoebe went on, "you can be creative and hating, loving and uncreative and anywhere else on the spectrum. What most delights the Divine are acts of love and creativity that evoke celebration, and celebration calls out the light and music in everything and everyone and makes all that exists grow in complexity and duration."

"Unfortunately," Aurelia countered, "the Warrior type still sees battle as the highest creative act, and that spills into other media. The general level of violence is painfully high."

"Yes, war keeps energy moving and changing," Phoebe agreed, "but not evolving in beauty and joy — which is not to say that those who engage in the actual fighting don't experience beauty or joy and meaning there. Goddess knows that for some, it is by far the most profoundly ecstatic experience of their lives. Eros lives in war; don't be mistaken. She is most especially present in any sublime complexity that involves the body. But evolving in beauty and joy and manifesting that sweetness with bodies is the real job; that is what keeps the Divine bothering with human beings. If you see beauty in war - which is really about trying to simplify things in some crude way — well, that is where your energy will flow," Phoebe responded. "The problem is too much rote simplicity bores the Divine and She will put us away like a game of checkers and turn her energy elsewhere if we bore Her to it."

Phoebe's existence on the Other Side, so close to intense Divine Presence, had taught her that if high wattage love is turned on in the direction of anything, without taking any other immediate direct action, the subject of that love would begin to shift and change, growing in complexity and joy the same way a good soaking Spring rain gets dormant plants to burst forth and grow. Goodness is always there in potential, like seed in soil, waiting for the right conditions. Studying and developing ways to do this was the legacy passed to Aurelia. Now it was getting to be time to intensify a wave of love in the Earth realm that would be greater than anything ever seen before to counter the growing fear of change. No one knew exactly what the outcome would be if the loving equivalent of an atomic bomb could be released — except that bloody pain and suffering would not be the outcome.

"You know, Aurelia, scientists have discovered that the crucial difference between natural and man-made things is that man-made things tend to be rigid, have little or no way to move and sway, and so they are brittle and they break. Men saw that 'give' in nature as a flaw and set out to tighten it up. But rigid things snap under pressure. It's nice those women scientists at Biomimicry are getting so many in all sorts of fields to study Nature and actually ask Her help instead of just trying to synthesize Her with incomplete understanding."

Phoebe took full advantage of the infinite information available to her on the Other Side to get professorial when the mood hit her. "The response of the Warrior is often to save what is, what they know, or practice strict preservationism — which is just a ham-handed strategy of low-level love, faulty warriorism, ineffective, and often with unintended consequences." Phoebe was on a roll, "Like me saving the caterpillar without checking the road first and getting myself run over by the very 'enemy,' the SUV driven by fool-headed men, that I was trying to save the little woolly caterpillar from."

"It makes me sad that you aren't here in the flesh to bring all this about, Momma," Aurelia sighed.

"Well that's the problem, isn't it? When you are part of something, forgetting that you are just a part, I wouldn't be 'bringing it about' at all, Aurelia, just one small part of a web of wonderful beings, some in human form, others as plants, animals, microbes. And me and others as spirits with a ringside seat! How do you think Jesus feels?" Phoebe chuckled. "Why, that poor man tried to get something going single-handed and got nailed to a cross for his trouble."

Men, for the most part, even fine ones like her Jerome, even Jesus for that matter, were a little inept in pulling off large-scale, positive change. Phoebe was convinced they lacked the patience and had a hard time working well with others. Plus, violent change, at first, has a satisfying immediacy and an exciting graphic nature. And, since for thousands of years, men have expected women to come in and clean up after, well, what happens after the destruction, it wasn't ever their highest concern.

"Momma, on another subject — Harvey had a dream that worries me. He saw a raven land in a field here at the Farm that turned into a dark woman. When he was telling me, I couldn't help thinking of Kali, you remember her?"

"You mean that little Charity Greenberg? Didn't she and her sidekick leave in a huff when we didn't go along with her idea of the wholesale assassinations of male politicians and other leaders?"

"Yes, Momma, she's the one," Aurelia replied. "She took the name Kali, from the Hindu goddess, before she left."

"Beating the men at the men's game, by the men's means, it never works," Phoebe intoned. "Didn't her mother get into that New Age movement that blended all the Eastern stuff with the Jewish stuff?"

"Yes, she brought Kali to the Farm for a mother/daughter weekend as a last resort and then sort of dumped her on us," Aurelia remembered with a pang of something she couldn't quite name. "Kali's a smart girl but she got scared off by the SAC work and that always made me nervous. She took that girl Diva under her wing; that was about the most loving thing I ever saw her do. She is an angry young woman!"

"I remember that the raven is her totem," Phoebe added. "She even has one tattooed on her chest. Said it was to make sure she'd never be buried in a Jewish cemetery. What on earth did her people ever do to deserve that kind of behavior?" Phoebe had become close to many of the biblical prophets on the other side who had finished their work and so no longer reincarnated into new bodies. She had a soft spot for the Patriarchs as they struggled watching their era transform into the next.

"And she hung around with that even skinnier little thing — what was her name? Diva, you say? She looked like a raven herself!" Phoebe fumed.

"Kali always thought we were too slow and patient. What if she has been planning a counter movement? Could you see it if she was?" Aurelia asked.

"Not necessarily." Phoebe considered. "If she plans it right, she could be working in exactly the same channels as the warriors; she always wanted to take them head-on. We can only see them from the outside, not the inside."

"I just wish you were here in the flesh, you know, to guide things," Aurelia sighed.

"Well, just call me 'Moses' — you know, I was talking to him recently, and he says his end was just like mine, an accident. They tweaked the story in the rabbinic period to get a little more judgment out of God during a stretch when the people weren't paying enough attention. Fact was, Moses was washed away in a fast moving wadi when he was out taking a pee. You know how a wadi can just rush up out of nowhere at times. By the way, Moses is very interested in Cronation."

"Well, he should be. The Jews got the ball rolling the last time when the God paradigm shifted from the many to the One. Cutting down the asherot and chasing the women out of the groves," Aurelia recalled.

"Well now listen to this: Moses says that right there is the key to the whole 'chosen people' thing. Chosen to take the fall, he says. He said to me, 'Phoebe, can you imagine this rag-tag bunch taking over anything? Chasing out anybody? Never mind a band of Goddess worshipping women.' I had to laugh.

"He says the Jews needed a war story for cover. It was time for that whole hero-warrior thing to kick in, and nobody else wanted to risk hiding Shekinah until the Cronation came around. That's why so many folks hate the Jews: they've been hiding the Feminine in plain sight all these years and, deep down, everyone knows it. It's all unconscious, of course."

Aurelia had long wondered if the changes in epochs really needed to be so violent. One archetype surpassing the next was inevitable. Why did humans resist it so?

"I feel plenty of sympathy for Moses, Momma. Gracious, it seems so hard sometimes to help the Shift! But we're trying not to forget the lessons of history. I imagine the cultic women were getting pretty insufferable towards the end of the Matriarchy when their string was running out, just like the men's is now. You tell Moses I can relate: the thought of the Shift really happening, it's a powerful thing. What a blessing to be a part of this one!"

I bet Moses didn't give a shit about getting into the Promised Land, Aurelia thought. He was just ready to rest his weary bones. I bet he jumped into that wadi feet first thinking about getting that stiff-necked people settled in the so-called Promised Land. He must have suspected how that was all going to play out down the road.

5

By the time I had a shower, a soak in the whirlpool, and was squeezed, oiled, and rubbed like a chicken for roasting by a woman with a black eye patch who hummed "Amazing Grace" the whole time, I thought I'd died and gone to heaven. I could barely struggle into the well-worn maroon sweats that the masseuse left on the chair after she finished turning me to mush. The sun was sinking below the horizon when Mattie reappeared in the locker room where I sat staring at myself in the mirror, slack-jawed, damp hair smelling of peppermint shampoo, but in no less of a daze than when I awoke in the backseat of the cab.

"You're done? great! Here's a mango-carrot-ginger smoothie," Mattie bubbled, "to hold you over until dinner. Isn't Magdalena a great masseuse? She lost her eye in a prison fight, but she surely sees the pain in a body with the eyes in her hands! I'm Mattie, by the way — sort of a Crone-in-waiting. I didn't properly introduce myself before. My mother more or less runs this operation; she's the head of the Crone Council here at the Heartscape cell. Her name is Aurelia Astarte. You'll meet her at dinner. Your friend Gina can't wait to see you. She's making Italian food tonight in your honor — that's your favorite, isn't it? It's all vegan, of course, but I think you'll love it."

Dinner. Yes, I am definitely hungry. I had a breakfast bar and coffee this morning, didn't I? Was that this morning? And the vodka, of course.

"I don't suppose there's a bar here?"

Mattie laughed, "We do have our own vineyards in California, Vermont, and several places in Europe. Wine is one of the economic initiatives we have in place for when the old order falls. Aurelia figures no matter what the world looks like after the Shift, every one will want a drink, and yes, the wine is shipped to all the cells under our special label, "Crone Nectar." And the Crones have revived dry farming, growing grapes with seasonal rainfall. The yield is smaller but sooo much better. So wine, yes. No bar. The Crones focus on the sacramental aspect of spirits."

What the hell is this joint?

"Ahhh, Mattie, what's with this place? Seriously, I'll sue the pants off Wentsouth for age discrimination if this is all some ploy to soften me up not to fight being fired."

"Well, first of all, you weren't fired, just replaced. And in case you've forgotten, age discrimination statutes haven't covered women since early 2003." Mattie recited the information in the singsong voice of a child in a catechism class: "'If an employer can show that a woman's youthful appearance is crucial to her success in the position she holds, he can fire her anytime after her 30th birthday' — or earlier, if he applies the five pounds per year exemption."

That rang a bell. I recalled a discussion in a continuing education seminar on business ethics about how gym memberships had become a legitimate tax deduction in tandem with the repeal of certain fair employment protections. The President made it sound like he was supporting health and business at the same time — brilliant, really. It was a strategy for dealing with the obesity epidemic. And, if you could be fired at any point for being five pounds over your government-mandated target weight, well, the good ol' government would certainly give you the means to keep those pounds off. I mean, that's democracy, isn't it? If you were a fat slob, surely your employer shouldn't be made to suffer. Your increased health costs shouldn't be borne by the workers who got up early and worked out, should they? This is what freedom is all about.

"And no offense, but that was a huge factor in Wentsouth replacing you with Candace. Age, I mean, not weight. You've kept yourself in shape in the traditional sense, rigidifying your muscles to armor your heart against the truth...." Mattie continued in a matter-of-fact voice, "But now you can actualize your true calling, although how that will manifest is still unclear from what the Crones say. But isn't that exciting?"

I was only half listening.

It was amazing to realize that we really had all somehow come to view ourselves through the lens of corporate expediency: the self as a product. Market value was ours to freely cultivate, like a social security account, health savings account, and personal education trust fund — all initiatives of the Men in Charge spun to sound like they would "get Big Government off the people's backs."

The government, meanwhile, in the sense of providing order and protection for people, had pretty much left the building. Bankrupted by wars, the Men in Charge had hit upon creating a Department of Emotional Well-Being, staffed entirely by former advertising executives (who created nothing but messages) to take the place of actual Departments like Health, Education, and Welfare. HEW ran their building with a skeleton crew now to make sure the building itself didn't fall apart. There hadn't been actual workers dealing with actual citizens and their "benefits" — a quaint concept, now passé — since the early 2000s. It was "free enterprise" all the way these days, free from ethics, free from regulation, and, especially, free from concern for women, children, and the environment.

For years, most of the debates on Capitol Hill revolved around refinements to the wording and means to enforce the Culture of Life legislation. Those debates, the equivalent of the Medieval discussions about how many angels could dance on the head of a pin, were downright scary — though like most people, I tuned them out.

I should have been annoyed at Mattie, but, I had to admit, these thoughts were floating through my own head. As she spoke, it all felt dimly familiar; but in my world it had all seemed somehow benign. I was doing my best, working hard, had good intentions. Besides, at the moment, I was experiencing a sense of pleasant relaxation that was as unfamiliar as it was delicious and, if you asked me my name, I'm not sure I could even spell it.

Mattie looked at me sympathetically. "I bet you're feeling confused right now. One of the things you'll find here is that coming into the Cronation vibration can sort of shock your system. Strands of thought that have been below consciousness will start to come to the surface. You may wonder how you didn't see it all before."

"Like what?" I said, but I sort of knew what she was talking about. The smoothie was restoring my energy a bit, but I definitely felt like Glad wrap was being peeled off my brain. And the rush of thoughts was like a breeze on a wound I didn't know I had.

"And what exactly is the 'Cronation Vibration'? Sounds like a nursing home game show."

Mattie laughed and shook her head. "We have a community of women living here dedicated to evolving consciousness. These women have been imagining and creating an alternative world — economy, health system, food production, educational institutions — all below the radar of the manifest system. A parallel process of loving and living that is virtually invisible to the Men in Charge. What that means is that as you begin to take a ride on the Crone vibe, your consciousness will get a boost to their level, and you will start to recall things you have overlooked. You'll start to make connections that your whole existence, your work life especially, conspired to keep you distracted from."

"So, in other words," I countered, "you intend to brainwash me with some kind of feminist, anti-business propaganda."

"Nope." Mattie gazed at me with an amused tolerance. "You get a chance to drop down into the heart level of your existence, the foundation of love that underlies everything. Cronation just gives you the space to recall some things you've been overlooking in your focus on work."

As Mattie continued to gaze at me, her eyes soft, a conversation I'd had with Marty ages ago popped into my head. I remembered when the Culture of Life legislation was introduced; Marty said it finally dawned on the Men in Charge that they weren't going to live forever. She said they were taking a page from the Cuban playbook, declaring a "special period" whereby the waning powers of male energy would receive the equivalent of price supports through a series of laws that curtailed women's rights and placed first dibs on their energy squarely into the hands of men, "for the greater good," of course. And, she said, the Men in Charge could conceive of no greater good than continuing, indefinitely, to firmly clutch the reins of power in their liver-spotted hands. I remembered laughing about it with Rae when they announced a "Viagration" program for the national water supply, similar to fluoridation.

"Viagrate the water to invigorate the country." It made headlines in all the papers coast to coast. Marty didn't find it as funny as I did. Come to think of it, the slogans on billboards began to be reminiscent of Cuba too — political messages, constantly repainted to stay fresh and maintain the status quo while the buildings they were painted on crumbled into ruins.

Mattie roused me from my reverie. "Look, Eve, has the smoothie restored you enough for a little Cronation history lesson?"

When I shrugged, Mattie said, "Great! Because I think you'll feel more comfortable when you hear some background. Let's go upstairs." She hooked her arm in mine and pulled me to my feet.

"We can start in the Hall of Women."

The scent of pine and lilies was strong as I followed Mattie into a long room. She switched on the lights.

"Over the first twenty years, the early Cronation cells gradually infiltrated and took over many well-known spas, retreat centers, halfway houses, and mental health and addiction centers, even some women's prisons around the United States. There were cells — small, decentralized groups of women in every city and town — meeting and learning, engaging in consciousness practices, sharing good food and fun.

"By the 1990s, you may remember, increasing numbers of women were also incarcerated for the smallest infraction of the so-called 'Life-Culture Legislation,' thinly disguised means of keeping women under control. These had been passed by the Men in Charge who still thought they actually were in charge, despite the serious wake-up calls Mother Nature gave them regularly in the form of hurricanes Camille, Katrina, Rita, Sandy and her subsequent tropical storm incarnations, besides wildfires, volcanic eruptions, and other acts of the Goddess Herself waking up and shaking off the deep sleep of the dark cycle. Many more women were ready and the movement really took off."

"I never heard anything about this," I said skeptically. I pride myself on keeping up with trends to do with women, so this is a sensitive point with me.

"Well, you weren't exactly the main focus of the movement, no offense. Phoebe — that's my grandmother — and the other founders felt that change comes best from within the groups most oppressed by the system. And well, you've bought pretty heavily into the status quo."

"I beg your pardon," I protested. "I wrote my business school thesis on fairness in the workplace. I plan to help women rise in the system as soon as I get to California."

"Yeah, well, hold on now, and let me go on a little bit before you get your back up. I'd like to put the 'system' as it relates to women in a bit of perspective for you."

"Can we sit down? This smoothie is great but I'm still feeling a little woozy." As I sank into an overstuffed sofa I noticed that the opposite wall was lined with photos of women and each had a ledge below it holding a vase of flowers; some had a candle burning or a stick of incense.

Mattie saw me looking and said, "Oh, I'll get to them in a second. We honor and call on the energy of many women from the past who made Cronation possible in the form we have today."

I pulled my feet up; Mattie was settling in for what seemed like would be awhile.

"The Farm, a.k.a. Heartscape, was a well-loved Midwestern spa that worked as a great cover in the early years as the women brainstormed their first initiatives. Phoebe got a job at Heartscape teaching yoga and working in the kitchen. She and the women from the initial cell received the Cronation blueprint via active imagination meditations during their time underground and refined it in regular gatherings at the Farm."

"What are you talking about? They made all this up?" I was appalled. This was exactly what my dad accused Mom and her friends of doing; "flights of fancy instead of doing the dishes," O'Malley would whisper to me when mom and her friends gathered at our house.

"No, they didn't make it up. They received it by opening themselves to the Creative Source, the Central Intelligence of the Universe, the Source of All Possibility, with the intention to be of service to the greatest good for all. Phoebe went underground with a group of women when the first Civil Rights Movement hit the skids. Each woman developed a different aspect of the plan through her special connection to the Creative Source. They learned that a new era was coming and would be governed by the Crone archetype, after centuries of the Warrior being the dominant archetype active in human imagination. If these wise women who'd reached emotional and spiritual maturity and dedicated themselves to 'the highest good of all' worked together, they could help the inevitable shift to be peaceful instead of drenched in war and conflict."

"Yeah, well, no offense to your grandmother, but it doesn't seem like its worked out so well," I sighed.

Mattie just smiled at me, which was slightly infuriating, and continued. "There were only a handful of women in those days who escaped the heinous scam of hormone replacement therapy, the cure for the newly invented 'disease' of menopause.

"For once it helped to be poor and black, outside the PR campaign of M.D.s eager to make money 'curing' this new 'illness.' All over the world, as the planet matured to Her Gaian Crone phase, unmedicated women awakened to a kind of powerful wisdom surging through themselves. In some places the shift was subtle. Where the men were less deluded and resistant, more women were elected to government office, and became heads of organizations and policy makers. And in many areas the women remained invisible, accomplishing their work while appearing to be simple laborers or office workers."

I suddenly remembered the woman on her knees scrubbing the floor in the Wentsouth lobby. "That's right, Eve, Esperanza is part of the Cronation Network. She does surveillance work with Lydia to discern women who are reaching the Shift point. Believe me, as a cleaning lady she witnesses plenty because no one pays any attention to her.

"Some of the Cronation women," Mattie continued, "have learned how to direct subtle energies to deflect angry diatribes in public discourse. They were deployed in news organizations and lower levels of regional and local governance. At advanced skill levels, even actual weapons can be caused to jam or otherwise malfunction. Women with these skills have infiltrated police forces around the world. Their interventions, while invisible to their male co-workers, have caused significant drops in crimes, which served as an ongoing deterrent.

"Others received intricate diagrams for inventions that would be required for the new society, like the plans for extracting excreted excess nutrients from the urine of well-fed First World folks so they could be kept out of the waste stream where they cause algal bloom in waterways. Cronation has a whole fertilizer industry from harvested pee! Some women channeled an advocacy system of law that encouraged individuals to take responsibility for their actions. Mediation, reparations and service have now become respected alternative means alongside the 'corrections' system of prison and punishment that has continued to writhe in a spasm of violence and decay."

"Really!? You remind me of my mother; this is the sort of pie-in-the-sky stuff she was always talking about." It used to drive my dad crazy when Mom and her friends talked like this.

"There is so much the women have done." Mattie showed no signs of wrapping up the lesson. "The Compassionista Brigades developed out of the Women in Black campaign in Israel and the peace vigils in cities around the world. You've heard of them, Eve?"

I nodded, trying not to think dark thoughts since Mattie could read them so easily.

"Women in Black had the awareness to let go of the angry rallies and protests of other eras in favor of silent witness to get their message across. That was a big step.

"But the Crones realized that standing silently got boring and women began to feel ineffective; a different sort of energy was needed. One day, Marisol, a Crone from Venezuela, began to see Kwan Yin, the Chinese Goddess of Compassion, as she stood on the plaza with her local group. She previously knew nothing of Kwan Yin and felt her visitation was a call for women to employ their imaginations more fully in their work. She urged each woman to ask the Divine for a vision or else to imagine the most compassionate feminine figure she knew: the Blessed Virgin or Our

Lady of Guadalupe, one's own grandmother. When the women learned to call on these energies, they created a vibration in themselves that evoked compassion in others.

"They began to gather outside of government buildings when important debates were taking place, creating a vibe of love and selflessness that began to open the hearts of lawmakers. Each loving decision was honored and celebrated by the Compassionistas with grateful gifts of flowers and food — until the Men in Charge declared it bribery when they received embarrassing publicity. Of course, since bribery is an accepted part of political life, the gifts could be and were slowly reintroduced in more subtle ways. More slowly, but still continually, decision making began to change as the intention of the gifts, for genuine gratitude, ebbed into the politicians and into whatever cracks and fissures there were in their personas."

"Yeah, well, this is a sweet story, Mattie, but frankly it seems a little bit delusional to me." I was getting a little impatient with this nonsense. "The world is a mess. All anyone can do is improve and protect their little corner and hope for the best."

"That's just the trance speaking, Eve. All humans have a deep awareness of multiple realities and interpretations of reality. What you just described is the dominant theme of the Warrior reality in its late stage of decay. Of course, since it's reinforced by the news and other media constantly, it's what most folks allow to guide their lives. Let me introduce you to some of the women whose spirits are guiding us. That may help." Mattie walked me over to a black-and-white photo of an elegant Black woman in profile.

"I've seen this photo before." The woman's gray hair was done in cornrows, her hands clasped under her chin. "She's a dancer, right?"

"No, she is elegant though, isn't she? That's Septima Poinsette Clark. She was the grandmother of the Civil Rights Movement. She helped Black folks get the right to be principals in the school system in South

Carolina, and she worked for pay equity. She also helped found the citizenship schools that helped folks learn to read and write and learn how to participate in democracy."

I felt a lump in my throat as Mattie walked me down a long line of women's photos. Ella Baker, Fannie Lou Hamer, Rosa Parks, each with flowers and candles burning. "I didn't know these stories," I confessed.

"Yeah, well, you have that fancy education and all, but there's plenty that gets left out. Without these women, there would not have been a Martin Luther King, Junior. These women did the day-in and day-out work, along with countless others."

I was embarrassed that I didn't know their names, but Mattie just said, "Look, Eve, we all have opportunities. Let these women inspire you, as they inspire us. There are so many more going back in history. Each and everyone of us has a part to play."

Next, Mattie took me into a library.

"Cronation has acquired information addressing everything from diet to advanced computer system networking for global communication to violence dissolution techniques. Intricate maps of the galaxy show the location of other societies of sentient beings, among which Earth is neither the least nor the most advanced. A great deal of ancient source material has been returned from the Akashic records showing in detail the evolution of consciousness and each individual's potential role in the grand scheme. These documents are exquisite fractal-like diagrams that showed how each human had a general task or role on Earth but infinite ways to choose how to fulfill that outline."

We moved over to a bank of computers and Mattie called up something that looked like a very cool screen saver.

"It became clear that the evolutionary trend was a natural unfolding, the big picture, yet each individual could choose how much or how little to invest in consciousness unfolding. These screens can be read by the women who channeled the code and who are working on creating computer programs that would allow the information in the fractal images to be displayed as text and image for the general reader, as you see here."

She clicked a key and the screen transformed into a text format like a magazine article complete with illustrations in color with explanations underneath.

"Eventually, when Cronation's New Age dawns, each child will receive her, and his, of course, own fractal document and be encouraged from a young age to experiment with how to manifest her uniqueness for the highest good of all.

"Earth has evolved through many ages, each with a dominant archetype. In the conscious memory of everyone presently alive on the planet, the world has been governed by the Warrior archetype — it's all we've experienced in gross reality — but it is rapidly approaching the end of its cycle. The greatest amount of creativity under the Warrior archetype was devoted to — you guessed it — war. Gradually, say over the last hundred thousand years, that archetype began to devolve or just plain run out of gas. As movies in the twenty and twenty-first century attest, there are only so many ways of shooting people and blowing stuff up. Blunt force trauma is a crude means of transformation."

There were plenty of women warriors throughout history, Mattie explained — small numbers compared to the men, and enough men with an integrated feminine wisdom — all powerfully aligned with the Creative Source, who kept the world in a kind of balance. When hormone replacement therapy became widespread in the 1960s, it blunted the fearlessness and fierceness necessary to be a woman warrior. Women were prevented from reaching their warrior years highly evolved in mind and heart. There was also a widespread misunderstanding of plant medicine as a way to drop more deeply into service to the Source. Lots of opportunities for evolving consciousness that appeared in the '60s had been reclaimed in their sacredness by the Crones.

"Since Hildegard of Bingen in 1100 CE there really hadn't been a bonafide woman warrior of major dimensions outside of the comic books, which were becoming an underground source of images to guide the Shift.

The '60s showed a flash of what could be, but at too many critical decision points poor choices were made; think about Bernadette Dorhn and the Weather Underground, for example. There needed to be a generation of older, wiser women who weren't enamored of the Male way of doing things."

Mattie clicked back to the beautiful fractals. Their slow spinning on the computer screen mesmerized me. "Can I see mine?" I asked.

"I think you've seen enough for now, Eve; you don't have to get it all at once. Look, let's get to dinner. I think once you meet Aurelia and get oriented to this whole movement you'll really be excited. Aurelia is going to report on her visits to Cronation cells around the country and tell us how their initiatives are going. We're building toward a major Cronation Wave starting at the Winter Solstice on December 21st. Ever since the hype about the Mayan calendar ending on December 21, 2012, there has been a major surge on that day. Some people are hung up on the Mayan calendar supposedly predicting the end of time on that day in 2012, but we think it will begin the Crone Era. Each year we prepare for one of the many rounds of the Divine's birth contractions."

"That's less than a month away."

I knew the date because I'd booked tickets to Belize for that very same day. I planned to be jetting off to bask under palm trees, drink piña coladas, and plan my move to the West Coast, not being hijacked by a bunch of crazy '60s throwbacks hell bent on getting a do-over.

"I know, isn't that great?" Mattie beamed. "The surges freak a lot of people out so it's good that they come on the shortest day of the year. Not that everything will be accomplished in one day — but, hey, once the full force of women's loving energy is unleashed across the world, Truth and Justice will roll across this country like a mighty wave and we'll be free at last," Mattie said, standing, misty-eyed, her hairdo moussed back into spikes, (no doubt with some sort of aloe-based organic product) since her stint comforting me in the backseat of the cab.

As we walked upstairs, Mattie continued, "From the beginning, Cronation recruited across class and income lines, not to mention race and age. The women who came to Heartscape — moms and daughters on special occasion getaways, groups of friends sharing pedicures and gossip, young moms out to recapture carefree girlfriend times — would all eventually be among the Crones of Cronation along with the bag ladies, shop keepers, and cleaning ladies, like Esperanza who you saw scrubbing the lobby floor at Wentworth and Wentsouth today. In every city and economic strata, hair and nail salons are gathering places for Cronation operatives.

"Women all over the world have taken positions where they could blend into the fabric of daily life while carrying out Cronation missions or surveillance. Each Cronation cell is interdependent and relies on the highly evolved intuitive functions of the individual members to tune in and act in concert with other groups. Dream groups share information, often disguised as knitting circles or book clubs, which are less likely to draw attention. In some neighborhoods women simply plan a communal time at the laundromat or market to share their plans and support one another."

Now I was wondering about every encounter I'd ever had with ordinary women. Could I have been blind to all this? I doubted it fully.

"Heartscape evolved into the nerve center for the entire Cronation movement." Mattie spoke almost without taking a breath. "Everything Phoebe and the others learned in their time of preparation guided them to assist the paradigm shift's final stages from the country's heartland. Here things move a little bit more slowly. Women began to recover from coffee-jacking themselves into a headlong rush away from anything that doesn't promise dollar signs or some shimmering chimera of pop-culture perfection. Phoebe saw her work as similar to that of the last runner in a relay race, carrying the torch that, when handed to the next generation, would light the fuse of change. But, instead of igniting a bomb (the transformational image of choice of late-stage warriors), it would ignite and burn up all the deadwood, detritus, debris, and dried-up ideas that clogged the flow of Love in each and every heart."

"I'm not going to wake up from this, am I?" I asked Mattie.

"Oh, you'll be waking up, all right! Cronation is all about waking up; this is just the beginning," replied Mattie, smiling as she hooked her arm in mine. "We are so fortunate to be incarnated in women's bodies at this precise moment when the long playing album of civilization is about to begin playing on the Feminine flip side!"

I stopped in front of some photos near the door: groups of smiling women.

"Those are women who've been part of different groups here. Some have gone back to their communities to work, some live here full time."

"Who are these women?" I pointed to a photo that included younger women.

"Oh, they attended a mother-daughter retreat a few years back and then stayed on as interns," Mattie said.

"Well, that one doesn't look like she's absorbed the 'vibe,'" I said, pointing to a scowling young woman whose eyes were sad and dark.

"That's true, Eve. Good call. She took off before she really felt the love here; she took that other young woman next to her along too. I hope they found some peace because they were sure angry."

6 ————————

Some months back Aurelia had been lying on the hilltop at the center of the Cronation property under the shade of a towering oak tree. "Momma, are you sure the timing is right?"

Aurelia knew that once the next wave of Cronation initiatives kicked in, there would be no stopping it. Each successive wave grew in strength and intensity like the contractions of any birth. Meanwhile, the manifest "order," if it could be called that anymore, deteriorated: roads, bridges, "public works" collapsed regularly from lack of maintenance and a cascade of the effects from extreme weather changes. At first it was mostly poor areas, like New Orleans, whose infrastructure has been cobbled together for decades — but lately even upscale areas were experiencing costly damage from severe weather, corrupt building practices, and lack of civic will to do the work of upkeep.

"That 'can-do' attitude is about 'can-done,'" Phoebe liked to say.

Aurelia understood that a great deal of what is commonly called "progress" would have to fall away before folks rediscovered what is essential.

"The storms, the avalanches, the fires and droughts, these are just Her own housekeeping chores," Phoebe said breezily. "If folks get nudged around like the spiders out of the corners when you scrub the pantry, well, so be it."

"Yes, Momma, but that's easier to say from where you sit. You see the whole picture," Aurelia grumbled.

"And that picture is endlessly shifting, brightening or darkening, depending on the intentions, thoughts, and actions of you folks living in the material world." Phoebe would not countenance any trolling for pity on Aurelia's part.

Meanwhile, agents all over the world had their tasks activated via a network that had been carefully researched, developed, and put in place over the last forty years by literally millions of women in every town, city, university, psych ward, strip mall hair salon, quilting bee, women's auxiliary, brothel, writer's group, book club, bowling league, prayer circle in every religious denomination, every ethnic enclave and political caucus. The secret banding together of virtually all women had begun slowly and sped up as the Great Awakening of the Goddess progressed in the mid twenty-first century.

Enough was enough, after all. While the Men in Charge knocked themselves out in war after war, the women bided their time as the feminine force of Nature paved — or rather, unpaved — the way for change. Aurelia knew this, yet something still made her uneasy. Patience was always one of Phoebe's greatest lessons. While the men exhausted the dregs of their energy and will to control things — like punch-drunk toddlers before naptime — flailing away at "terrorists" in new wars or focusing on new improved computer features in cars that were already so complicated that the average driver couldn't even change a tire, the women of Cronation practiced stillness, waiting, silence, imagination, and peace.

The Western women had much to learn from their sisters in burkahs, hijabs, and purdah who knew that they could use, required even, the solitude afforded by their customs to concentrate and increase the strength of their transformative energy. It took a while, but the Western women had finally come to understand not only "right action" but also "right inaction." They no longer squandered their energy in anger or protest or in trying to reform and enlighten men. The overt repressive efforts of men worldwide had only focused and increased the women's energy, even while superficially seeming to shut it down. The strong polarization of forces was necessary to complete the paradigm shift.

Aurelia worked diligently to dissuade the women from complaining and blaming the men, yet sometimes she struggled to put her assurances into words. "Blame is lame" some of the younger women said, but Aurelia knew that even the impulse to blame came from a spot of blindness she couldn't quite put her finger on. The women understood, with varying degrees of clarity, that they were participating in a natural phenomenon that would manifest with the highest and most complex good for all involved in direct proportion to their clarity of intention, their generous compassion of heart, and their unfettered willingness to hoot, holler, dance, sing, and have fun. "Recalibration to the Celebration Via your Imagination" was one aphorism that seemed to hit the spot.

On the other hand, to men, the Shift of eras felt like a noose slowly strangling the life out of them as a punishment for all their bad deeds. As long as they were blamed and felt blameworthy in their own hearts, they caused energetic static and resistance in the change process.

"Look, Aurelia, I wish I could just yell 'time out' and send the men to their rooms," Phoebe sighed. "I wish I could pull the plugs on all their headphones, microphones, and other devices and escort each one off center stage. Lovingly, of course, but firmly. Maybe sit each one down in a nice comfy chair in front of a wide-screen TV and some football. But they get to write their own finale. It's been their show."

"They've done so many fine and wonderful things," Phoebe catalogued, "the printing press, the radio, x-rays. Land sakes, Mr. Kodak and his cameras, all those computer boys who started out in their garages. Then of course there's Moses, Plato, Jesus, Percy Julian, W.E.B. Dubois, Martin, of course, Nelson, and Desmond…"

"Will we be different, Momma? Have we learned enough from their mistakes?"

Phoebe continually cautioned her daughter and all the women to hold a place of compassionate disinterest when thinking about the Men in Charge, or anyone else for that matter. "If you get all caught up in the 'poor men' or the 'bad men' thing and don't keep your eye on the work, I guarantee you they will suck your energy right into the war machine. If you really focus on what the men do and say, why you'll have no choice but to protest twenty-four hours a day — or just throw yourself into the nearest river.

"It is not your job to fix the men. The ones that are too far-gone will crash and burn in ways too numerous to list. The ones that are open to change will get sick and have all sorts of healing crises to scare the daylights — or actually to disintegrate the crusty accumulations of terror — out of them. Those who have the stamina, or support from wives and daughters, will soften and come around. Their own latent feminine energy will start to light up just like the women are lighting up."

Like her forebears in the early Civil Rights Movement, Phoebe was a "womanist." Men were not the devil, not to be criticized; that was a waste of time. Neither were they to be kowtowed to or coddled. Just seen, like all of imperfect humanity, with soft eyes.

"You all can spend more time doing your own work, looking at your own shadow, because as the Shift comes, the men will be mirroring your own worst selves. As their feminine energy starts to percolate, so will the male energy in the women. There'll be more switching up than a Virginia reel square dance!" Phoebe laughed.

"Women will screw up plenty when they get the chance, don't worry," she told Aurelia. "We're no angels, as the angels never tire of reminding me. As women's male energy rises, you can expect them to channel their own versions of knuckleheadedness in the worst ways. You are lucky to be in those glorious women's bodies. If you pay attention to the wisdom that arises every minute from that beautiful body, you'll do a damn sight better. Not perfect, Goddess knows. There will be new challenges and plenty of chances to screw up. We'll just have to see.

"Remember, that 'transition' as they call it, when your body suddenly decides its time to push," Phoebe liked to remind Aurelia of the birth process for women, "your little old uterus tightens down like the Goddess Herself is squeezing the last drop of water out of Her laundry and is about to shake it dry. When the whole thing gets going and there's no turning back. The Men in Charge are going to clamp down on women in response to their own fear as well and you have to be ready to meet their terror with love and light. That's the difference between a baby getting stuck in the birth canal and needing to be pulled out bloody with forceps, or a woman getting sliced open like a watermelon at a Fourth of July picnic and having her child pulled out by the ears — instead of sliding out like she's coming down a waterslide at Great America! Do we want the next era to be a fun and amazing theme park of love or another damn endless war?"

"You'd think," Aurelia fussed, "that a few of them would recognize that they are just projecting their fears all over the place and seeing the world just the way it is inside them."

Phoebe snorted and a flock of blackbirds lifted off the high-tension wires that ran along the country road bordering the Farm. A cloud appeared that looked for all the world like a kicking mule.

"So, to answer your question, Aurelia — yes, it's time, for goodness sake! You got the dumbest passel of men in charge since Hoover ran the FBI. It's an opportunity. They get more repressive by the minute and even they don't know why. It's time all right. If you think you can wait for them to wake up all fresh and easy on their own, you are sadly mistaken. You, of all people, Aurelia, ought to know that when anyone is in the grip of an archetype and others project all their energy in that direction, waking up is doggone hard to do. That's why consciousness and change always seem to come from out of left field, from poor people, 'crazy' people, whoever hasn't worn out their energy being in charge. You can't be channeling the new script if you still have a speaking role in the old one, now can you? No, you cannot.

"No, you definitely cannot," Phoebe repeated. "Men like Harvey who get the simple truth that it's time to be in service to the Great She, they know it's nothing personal, get that it's not about knowing everything and having a blueprint. We just focus our light and de-light in what unfolds. It's not like putting in an order at the take-out window — that's a distortion of how things work. Humans' job is to focus on the values, cultivate the qualities they would like to see more of in the world, leave it up to the Great She to decide what it will look like. Otherwise it's no fun for Her. She is not about predictability and it's time to stop reaching for that stale, old tonic and celebrate not knowing."

Aurelia knew in her bones that they were being divinely guided; she just needed to hear Phoebe get excited sometimes and reassure her. And it was true that they had had many moments of reassurance along the way. The government's denouncement of estrogen therapy in 2004 was one of the prophetic signs that Cronation was nearing its birthing time. It had taken years to get the women in place at NIH for that one. Estrogen "therapy" had kept women in an emotional trance of placidity and terror since the 1950s. Getting vast numbers of women off synthetic estrogen really helped speed up the cause, just as the sages had predicted. Millions of women began to wake up as the excess hormones washed out of their systems.

Estrogen replacement prevented women from reaching emotional maturity and attaining the spiritual evolution that is a natural part of aging. Instead, wandering lost in a perpetual adolescence, feeling a lack of something they couldn't quite name, women took endless workshops and read piles of self-help books, choked down vitamin and mineral dietary supplements, and consulted therapists, coaches, healers and shamans, even magazines at the check-out counters in an effort to figure out what was missing. Their collective energy was frittered away in a melee of talk shows, shopping trips, and diets. Aging continued unabated, of course, and cosmetic surgery soared. The net effect being that women were neutralized as a potent force for change and turned into profit centers for surgeons, psychologists, and assorted New Age snake oil peddlers. These pursuits kept the majority of women busy and distracted while the Men in Charge looted the till at home and abroad and fought over whose ersatz version of democracy should carry the day. Once the fantasy that estrogen was helping to protect their health was shattered, women dropped the pills like the poison that they were to their maturing systems.

The whole Cronation Movement was about carefully developing, nurturing, and then unleashing the power of women at the exact moment when the Old Order was at its weakest, but not so far gone that the end result would be cataclysmic.

"The time is right, the Hair Initiative is beginning its last stage," Phoebe said firmly. "Remember, that has always been one of the markers that the time is near."

Under the cover of "The Foundation for Women's Health and Appearance Tools," (W.H.A.T.) a fake right-wing outfit whose mission was "To keep women looking their best for the common good," Cronation had begun the Hair Initiative. Hair dye was causing cancers in countless women trying to stave off an aging appearance, not to mention the legions of hairdressers, male and female, who had a shocking incidence of bladder cancers from exposure to the coal tar chemicals in the dyes. Cronation research indicated that going directly at the hair dye and trying to get women to give it up would never work; women knew that their desirability hinged on seeming younger. But, as they began to abandon synthetic hormones, they began to notice how artificial dyed hair really looked and came to appreciate and prefer their own natural hair color. The proliferation of gray-haired women was an unconscious signifier that tripped a switch in men's plural brains, signaling their era of domination as coming to an end. (This, of course, increased their fear, since they expected reprisals. Cronation taught that simply noticing men's fear and not responding to it was the best approach.) Attractiveness began a slow re-definition. Gradually the image of the fit and funny gray-haired woman began to creep into the culture and undermine the top-heavy Barbie doll blonde as the main archetype of beauty.

Even W.H.A.T., the group who also invented hot rollers that plugged into the cigarette lighter in a car so women could set their hair on the way home from work and look fresh for their husbands when they came in the door, found that as long as gray hair looked neatly coiffed, most men didn't register the change, men being less visually astute to begin with. The W.H.A.T. hot roller device became standard issue in minivans in 2002.

The husband's right to an attractive spouse, put in place by years of viewing sitcoms where average looking men were always paired with exceptionally attractive women as the culture defined beauty, was a key provision of the Culture of Life Laws. That scenario, universally reinforced by TV viewing, ensured that when the proposal to make it law was introduced, there was a bipartisan majority on the very first vote. Even a few women voted for it, but they were probably still on HRT.

"Momma, it just seems like you should be here leading this. Can't you just get into a body and come back?" Aurelia was surprised to find her eyes filling with tears.

"Now, Baby, this is to be expected," Phoebe comforted. "You are feeling the residue of outworn ideas. There is no one leader, one person to rely on. All over this good earth there are cadres of women taking turns leading the way. And, gracious, I am here for you so completely now, why, I know it if you eat too much falafel at lunch and get some gas — that's how tuned in I am! No, we are all exactly where we need to be. You are enough, you are magnificent, you are here to lead along with all these women and to usher in the Era of the Crone. Remember all the women out there suffering right now. Remember all the Divine guidance we've received and all the steps we've taken to put this into place."

"You're right, Momma, I know there are so many sisters locked up for nothing more than having their own life source energy stolen from them." Under the "Muse Clause" in the Culture of Life laws, a woman could be put on trial if her husband's productivity in the workplace fell below a certain level on the assumption that his helpmeet was culpable somehow.

Phoebe resumed, "Your women monitoring the Hair Initiative say you're close to critical mass, don't they?" Phoebe asked.

The Cronation counter mission embedded microchip broadcasting devices in the hot rollers in the mini-vans women drove to and from work so that a woman could beam up information to the Cronation mainframe from a secure, moving site — her car. W.H.A.T. funded some professors at Tufts University to do a demographic study to discern the point when the widest age spectrum of women would turn gray. Cronation sages determined that when a critical mass of 75% of the eldest women worldwide turned gray, the criteria for a more public Cronation initiative would be met. The overt purpose of the study was to research the most effective ways to reeducate those women who were unwilling to dye their hair due to health concerns, neo-feminist psychobabble, or downright laziness. Free kits for "hair makeovers" designed to covertly lure the hair dye crowd to give up the practice were offered at grocery stores and malls in red, white, and blue packages that also contained a message about Cronation and a phone number to call for more information and a website that the FBI hadn't found because it was coded to come up only under knitting, gourd art, and recipe sites. Cronation had learned a few tricks from the Men in Charge about counterintelligence.

"Yes, Momma, of course. Actually we've been hovering between 65-70% for months; something is bound to happen soon to push the edge. We're due for a visit from Lorelei soon, too."

Lorelei Winger, consummate double agent and member of the Crone Council, was the wife of Wright, the current Man in Charge (the various elected offices dropped away in meaninglessness once electronic voting machines programmed by the highest cash bidder became standard). She sat on the W.H.A.T. Board. She oversaw a huge NIH grant that ostensibly funded a "health campaign," to study preventative measures to arrest aging, which was supplemented with money from Homeland Security. Too many gray-haired, wide-awake women were definitely a threat to national security and to the inalienable rights of men to have the most attractive partners and keep on doing what they were doing. Most of the funds were funneled to Cronation cells around the country by Lorelei and the other dedicated women who balanced a double life with grace and aplomb.

"How Lorelei has held her tongue all those years is a mystery to me, Momma," Aurelia shook her head.

"Well, let's just say she is one old soul. Believe me, nobody wanted that job. She's like your wonderful Lydia, deep cover where the Men in Charge least expect it, and compassionate too. Such big hearts these women have! They are vibrating at a very high level, let me tell you!"

Lorelei and Lydia were both part of the covert "Crone Archetype Activation," a major special operation, "Code Purple" after the book When I Grow Old I Shall Wear Purple.

"Imagine any woman in her right mind waiting 'til she's old to wear purple!" Phoebe had laughed when the book became popular. "Such a clever way to bury the meaning in code."

Some women married to government officials took to wearing wigs to cover their graying hair, not wanting to compromise the Hair Initiative or draw attention to themselves. Everyone remembered what happened to Martha Mitchell when she tried to speak up during Watergate. Many of the wives of Men in Charge were among the greatest adepts in biding time.

"Remember, Aurelia, advertising science had long shown that whatever image one sees most frequently becomes the most attractive over time. That's how we got that awful 'anorexia chic' in the '80s. It's a survival mechanism that was totally co-opted by Madison Ave. Back in hunter-gatherer times, it was 'love the one you're with' or the species couldn't continue. That he had a face like the back end of a rhino didn't matter a bit. If he hung around long enough, gatherer woman would be convinced to mate with almost any post-primate that stayed upright most of the time."

Phoebe had chaired the Economic Entanglement Committee in the Cronation underground for years. They studied the economic ramifications of every aspect of women's behavior and ran intricate statistical tests to determine which ones were most amenable to change and would also have the most far-reaching positive effects without negative unintended consequences. In recent times the media had come to have nearly total control over what was considered attractive.

Six to nine months after the Cronation-recruited cohort stopped dyeing their hair, the numbers of fully gray-haired women would reach a critical mass and suddenly seem both exotic and desirable. Aurelia mused that gray really would be the new blonde in ways no one would have foreseen.

"I guess we can thank advertisers for shortening the average attention span to nanoseconds," Aurelia said.

"Always, always," Phoebe replied, "be on the look-out for unintended consequences that you can use to your co-creative advantage."

The shift to make older women the most desirable was one of Cronation's greatest, most subversive, and dangerous achievements. The aging Men in Charge were actually turning on the younger men over this one, a real split in the otherwise monolithic men's world culture that was closing its grip around its own throat. Confused by younger men's interest in and respect for older women, the older men, as usual, lashed out with misguided measures. With surreal logic, the men who at nineteen vowed to trust no one over thirty, put a bill before Congress to make electronic surveillance of any man under the age of sixty legal without a warrant — until it came to light that only men under thirty had the skills to design such a sophisticated surveillance system and they weren't playing. The appreciation and attraction younger men felt for the Crones helped to balance the fears of some of the older men in the big picture. While many of them projected their terror at losing power onto older women who, they claimed, would (like the "witches" of old) steal it, some felt a stirring of their own long-denied feminine side. For those older men, new interests in art or gardening marked a wonderful blossoming that contributed to softening the changes taking place.

Phoebe had chuckled when Aurelia asked if pitting the men against one another might not have some drawbacks.

"Like what? They stop thinking up countries to invade or wildernesses to plunder? Slow down the production of some damn chemical plant? These are just playground squabbles. Let them keep each other busy for a change. Besides, enough feminine energy is active in the young men that they can just chuckle at their chuckleheaded elders. And they all know tai chi; they can take care of themselves."

Aurelia was well versed in the strategies necessary to turn the tide in society. She was part of the academic elite of her generation who wrote papers in her anthropology class such as "The Coming Eroticization of Age" where she showed that Baby Boomer demographics were such that, as their wives aged and entered their spiritual and sexual maturity, without the interference of synthetic hormones, many of their husbands meanwhile would be losing potency at an equal and opposite rate.

The long-term effects of eating too much meat caused Proteinosis, a syndrome where men more or less calcified like Lot's wife into a pillar of salt. One day the man would be watching the hockey game like always and just be unable to get up off the couch, his knees locked in place. The physical rigidity, compounded by the planetary realignment as the Warrior archetype waned and the Goddess/Crone began to ascend, was causing men to seize up or break down at unprecedented rates while women filled with light and kindness that made them very attractive to younger, more conscious men. The tide of Goddess energy lifted all women's boats. Even elderly women were getting a second wind, drawing amorous glances from young delivery men, and even in retirement communities, fending off advances from men a generation or more younger.

Meanwhile, younger women, like the one who replaced Eve at Wentworth and Wentsouth, benefited from the final frenzy of macho values. While CEOs and politicians fought each other to the death, locked in impotent brain freeze or self-destructed from terminal hubris, women were busy methodically taking over the reins of power in the public sphere, ready to guide the transition to the next chapter in the Life of Gaia, the planetary awakening to Cronation.

Aurelia published her theory in major academic journals and introduced it into enough blogs that it became a meme: younger men who were waking up to the return of the Goddess and the dawn of a new era were going to be fascinated by the older gals and would enjoy these women who evoked the Earth Mother archetype that was recouping Her power, coming into ascendancy after centuries of lying dormant. The new young female corporate execs would remind the young men of their fathers and throw a real wrench into sexual attraction between age peers, causing an epidemic of impotency, low birth rates, and dysphoria within the same-age cohort. This would delay their production of offspring until the paradigm shift was fully underway.

The Crones in the Tantric Teams were versed in the ancient sexual arts. They worked with these young men closely, all in the line of duty, of course. The tantrikas would keep the young men occupied while at the same time training their skills and stamina. Eventually, once they'd been trained in the art of making transformative love, the Tantrikas would turn the fellows over to the younger women, who had served out their time remaking the corporations and world governments. It was a loving thank you to these young women for the sacrifices they made as the last of the corporate women warriors. Their enlightenment would come as a bolt of insight as the men's club crumbled and they found themselves still standing as if virtual reality goggles had been removed.

"I'm still concerned," Aurelia worried, "about the effect of a chemical deluge into the water table. If too many women dump out their dyes at once…"

"Oh, don't worry, Sweetie," Phoebe laughed, "there's enough die-hards out there who will be lying in their caskets with skin like Corinthian leather pulled tight over those cheekbones, and L'Oreal tawny blonde #5 on their tresses and fake boobs pointing hard and fast toward heaven like Twin Peaks. We may not reeducate every single woman who dyes her hair, though Goddess knows, we've tried!

"I'm more concerned about the surge in libido that comes once the hormones are gone. Women are Croning much more robustly now that they don't have to purge the synthetic estrogen out of their systems. I've never been completely satisfied with the numbers in the Tantric Teams! We have to figure out how to get more women signed up. A woman of fifty with a full-surging libido and no Tantric training can be as unpredictable as a bull on speed." Aurelia could hear the smile in Phoebe's voice.

"You and Harvey have done a great job getting the idea across to the younger men, but why more women aren't signing up to make hay with these healthy, sweet men is a mystery to me."

"And," Aurelia continued the thought, "we can't get a media campaign out saying 'Tired of the old codger in the sack next to you? You can do better.' Not in this political climate. You'd be arrested by lunchtime."

"I know," Phoebe sighed. "We tried a PR campaign like that back in 2004 to pave the way, but we didn't predict that the number of fifty-somethings tuning into that L Word show would go through the roof. Once they saw full-frontal lesbian love, I don't care how sweet the man is, he just can't compete if the woman is beyond her mating years. Back then if you mentioned the word 'Tantra' to a menopausal woman before the hormones were fully flushed out of her system, she'd likely stuff her last tampon down your throat.

"Well, those Focus on the Family fellas sure capitalized on this one," Phoebe continued. "It makes sense in that small way that those folks tie sex so completely to procreation that you can talk women right out of birth control of any kind. But, with men drying up, they don't have the juice for sex after their wives are done childbearing anyway. Those women have turned their energy to crafts, I guess. But how many gourds can a woman paint like Santa Claus before she notices the blessed squash is shaped like a dildo?" Phoebe chuckled.

"Maybe we can come up with a catchy yet non-threatening name and get the classes back into the community centers on the local level," Aurelia suggested.

"And then there are the women who remember the public beheadings when the Muse Clause was first introduced." Phoebe shuddered.

"Oh my, yes, that was awful!"

Aurelia remembered when the government came out with a study that showed that worker productivity had taken a real nosedive in the U.S.

When someone looked at the data carefully and realized that a drop in male productivity was responsible for ninety per cent of the net loss, a crisis ensued. A few zealous female researchers thought publicizing this finding would finally win wage and benefit parity for women workers; needless to say, they weren't part of the Cronation movement. Aurelia could have told them that such a naïve assumption hadn't worked since the Garden of Eden. Men are hardwired, when up against the wall, to do just one thing: point the finger at the nearest woman and say, in unison, "It's her fault."

The Muse Clause was diabolical. It recognized the importance of women by quantifying every individual woman's contribution to an individual man's success; they even called it the "Gratitude Index." Every man was given an opportunity to assign responsibility for a percentage of his work product to a woman or women as a sign of supposed grateful collaboration. They filed it as a part of their tax forms each April. The Men in Charge called this a breakthrough for women, a recognition of the importance of her labor.

Wives bore the brunt of the Muse Clause, of course, but mothers, daughters, even neighbors, and, in at least one case, a female Labrador retriever named Peaches, were incarcerated if it was ruled they, through less than total devotion, diminished the man's output in any way. A woman could be blamed for a man's lack of work-related dedication or production if it could be shown she provided bland meals, poorly ironed dress shirts, or not enough praise. A dozen women were beheaded in Times Square as a warning to the rest: Behind every successful man is a woman — trying to avoid the guillotine.

Charity Greenberg, the young woman who was now the cause of Aurelia's concern, had found Phoebe's counsel of forbearance, in the face of this absurd and tragic slaughter of women, ridiculous. Actually, it was when Peaches was banished to a remote corner of Labrador for allegedly distracting her owner from working by her need to play catch that Charity declared Cronation a failure, renamed herself Kali, gathered up another young girl named Diva, and took off from the Heartscape compound.

"Momma, back to the timing question. Could a rogue woman with her own agenda undo all we've done to enable this Shift to unfold light instead of the usual chaos and darkness?"

"Well, she'd have to be one powerful dark woman, Aurelia, with her own light dampened down. But even then she alone wouldn't have enough force to upset the apple cart. She'd have to have more than just herself."

"I just wonder if the sparks of revenge that must be smoldering in some women's hearts could be fanned and multiplied by the surging energy," Aurelia said. "It's just a funny feeling I have."

"Well, Darling, women are complex creatures and this upload of power and energy is a first of its kind in history. No telling what it might set off in any given heart. You know what I always say, 'Follow the shadow to the root' if you want to learn what is casting the darkness."

"Thank you, Momma, I will do that."

7 ———————————— ⬡

Mattie steered me toward a clapboard house, and I could hear the sounds of women's voices, talking, laughing — a "hen party"— O'Malley would have said. That's what he called Mom's women's groups when they met at our house while I was growing up. As Mattie guided me through the crowd, I saw women of all ages, but the vast majority were older, gray-haired yet lively and somehow ageless, as if one of Mom's groups had been multiplied tenfold and gone swimming with the cast of the movie Cocoon. These women were raucous, beautiful, all colors, all sizes and shapes. I couldn't take my eyes off them. Some must have been in their nineties or more, but I didn't see a walker among them, though near the door I almost tripped over a large terracotta pot that held half a dozen carved walking sticks.

Women greeted Mattie with hugs and kisses and smiled or squeezed my arm, "Welcome, Sister, welcome." Suddenly an ancient-looking woman with mahogany skin banged the floor with a walking stick carved with the head of a lioness.

"All right, everyone, all right. Finish up your sherry and let's commence to moving over to the barn. Nearly everyone is there already. Aurelia will be there shortly."

"That's Elsie," Mattie whispered as she steered me through the crowded room.

"She must be ninety years old," I said.

"One-hundred and two actually," Mattie smiled. "Many of the women here, the eldest elders, were tuned in very early to the Great Shift. They were able to draw energy straight from the Source and remain healthy because of their bodhisattva vows."

"Their body what?"

"Bodhisattva," Mattie explained. "They forgo returning to the Eternal Void in order to help others reach enlightenment. You know, stick around on earth to help the rest of us get it right, instead of going to their well-deserved rest."

"Oh, yeah, that." It did ring a bell from some Eastern religion course I took in college. "Are they Buddhists?"

"Women of all religious backgrounds are part of Cronation, but we realize that those distinctions are mostly an artifact of the past era of separation. The Crones recognize one Source, infinitely manifesting, and they commune with Her directly. They define life as celebration. Oh, look, there's Sarah Leaf."

Mattie was waving to another woman, one of the younger ones, across the room. She dragged me along.

"Rabbi Sarah, this is Eve. Her Momma was Jewish. Eve just got here today."

"Hello, Eve, shalom and welcome. It's great to meet you. Mattie tells me your mother was very involved in the Jewish Renewal movement."

"Yes," I offered, "My mom and Mattie seem to be great pals; she seems to have much more direct access than I've had since Mom died."

I shot Mattie a look, but she was hugging a tiny woman in a sari and trying not to spill her sherry.

"Rabbi, is this some sort of 'Happy Hour'?" I said as politely as I could, hoping she'd get me a drink.

"Call me Sarah, and, yes, exactly! Here, let me get you some wine and we can sit down and chat for a moment." She led me through the crowd to a couch near the window and picked up two glasses of sherry along the way.

As we sat down, I took a huge gulp before I realized Sarah Leaf was holding her glass reverentially with her eyes closed. She recited a prayer, but not the regular one for over the wine. "Nivareykh et eyen hahayim matzmihat p're hagafen."

"That doesn't sound familiar," I offered, wiping my mouth and hoping the Rabbi hadn't noticed my faux pas. "Not that we were observant or anything. My dad was Catholic. Irish Catholic. No use for religion at all, except for the blessing over a drink. That made sense to him."

Was this place going to turn out to be some sort of multi-religious cult? Sarah Leaf looked at me kindly. With her curly red hair, she could have been one of my cousins on O'Malley's side.

"The prayer you're used to hearing focuses more on saying the blessing because we are commanded to by a king," Rabbi Leaf explained. "This version of the blessing just shifts the focus to the Source of Life as it flows into being, more in concert with the aspect of the Divine we aim to invite to show up. Don't worry, Eve. Cronation isn't about religion. It's about the Spirit that infuses all beings and all things."

I must have looked relieved.

"But, we Jews do have a special connection to the Crones." She beamed. "You wouldn't have heard about it in Sunday school, even if you had gone, but the Jewish people have been serving and protecting the Goddess for thousands of years. We've been in exile with Her, waiting for this era to begin."

"You don't say?" I was beginning to relax from the sherry. I drained my glass and fingered the stem, but the rabbi didn't take the hint.

"Yes, the Kabbalists, our mystical teachers, say that when Shekinah — the feminine aspect of God — returns, a new era of peace will begin. One esoteric understanding of the journey of our people is that they volunteered to remember the Shekinah until it was time for Her return. During those few thousand years of patriarchy, the Jews have been guarding Her while She slept, if you will, gathering Her power for the next feminine era. Our people have always kept the lunar calendar, for example, in Her honor.

This service to the feminine is also at the root of anti-Semitism. Unconsciously, men from other groups have always known that the Jews were never entirely down with the patriarchal program. And there's, you know, the burning of witches and all that."

I didn't quite have the focus to dredge up any of the arguments Mom's friends would have made about how patriarchal Judaism itself was; I never paid close enough attention to them. O'Malley's approach of throwing out the whole business of religion always seemed more practical than trying to sift through the stories for some grain of truth.

"No offense, Sarah, but I'm sure my mother would really appreciate this a lot more than me. I take after my father, practical more than mystical."

Sarah Leaf laughed, "Well, one thing I've learned from Aurelia and the Crones is something about walking the mystical path with practical feet."

Whatever that meant.

Mattie poked her head in at that moment. "There you two are! Come on now, it's time to get over to the barn. Momma's gonna speak a bit, then dinner. Eve, you must be starved." The three of us walked to the barn arm in arm, and I have to say, there was something sort of thrilling in the excitement and energy I was beginning to feel.

We entered the barn through a rear entrance. When I laid eyes on Aurelia Astarte Marx for the first time, her hands were lifted, her caftan billowing at her sides. She had feathers and beads worked into the gray dreadlocks that hung about her face like Spanish moss. She was addressing a collection of women who looked like they'd been milling around Yasgur's Farm since 1969, aging but not necessarily changing clothes. She was enveloped in a pulsing golden light that, at first, I thought came from an overhead fixture until I realized there was nothing above her except the high, rough-hewn barn-board ceiling.

Every surface of the barn, walls and ceiling, even the floor was covered in painted imagery. Snakes, flowers, stars, and hundreds of images of women, faces and whole figures, dressed in colorful outfits, naked and dancing, climbing trees, in every color, size and shape, flying, some masked, others in wild robes, across starlit skies. The barn, in fact the whole scene, reminded me of my mother's description of her one and only LSD trip at a woman's retreat in the 1970s.

"It's gonna be like that, Eve, one day it will. You mark my words," Mom declared. "You kids have to figure out how to do it without relying on the drugs; they can give you a glimpse, but it doesn't last."

No doubt, Rifka Weissman O'Malley would have loved this scene and would have fit right in. The average age of the women in the barn had to be sixty or seventy yet there was a spark and glow to their faces combined with the colorful get-ups that felt anything but old. Women were grabbing Mattie and Sarah for hugs and smooches as we stood at the back of the room. Aurelia was working the front of the room, smiling and hugging, laughing and swaying. I was becoming dizzy looking at it, at her, at the assembled throng. And the dogs: some of the them gathered around Aurelia were curled up and snoozing; some had their heads back, howling, at any or all of the painted moons, in every phase of waxing and waning that hung in indigo and purple painted skies festooning the ceiling.

As I stood watching, some of the women began a snake dance, their bodies shifting into filaments of light. I blinked my eyes. The same light

I saw emanating from Aurelia pulsed out of the women too, from their heads, their fingers. They traced light lines across the air as they danced. I felt my hands and feet start to buzz. Was there something in that sherry?

Aurelia hit a gong that reverberated through the room and the women melted the snake dance they were doing, and the vocalizations they were making faded as if by magic, and the women took their seats. Mattie, Sarah, and I, at the back of the room, sat on backless stools against the wall. An ancient-looking woman with gleeful brown eyes next to me reached across and gave Mattie a squeeze. "Your mother is Kwan Yin, Buddha, and Whoopi Goldberg all rolled up in one!"

"Yes, Honey, and then some!" Mattie laughed.

The dogs had finally settled down and Aurelia, swaying slightly, her eyes half closed, began to speak.

"Sistahs! As you know, I have just returned from visiting many of our magnificent, brave, and wonderful sisters all across this sweet and aching land."

"Tell us, Aurelia!" they clamored and several dogs howl.

"In Baltimore, a group of our Compassionistas surrounded the city hall practicing our Mothers of Compassion meditation. They were completely incognito, some disguised as meter maids, others as gardeners, some as street sweepers, some as shoppers, some just out with a baby in a stroller getting some air."

Sarah leaned over and explained, "The Compassionista Brigades developed out of the Women in Black campaign in Israel and peace vigils in cities around the world."

I nodded, "Yes, Mattie filled me in on some of this. But frankly…" I wanted to put my skepticism into words but I felt woozy. The place felt like what I remembered of story hour in the bookmobile that used to come to my neighborhood when I was small: magical and otherworldly, but with not quite enough air.

Aurelia continued to speak, "Each one held in her mind's eye and her heart's eye, a vision of kindness and love embodied in a female form so strong for her, so strong!"

I actually remembered the face of that bookmobile librarian. She seemed as old as God with tightly permed white hair and a blue cardigan sweater over her shoulders held in place by a chain with pearl clips, but with a smile that made me feel warm all over.

Aurelia's voice rose, "Well, Sisters, let me tell you, in that session, the Baltimore City Council voted unanimously to disarm their police force, just have them turn in their guns. They voted to empty their jails and to immediately begin building housing for all who are without it."

The women hooted and cheered. I looked at Mattie who was grinning and clapping too.

"Is she nuts?" I whispered to Mattie. "If that actually happened, the National Guard would be in Baltimore shooting Thorazine into the City Councilors so fast your head would spin."

Mattie shushed me, "Just listen, Eve."

"Of course, dear Sisters, once the women finished their meditation, the council members came back to their own reality, gray and paltry as it is, and resumed bickering over whether Walmart could have that parcel of land down next to the harbor."

I watched the women around me all nod knowingly, as if Aurelia was explaining something as plain as the nose on your face.

"We have, as you know, been active for a long time in Baltimore, as in other cities, with our Crones who work the video recording of the Council sessions. They have found a way to embed the Compassionista meditation images into the regular council video just a few frames at a time — so now everyone in Baltimore is receiving that message subliminally. They have also saved the segment when the council acted with love to undo violence; this will be held until the right time."

"Nobody watches that local T.V. crap," I said to Mattie. "This is a joke! Anyway, that's coercive — implanting mind messages? Pretty 1984, don't you think?"

"Our sisters are working all over the country and the world to disrupt and destabilize the fixed ideas of scarcity, fear, and violence, and to activate the dormant images of love from the Great Source." Aurelia continued, "This can only succeed through our vigilant practice of compassion in each and every woman's heart, and each and every interaction we have."

Mattie shot me a "See? It's all good" look.

"Now, those of you who are here to prepare for the next weather project, our Crones at the international weather station are saying you should be ready to travel next week. We don't know exactly when the storm will hit, and we want you to be comfortable and situated with your host families well in advance."

Mattie leaned over and started to explain, "The Crones discovered that global warming partly is the Earth's own hot flash as She awakens to her planetary menopause. Of course it's exacerbated due to all the stuff humans have done to stress Her out. Just like any woman who has a bad diet and too much stress screws up her own change of life. We are meant to take that time to go off and meditate in nature and get our vision for our Croning; that's what menopause is for, you know. And the Earth needs the same thing: rest and re-vision. The question is whether or not she needs to get rid of humans to do Her work. We're hoping not. We've discovered that if enough Crones gather near a storm center, their vibration reduces the damage and the fear in those affected. Isn't that awesome?"

I started to respond — but the dogs were howling again and the weather women were taking a bow and getting applause from the crowd.

"Awesome," I muttered to myself wondering if this Aurelia-in-Wonderland was a certified crackpot, what loony bin she had escaped from, and what on earth was I doing there — or if there was something to all this.

Sarah Leaf seemed sane enough and she was listening and applauding along with the crowd.

"Now we will hear from Jean, a beloved sister from Seattle." More cheering. Aurelia stepped aside.

A diminutive woman who seemed to be about eighty years old, wearing a purple beret and lieder hosen, came to the front of the room. She pushed wire-rim glasses up on her nose, cleared her throat and began:

"Hello, my Sister Crones. Last week we organized a continuous flow of women silently walking a labyrinth we built on a vacant lot near the downtown. It was beautiful. We used all recycled materials to mark the labyrinth — pop cans, empty bottles, and such. You can see a picture on the Cronation website. Anyhow, women signed up for hour-long shifts and during that twenty-four hour period simply inwardly chanted our generosity mantra — you all know the one, 'give freely, love freely' — and there was a 70% decrease in traffic accidents and petty crime. The Bill and Melinda Gates Foundation made the decision to increase giving by 50%.

And this was a completely unexpected outcome — especially for Seattle: hold onto your hats, there was a 60% drop in coffee sales throughout the city! Except at that drive-thru place where the young girls wear bikini tops; their sales went up, but I think that shows that customers aren't really going just for the coffee. On some level those men know they're seeking the ministrations of the Great Goddess and Her love when they see those girls. It's a sacrament really. Rabbi Sarah, don't you think so?" Sarah nodded and smiled.

Again the cheering began and the dogs scratched and howled. There were several women cued up behind Jean, notes in hand, to report on their local good works. I felt the way I did when my mother couldn't get a baby sitter and O'Malley was working and she dragged me to her women's group meetings. The whole thing was sweet but just absurd.

As the women continued their speeches, I noticed Aurelia making her way down the side aisle to the back where Mattie and I were sitting. My eyes suddenly started to water and my head was throbbing. "Mattie, I'm feeling a little faint…"

The next thing I know I'm lying on my back on the floor. Mattie is holding up my head against her knee, trying to get me to sip some water. The barn is now silent and still. Aurelia gazed down from what seemed a towering height, a radiant smile on her face; I gasped and began to writhe in pain, electricity prickling through my skin like when I put a fork in the toaster as a kid to get my bread out.

"Oh, child! You poor little manikin!" Aurelia murmured. "Take her down to level 'B,' Mattie. Call ahead for the SAC chair to be set up."

That, and the mournful howl of a part Blue Tick hound, was the last thing I heard as I was swallowed up into dark oblivion again. Mom would have loved this place.

8 —————————

Mattie stood before a council of the elders in the Wood Room, where the Crones held meetings: Aurelia, Rae, Marty, and several women of Phoebe's generation, Elsie and Vivian. She offered her report on Eve: "It's much more intense than I would ever have dreamed from just looking at her." She looked gravely at the older women.

"We don't realize how much the average woman is carrying in her cellular level memory, never mind the average manikin," said Vivian.

Aurelia stood up and paced across the floor, shaking her felted hair as if to clear her head. "If the women are in such bad shape, how bad must the men be? Maybe it is too soon to initiate Cronation." But even as she spoke these words, Aurelia knew they didn't express what was really on her mind.

"Or could this be a blind spot?" Marty wondered aloud. "Are we so concerned that the men have made a mess of things that we have failed to see that it's the women like Eve, the ones who seem so 'successful,' who've borne the brunt of it all? The recognition that even seemingly successful women are deeply harmed could unleash a lot of anger and a desire for revenge."

Vivian spoke next: "You know, Aurelia, you and some of your generation were shielded from this particular curse, and you taught

Mattie's generation how to work around it. You grew up knowing there were multiple realities once you understood what Phoebe and the other women were doing in their work. You were taught to stay awake to the truth you knew in your body while living in a world that denied that truth in every way. Mattie not only takes it for granted, she can travel back and forth between multiple realities like crossing the street."

"Phoebe always said that was the hidden gift in being the people in the margins," Elsie spoke gently, looking at Aurelia's bowed head. "We had to really see the reality of the oppressor just to survive. That's why this movement is so powerful. We have made a home for all the tired, so-called outsiders, failures, and misfits. We've gathered them and their gifts for this time."

"But the manikins," Aurelia sighed wearily, "women who come in as kin-to-men or become so due to circumstances, look so strong, so able. They come so close to the false ideal and get rewarded for it — they don't see what they're giving up."

"Yeah, but they don't have the built-in protections that men have," Marty added. "Most men don't take in what doesn't fit in the compartments already established in their heads. But the manikins do; they just don't know it. It's like they have another program operating in the background, a honeycomb of spaces in their souls and memories that just stockpiles the pain of the world. It can't get broken down and moved out of them unless they happen to be artists of one kind or another or experienced energy workers."

"Or disease sufferers," Elsie noted. "The manikin's physical system takes a terrible beating from all these other stories running in the background. That's why cancer for women became so honored as a cause, on the deepest level we all know it is an act of service, however misguided. And the Crohn's disease sufferers. These women are this era's sin eaters; they just take it all in with no way to digest all that's wrong."

"Bless their souls," all the women responded.

"Well, this Eve is no artist," Mattie said. "That box is M-T and locked up tight. There must have been some powerful messages that art wasn't a worthy pursuit. She does know tons of art history though. Parts of her scan were like a survey course slide show. And her CT scan is clear. So far, she has some minor calcifications but no tumor or other disease activity. It's amazing, really."

"We forget how wise all you elders are," Aurelia smiled at Vivian and Elsie, taking their hands in hers. "God bless grandmother Riva for sending me into the barn to paint!"

"Bless her soul," they all intoned.

Riva had passed on to the level of existence that is pure light. In her time she had cleared much of the accumulated damage of slavery for herself and others and so many wrongs by teaching about the time to come — not after death, but in this world, reawakening the women's trust in the natural world and initiating others into creative pursuits, the ultimate antidote to slavery. She didn't speak to them the way Phoebe did to Aurelia, but the women of Cronation often felt a surge of light, warmth, and inexplicable love whenever Riva's name was mentioned.

"Well, no doubt, the central teaching Phoebe got from the Source was how to manifest in a large way what Riva just knew in her bones." Aurelia continued, "If you all can just keep creating with love, you can get it right. Life is like a painting, sometimes it looks downright ugly until you rearrange it all again, keep it moving. The light is there and all the colors — you just have to learn to keep working, to play with it until it shows you what you need to know and how to be unafraid. You love it into being."

"Until the beauty shows up," Elsie said.

"Tell it, Sistah," the women murmured.

Aurelia straightened up, "So what about this girl Eve? Mattie, what are you saying?"

"You all saw her faint when she was in Momma's presence yesterday," Mattie answered. "Her own momma and daddy loved her plenty, but they've been gone awhile. I think she's forgotten what love feels like. And who knows when this lady last had any real bodily pleasure? I say we give her to the boys to practice some Tantra."

Marty laughed. "That's a great idea, but I've known Eve for years and I bet she's forgotten how. Maybe we can put a big bottle of Cannabis Crone Cream in her room and hope she takes the hint?"

"I'd like you to try again," Aurelia replied. "Schedule another session in the Story Alignment Chair, if she is willing. Sex might be overwhelming. Remember, fear is fear. It's all about unlocking her natural healing vibe and breaking up the fear."

The image of an icebreaker ship in Arctic waters came into Aurelia's mind. She shivered. "You know, Mattie, try some warm baths and paraffin soaks too. Some parts of this girl just need to thaw out. I bet she lives on frozen food, damn Lean Cuisine! See if you can get her to spice her food a little too."

"That's right," Elsie chimed in. "Don't ask those Tantra boys to do all the heavy lifting. The Cannabis Crone Cream isn't a bad idea, though. Let's give her system a chance to right itself. That's one of our core beliefs, isn't it?"

"Yes, Ma'am, it is, 'Support the system as it unwinds and heals itself.' I know Phoebe favored sexual healing — but then she grew up listening to Marvin Gaye, rest his soul, and she never got over losing Daddy." Aurelia let out a long sigh.

"There's enough time for that — we're looking for the key to heal a whole generation, one that has equated sex with a whole lot of fear: HIV, STDs, infertility. Great Lady of the Lake! They're suffering!" Vivian shook her head. "Maybe two bottles of the Cream."

Mattie grumbled as she walked back to the barn. "Afraid of sex, afraid of food, afraid of images, dreams, boogie men under the bed! Well, no one said flipping the switch in the manikin would be easy."

Mattie kept Eve in a twilight state after each session in the Story Alignment Chair. After the first session she began to map the terrain of Eve's inner fear landscape. Once she had that drawn, the healing could unfold. Scenery was pretty much the only thing that worked for the first sessions. Eve's system got that nature is Divine. Pretty elementary, but at least it was a start. Mattie decided to slowly introduce some aspect of bodily pleasure at the end of each session. While Eve was still in a light trance, she'd have Harvey come in and do a foot massage or a hot paraffin foot soak. She kept the temperature in the room up and covered Eve with an afghan crocheted by women in Cronation cells under cover in nursing homes and state hospitals.

"Thank Goddess she's not ticklish, or I don't know what we'd do!" Mattie told Harvey when he arrived for the second session. Mattie set the audio to a medium level of entrainment. A home tone provided by a drone sound playing on an endless loop provided support for the soul. She wanted Eve to begin to associate the time in the chair with pleasure. She would lower the lights and sit off to the side to watch Harvey work. Mattie had come to love Harvey. Watching his kindness as he gently handled Eve's feet awakened something in her that she rarely felt: a longing for strong arms around her, men's arms. Mattie had no memory of her father, who died when she was a baby and her life was so woman-centered for so long that whatever crushes she'd had and the few love affairs were all with other women.

"How humans didn't realize we were getting off track," she mused, "when something as simple and sweet as sex became so dangerous and complicated! I wonder what relationships will be like once Cronation brings Her full power into being."

* * *

As Mattie left, the rest of the Crone Council was getting tea. Aurelia touched Vivian's shoulder: "Vivian, did we all sound a little 'mannish' just now? It sounded to me like we were reducing this child Eve's distress, not respecting her pain and how she and so many are carrying it for the whole world. I felt a 'mannish' tone, like 'Oh all she needs is to get laid.'"

"Well, now that you mention it, Aurelia, that may be so." Vivian turned and took Aurelia's hands in hers, which were as brown and gnarled as tree roots. She looked deeply into Aurelia's eyes. "I see you're troubled, child. Do you want to speak about it?"

"Thank you, Vivian, what I needed is your loving witness." Aurelia embraced Vivian and felt the strong pulse of love emanating from the older woman's slight body.

Vivian smiled. "I know you'll speak of it when the time is right."

Aurelia decided to keep her own counsel about what was really bothering her for a while longer. It wasn't just a nagging concern for the men, that much she knew. If Eve represented deep freeze as a way of dealing with pain, Charity Greenberg represented apocalyptic fire. It was no wonder she chose the Goddess Kali as her model. From everything Mattie said Eve believed she'd learned to work successfully within the existing system. She had earned the respect of the Men in Charge. She was sure she could — through reason — influence them toward fairness and equity. After all, they valued her clear thinking, applauded her work ethic. With her sensuality pretty much in limbo like a fish in winter — not dead but under ice and fast asleep — Eve wasn't prey to the kind of man who controls through sexual or romantic love. Aurelia felt certain the detoxifying work of Story Alignment would work for Eve, once she became conscious of all she was holding and was given a way to release it, she'd see her next path clearly.

Kali was another matter all together. SAC hadn't worked for her. The process wasn't as fine-tuned when Kali was at the Farm. And she had suffered an early life betrayal far more profound than Eve's at Wentworth and

Wentsouth, and she had only been a teenager back then. Aurelia looked up as a huge black raven landed on a ledge out side the window of the Wood Room.

Just then Rae knocked and came into the room where Aurelia had been meeting with the Council of Elders.

"Aurelia, Lydia has arrived with Lorelei Winger."

"Good, get them settled in their rooms with some ginger tea and ask Lydia to join us right away."

Lydia was still wearing her office clothes and looked out of place among the Crones, most of who dressed in cozy sweats or some form of flowing multi-colored clothing, sandals, or sturdy gym shoes. A few carried hand-carved walking sticks that doubled as canes for support and also talking sticks when the need arose.

"Namaste, Sisters," Lydia greeted them, bowing slightly.

Lydia often accompanied Lorelei Winger as an aide. The entire Winger dynasty now lived in the White House compound which had expanded to take over several additional city blocks surrounding the White House itself, which had been made into a bomb-proof fortress after Wright Winger had lost every shred of support and declared elections a threat to national security. Government was a shadow of its former self, with faceless corporations pulling the strings while special interest groups quietly privatized everything from water and electricity to the national parks. Lorelei and Lydia had developed elaborate cover stories to gain information from a government grown pathologically secretive. Lorelei was a virtual prisoner herself, except for her work in the few Right Wing organizations, like H.E.L.P. and the Flicker Foundation that they'd helped to establish as fronts for Cronation.

Lydia pulled up a chair to the council table and cleared her throat and then looked gravely from face to face. "I'm afraid I have some serious news. Lorelei Winger was able to tap into a briefing at the White House.

She says the Pomeranians are about to put their entire female population under lock and key — literally confining most to their homes and posting guards on every block, as well as imprisoning any woman who is in a leadership position of any kind: teachers, doctors, even store managers. She says President Winger is so freaked out he's considering imposing martial law on the whole country and says the European Union is considering doing so as well. The Pomeranians say they have intercepted a plan to bomb strategic places all over the globe where women's rights have been restricted, in the hopes of conquering all the repressive regimes in one fell swoop. They think their women are superior and want to preserve them to repopulate the planet in the event of a disaster. No one seems to know where the threat originated. No group has claimed responsibility yet. The Muslim world thinks our women have too much power in the business sphere and are pointing the finger at us.

Who knows what groups are really involved?" Lydia continued.

"Or if our own government is just manufacturing more disinformation," said Elsie. "Those men only seem to feel safe when they're clamping down on some womenfolk."

"We hear that, Sister," several of the councilwomen replied, shaking their heads.

Lydia continued: "The Senate is going to be called into secret session to allow the President to invoke the emergency Preservation of the State clause in the Culture of Life laws. If he does that, we could find martial law imposed on us too within twenty-four hours, ostensibly for our own protection."

The women gasped.

"This could ruin everything!" Marty cried. "I understand the Pomeranians probably see themselves as saviors, but everyone knows another war could be cataclysmic, especially another one without a clear enemy. Anyone can be a target."

Aurelia stood up. "'The Men in Charge' — it galls me to call them so — have diminished their systems of reflection to such a point it's as if they have plugged right into the reptilian brain and edited out any chance of feeling, nuance, or compassion. Fear, fight, take the spoils are all that's available in their mental menu. It's a chance for war preparation, another distraction from the economy, the erosion of rights, hope and freedom tanking — and they're going to say this is for women's safety and homeland security. Trifecta!

"We have to think fast," Aurelia said firmly. "Are any Cronation operatives implicated in a counter-movement in Pomerania? Have there been any reports from underground women's groups monitoring the Internet? Maybe they have uncovered something that gave the Pomeranians an opening for thinking this?"

Aurelia's mind was racing. Could Kali have something to do with this?

"We haven't really got a team online monitoring this sort of thing," Marty replied. "So many of the women have spent years practically chained to a desk and a computer screen they just can't bear the work, and the health issues, carpal tunnel, eyestrain! We've needed all the ones who are really good at tech stuff to do direct Cronation work, staying in contact with the cells around the world." Marty managed IT for Cronation and it was her personal spiritual practice to remain compassionate and not judge the rampant technophobia of so many of the women.

"We haven't heard yet what the precipitating event was. They're holding back that information, if there is any, for 'international security purposes,'" Lydia said.

"The Pomeranians have been more neutral than Switzerland for decades, for Goddess sake. Most people will automatically accept this — 'if the Pomeranians are fearful, it must be a real threat.' I can tell you this: just being in Washington and watching the men fragment; you can feel the underlying chaos. They all seem like digital movies pixelating and dropping frames. They start talking and then lapse into terrified gibberish."

"War has always been their drug of choice," Marty said gravely. "This seems like another sign that the Goddess is getting ready to push. They need that rush of a new conquest to feel alive and beat back their fear of their own deaths. These men have never liked dealing with what comes after the quick fix; I'm sure they haven't thought ahead to what comes next."

"You're right," Lydia added. "Can you imagine their surprise when after they round up all the women and lock them down, the whole economy grinds to a halt?"

Aurelia sighed, "Okay, we can figure this out. We've always known that the return of the Goddess would happen at some point in the process of establishing Cronation; we just didn't know exactly when. We know we have to expect chaos and uncertainty in spite of all out preparations; we've ridden the waves many times. We know that things will get very dense and constricted right before She comes. This clamp down in Pomerania could be the first contraction."

"Yeah, like any old birth," Elsie picked up the image. "You just keep the towels ready and when the contractions commence, well, you roll up your sleeves, but that calve could be coming out sideways or upside down. You just deal with it." Elsie started to laugh, "Well, I sure am glad to be here with you ladies for this! Reminds me of when that big old Brindle cow had twins back in '54. That bull began kicking in his stall, you'd a thought he was the one giving birth. Right up until he passed out cold."

"Men are going to experience this as absolute annihilation," Aurelia cautioned. "But of course many of them will project it outward as the end of the world. It's up to us to hold the space steady as we can."

Aurelia looked fondly at Elsie, "We are so blessed to have you and all the Elders with us. Elsie, can you channel Phoebe and get her take on this new development? Marty, you get over to the GPS lab and get us the readout of the prevailing estrogen levels worldwide, but especially surrounding Pomerania. Lydia, get back to Lorelei and see if she can prepare a briefing for the whole Farm for right after breakfast tomorrow; tell her to keep it simple. The rest of us need to get into the studio and paint. We need as much direct guidance as we can get, and right away. And Rae, call Mattie: please get her to work with Harvey as soon as she can. He had a dream that needs decoding and aligning right away. He should be done with the scan by now. Chaos may break out on more fronts than we've counted on."

Aurelia wasn't sure why she was holding back telling the rest of the women that Kali might be back in a new, improved, and scarier form, but she trusted her gut on this one. A time-honored Cronation aphorism was this: "Seeming mountains often turn to dust and blow away if not given a lot of energy." Of course, another adage, "A stitch in time saves possibly blowing the place to kingdom come," had its merits.

The nagging image of frightened men with triggers of worldwide destruction within reach was just as frightening as Kali's potential for tapping into the energy of her namesake Goddess for misguided ends.

9

"I just did a quick scan when we brought you down after you passed out." Mattie was projecting images of colorful chromothermophotography charts onto the wall. I vaguely remembered being in the barn and Aurelia coming towards me and feeling something like an electric shock go through my body.

"You're what we call a 'manikin,'" Mattie continued, "A woman who is functioning mostly in alpha-male brainwave patterns. You don't feel much pain, can work for long periods with a single focus, have few relationships, and channel your libido into your work. You easily override an empathic response to another person if work demands are being made concurrently."

"Sounds like a sociopathic boy scout on steroids," I responded, miffed at her tone of concern. This evaluation was almost identical to my last performance review at Wentsouth, one that garnered a substantial raise, I might add. In a different language of course: 'not distracted by sex' in corporate-speak would be 'on-mission,' or a 'pro-tasker.' No need for harassment suits after all.

"I'm pretty well known for being fearless. I've been white-water rafting, you know. I think you might want to check the dials on your Way Back machine there. Besides, I have lots of friends and good relationships. What about Rae and Marty and Gina?" I felt a definite need to bolster my case. "So what if I never knew they were all part of some wacky feminist underground? And I've had sex." Wow, did that sounds unconvincing!

"That's right, you compartmentalized relationships that were formed before you became completely manikin. We're not sure about all the parameters of the syndrome. It might be like alcoholism: you could have an underlying propensity but it takes the right conditions for the process to develop. It might exacerbate with age. Your image of those women friends remains exactly the same as when you were all in college. I bet you never even knew that Gina became a vegan chef."

"Gina, a vegetarian? That's ridiculous! She loves meatballs; she's Italian for God's sake…" Come to think of it, I had noticed she only ate the salad at Spiaggia the night of my birthday. I figured it was a weight issue so I didn't want to bring it up.

Mattie continued, "Remember how in Hitler's Germany the SS guys could play with their kids, have dinner with their wives while listening to classical music, and then go back to the concentration camp and shoot anyone who looked at them cross-eyed, just for the hell of it?"

"Now you're calling me a Nazi?"

"No, no, they're just a great example of the human capacity for compartmentalization. Most people compartmentalize to a degree. But the Nazi's were especially good at it. Anyway, that's not the most interesting part of your scan. Up until now we've mostly studied our voluntary recruits, women who've come into the movement by choice or who have had trouble with the dominant paradigm, women who were locked up in jail or in treatment programs. Anyone who's gotten into that much trouble usually has enough consciousness to know that the status quo is seriously out of whack. By the time we got them, they were halfway into recovery from the culturally imposed illness. Once they receive a little affirmation for their truth, they just unfold their power like a sail on a great schooner."

This lingo was starting to piss me off.

"Unfold their power? What the hell does that mean? Are you talking about those crazy tattooed, nose-pierced crackpots who want to write poetry for a living? Why don't they unfold their laundry and iron it for a change? You know, I had a program at Wentworth and Wentsouth for interns, young women with promise who weren't afraid to work hard and weren't all hung up on the 'patriarchy' and didn't think wearing a nicely tailored suit violated their basic human rights...."

"Whoa, Eve honey, simmer down! Can you see how the strands of male-interpreted reality have informed your discourse? Being a manikin is nothing to be ashamed of. We have great data on the resiliency of women in general but we haven't ever had a true, bona-fide, high-level manikin to work with before. We tried to monitor Condi Rice for a while but we couldn't get the equipment close enough to her for a long enough time. Do you know she does her own hair and has perfect teeth, never needs a dentist? And she knows karate. We tried to kidnap her once. Our Crone squad knocked down her Secret Service detail with ease, but she got the better of the two women in the operation. They claimed they just wanted her autograph, so she let them go."

"What is this 'manikin' stuff? Isn't that a store window dummy? This is insulting!"

Mattie looked at me and grinned. "That's the definition in Webster's, and I guess you could say it applies in a way. You manikins are window dressing for the Men in Charge. Actually, our use of the word is this: man-i-kin, women who have evolved as kin-to-man, closer in functioning to the acceptable current male archetype than to genuine women. Aurelia has done a great deal of the research on the gender spectrum and she thinks that it's a genetic evolutionary thing that affects the production of hormones. If you pair a woman with a high level of consciousness with a man without much alpha, the core identity can shift over as few as two generations."

"Are you calling me some kind of hybrid freak? Are you calling my dad a pansy?" Suddenly I was channeling an old-fashioned Irish barroom brawl. I wound up to punch Mattie in the nose when I felt an electric shock course through my body, dissolving me into a heap.

"I'm sorry, Eve, but now that we're giving your system a chance to unwind, you will find your behavior a bit erratic. See? That's what we call 'testosterone flashing,' an alpha male response. You're fearful, so you go on the attack."

"How did you do that?" I had an excruciating pain in my elbow where it banged the wall. "You have a cattle prod I didn't notice?"

"Oh, no!" Mattie laughed. "I'm a gold belt in mind-jitsu, a martial art that is done entirely by directed thought."

"I'm so dangerous you need to throw me against a wall?" In addition to my throbbing elbow, my feelings were hurt.

"It's only possible to master this form with level nine compassion. At that stage, the intention to do no harm is practically engraved on the soul. There's nothing personal left that would make it possible to misuse mind-jitsu."

"Oh, yeah? Tell that to my fractured tibia and pounding headache."

"That's an illusion," Mattie elaborated. "If I showed you a CT scan of your head, you'd see there was no organic trauma. I simply planted a thought in your mind consistent with the story you were enacting: let's see, Irish barroom fisticuffs, I believe it was. If I showed you a videotape of what just happened, you'd see yourself just buckle and slide to the floor. I never moved an inch or lifted a finger."

"Well it feels like you took a Louisville Slugger to my head." I wasn't letting Mattie off the hook. This whole situation since I arrived at this "farm" was just too weird, and although I'd given up expecting to wake up in my bed in Evanston, I wasn't jumping on board either.

"Look, I'm sorry, I know all this is a lot to take in. But here's an exciting discovery — Aurelia is going to flip out when we tell her. You are actually accessing massive amounts of information in the feminine mode too. Your system just isn't bringing it to consciousness. Remember those cartoon joke renderings of a male brain? There would be like a big section labeled 'sports,' one marked 'beer,' and those would have huge activity, then one marked 'feelings' and it would be empty."

I was beginning to tune Mattie out. I was starting to see patterns in the projected slide: a dog chasing a cat.

"See? You're doing it now!" Mattie was really excited.

"What? What am I doing?"

"You're spacing out on what I'm saying, just like a guy would. The male attention span — except for work, food, and sex — is approximately 44 seconds. Yours is actually a little bit higher or no woman would be able to stand you for five minutes. You don't key into sex and not even food that much so your random, non-work span of attention is actually close to 60 seconds. That's why you were so effective in the business world. A high-grade manikin is worth half a dozen regular men; a manikin doesn't waste time on football pools or fantasy baseball or Internet porn. She has just enough emotion and feminine attributes to hook men into conversations about work but so few of the usual feminine concerns that they never notice she's arousing their libido, while directing it into the work arena. She doesn't even really know it herself. What libido you have is kind of halted at a pre-adolescent level. Real sexual arousal is beyond your grasp."

I felt I should take offense at Mattie's description of me but I guess I had my own doubts. I remembered Marty once urged me to get my hormone levels checked; I did get the tests done but I kept forgetting to pick up the results.

"A really brilliant manikin," Mattie continued, "has a man leave a meeting with her psyched to keep working and emotionally feeling like he just got a hand job. If there had been a Manhattan Project to develop the American manikin, the economy might not have gone down the shitter. Believe me, the Asian manikin is unstoppable. Wentworth and Wentsouth must have loved you. There is no trace of awareness; you aren't playing a game so you reinforce the perception that you really are the same as a man."

"I've always had a very strong work ethic which was highly respected at Wentworth and Wentsouth," I sniffed, but then winced remembering Candace and how Wentsouth replaced me with her at the last minute like I was some kind of widget.

"You mentioned some kind of discovery?" I really wanted to change the subject.

"Yes, you have the full feminine mode operating in the background like — no offense —a computer virus sort of sent all your files into some hidden off-line mode. All we need is the password, if you will, to get into that area and create a bridge to your 'mainframe' consciousness. You've been ultra-sensitive to every world conflict, catastrophe, relationship problem around you, but only on a sub-conscious level. You're really very intuitive and deeply sensitive. When I hooked you up in the Story Alignment Chair you went straight for Belfast. I'd like to go back in with the image projector turned on and we can see what the content is all about. Would you be willing to do that?"

"My dad was Irish. We never talked about the 'troubles,' I just knew it was a sore point. I think a couple of my uncles were in Sein Fein."

Mattie was starting to freak me out. I never liked tarot cards or psychics. In college when everyone else was trying to tell the future, I was reading the Wall Street Journal for my future predictions, and this stuff was coming too close to fortune telling for my comfort.

"I don't really like being talked about like a piece of hardware, you know…"

Mattie smiled sympathetically and patted my arm. "When I tuned into what is essentially your cell memory storage — a kind of molecular library that imprints everything you've ever been touched by — you have everything in there: fires, earthquakes, Vietnam, the Spanish Inquisition, the wreck of the Hesperus, witch burnings, Mount St. Helen's, the Gulf War...! You are really special, Eve."

"Look," I interrupted her, "I appreciate your machine and all its fascinating powers, but what the hell does this have to do with me? Are you going to do a brain dump and send me on my way, a reformed femmiekin? Are you any better than the advertising industry? Just implant a few revolutionary slogans and wind me up, another post-global drone against the machine? Is this what this place is all about? Kidnapping women who have actually succeeded and reprogramming them?"

Mattie's eyes widened, then she furrowed her brow. "Where is all this coming from, Eve? Is this a conversation you wanted to have with your mom?"

"I have every intention," I countered, "of setting up all sorts of incentives for women in business when I get to the Coast. I'm just as much of a feminist as my mother was; I just never liked all those touchy-feely weekend retreats with women in stretch pants singing to the Goddess in rounds. She used to drag me to mother-daughter rituals the way other parents took their kids to Chuck E. Cheese. Do you know any ten year olds who like tabbouleh? To this day the scent of Nag Champa incense makes me gag."

Mattie shook her head and looked at me the way you look at a hopelessly clueless aunt who asks you why if the Internet is so great it doesn't have Grandma Lula's rum cake recipe in it somewhere — sweetly, but with nothing to say.

"The most interesting thing," Mattie continued, "is that you've stored emotional and intellectual data on everything that's gone on but — here's the amazing part — you still have enormous unused storage capacity. Like computer RAM. You may have the potential to be the bridge between worlds that will keep the men from freaking out and destroying everything in terror when the Return of the Goddess starts and Cronation takes over.

"Look, I know this is a lot of information, Eve. And the detox aspect of SAC takes more than a few sessions. Why don't you have some chamomile tea and do some deep breathing, relax for a bit. I have to check on Harvey, he's having a dream scan next door. When I come back we can start again this time with images, I think you'll be really amazed."

Mattie left me to drink my tea and wonder if things could get any wackier. I decided if I couldn't get something stronger than herb tea, I might as well take a nap. Maybe I'd have an "instructive dream"; Mom was always big on those. If I went to her for advice, she'd tell me to write down a question before I went to sleep and put it under my pillow. I'd never remember to wait for the answer in the morning. Once my alarm clock went off, I always hit the ground running.

The SAC was pretty comfortable. Before I knew it I was asleep.

I awoke in the dentist-like chair, with nylon webbing strapped across my chest, over each thigh and calf and across my wrists. Mattie apparently took my presence there as informed consent to continue her program of scouring my brain. My head was held between cushioned pads with embedded speakers playing music that sounded faintly Indian — I could make out a sitar and tabla. As my eyes began to focus, I saw Mattie lowering a projection screen in front of me with a remote control but I felt too drowsy to speak to her. The lights in the room dimmed even more and the music got louder. A Celtic knot form began to draw itself in pale gold against red, mandala-like on the screen before me. I felt relaxed, like I was melting back into Magdalena's great massage.

Almost immediately images of Northern Ireland began to appear on the screen. Bombed out landscapes, graffiti on crumbling walls, pale children running, a car exploding, cursing in Gaelic, women sobbing and keening, sirens, guns flashing, a funeral procession going into a dark church, hymns in Latin reverberating off ancient stone walls. Tears streamed down my face. Then flutes, fiddles and pipes, and bells began to weave into the music and the images on the screen gave way to images from the Irish countryside: rolling emerald hills, black and gray wooly sheep crowding and baaing along a dirt road, the sea crashing against the granite mountainside.

The image started to slowly spin. Then I was above it, a bird's eye view of a green island set in a steel-blue sea.

"It's all one, it's all one," whispered a quiet woman's voice over and under the music. My breathing slowed and I realized I'd been straining against the straps. I sank back into the chair, and closed my eyes.

The sound shifted to a gently roaring ocean. The rhythmic crashing of the waves soothed my raw nerves. I may have dozed off. When the Celtic music resumed, I opened my eyes. The image of the emerald island was slowly spinning back down to earth. This time the earth was lit from within with a golden light, glowing and impossibly beautiful. I could still make out all the contours of the land, but now I could see the ancient burial mounds, the stone walls that threaded over the hills. I could see into the ground itself — the roots of trees, even the grass, were like pulsing golden wires plunging into the dark earth. I saw the skeletons resting below the mounds and the slow pulsing light they emitted; there were slight variations in the color and intensity of the light. Tears flowed from my eyes again, but now they were tears of awe. I longed to dissolve into this great beauty, add my little light and just merge with the scene.

"Not so fast," I heard Mattie say, or maybe it was my mother's voice. "You can't just check out on level one. We need you here!"

The Celtic knot mandala reappeared, this time in silver against a deep blue-green background. Imperceptibly it faded and the sheep and their herdsmen came into view. I saw them light up from within like budding trees, thousands of little golden twinkles fit within the outline of each sheep and man. That faded too, and in slow motion the streets of Belfast came back into view. I felt my body go rigid; I gripped the armrests and the scene slowed even more.

Barely discernible flickers of light appeared in the scene. First in the scraggly trees lining the pavement, then in the ground itself. The scene appeared as if dawn was breaking, but the source of light was within each element in the landscape. There was the faint outline of light in the walls, the cars, the litter on the pavement. I strained forward, squinting my eyes and breathing more deeply; as I did, I began to see quivering lights like candles in a breeze in the hearts of the children running in slow motion toward me, their mouths forming silent screams; in the man crouched on one knee, a black ski mask over his face, an automatic rifle against his shoulder, shooting at an unseen enemy. Now I felt a dull, throbbing pain as my breath became shallow. The light flickered and I heard myself cry out, "NO, NO!" But this made the light flicker even more frantically, then the screen went dark.

"That was amazing, Eve," Mattie's voice was soft. "You're a natural for this work. It's amazing to see how it clears things on the level of cultural work for the collective. Can I get you some more tea?"

Mattie pressed a button on the remote and all the straps holding me in the SAC slowly retracted. I sat up and took the tea she poured for me. I actually felt pretty good, refreshed, even. "So what was that all about?" The memory of the images and feelings was receding quickly.

"The SAC was a key invention channeled by Phoebe's group, and it inspired Aurelia's work as an undergrad in engineering at M.I.T. It could be rigged to look just like a dentist's chair or one in a salon or barbershop — which is where they had some set up for the initial research. Except that the little headrest has sensors that picked up information through the skull or were placed in the seat behind the shoulder blades, tapping into the rhythms of the cerebral-spinal fluid. Eventually a lightweight version will make work in the field easier, once more people accept that they can undo their cultural programming.

I nodded and Mattie continued. "One day, maybe soon, folks will be able to get a SAC session at walk-in clinics or the supermarket. A light trance is induced via the harmonic mantra and all the fear-based ideas, memories, and cultural residue get projected on a screen; that's what we saw just now. It can also happen in a remote location. The person in the chair could just be getting a haircut or their teeth cleaned, for all any-one knew. The cultural transformation can be carried out in plain sight via the Cronation network. A Crone operative counters the fear images with transformative word association spoken at a subliminal level via a comput-er terminal off-site. The two-way sensors transmit the spoken words back into the brain fluid, which carries this counter-information throughout the body via the nervous system.

"I didn't need to do that for you today; we were able to watch the images together. Usually the Crone operative monitors the images on the screen and a sensitive meter reads out how much life force energy is puls-ing in each image, hence how much reality the subject is investing in its existence. After the session, the recipient and the Crone go over the images and the readout of the energy levels and decide on which ones to shift."

Mattie poured me more tea. "These images are viewed on the screen. Then they can be paired in a trance state with an alternative verbal script. The ego gets gently destabilized and begins to loosen its hold; the ideas and memories break up and dissolve. Eventually strong transformative counter images are interspersed with the old images, projected internally and wirelessly onto the retina — at first in too few frames to be seen by the eye but enough to allow recoding in the cerebral cortex and then, eventu-ally, a more balanced set of images develops that reflects the individual's destiny and purpose. These are actually 'downloaded' from the subjects' own brain files. It seems that each person has a series of images and ideas they come in to life with the potential to understand and manifest. Since normal education does not teach youngsters how to access the codes to tap into these files, most get deflected from actualization, and the huge files go unused. Locating those files in the vast resources of the brain was a major breakthrough that should have earned a Nobel Prize, but the worldwide Crone council agreed that discovery couldn't be made public — without prompting a new age witch hunt, if it were revealed that anyone could break out of a consumerist trance at will.

"Instead, celebrations of this gift from the Divine Source were held in Cronation circles worldwide," Mattie continued. "There was a three-day feast of dancing and singing, along with a ceremony inculcating a vow of secrecy. If the Men in Charge got hold of a Story Alignment Chair, they might try to use it to program who knows what. In the detox process, finally, when the subject begins to detach from her cultural programming, she is given lots of visual and verbal reinforcement.

"It can be hard to tell when the detox is completely finished. Buried layers rise up as the more superficial surface ones are cleared away. The 'dentist' or 'hairstylist' brings the subject out of the trance and all memory of the SAC reprogramming sinks back below consciousness, if the woman chooses that option.

"Women return for another 'haircut' when they feel the gray sludge of fear rising, dulling their light and life source energy. The detox process is strictly voluntary and made known through a word-of-mouth network of beauty parlors and health clinics, usually in poor neighborhoods and communities of color where the Men in Charge would never imagine their own future was being plotted — not in violent payback that would certainly be understandable to them, but in a far more gentle pulling out of the energetic skids from under them."

"Don't the Crones want some retribution?" I could imagine they would.

Mattie shook her head. "No, the Crones have a deep sympathy for the Men in Charge that they scarcely deserve on the face of things." Mattie replied. "But what's amazing, Eve, is how quickly you cleared some powerful images. I'm sure you will have something very important to contribute to the work."

"Yeah, well, for now, maybe I can just finally get something to eat!" I was really hungry and it seemed every time I was close to a meal some great Crone event conspired to keep the food out of reach.

"I believe you mentioned Gina still makes great Italian food?" I said hopefully.

"Well, you're right," Mattie grinned and tousled my hair. "We have been at this quite a while. Let me go see what I can do."

10 ————————

In the art studio, Aurelia lit a stick of Nag Champa incense and placed it in a holder on the table that serves as an altar. One side of the altar hosted a collection of natural objects: bones, a cow skull, dried pomegranates, acorns, small figures of creatures associated with death and transformation — snakes, crows. The other side sported a vase of fresh flowers, some apples, a bowl of water, various colored stones, and tiny fertility figures. In the center was a bowl filled with scraps of paper on which women had written prayers and intentions. It was a Cronation custom to light a stick of incense before beginning to paint. At the end of a session, they burned the notes in the bowl to signal their intention to release any resistance to the new information that arrives via the images.

The fragrance of the incense calmed Aurelia's nerves and allowed her shoulders to drop and relax. She picked up an obsidian sphere and rolled it between her palms to absorb any negative energy. "Oh, Divine Source, I offer my fears, my limitations, my blindness, my striving for answers. I pray that You open me and all of us to Your wisdom and Your truth in gratitude. Infuse us with Your courage to conduct ourselves with imagination, truth, and compassion at all times, and for the highest good of all, and for Your greatest delight. May we always remember that You call us in love and joy to aid the blessed unfolding of the life that we co-create together with You. Amen."

"Amen, Sister," the other women echoed.

They set about opening the paint containers, filling jars with water and unrolling large sheets of paper and taping them to the wall. Aurelia chose music by a Hungarian women's choir from the music files and adjusted the volume to begin quietly and rise in volume imperceptibly as the women got to work in the studio. It was the closest thing she had to Pomeranian music and she figured it would invoke the right mood and help the Crones journey into the energetic place where they could receive guiding images about what was taking place in the world. When the work went well, it was as if each woman had a golden cord of energy arising from her crown chakra spiraling up to the Source Herself. If you had the gift of seeing energy, as many of the Crones did, when you came into the studio it would look like one of Alex Grey's paintings had come to life, each woman lit up from within in patterns of awesome complexity. You would see cords of light connecting each woman to the others as well as to the One. The lines of energy also spiraled down into the Earth from the centers of each woman's feet, keeping them grounded in everyday reality while they painted.

Still, many of the women at Cronation couldn't come near the studio when the Crones were painting without fainting. Others would lay outside on the grass in warm weather and absorb the vibe; this practice alone could raise a woman's consciousness several degrees.

"Now let us remember," Aurelia intoned, "our purpose together is to create and hold a space where all our thoughts are welcome and can rise and fall. We allow them to be seen — our hopes and our fears. Let the chaff fall from the wheat and let us see what's what."

"We hear you, Sister," the women chorused.

The Crones sat down at tables with their journals. Each woman carefully crafted and wrote down her own version of the intention they all shared. Whatever words they used, each ended with a plea to be used as an instrument of peace and to manifest the highest good for all and the most joyful delight of the Creative Source. This work of shared intention to be of service is the CIA — Collaborative Inquiry through Art — a major initiative of Cronation. After all, who but the Source is the Central Intelligence Agency? Decades of close work with the creative process had yielded this joyful and reliable method to get guiding information in a pleasurable and joyful way. CIA allows each person participating to show up fully in her uniqueness while offering her special insights as gifts in service to the group intention. The wisdom imprint of such work is like a complex energetic mandala that can be read and sourced by all involved.

Source, let me do no harm, Aurelia wrote, *and forgive me for any unintended harmful consequences. Release all my fear. Guide me to wisdom about Kali, or should I say, Charity Greenberg, and if it is right for me to know, grant me insight into what she might be up to.* Then she took a few quiet breaths and let her intentions melt away, giving them up completely to the Source.

What Aurelia had learned many years ago while painting in the barn behind Riva's house was that the highest human purpose is to help the Divine unfold in ever more interesting and wondrous ways. The Source delights in patterns, complexity, simple elegance and color, a good story, and a well-told dirty joke. But the Divine does not control the vision you choose from the infinite possibility, from war and pestilence to white-robed angels plucking harps. Your imagination, intention, and the clarity of your vision are the only limits. Many times Aurelia asked for specific outcomes — the healing of a particular woman's pain, for example — but she always qualified her intention by asking for the highest good for all to manifest. She had no doubt that a Divine Order existed, grander and more complex than she could see. Every time she turned control of the details over to the Source something manifested that was so perfect, so beautiful, so far beyond what she could have planned, she was left with awe and the deepest gratitude.

"That is the unique gift of being human," Phoebe taught. "We can choose not to do what we can do, to let our gifts lie fallow. Or we can turn our imagination to a higher purpose. But just because we can figure out better and better ways to propel bits of lead into each others' precious bodies, for example, well, that is no reason to decide that a gun is the be-all and end-all tool of change." The human love affair with guns was one manifestation of human creativity that Phoebe just couldn't abide. "We can choose to privilege the welfare of the whole over our individual, fleeting desires and come to learn how we are held completely in the more generous intention. There is no self-denial in dedication to the highest good of all. Unless, of course, we have a God complex and think that we know exactly what that looks like."

Phoebe did all she could when working with souls about to reincarnate to get them to undermine the love of weapons. It was slow going. Somehow the gun had replaced the magic wand when humans lost awareness of the way energy works. What they used to be able to do by pointing a finger and sending their focused energy they now they could only do crudely and so messily with bullets and guns. It was that bedrock of fear, she supposed, that kept the blinders on. It was the illusion of the once-and-for-all-ness of shooting someone that seemed to comfort humans, as if that stopped the energy of the adversary. That fearful desire to stop the flow was probably humans' biggest error, and Phoebe did her best to instill that lesson whenever she could.

Painting in the studio was one thing Phoebe missed terribly, but at least she could visit, watch and talk to Aurelia while she worked. Today would be a great session, Phoebe sensed, as she settled in to listen and watch from the other side.

"To keep energy flowing, imaginings need variety, spice, and joy."

Phoebe offered Aurelia some supportive reflection. "The Divine Herself is all potential, endless possibility — and we are She. It is actually Her humans that decide what is and is not okay, and She as Her Goddess Self loves us for that. As the Source, She has no sense of what humans call 'morals.' From inventive serial killers, to Leonardo da Vinci, the Source is an equal opportunity enjoyer. Why, the Marquis de Sade scored pretty high points imagination-wise."

"The Marquis de Sade? Really, Momma?" Aurelia wasn't a fan.

"It's tough to accept, but that's the way it is. The Source does not get hung up the way humans do on life and death, because that endless energetic spark continues to unfold in form after form. The Hindus expressed this truth in their renderings of Kali giving birth on the shores of the Ganges, picking up Her children, playing with them like dolls and then eating them, before birthing them again, then repeating the cycle endlessly with variations. She appreciates all categories of imagination — a surprise to most humans, especially religious fundamentalists of any stripe. When you understand the true meaning of eternity as eternal change, the rising and falling of each and every existence is cause for awe and wonder; but the need to cling to any particular one existence is gone. Just love it, honor it for all it's worth while it's here. In a way it is always here, just as in a way it is gone."

"Speaking of Kali, Momma," Aurelia interjected, getting to what was uppermost in her mind, "what could that girl be up to? There was a time when I thought Charity Greenberg would become a leader in Cronation, another woman of Mattie's generation to lead them onward. When she took the name Kali, though goodness knows she doesn't understand it really, I realized I had underestimated the girl's pain and her brittleness, Momma."

Her memory of Charity/Kali made her uneasy.

"I know the truth in the big picture," Aurelia continued, "and I'm pretty good at getting it right in the moment — though with that child, I just don't know… and that murky middle ground where most of life takes place and your work gets all entangled with everyone else's… Source, help me see my own failings there," Aurelia stopped painting for a moment and added these words to her intention in her journal. Her firmly held beliefs floated through her mind like flags or pennants on the cords of light that held her to the Source as she painted.

Phoebe sighed, "To the Divine, it really is all one: eternal and time-less energy. What manifests through human effort is only momentary, so why sweat the small stuff? Enjoy, respond, move on, see what comes next. Oneness doesn't mean one God in the literal biblical sense, one Great Old Dude, one temperamental old white man in the sky, loving but strict. It means divine golden light, that life force energy is one energy, in every-thing, of everything. For eons humans were fascinated by the natural world as it is, happy to wander from beautiful place to beautiful place, foraging only for what was needed in the moment, resting when tired and making up songs of praise. Eventually the magic of cultivating plants captivated human imagination and that required staying put, to watch things grow and celebrate the miracle of food showing up in orderly rows instead of serendipitous discoveries by the side of the path. Imagination was then freed up to be used in the service of storytelling. Mostly, folks would sit around for hours on end singing, making cool stuff like pottery and carved wooden bowls. These developments delighted the Source because She could feel Her creation grow in complexity as She watched humans sow and reap, shepherd animals, and come up with new recipes and new tales to tell. Humans still loved Creation then. They loved animals; they loved plants; they hadn't entered the era of separation from one another and from the other beings. They could still hear the slow deep voices of the rocks and the sighing stories of the trees. The animals spoke to them easily. There was little difference between dreaming life and waking life."

"That sounds heavenly to me, Momma. Why did that have to end?" Aurelia loved giving Phoebe the chance to go on, as if all the lost opportunities for childhood bedtime stories could be reclaimed. The other Crones, used to hearing what seemed like one-sided conversations when Aurelia connected with Phoebe, were lost in their paintings and in the music.

"Well, Aurelia, after eons of life in that circle, the beauty of the endless round got a little bit tiresome. Humans began to tell stories that grew in complexity and they got bored with the stories of the trees and the rocks. They began to notice differences in one another: some seemed to get better results with their crops, others had herds of more robust sheep. Some human offspring were more comely or clever than others. They created the job of poet to keep the older stories alive and to continue listening to them. Other things began to captivate the human imagination: figuring out ways to reliably increase the flocks, get more beans out of each planting. The theme of 'more' replaced 'enough' and that was fine — for a while. The great She really loves the spiral: 'That which leads to the next iteration is privileged.' Variations on any theme make the rule of the circle extend into another dimension. When humans learned to pull the circle up into the spiral, why, She was delighted!"

"Then for humans," Aurelia picked up the leitmotif, "the job is to notice what kills the theme. What makes the thread break? What causes that which has been unfolding to crash and burn? Sometimes we get stuck and want to return to the safety of the circle. Sometimes we want to push the spiral faster and faster."

"How you work this out is endlessly fascinating to the Source, and now, to me too," Phoebe laughed. "My, that painting is getting dark, Aurelia!"

"Momma! You know the 'no comment' rule! You taught me that side by side with the strands of light and delight created by storytelling about the world and all the new discoveries humans made, there are always dark strands of the unknown."

"That is for sure," Phoebe agreed. "Sometimes in experiments to breed more animals with a certain trait a monstrous goat would be born. This sort of occurrence awakened a dim sense of power in some that pointed toward bigger and newer discoveries in the unseen dark ahead. Some humans were fascinated by these stories yet to be told, others shied away from the dark in fear. The mystery of life and death, the creation of weapons, the organized killing of war, these loomed ahead of humans like dark clouds of potential — possible, but not inevitable."

"Could we have avoided any of that?" Aurelia mused.

"I don't know the answer to that, child. When interpreted through fear, the clouds crafted themselves into stories that produced fearsome realities. Throughout the ages the dark and light strands wove stories of complexity and beauty as well as brutality and horror. In some eras, fearsome knowledge was punished as a threat to peace and order and was suppressed. Women often suffered as the symbol for Nature's potential at such times. In other times, such knowledge proved to be an awesome aphrodisiac, women were seen as just another part of Nature to be controlled, causing some men to believe they rivaled and could even control the Source Herself."

"When the Crones who tend the various libraries of humanity look back on the fractal vision of human history, they duly note each dark part of the weave," Aurelia affirmed. "The women who journeyed into the dark places to learn more each came back with one insight in common: regardless of the details, the time or place, the actors and outcomes, when the dark stories were told through a lens of fear and separation, suffering was produced — which led to more fear and sometimes cycled around and around in a terrible way, until humans exhausted themselves."

"Whenever we try to hold on to the circle, or worse, go back to it after it is done, suffering is bound to follow, that much I do know," Phoebe answered. "And, while the fear was sometimes fear of neighboring tribes, sometimes fear of particular animals, often fear of women; when it came right down to it, the strands found in every dark story were fear of Nature itself and especially fear of change, which is what Nature is. And at bottom was the mistaken belief that the ultimate truth is that we are forever separate from the Source, from Nature and from one another. Now, the explanations for how things change are always made with whatever information is at hand. So if women singing and dancing in the groves seemed to make the sunrise and sunset and cause the animals to give birth to healthy offspring, well then, jolly good. But if storms come too often and crops die from too much rain, a womb or two or three is barren — well, it might be the fault of those women in the grove, might it not?

"In some communities there were elders, men and women, who took it upon themselves to journey into the dark seams between the old stories in which they were living and the new ones that were beginning to appear. They were able to travel out of time and place and hover at sufficient distance that they could see the patterns of life clearly and watch them as they shifted. They would return with clarifications and interpretations of the emerging stories and create rituals to lessen the fear. Fear tends to make things go rigid. Many animals become stock-still until a predator passes. Humans who get afraid want to hold on tight.

"Once humans began to develop imagination," Phoebe went on, "they tended to have a hard time discerning real dangers from the ones they cooked up in their minds. Unlike animals who will seek a quiet place to sleep through a storm that doesn't really threaten them, humans get agitated and try to hold everything in place, the opposite of what the Source expects. She is offering a new gift, based at least in part on their imaginings, and Her children close their eyes, scream and push it away. Or, for those completely convinced that separation is the ultimate truth, the gift appears as power stolen; they seize it, fashion it into a weapon to be used against others and even against the Source Herself. That's what you are seeing now in the world, Aurelia. I know those men are tired and afraid, but for the life of themselves, they can't just stop defending what is ending."

Rabbi Sarah Leaf was painting next to Aurelia, and while she couldn't hear Phoebe's side of the dialogue, she had been listening to Aurelia's.

"There came a moment," Sarah chimed in, "when, in the Earth's own life cycle — for one story of reality is that She, the very planet and the greater all in which She is located, is a sentient being Herself, and we humans are surely parts of Her — She went into a kind of dormancy. She pulled into Herself, a 'tsim tsum,' our Jewish mystics call it, to generate the energy for the next round of unfolding. It feels like different things to different humans who have separated enough to have consciousness. The cycle of simple coexistence in the natural world began to lose energy; the expected order did not prevail. Like when a mother takes a nap and children are left to their own devices, the children might get bored and get into various kinds of mischief, feeling an absence of the energy that had guided them and held their world in place. Having no sense of time, it feels like a new forever has replaced the predictable forever that used to be. It could be fifteen minutes, but never mind."

Sarah was painting a bride with wings, an image of Shekinah, the feminine face of God that often came to her. "Our Sabbath," Sarah continued, "is a practice that tries to prepare us for such a timeless time. It helps us get used to letting go of the era of making and doing for a little while, to remember the sweetness of the circle and of rest and through praise and prayer raise the circle into a spiral up to heaven."

Aurelia turned to Sarah, "Go on, Sister, you have a wisdom I need."

"This energy that the mother provides is a force that a child scarcely understands; likewise, they do not understand its absence. Feeling abandoned, they might turn on one another, pointing fingers of blame, or decide one child is at fault. A new story is needed, and children will listen to whoever seems to have a way to manage the terror that grows in such moments. Instead of napping, the children think their Mother is dead or has run away or never existed."

"That's why on Shabbat you welcome Her back as a bride?" Aurelia brightened. "You're practicing for Her return?"

"That's right." Sarah nodded as she added layers of pink to the golden wings of her Shekinah. "A common response to such an awesome fear is for one person to act the role of the Mother as best it is understood, choosing a child or children to sacrifice. Since the Divine reclaims each and every one of Her children eventually, this practice is seen as a way to mitigate Her power. It's a way to take control and play Goddess. Like saying, 'Here, take this one and leave the rest of us alone.' Those with a god complex imagine bargaining with a cruel and capricious being."

"That was how Riva taught me to understand the story of Abraham and Isaac in the bible," Aurelia said. "'What kind of crazy man thinks that God wants him to kill his son? Did he ever think about talking to Sarah before he went off like that?' I asked Riva."

Sarah chuckled. "Yes, as her namesake, I've always wondered what Sarah might have said. What did your grandmother tell you?"

"Riva said, 'One who is afraid that God has left him is feeling all alone and acts from fear. Remember when your Momma left, you wanted to kill all those other little children? Nothing made sense to you. Why would your Momma leave you?' One day she came behind the barn and I was fixing to choke this little boy Oscar to death. His momma left too, so I decided it must be all his fault; he was bad, his momma left and took mine with her. I just made up a story with what I had at hand."

Sarah smiled and sighed sympathetically.

Aurelia put her hands on her hips, "I still said, 'Yeah, well, Abraham had no excuse; he was a grown man.' And Riva said, 'Any grown man can be as full of fear as any little child. That is something you must always remember, because many times they forget. Remember always to see the child in those consumed by fear.'"

"Those biblical days must have been fearsome times," Sarah shook her head. "As the rituals that had held one worldview in place began to fail, humans discovered that while they did not control the natural world through their rituals, perhaps they could through their words and actions. That's where my people came in.

"At the time that the discovery of words became important," Sarah continued, "humans discovered that they could create using words as well, an exciting but confusing discovery. Most people forgot that they had a Mother at all as they got more and more caught up in events and ideas that seemed strictly of their own making. The circle was traded for the line, and the line led forever into the future. Even with the observance of stars, the moon and the seasons, they forgot the round. They didn't yet understand the spiral, so they codified what they knew in the calendar and clock to try to keep it safe and same." Aurelia laughed, "We sure do like to think we author eternal truths!"

Sarah continued, "And the women, whose rituals had seemed to hold the world in place, began to be viewed in a different light as men discovered their own powers. The men had learned they also had a role in making new life; it was they, not the moon that impregnated women. Maybe they felt tricked, who knows? Maybe the women already knew it and kept it from them."

Marty joined the conversation; she had been enjoying listening to the two women speaking. "Imagine the first men to figure this out, a real leap in abstract thought. Hey, this sticky white stuff might be important. Maybe a guy was noticing animals doing it and put two and two together. To be the first guy that reduced all that mystery, the touch, the taste, the sounds of humans coming together in a most unlikely act to create new life."

"Yes," Sarah stopped painting for a moment, "Think of it! With nothing but the unutterably astonishing human imagination that can pick up clues and hold them in the mind until a picture and a story forms. Amazing! I always wondered if the others scoffed. Was the messenger as unwelcome back before history?"

Marty laughed, "Yeah, did the other men say, 'No way, dude, don't let the women hear you, they'll cut your dick off.' Did they get together and talk amongst themselves during the early Goddess era? I can imagine: 'You don't think the new ones come from the moon?' and 'Yeah, I know the women's bellies look like the moon, but have you ever noticed, no woman gets round like the moon unless one of us puts his stick in her first?' Like, 'Whoa, Gork, what are you saying?'"

"'I'm saying, this stick is a magic wand: it gets stiff, it softens up.'" Marty was swinging her arms in a parody of a caveman. "'Stuff comes out of it, I know, I know, not blood like what comes out of the women — like when we slaughter a bear, except women, they don't die. But what if it's some kind of magical white blood, with seeds in it or something, huh, what about that?'" Some of the other women painting nearby laughed at Marty, and Aurelia shot her an amused look. "Don't be making such sport of our ancient brothers, now, Marty, we have no idea how they felt with the women in charge back then."

Sarah continued, "And so they started to pay closer attention — maybe Gork was onto something. Maybe he was a proto-nerd, good at counting and keeping track of who put his stick in which women, maybe noticing a family resemblance in the offspring," she offered.

Phoebe was enjoying the women's banter.

Elsie joined in the storytelling, "As the earth seemed less predictable, and men exercised their new found powers in creating order, women seemed the cause of the disorder. This is simplifying something terribly complex and mysterious, but you get the idea. Humans are story makers, imagineers — and stories need sets and props and the imagination is great for coming up with stories and props and so forth."

"And so it went for millennia, stories and props," Elsie elaborated, "fear and love, war and peace. Sometimes the stories evolved in gentle ways, sometimes fear forced them into twisted contours that caused great pain. But once that story of the Earth and Nature and women as the main authors got overthrown, once She got down for Her nap, well, the men, most of them, worked out their fear of the change, and got busy and occupied with thinking stuff up.

"Women could be in charge of making babies, though eventually men pretty much took over the management of that when they could. Same with growing food, building shelter. Man as manager, man as maker, became versions of man as warrior. Women got to be spectators for the most part. The female imagination wasn't so welcome. After all, it seemed like she'd messed things up, didn't it? Imagine them hitting their foreheads, "'How did we not see this before?'" Elsie sighed. "And so he created God in his image and we all know how that worked out."

"Momma, do you think that without realizing it, men hold a grudge against the Divine Source, their true Mother, and feel abandoned by Her?" Aurelia spoke out loud to Phoebe, knowing the others would understand.

"Certainly, Aurelia, and women bore the brunt of this grudge pretty much up until now. As She awakens and things begin to shift, the old stories creak and fray and begin to fail. The male imagination, despite the amazing things it has wrought, has run out its string, much as women's did back in Moses' time. The spiral winds around and it's women's turn again to take the helm. For a minute at least, until they take a crack at the Great Marriage again and see if it takes this time, that humans learn the lesson of balance. It's a natural unfolding when seen from really far away, like as far as the edge of the galaxy maybe — but up close, it is awfully messy and the mess we see from here seems to be maybe all men's fault."

The rest of the women continued painting silently until Marty said, "I bet I know what Phoebe said to that question!" and they all laughed. They had all heard this story many times before but still loved the re-telling, the reminding. Every Crone knew that the Great Marriage, the Hieros Gamos, the balancing of male and female, active and receptive energies both in individuals and at every level of the cosmos was the great project that they were all experiencing together. The coming into alignment of enough individuals might be sufficient to align the bigger picture, so the Crones believed.

Phoebe resumed her thoughts and spoke to Aurelia, "For a long stretch, humans had used the imagination mostly for thinking up the creation and manufacture of stuff, early on using just what was at hand and saying please and thank you to the tree that became a dugout canoe or the deer whose skin became moccasins and a blanket. Later it got wild: appliances, fashion, processed food, prescription medication, and laborsaving devices of every description.

"At first this was exciting," Phoebe remembered, "but it began to get really tedious sometime in the 1960s, when plant medicine and hallucinogenics gave some humans a peek at what life could be like, if they just didn't go so fast to fear! Although no one would admit it, very shortly there was enough stuff to outfit every man, woman, and child in the world with waffle irons, video games, and high-performance gym shoes. But though we created the desire for all these things, we never got the hang of a good distribution system or how to tell when enough of a good thing was enough. Landfills became a sad solution.

"It was when humans became adept at making things with less and less energy and more and more material, since they tended to still think matter and spirit are separate, that things became messy," Elsie said, sadly. "Problem was they couldn't figure out what to do with the excess energy. Stuck on the concept of money, and exchanging it for more stuff, they just couldn't get the part about pleasure. Feedback loops just weren't working when groups got too big. Where they could have gotten immense pleasure from sharing, passing stuff around, they instead hoarded."

Phoebe sighed and continued the telling, "The Divine Source is easily bored with predictable outcomes. Without doubt, humans have provided Her with endless amusement as well as challenges. She is often sad that so few of Her creatures emulate Moses and call Her out on shit like the fire and brimstone stuff or the terrible threats of the Book of Leviticus. The feedback loop with the Divine is the most important one of all. So She obliges by manifesting as much natural drama as She can to try and get our attention and bring us back to each other and to Herself. Humans just seem to respond quicker to fires and floods than to a beautiful bird landing in the backyard."

She can't get over how people continued to enslave themselves, creating unnecessary needs and then working so hard to fulfill them. The Divine recognizes the mirror-like relationship with Her creation. Her creatures can't sit still for long, being what they called "idle" — yet really, that's a lot of what they were made for. Can't you all see you could just get together and make music and dance and sing? She just likes watching you experiment and create and play and figure out ways to connect with Her," Phoebe said.

"I know, Momma, I know." Aurelia hummed along with the Hungarian women whose voices and music filled the room. She learned during her years of painting and talking to Source that the bottom-line relationship to the Divine is one of call and response. She realized the potential of every little prayer, curse, and complaint.

"And if I didn't call on Her for a while, She calls me, through a pain in my body, a dream, or a natural occurrence like a storm," Aurelia murmured and the women close enough to hear murmured back, "Amen, Sister, amen!"

Painting and drawing, any kind of mark making, helped to tap into the infinite well of the imagination that was one aspect of the Divine Source. When she was young Aurelia would challenge the smaller children to create something never before seen, a color, a flower, or an invention. Sure enough, before long there would be a story in the New York Times about a discovery of a new flower or an extinct bird suddenly spotted by some ornithologist who was paying attention and also wasn't so hooked into the idea of "extinct" that he was blind to the creature's appearance.

Of course, few people had the ability to access imagination the way those children did who'd been raised up in Nature by Riva and Aurelia and never went to school. Fewer still knew the real power and purpose of art was to renew and increase love and happiness, and celebrate the infinite diversity of life. The cultural trance of repetitious video games, TV shows, computers and just plain cacophony of modern life put the imagination of most people out of reach. The feedback loop to the Divine was just broken for so many. It was a damn shame.

Aurelia had mixed colors for a long time before she placed a single mark on her paper. "Now, why am I feeling drawn to that pale shade of peach that white folks like to call flesh color?"

The other Crones knew better than to answer that question.

"No comment" was the one abiding rule of the art making process. As long as women were engaged in bringing forth an image, the image was given primacy over the naming or interpreting that humans love to do. Naming stops the unfolding, usually at the limit of what is already known. The idea of Collaborative Inquiry through Art is to bring in new information, new images. Understanding comes later, not as a solely intellectual act but rather like the deep gift of the image seeping into body and soul.

Aurelia felt a wave of resistance at the impulse to paint with the peach color, but she just focused on her breathing and let her hand move across the page. Although the women painted side by side, standing at the wall, each one was deep into her own flow. Each one released her intention into the Void and gave herself over to the pleasure of paint stroking onto the paper, or in Rae's case, squeezing some tin foil into a doll-like figure. Lydia was working in charcoal; her face and the apron she'd donned to protect her dress smeared where she'd absentmindedly wiped her hands. The Hungarian women were chanting, pounding drums, and shaking rattles and bells. The women creating were pulled so deeply into their flow zone that they ignored the bell signaling mealtime — and the one signaling evening yoga and meditation — and the final one for lights out.

When they finally put down their tools, it was well past midnight. Gina sent over some bowls of fruit and nuts which they sampled as they looked around silently at the images each had made. It became apparent, regardless of size or medium, whether two or three dimensions, whatever style or technique, that while each work of art was a unique creation reflecting its maker, they were all possessed of a commonality as well. Each image was a rendition of the same subject: forces of dark and light, in some a figure of a woman in a wrinkled navy blue business suit standing in a burnt out landscape facing another woman dressed in black leather; many showed a black bird, swooping down from a Roger Brown sky about to land on the shoulder of the black-clad woman.

Aurelia gazed at her own painting. There was no mistaking the resemblance of the figure in black to Kali, previously Charity Greenberg, and the woman in the business suit surely looked a lot like the newly arrived Eve. But, knowing better than to come to any conclusion about what it all meant, Aurelia put down her paintbrush and just let the feelings evoked by the images wash over her.

11

Harvey sat back in the snug enclosure of the SAC with the setting on dream scan. He pressed the switch on the armrest that slowly lowered the lights to off and focused on his breathing. He felt his muscles relax into the chair as he recited the mantra for dreams: "Now to the river where dreams flow, deepest wisdom may you show me. Drop me like a pebble I hold, into the dream, let the story unfold."

The dream figure of the dark woman dragging the sack began to materialize out of the hazy gray static of the screen. Mattie came in quietly and took a seat on an upholstered stool next to Harvey, just about at ear level.

"Okay, Harvey, just notice her, really notice." As Mattie spoke the figure on the screen brightened in color and details appeared and grew sharper like someone pressed the enhance button in Photoshop.

Harvey spoke: "Her hair is long and black, curly and springy. Her features are kinda sharp — man, she looks a little scary!" Just as Harvey spoke the last words, the figure looked directly out and locked eyes with him, then blurred and faded away.

"Okay," Mattie said in a soft, measured voice, "'Scary' is a judgment, it breaks the flow. It's just an image, Harvey. Can you release 'scary'? Just stay with the image. Remember, when we judge an image, we send it down the path of our judgment towards manifestation in that form. 'Scary' is just one element of this figure: one possible story is a scary one. We want to learn more about her."

"Yeah, right, I'll try again." Harvey took a deep breath, clenched and relaxed his fingers. "The woman is tall. She is wearing boots with pointy toes and high heels." The image began to materialize from the feet up on the screen. "The scene is kind of dark, like it's dusk or early evening. She's trying to get somewhere in a hurry. Her sack seems very heavy."

"Okay, good, the image is coming back into focus," Mattie prompted. "Can you see the difference? You say it seems heavy because you observe that but in a neutral way. It's the emotional charge that we add with our judgments that gives them so much power to control what manifests. Can you try some simple dialogue?"

"Yeah, 'What's in the sack, Miss?'" Harvey began.

At that moment, there was a dark flash on the screen, a raven flew up out of the flash and the woman with the sack disappeared. The screen filled with static.

"Oh, man, I'm sorry!" Harvey pounded the armrest.

"Don't worry," Mattie got up to leave. She patted his hand. "You're doing great, just chill out a little, do some breathing and try again in a little while. Take it slow. I have to go check on Eve."

Harvey focused on taking deep, long breaths; he re-set the dial on level one and revisioned the initial dream image with new details: a tall, dark, thin, sharp-featured woman with curly black hair dragging a large sack. This time he focused on the background.

"I'm not gonna get shot down again. This thing could have real possibilities for helping guys," he thought. "Imagine if you test-drive your bullshit before trying it out on a real woman. Watching a screen go blank sure beats the hell out of being turned down for a date." This line of thought caused the image to pixilate, but when he banished the idea of a dating application the image righted itself and came back into focus.

Harvey had watched numerous times as Mattie worked with one or another of the women to bring a dream image into focus and then get it to evolve into a full-scale story while also explaining the process to the dreamer. Usually the subject was a personal dream and the woman was used to telling a particular story about her life that cast her as a victim or simply wound round and round in circles. Mattie coached the women to explore different narrative paths for the image while they watched how the story changed on the screen.

Like the woman whose dream ended when a tall figure chased after her with a knife. She always woke up terrified before anything but the chase happened. In one new alternative version, the woman imagined a knife sharpening shop, slowed down the man's pace had him bring the knife to her to be sharpened. At first she couldn't get past her fear though, and once she sharpened the knife, all she could imagine doing was plunging it into the man's chest. Mattie coached her to slow down the unfolding of the story even more, to stay with the fear and keep breathing. She knew that if the woman could do that, the fear would shift into something else.

"It's a dream," Mattie would say, "your dream. You can dream it forward in any way you like; the Source will support you."

After a few tries, the woman had imagined that the man ran into the dark while she crouched there and watched him run past. He came to a cord that he cut with the knife and that action opened a flood of light into the space. The knife melted in the light and the man fashioned it into a crown. He called her name and then he placed the crown on her head. They embraced and the cave was filled with a kaleidoscopic rainbow of light. "A classic 'Hieros Gamos,' the alchemical inner marriage," Mattie had told the woman. "You are meeting and embracing your own inner active energy which is symbolized by the male figure. But, at the same time, you are also untying a knot for the collective dream time of all of us by transforming a dream based on fear into one of joining with your own power." Mattie assured the woman that she was increasing the possibilities for all dreamers through her work and doing so with compassion. Harvey was excited by witnessing the work and wanted to be a part of it.

It was always exciting to see a woman realize she could direct the narrative: "dreaming the dream onward," Mattie called it. She explained how she grew up learning the skill in a much more low-tech way through the painting process she learned from Aurelia. At first the whole thing — entering dreams and painting pictures to talk to the "Creative Source" — seemed kind of crazy to Harvey. He'd been raised with a pretty conventional idea of God: Big Guy, knows everything, sees you when you're sleeping, knows when you're awake. No, that's Santa Claus, but same difference. A powerful old man who can zap you on a whim. Not unlike Harvey's dad who sometimes took off his belt and threatened Harvey or one of his brothers with a thrashing if they didn't behave, though he never actually beat them like some of his friends' dads did.

"Your dad didn't have to really beat you," Mattie once said, "because Sunday school made sure that a picture of a bigger, more powerful dad — a.k.a. God — could turn you to ash with a touch. It's classical stimulus/response conditioning. For most children, the actual angry parent and the view of God they are taught become enmeshed. Remember Pavlov? The dogs eventually just start drooling at the sound of a bell."

What helped Harvey buy into the dream and painting stuff was when Mattie compared it to playing with plastic army men, something Harvey and his brothers had spent hours doing on rainy days as kids.

"Tell me you didn't make up stories, have those guys talking to each other, giving orders of who to blow up and who to shoot! We are here on this earth to play. We just need to realize that the play stories become the real stories."

Mattie made it sound so simple, but to Harvey the idea of (as Mattie called it) a "co-creative, loving Universe" where each person's thoughts, feelings, and actions determined what life looks like — well, at first, that scared Harvey to death. "So my dim bulb of a cousin, Eddie, he gets together with his dim and dimmer friends, and their thoughts create the world? All those guys can think about is who's got what and how can they get it."

"Exactly," Mattie replied. "Hence we have strip malls, strip mines, strip clubs, and strip searches. You got it; I want it; I'm gonna figure out how to take it. The male mind tends to go straight for its identified target. And, at first glance, that seems so obviously smart. But it disregards the law of unintended consequences. When you are dealing with anything in the natural world — and that includes women — a circular approach that lets you see alternative possibilities is better in the long run."

"Point A to Point B," Harvey retorted. "Why waste time?"

Mattie laughed. "Time, ah yes! There's the culprit! Time is an illusion, a construct created by the slightly more conscious to perfect what your cousin Eddie does: getting what's yours from you."

"You make it sound like a rigged game that you know the 'rules' to," Harvey had protested, "and men are just stupid shits and now that you women have the upper hand, you're gonna show us just how stupid we are."

Harvey had gotten used to Aurelia in his early days at the Farm, but Mattie — younger than him, so smart and, well, so sexy — sometimes got him mad when she explained things.

She had looked at him and smiled that day.

"No, Harvey, really, that's not it. It's not men: it's when only part of the brain is working, I call it the masculine part, but of course women do this too. That 'Point A to Point B' as you call it, that all comes from a faulty underlying assumption."

"Oh, yeah? What's that?" Harvey remembered how he'd felt kind of queasy, a little bit sick to his stomach, when he looked directly into Mattie's eyes.

"The assumption is that there isn't enough to go around: You better look out for number one, and the universe is a cold, scary, capricious place that doesn't give a damn about you. That underneath it all, God is the cranky Father who you can't depend on and can't trust because you don't know exactly when He's gonna go off on you. Because you're basically bad, a 'sinner.' And enough actual fathers are like that, unpredictable, so the story comes true. Or so I've heard. I never knew my daddy."

"I'm sorry, Mattie, I didn't know that. I guess I just thought…" Harvey began.

"Thought what? The Crones found me under a cabbage leaf? I sprang full grown from Aurelia's brow?"

"Well, none of you seem to really need men…"

"Look, Harvey, I have been loved and honored my whole life by incredible people. Yes, they are women. But don't imagine there isn't an ache in me, a curiosity, an empty place. Most of the time I'm fine with it. I trust that the world is sacred and more complex than I can imagine. I praise What-Is."

Harvey had only been at the farm for a few months when he and Mattie had this conversation. "Well?"

"Well what?" Mattie answered. "Haven't you learned anything about a different world view from Momma? Why wasn't she angry with you after you ran over Phoebe?"

Harvey felt flustered but he tried to remember what some of the things he and Aurelia had talked about when she visited him in the hospital as he recovered from the injuries he had sustained in the accident. "She said time doesn't really exist, that multiple realities coexist, that she and your Grandma and all sorts of women all over the world are working to shift reality from that point A–point B thing to some other way where everybody will be well fed and stuff."

"Point A to point B works really well in a crisis when you have to rescue a baby from a burning building and there's no time to waste," Mattie explained. "Then a whole other whole level of your brain actually kicks in to do the circular reasoning — I'm talking about at a kind of warp speed — you don't even realize is happening. That's why men love to create a crisis: it's the situation they feel best equipped to deal with."

Mattie could tell that, although Harvey got it on some level, he didn't totally get it. He was still back on wondering why she didn't know her dad. Mirrored back in Harvey's eyes was something else: compassion, a bit of sadness, but also an electrifying something Mattie had never felt before.

"Alignment," Mattie said. "Loving alignment with what is. That's what life is about. And when you get into alignment with What-Is, things unfold better than you could ever plan."

Then she kissed him. And while his brain remained somewhat confused, Harvey and Mattie experienced the form of alignment as old as humankind. Lesson learned.

"I promise to ease up on the lectures," she said as they lay together afterwards in each other's arms. "And Harvey? That was beautiful, thank you."

Harvey started to cry, slow tears rolling down his cheeks at first, then he gasped and doubled over and started sobbing. He was hugging his knees to his chest, images flooding his mind: Whiskers, his pet rabbit who died when he was eight; Mrs. Ellis, his favorite teacher, who yelled at him in the second grade; the moment right before the truck hit Phoebe with that sickening thud. Mattie leaned into him, stroked his hair and whispered, "I'm sorry, Harvey, it's painful when the walls come down."

"Don't be sorry. I get this, Mattie, I really do. Maybe I can't explain it — not maybe, I can't. But I get it and I'm grateful."

They lay together listening to each other breath for a long time.

* * *

Harvey sighed. He had a ways to go on the dream stuff. Mattie, of course, grew up doing this; for her it was as natural as breathing. Deep breath, repeat the mantra, the image returned vividly.

"Where are you?" he thought as he gazed at the woman on the screen, focusing on his breathing. A street scene started to come into focus. Instead of trying to engage the woman, he observed: "That bag looks heavy."

The woman looked up and made eye contact with Harvey. This time he stayed steady and sort of put his eyes out of focus a bit.

"It sure is, asshole, it sure as hell is. And it's full of pictures you don't want to see."

Harvey kept his breathing even, noted his excitement and let it go. The image wavered only slightly. No rush, steady breath, let the image set the pace. Harvey returned to noticing in this half-focused way, like he was looking right next to the woman but with his field of vision open enough to include her. The woman's eyes were dark amber and probing, but sad and hard. She was wearing a black turtleneck and black pants tucked into boots, boots with a high heel and an exaggeratedly pointed toe. They made her seem even taller, thinner, more dangerous, like a walking stiletto. Harvey just watched these thoughts float by while he focused on her surroundings: traffic and buildings came into view, a busy city. He could hear the sack scrape along the ground, a sidewalk.

"Won't the sack wear out, being dragged along the street like that?" Harvey asked slowly.

"What sack?" The woman snapped her wrist and the sack retracted into a stylish black leather shoulder bag.

"My mistake," Harvey said in as neutral a voice as he could. "What's your name?"

"What's your name, hot stuff? How did those hags make a monkey out of you? You look a little old for the sex camp. Well, I guess they need someone to do the heavy lifting around there. You must be the token dray horse, huh?"

Harvey kept breathing steadily, listening to the insults and not responding, but he could feel his heart beating faster. Keeping his eyes focused just off the dream figure, he began to notice the surroundings. She was walking towards an office building. A raven that had been in the background, sitting on a pole, then on a mailbox, landed on the ground and turned into a small woman. The two approached the building together. The image grew faint. As the tall woman reached for the door handle, the smaller one turned and made eye contact with Harvey, held her hand up like a gun, pointed at him and mouthed the word: "Pow!" She grinned and blew on her finger like a gunslinger from an old Western movie then followed the tall woman into the building.

Harvey felt a spasm in his chest and the screen went to static. He kept breathing deeply, fixing the images of both figures in his mind. Although the smaller women's antics seemed somewhat playful, Harvey had a bad feeling. Suddenly the static dissolved and the dark woman's face appeared and looked right at Harvey.

"Point A to Point B, Mister. That's still the shortest way to reach the objective."

"Not anymore," thought Harvey. "Not anymore."

12 ———————

In the art studio, the women did some chi gung exercises to get their energy flowing. They did the "Crane in the Creek" form together, moving their arms and legs up and down, placing each foot down mindfully toe first, undulating their arms to resemble the graceful crane and loosening their chest muscles to open their hearts. Even after staying up all night, the ancient Chinese movements never failed to restore them. They gave thanks to their bodies for supporting them in their work, made a promise to nap later, ate lightly, and then gathered around one of the tables with Aurelia to share the words that had come to each woman in dialogue with her image.

"We are getting very close to a major point in the Great Shift and some considerable chaos is inevitable. We have always known that the Shift will not look exactly like whatever we can imagine; it is beyond our human imagination. We cannot plan it but only prepare for it by becoming flexible and ready to dance, to train our ears to hear new music. So, before we read our witness writings, I'd like to make an invocation." Aurelia closed her eyes and began: "Let us not lose our way. We ask for all fear to be released from our muscles and sinews. Make us limber and joyful. We ask for our hearts to be open for the clearest compassion to flow from our every act. We ask to be ready for surprises and to be courageous enough to welcome whatever aid arrives, in whatever form, however unexpected."

"We feel you, Sister," the others murmured.

"The last may not be first," Aurelia continued, "they may just be somewhere in the middle of the pack. The dark may be light. The sweet may taste sour — it may taste sour, sweet, and salty all in the same mouthful. Every cherished belief will need to be re-visited. The Sacred holds nothing inviolate, She has a sense of humor, She elevates whomever She sees fit. We ask for the grace to dance alongside Her in the Great Changes to Come. Amen."

"Amen now!"

The songs of the Hungarian women were silent, the incense long ago burned to ash. Aurelia felt the familiar knot in her stomach that often accompanied seeing the images before the witness writings were read.

"I'll go first," Lorelei Winger spoke up. My intention was: *I tune into the Pomeranian situation and see if that is where we should focus our resources.* The women gazed at Lorelei's painting. It was rendered in a colorful, impressionistic style: daubs of paint placed next to each other converging and vibrating to convey an image of scores of beautiful women reclining in grassy fields talking and eating fruit together; a bright blue sky festooned with fluffy clouds formed a pleasant backdrop. Lorelei began to read:

Are you the women of Pomerania? We heard you are being rounded up and locked away...

The plump blonde woman reclining under a spreading oak tree replies to Lorelei's query: *We beat them to it. Our Minister of Women's Affairs issued a proclamation last week at the new moon. She said it was time for the women to take a retreat in honor of the first queen of Pomerania, Elsa. She said she'd had a dream that directed this action and urged all employers to be flexible and allow their women workers to go to the countryside. I reply: Oh, what a great signal to the women of your country and the world!*

Another figure in the painting speaks:

Yes, the women in our Cronation cells all know the signal. Whenever we speak of Elsa, the first Queen, they know we mean the Divine Source.

What advice do you have for us here in the West? Lorelei continued to read her witness.

As we have all known, the defining action will begin in your country and send its ripples out to the world. Beyond that, simply stay in love and banish fear.

Thank you, Lorelei closed her reading.

As was the custom, the women did not comment on Lorelei's message but simply nodded or slapped their hand on the table or their thigh. They would wait until each woman had read their dialogues aloud before shifting into any discussion. By concentrating the energy of the revelations in this way they could feel their way into the levels of the message more fully and be guided toward right action.

Lydia stood by her charcoal drawing.

My intention: *Please guide us to see what must be seen that may present a danger to the Shift.*

The women murmured appreciatively. Lydia, who spent so much time in the business world, could often tune into the darker aspects of reality more easily than many of the women who lived in the relatively idyllic setting of the Farm.

She read: *I see dark swirls that emanate up from the bottom left hand corner of the paper. At the bottom they are dense in form but they spread out and become lighter above. Can you speak?*

Recognize me for what I am.

What are you?

Smoke.

Where there is smoke, there is fire? Is this your message?

And fire in the human realm may speak of a deep rage.

Yet you are beautiful in form, why is that?

There are those for whom rage is so true as to be beautiful.

Thank you.

And so it went around the circle, each woman and her image bearing witness to some aspect of the truth of the moment, of the situation that was underway — a great shift in the planetary energy that the Crones had been preparing for for decades, that had been unfolding since the world began. Like the ancient oracles of Greece and Rome, the Crones accessed the deepest wisdom of the Source through their dedication to the Creative Process. By using paintings instead of just dreams, they had created a means for any woman who chose to activate her oracular capacity to add to the wisdom that informed them all. They had learned how important it was to have many voices in order to see a situation fully. Though Aurelia seemed to be their leader, she was just one voice among the many wise voices of the Crones.

As each woman spoke in story, metaphor, or aphorism, threads of light formed a shape around them. Initially the threads traced a simple glowing triangle of white light lines between the first three who spoke — but as they continued, additional lines began to form in the chakras' rainbow of colors evoking different facets of wisdom and different levels of insight. Not every woman could see the auric lines easily, but for those who could, the emerging pattern provided a means to know where blind spots remained in the vision being transmitted. A complex 3-D tetrahedron, for example, with bright lines in red, orange, yellow, green, turquoise, blue, indigo, and violet, confirmed a complete plan on the physical level. When another version in the pastel hues of these colors was present, the women were also confirmed on the causal level, which meant that the guides and angels in the next realms were also present and assisting them. If parts of any form were faint or missing, the women knew to wait, paint more, ask for increased clarity, to discern where they were missing alignment.

By the time Aurelia read her witness, a fuller picture was taking shape in the imaginations of the women. Aurelia could sense what was needed but she didn't know yet how they would accomplish the task. She noticed that some of the lower chakra colors were missing: red and orange strands had yet to appear. That suggested some foundational learning was yet to unfold.

She read: My intention is: *I open to the highest good for all and for this beloved planet that we call Mother. I ask to be used as an instrument of peaceful transformation, if She can allow that, so that the shift that must come can be one that leads to joy and celebration and a recognition of the Divine in every being.*

She felt a twinge of fear and shook her head. All these years, all this practice, and still there is a bit of fear before ever unfolding truth. How fearful must others be who have never learned that the ground of all life is love? Standing on the boundary between separate self and the Great All within a community of women was an awesome vantage point. Deep breath, she continued:

My witness: *I see a woman who looks an awful lot like Eve, our newly arrived sister. She was brought here after being identified by Lydia as ready for her own shift and with possibly an important role to play in the big Shift. Here she is wearing her business suit and standing facing another woman who is dressed in black. This woman reminds me of Charity Greenberg who was with us a short while some years back. Can either of you speak?*

The dark figure replies: *Kali, the name is Kali. That's one thing I took from you, Aurelia. At least I got a name that fits me.*

Welcome, Kali. How have you been?

Aurelia nearly bit her tongue holding back some of the things she wanted to say. If Kali herself had been in front of her she might have been tempted to shake her. She had been so bright, so hungry for the truth; she fought with Aurelia in a way Aurelia loved, sparring and challenging, but in the end, Kali fled from the love that was such an important part of the

Cronation message. Aurelia always felt in some way that she had failed the younger woman.

I have my own plan, thank you very much. I always agreed with you about the 'what,' it's the 'how' in your program I couldn't get. See, Aurelia, I think you don't see a piece of your own shadow. 'Black Power,' wasn't that the phrase? Your people had the guns; they lacked the nerve. And so do you.

There was a soft gasp from the women. Aurelia sat for a heartbeat or two as the impact of her own witness washed over the room. The words of a witness, written as they are in a stream of consciousness flow, had another level of power when read out loud in community.

The guns are what killed my father, Aurelia read the words so softly, the other Crones had to lean towards her to hear.

And you've been afraid of them ever since, but I'm not afraid, Kali snapped.

Aurelia stood up.

"I'm not feeling very well, Sisters, I need to lie down. Please continue — someone else can read; I'll listen from here."

Aurelia sank down onto a couch in the studio near the circle of women. She waved them away, "Please continue," her eyes glistening with tears.

The women were silent and until Lorelei finally spoke: "Aurelia, dear one, you have done so much, everything the Source has asked of you. You have given up your father, your mother, your dear husband William. You have dedicated yourself to the Source and to our wellbeing. Let us help you now and continue this difficult dialogue."

"Yes, child, let them help you!" Phoebe was present and speaking to Aurelia as she had throughout the painting session. As she laid on the couch, ashen, her eyes closed, Aurelia raised her hand to Lorelei and pointed upwards and said, "Phoebe."

They waited silently as Aurelia communed with her mother. "It's your 'Moses Moment,' Aurelia. He said you'd get one. You need to get out of the way. You can't do it all. Let these strong women help you and you just listen to hear the message. It will free you and do a healing throughout every level of the cosmos, don't you worry."

Aurelia opened her eyes and gazed from face to face, tears in her eyes. The love radiating toward her from each woman was unique in color, vibration, and even sound. She felt herself being rocked gently as if whatever last bits of resistance still held in her being were being released and replaced with love. Suddenly she felt a sharp pain in her gut. She doubled over and moaned.

"How could I have been so blind? How could I have not seen that my insistent love was too much for that poor child? Kali dear, I am so sorry," she wailed.

The women murmured, "Let it go, Aurelia. Sister, forgive yourself."

Rae rose from her seat, taking up Aurelia's witness writing and, once Aurelia's sobs quieted, she began speaking, reading from the page the words spoken by the Kali figure from Aurelia's painting as recorded in the witness.

Your people were cowards, Aurelia. They could have risen up and killed the Men in Charge in 1968, and we'd all have been better off. But your mother slunk away and abandoned you to make this fantasy world. You have enslaved more women in this stupid dreamtime than any man in any kitchen or factory. Freedom comes from the barrel of a gun. You know this, Aurelia, don't you? Mao said it first and the Panthers agreed.

Lorelei stood next, Rae handed the pages to her. She would stand in for Aurelia who lay unable to move, silent tears streaming down her face.

It is true that there were cowards among us, in that era, as there are the fearful in every group. But it was not the cowards who led Phoebe to that fruitful exile. It was the spirit of her sisters in the struggle: Mary McLeod Bethune, Bettye Collier-Thomas, Ella Baker, and Septima Clark. These women knew better than guns. To take up the gun was to lose the very soul that the Men in

Charge had tried and failed to deny and steal through slavery, to hand it over to him on a platter. These women did not succumb to hatred. They knew that under all that hate was fear, and under all that fear was the desperate lack of meaning that fills any space devoid of love. This is what we call 'terror' today, the swirling mix of hate and fear and dread of what is coming.

These were the words Aurelia's soul had spoken back to Kali's challenge.

All of the women were crying now, but new strands of red, orange, and yellow were pulsing radiantly between them. This had been the foundational piece just outside of Aurelia's awareness and necessary for the insights to be complete.

Lorelei continued to read from Aurelia's witness writing: *The very fact that there were slaves who loved those who enslaved them, loved their children, was the root of the fear, the terror that filled the souls of those men in power. In a way it would have been a kindness to have taken up guns and killed the white folks, for that is what they understood they deserved. But as you know, Kali, it is love freely given in the face of hate, in the face of fear, in the face of rejection, that wounds more deeply, has more power, than any bullet, for it causes the heart to swell against its own limits, against the strictures pulled tight and then finally, finally, of its own accord burst and break open to love and forgiveness, remorse and the desire for justice.*

The women in the room began keening, a sharp cry of mourning. Wave upon wave of sound washed over the room building energy like a fever that needed to break. Aurelia lay on the couch engulfed in a love that dismembered her in its ferocity and cleansed her heart like a torrential river. The words of her soul's wisdom never failed to amaze her.

"Bless the Source," she whispered.

13

Mattie came back with a tray, "Here you go — Heartscape's finest. I even got you a bottle of Crone Nectar. Oh, and I told Harvey to join us. Once he's out of the SAC and done with the dream scan."

"There are men here?" I certainly hadn't seen any so far.

"There are the Tantra guys, young men that come to do internships in Tantric love making. They live pretty monastically though. You won't run into them on the grounds; their compound is kind of far from the main buildings. They cultivate the Cannabis crops as part of their service too. But Harvey is a special case; I guess you'd say. He was in a car full of hunters last year — his cousins and brothers were driving to go hunting — and they ran over Phoebe, that's my grandmother. I told you about her."

"What?" I was famished and probably eating a bit too fast, but I nearly choked on my lasagna. "He ran over your grandmother? Is he here on some kind of work release program?" I'd read about "creative sentencing." It used to be something a judge could mandate to teach a first-time offender a lesson, but for the past ten years it was also used as a half-assed cost-cutting way to get around overcrowded prisons.

"We had a work release guy at Wentworth and Wentsouth for a while." I wiped my mouth and tried to compose myself. "But he didn't work out. Mr. Wentworth sent him to bring up his Mercedes one afternoon and the guy never came back. They caught him in St. Louis."

"Eve, Harvey isn't here on work release. Momma didn't press any charges. Harvey asked to come and make some kind of restitution and Momma said yes. He lives here now and tends the orchards and does other stuff. He's just had a dream with collective imagery so Momma asked him to come work on it."

"Are you sure there isn't any meat in this?" I figured changing the subject wasn't a bad idea and frankly the food was amazing.

"Nope," Mattie grinned. She did that a lot. "Gina spent ages translating all the recipes she got from her grandmother, her aunts, and her mom into meatless versions. She's an amazing cook. Her vegan pizza is my favorite."

"The wine isn't bad either," I said though the label was a bit shocking, a naked goddess woman with wine streaming from between her legs into a cup held by a man. "I guess you aren't planning to distribute through Walmart, huh?" I passed the bottle to Mattie who poured a glass for herself and one for Harvey who was just coming through the door. He settled himself on the floor opposite the couch where Mattie and I lounged. Harvey extended his hand and I wiped off the garlic butter on my sweats. He had a firm, regular guy handshake. For some reason that surprised me.

"You must be Eve. So how'd it go?"

"Okay, I guess. That image thingy is pretty cool."

Harvey smiled. "Yeah, I've been working on a dream myself. This stuff is amazing."

"Eve is a key person for activating the Shift," Mattie told Harvey.

I paused with a piece of whole grain garlic bread in midair. "Mattie your language is making me very uncomfortable," I said evenly, calling on some past workshop in effective, nonviolent communication. "I'm not some frigging messiah widget you can just plug into your 'save the world' program."

"Everyone comes into the world to do something, play a part," Mattie countered earnestly. "You may be the one we've been waiting for. Aurelia said there would be someone who would provide the tipping point, like a transitional person. You may have a piece of information you don't even know is important, or a capacity to take a certain action. She didn't know exactly how or what that would look like; we all know it isn't some guru or prophet like the old stories."

I must have looked pretty skeptical. "It's not like we're gonna nail you to a cross or something. I'm sure she and the elders are in the studio right now painting to find out."

"Painting?" I almost laughed out loud. "They're painting to find out? Painting pictures?"

"Yes, it's the form of conversing with the Source that Aurelia was gifted with many years ago. Painting and witnessing the image has proven to be a pretty reliable means of accessing wisdom and guidance. And it doesn't wear you out, like the trances Edgar Cayce used to go into? That poor man was old before his time. Painting is actually rejuvenating, and anyone can do it. It's not like you have to be a trained artist or anything — in fact that can get in the way sometimes."

"You don't say?" This whole thing was sounding again like some really elaborate practical joke by Marty and the rest of my so-called friends. They all still remembered when I came back to college freshman year after winter break and changed my major from Art to Business.

"Okay, so when is Marty gonna pop out from behind a door and present me with a gift certificate for a class at the Art Institute so I can uncover my inner Van Gogh? Oh no, of course, it would be my inner Frieda Kahlo, wouldn't it? Nixing Art as my college major was one of the few things my parents ever agreed on," I confessed. "I bet they're kicking themselves around the block over on the 'other side,' huh? Maybe they're in some 'Divine Reeducation Program' up in heaven studying art appreciation right now." I was really losing my patience with this.

"The whole thing about the Crones," Harvey broke in, trying to ease the tension, "is that they really see you, I mean they see your soul."

Mattie nodded at Harvey. "Oh no, Eve," she continued, "I'm sure there was a reason in the Divine scheme why it turned out this way. You're so sensitive, if you made art, you'd be able to access so much pain that you'd probably wear out and be dead right now."

"I thought you said painting is so 'rejuvenating'? Huh? What about that?" I had her now, with her stupid New Age double talk, "everything unfolding according to a plan."

"Aurelia has painted this way since she was a teenager. It's a sacred calling. I don't appreciate you making fun of my mother." Suddenly Mattie looked like a little girl, ready to put up her dukes and pop me one.

The look in her eyes softened me. I felt like I was back on the playground at St. Bernadette's elementary school. "I'm sorry, Mattie, truly. This has been a really strange experience for me. Your mother makes me faint; you've had me strapped in a chair —reading my mind, 'realigning my story' — and now you're telling me I'm some kind of chosen one. Isn't this all a little too much?"

"Wow," Harvey said earnestly, obviously relieved, "I thought I might have to break up a fight here." Apparently Mattie had never used her 'mind jitsu' on him.

Mattie started to laugh. "Look, Eve, don't get so hung up on the words. That's what has caused humans so much suffering for so long, while we've waited for the Shift. Think of it this way: there's a long story unfolding, it can be dark and violent, or it can be fun and funky and full of color. What if you stepping up to your role in this moment is what tips the scales for fun? Wouldn't you go for that, be willing to do your part? Harvey was pretty clueless about all this, but now he's doing dream work and everything. We never know where we'll be called." She grinned at Harvey who blushed from head to toe.

I had to admit there was something irresistible about Mattie. As I looked at her, spiked hair, hands on hips, kind of like an overgrown eight year old, I suddenly remembered myself scrambling over rocks, playing pretend in the yard — and I smiled. "Yeah, whatever, okay," I surrendered. "Candace has finished her presentation by now, I bet Aversmith didn't even notice it wasn't me."

"That's it, Sister!" Mattie exclaimed and hugged me. "Cronation is about celebration. We don't have to be so serious all the time." Harvey grinned back at her like some dopey high schooler so I knew her charm had gotten to him too.

"It's been a long day, let's all go get some rest." Mattie pulled me up from the couch and I looked longingly at the empty lasagna plate. "Brunch is amazing too. You'll see tomorrow, food is always a celebration here."

Harvey and Mattie walked me back to the house with the wrap-around porch where we'd gone for the Crone version of Happy Hour. Mattie took me up to a lovely room on the top floor and hugged me. "I think you'll be comfortable here, Eve. Sweet dreams."

When I went to the window to pull the shade, I saw her and Harvey walking down the path together, arm in arm in the moonlight. Seeing them together, I realized I'd never asked for more details about this Tantra business, I had been so in love with the lasagna.

Before I'd bailed out of the art program in college, I'd had a brief encounter with one of my professors, Stan Stanoslav — a conceptual artist who claimed to be an expert in Tantric art. Stan was a free spirit. Department legend had it that every term he picked one lucky student and "initiated her," or him, into Tantric sexual practices. I recall him fixing his smoldering Russian eyes on me at the end of the semester. A small group of students from his class, "Morphological Considerations in Conceptual

Art," had been celebrating the end of the term with hot chocolate laced with Stan's peppermint schnapps in his office in the basement of the department. When the gathering began to break up, he'd said: "See you after the vacation, Ewa," grasping my hand. I had already transferred to the business major for next term, so I missed my chance.

I probably would have reported him for sexual harassment anyway. Still, seeing the spark between Mattie and Harvey, thinking of Stan, I felt an unfamiliar shiver of — pleasure, I guess, as I drifted off to sleep.

14

It was after brunch on Sunday morning when the Crones decided they were finally ready to address the women of Cronation again with the results of their time together visioning in the CIA process in the studio. The buzzing at Heartscape had been intense when none of the Council came to dinner the night before. The women all knew that the lights in the studio had burned late into the night, and that meant something big was going on. Each woman on her own, before settling herself down to sleep, had taken extra time to meditate, light candles and incense, and align herself for any instructive dreams that might come.

The Crones slept together in the studio, as Aurelia had done as a girl in Riva's barn, to allow the energy to fully permeate them and to remain in collaborative consciousness. Come morning, they stretched and yawned as they put away quilts and sleeping bags and gathered once more in a circle. The Crones were quiet, somber almost, as they looked to one another. The energy felt slowed in the way it does before a storm.

Aurelia was still feeling the effects of hearing her witness read aloud by the other women. She felt shaky and light, as if she'd become transparent or a weight she hadn't known she was carrying had been lifted.

"Remember, Aurelia, you have always asked to be used as an instrument of peace." Elsie embraced Aurelia and the other women crowded around them. "It was very powerful and so necessary for all of us to hear those words spoken. It was no failure that we didn't take up arms against the government in those dark days; it was the blessed hand of the Source on our shoulders, leading us through the Valley of the Shadow, through our grief to this day. Thank you, Sister, for bringing that message through for all of us."

"Yes, thank you, Sister," another woman echoed Elsie, "for holding that shadow for all of us. I feel the freedom of loosening bondage in all of us."

"Well, I have never felt such love, such a fine strong holding," Aurelia smiled. "Are we ready to share what we've learned with the others?"

The women closed their eyes and, sitting together in a circle holding hands, breathed in and out as colored strands of auric light wove themselves into the complex form of an octahedron. The form grew brighter as they relaxed and their breath aligned into a shared rhythm.

Aurelia reached for a small chime and struck it. "Let us follow the sound as it fades from our perception and know that when we reach the silence again, the truth of all our witness will be inscribed upon our hearts. Are we ready to serve the Divine Source?"

"Oh yes!" They all agreed, squeezing the hand they were holding and getting up to set out across the field for the dining hall.

As she entered the hall, Aurelia touched the mezuzah on the doorpost, a gift from Rabbi Leaf. She traced the ancient letter "shin" carved on the wooden rectangle that held the parchment reminding all that love is the greatest teaching: love one another; love the Source.

"Remind me, oh Source, that you guide me always," she whispered as she crossed the threshold. Aurelia took her seat with the other Crones in a semi-circle of chairs set up in the front of the room as Lorelei Winger stepped forward to begin. A hush fell over the women facing the Crone

Council of Elders. Some were excited to see Lorelei Winger, whispering among themselves about how much prettier she was in person than in the newspaper or on TV. Some strained forward to hear her words and others offered a silent prayer of gratitude for being present at this auspicious moment.

"Namaste, Sisters," Lorelei bowed slightly. "I am so glad to be here with all of you. As you know, the Crone Council of Elders met through the night, painting and witnessing to receive guidance from the Source. I beg your forgiveness for not joining you all for the evening meal last night. As you know, the Source is timeless and sometimes She takes us to that great space without time when we are in Her service. Thank you, Gina, and all of you who brought by food for us. Know that we enjoyed its sacred nourishment and were grateful for it. I have come here now because the Shift we are all working for has begun to manifest in the country of Pomerania."

At this there were murmurs of alarm and excitement among the women.

"Don't be alarmed, Sisters! We've learned that the Pomeranian women are in full alignment with the Shift. Their minister of Women's Affairs has issued a proclamation that the women of Pomerania are to go into the countryside to celebrate the Shift under the cover of a day remembrance for their Queen Elsa, which is their code word for the Source, blessed be She.

"However," Lorelei noted, "they have always been seen as the most neutral of countries, so any large movement is likely to be misinterpreted by other nations out of fear. Our concern is that many other countries may begin locking down their women, restricting travel and communications, if a distortion of their actions gets into the mainstream news. We believe that what this action on the part of the Pomeranians means is simply that the time is now for the next wave of change. As all of you who have ever given birth know, the contractions come, followed by a space for recovery

— which can be minutes or seconds. In terms of the Divine re-birth, that could be days or weeks.

"So the communications cadres must put out an alternative story that will undermine and help counter the fear-based narrative that will inevitably be shown on the nightly news." Those women whose task it was to blog, send press releases, and write for alternative publications nodded and looked up from taking notes. They would leave for the Cronation communication center after the meeting and begin to saturate the Internet and news sites with alternative stories about Pomerania and the Shift in general. Some would concentrate on alerting cells of women around the world, and others would focus on monitoring mainstream and alternative media sites.

Lorelei paused and looked out at the faces of the women before her. "We don't know how close the Divine Source is to birthing the age of the Crone, but we know it will be soon. As in any birth, all the preparations we have made leading up to the blessed event count for a lot. But not everything. The actual handling of the birth moments, the atmosphere of either fear or love — these determine a great deal about the future." She smiled at them with tears in her eyes as the steady pulse of loving energy emanated from the eyes and bodies of each woman present.

"I feel so blessed to be addressing you all, who have done so much to make the coming age one of peace and love. You have all labored to raise your own consciousness and that of all of us. You have worked to untie knots of regret and fear; you have reworked old hurts. You have built shrines of peace in your hearts. You have served in the most humble of ways, foregoing fame and fortune. Many of you have suffered in this incarnation on behalf of the collective human family. Thank you for your service.

"All over the world women are ready for this moment," Lorelei declared, "ready to embrace the chaos, ride the wave as it crests, and then stand in the full glory of their wisdom to lead the new era of compassionate generosity that you have learned to embody and so bring into being in the world."

The women cheered and stomped their feet and their walking sticks, clapped their hands and whistled and vocalized sounds of joy. They hugged one another and began the traditional Cronation snake dance around the room, chanting, singing, and laughing, the dogs joining in and howling along with the energy.

Lydia stood up and embraced Lorelei for a long time. Then she turned to the room of women, alive like one organism, moving to a larger rhythm. "Sisters," Lydia called, "let us return to our seats so that we can hear from our beloved Crone, our Sister Aurelia. She has much to tell us."

Now it was Aurelia's turn. The air was charged, the faces expectant. Memories flashed through Aurelia's mind as she waited for the women and hounds to settle down.

She opened her eyes when it was finally quiet and channeled a surge of loving energy so strong that the women in the first row felt like an oven door had just been opened in their faces, blasting them with the cinnamon scent of apple pie, fresh bread, and homemade cookies, all at once. They beamed back at her an equal amount of loving regard in the ancient call and response of pure, unadulterated joy.

"Sistahs! At long last we are coming close to the day of reckoning and freedom. We have watched and waited, worked and prayed, dreamt and painted as we made ourselves ready for this day. We have employed the minds and hearts of the most brilliant women of this era to devise the means to midwife the Great Shift's manifestation: We have studied science and found ways to mend broken, fear-filled minds. We have recovered methods from ancient texts that have taught us how to empty hate-filled hearts. We have channeled the sages of ages past to learn how to soothe the deranged spirits of the power mongers among us so that we do not repeat their errors and bring about change through war and mass destruction. We called forth the future and have created a parallel system of food production, housing and governance, so that as the old order falls — and you know it is has been failing and is now falling — we fall into the loving arms and capacious lap of the Goddess.

"The Great She, embodied in each and every one of you and countless others like you the world over, She will be there to catch us all in Her lap of endless loving grace through the ministries and good offices of Indra's safety net, womanned by the good Crones of Cronation the world over. In doing these things we have been preparing ourselves for what is a matter of natural unfolding of the Creative Source in response to our call: we beseech Her to renew Her bond of love with us and all creation as She wakes from her much needed rest to return Her energy to the next turn of the Great Spiral of Life. We can't wait to share with everyone what we have learned.

"And may She be pleased.... This is not a revolution of ideas...."

"No, it's not," they answered, clapping and whistling.

"And it is not a plan or a strategy, not a program, nor a panacea." Aurelia's voice surged like the tide of a mighty ocean.

"No, Sister, no panacea — you tell it — what is it now?" they chorused.

"It is not the brain child of any person, though many are they who have dedicated their fine minds to it," Aurelia continued, building up steam.

"Not a brain child. No, Mam!"

"Is not a patented invention nor is it copyrighted in any book that is for sale."

"No, Sister, no copyright, no patent pending!"

"This is not an unfolding of events brought to you by some corporate sponsor!" Aurelia thundered, "Although through our alignment with the Creative Source, the Holy and Profane One, Blessed and Debased One, He and She and It — blessed be — through All That Is, we have been graced with innovations that speed the plow and break the chains of all those enslaved by the meaningless make-work of the late capitalist era debacle."

"Tell it, Sister Aurelia, tell us right now!" The women were again standing and stomping their feet, howling as punctuation to Aurelia's preaching the word.

"This revolution I speak of is a natural unfolding, a birthright of all and everyone who lines themselves up — body, mind, heart and soul — and lets the Spirit move through her, untying the knots, clearing the path, commencing the waters of grace to flow to the river... the River of Life, our reconnection to the river of life. It is a mighty righting of many wrongs. It weaves the dark and the light, the high and the low. It is a birth in fact, a mighty birth and rebirth, and we are the midwives. Like Shifrah and Puah of biblical fame, we have been building, through our Crones in their beauty and wisdom, the strength of our nation, of our crone nation, of CRONATION!!!"

Even the hounds began to scratch and howl. By this time the women were all back on their feet, testifying to the message, whistling and cheering, hugging each other with tears of joy streaming down their faces.

"We have gathered so many."

"SO, so many!" came the response.

"We have called them from the factories, from the farms, from the streets, the universities, from the gutters and the boardrooms, the whore houses and the high-end retail emporiums, the shoe shops and couture salons, the flea markets and the church basement rummage sales across the land. From behind the mehitzas, out from underneath the burkas, out of sweatshops and dry cleaners and chauffeured limousines. From the highest heights and the lowest lows we have called all Her children who have ears to hear! Do you hear Her?"

"Hear, yes! We hear Her. We hear Her, Sister Aurelia!"

Aurelia lowered her voice to a deep intonation. "But we can't call them all. We have the legions of the willing who are ready to ride the wave as it crests and to care for those who get washed over by, swept away by that wave. You, assembled here, you are the riders of that next wave that clears the way for Her Great Awakening!"

The women spontaneously broke into a serpentine line dance, snaking around the room, while simultaneously moving up and down in a wave-form that used to be popular at concerts and sporting events — except these women were in a full trance, dancing, clapping, whistling, vocalizing in ecstasy. Many of these women, before they joined Cronation, could barely get out of a chair despite their mega-doses of glucosamine; now they dipped and danced with the grace and agility of women half their ages. Such was the power of awe and celebration that Aurelia called up in them.

After the women had celebrated for some time, Aurelia called them back. "Sistahs, I must tell you the most profound thing I learned today."

"Tell us, Aurelia!"

She turned and swept her hand across the group of Elders seated behind her. "I learned I had to purify my heart: there were dark places, unseen fears and pain in me leftover from another era. And I learned I could not do that alone. Now you might say, 'Well, of course, why is she telling us this? We know this simple truth!'

"But I saw how it was an act of my love that had harmed someone, one of our sisters who left us sometime back: Charity Greenberg, who now calls herself Kali after the great Hindu Goddess of Truth who cuts through all our illusions and self deceptions. An image of this young woman appeared in my painting. Charity, as Kali, challenged me to go even deeper into my soul and see what illusions I was clinging to. I saw that I had used my love on her like a hammer to a lock, trying to break through her closed heart when she was with us. Before you all, I ask her forgiveness, and yours.

"And, I ask you all to search yourself for where you may be holding onto false pride, where you may be harboring a grudge, where there is a lover or a parent or the Source Herself that you are withholding yourself from. And I ask you to forgive them — and yourself — and to let the truth in."

The room was silent. The women radiated love back to Aurelia as she had so often given love to them.

"If you find fears in your heart, tell them to one another," Aurelia said gently, "release them to the earth and see them for what they are: an old protection that you will no longer need. As the Shift happens, it is this forgiveness and vulnerability that must lead us to the next place where we can stand together. We must become as clear, as transparent as water. Thank you, Sisters, for being my witnesses."

A soft, slow chant began among the women and rose like the buzzing of a hive of bees. Many of the women came up to Aurelia and hugged her in thanks, and then settled down to see and hear the messages that the images and words the Crones had received in their session of painting and creating, the wisdom and guidance, revealed for the community.

15 ———————

Kali, the former Charity Greenberg, bit into a dried Calymyra fig, tearing a leathery chunk off and gesturing to the women facing her around the black granite topped conference table. "Have you ever noticed how much a dried fig resembles an old man's testicle?" Her dark eyes narrowed as she looked intently from face to face.

When none of the women answered, she snorted and went on. "Well, how do things stand? Are the assassins in place?"

"Actually, not all of them," Diane answered. "There's been trouble getting Esther into the White House. Seems Lorelei Winger left on some kind of trip unexpectedly. Esther was going in as her pedicurist, but the salon called and cancelled this morning."

Kali stood up and leaned forward, splaying her plum-polished fingers across the table.

"Some kind of trip? Diva?" Kali addressed a large raven that sat on a perch at the end of the table.

With a flap of its enormous wings, the raven transformed into a small, black-clad woman who slid into a chair opposite Kali at the end of the table. "She headed for Cronation Central, got there yesterday."

The other women at the table, all dressed in black, each held her breath waiting to see how Kali would react to the news.

"Oh really? And when were you going to share that juicy tidbit? After our whole operation goes in the tank?" A slow smile twitched on Kali's face. The rest of the women watched nervously as she got up and began to pace slowly around the room.

"This may not be such a bad thing. If Wright Winger is left alive, it will create even more chaos. Everyone will assume he had something to do with the assassinations. I'd like nothing more than to see those men running around pointing fingers at each other for a change.

"Diva, you stay," Kali commanded. "The rest of you get to Cronation and pick up the target — and do it as cleanly as possible. We want the maximum time to strike before Earth Mother Aurelia gets wind of anything and tries to stop us."

The other women filed out, each bowing to an enormous granite statue of a black raven, wings unfurled, sitting on a ledge near the door. The tiny rather sprightly looking young woman named Diva pulled her feet up into the chair and pushed away from the table, sending herself across the room.

"I can't believe you didn't tell me Lorelei Winger was at Cronation!" Kali whacked Diva's shaggy head. "Are you trying to wreck everything?"

"Just a minute. I have to crap," Diva interrupted. "Sitting on a perch and concentrating on controlling my bodily functions isn't a cakewalk, you know."

Kali sighed. "Hurry up. We have work to do."

By the time Diva returned, Kali was studying a map of the world that had red pushpins marking major cities across the earth.

"How'd you like to fly into the White House?"

"Ha, ha. I don't think a raven would make it through security and I doubt they leave too many windows open these days. Or did you mean fly into the White House? No way! I'm no suicide bird. I'm finally getting the hang of this shape-shifting business and it's way cool. Anyway, it's not like I could crash into a window and they'd nurse me back to health in the Lincoln bedroom. That crew isn't exactly known for their 'compassion for all beings.'" Diva said sarcastically, making air quotes around the phrase that referenced the Cronation movement.

"True. It's a shame that the Crones can't get over that irritating little blind spot. Compassion for bad beings is just stupidity. But once we clear the way, their do-gooder programs might actually have a chance. They should thank us."

Diva shook one foot, distracted. "I'm having some trouble getting the claws to retract completely when I shift form."

"That's because you're so hyped up on Red Bull that you can't concentrate."

Diva's bright black eyes and self-inflicted haircut echoed her raven shape-shift. She grinned at Kali. "Nah, my mother was a meth head when she was pregnant with me, she messed me up. The Red Bull just keeps me even. Of course it wouldn't hurt if we had some decent food around here. Speaking of mothers, won't yours try to stop us? She believes that every word that Rav Wendell dude ever said is true, no matter what we said. She'd be pretty pissed off to know you were behind getting him knocked off."

"Diva, first of all, Wendell — or Rav Babka as he now styles himself — is not the only target of our mission. Killing him is incidental. We are just as committed to freedom for all women, even for those freaks at the farm; we're just more realistic. There is no way a new era is being ushered in without some serious cosmic housekeeping. Babka may be as overblown and sickening as his pastry namesake, but his evil is stupid and pathetic, pumping up deluded women like my so-called mother with pseudo-spiritual psychobabble and getting them to sign over their stocks and bonds. Nothing L. Ron Hubbard and plenty of other smooth-talking sacks of shit hadn't perfected long before Rav Wendell set up his tent. Killing him is no more significant than stepping on a cockroach."

"Yeah, well, funny you should call him a cock-roach. They just shit everywhere. They don't screw children," Diva slyly replied.

This was a sore point between Diva — who'd been sexually molested by nearly every man her spaced-out mother ever got involved with — and Kali, who claimed she had no such experience, but had such an emotional and unshakable belief in the venality of all men that Diva felt it must have originated somewhere in a similar traumatic experience.

"Look, I told you, if you want to be the one to personally dispatch Babka to his just desserts — ha, ha — you are welcome to him! Every one of us has to directly kill at least one man in charge of something, as long as he meets the Nemesis criteria."

A large painting of Nemesis, the Goddess of Just Revenge, hung on the wall behind the conference table. After considerable research, Kali had named her operation for Nemesis, and was quite proud of the aesthetic and symbolic precision of her choice. Her plan was to simultaneously as-sassinate world leaders in both major and minor countries as well as heads of corporations, religious institutions, and universities. The criteria for the men named as targets: prolonged misuse of power as manifested through any one or combination of the seven deadly sins. Of course, they'd start with a small number of men known to the members of Nemesis. Once they got a buzz going in cyberspace, recruitment would skyrocket and she was bound to hear from women all over the world — that was the plan.

A list with photos of the world's worst dictators was taped to the wall. Kali spent hours online monitoring websites that ranked the men in power around the world. The pins in the map each stood for a target. She assigned the women she recruited to her project each a different category of heinousness to research — if possible connected the each woman's own trauma — and had them compile lists. Men who beat their wives, men who mistreated animals, men who embezzled pension funds, CEOs of corporations that made soda pop or cigarettes and sent the extras to third world countries, men who oversaw the clear cutting of forests, heads of fracking companies, politicians who'd taken bribes to gut environmental laws, religious leaders found to be abusing those in their care. The lists were endless, the categories always being revised, depending on which news channel Kali was watching or the day's headlines on her Internet feeds.

Men who committed crimes against children were the worst. Those men, Kali felt, should be killed up close, preferably by the victim of their evil — or if that was not possible, then by a woman of similar age and appearance to the victim. She felt the men needed to understand that revenge was being enacted, rather than some kind of random attack. In fact, for Kali, revenge killing was a form of performance art — and in her mind the theatrics were part of the thrill. She considered having the men sign a confession first, giving them time to become duly aware of what was about to take place, but she worried that the assassin might be overpowered: even stupid, bad, pathetic men were almost always physically stronger than their victims.

She was a connoisseur of such films as *I Spit on Your Grave* and *Kill Bill*. She also spent a lot of time watching the increasingly professional videos put out by terrorists and picking up tips. Kali felt akin to jihadists although she thought suicide missions were just plain stupid. Once the wrongs were righted by eliminating the men, the women avengers would be needed to run things, redistribute the wealth, take over the corporations, rewrite the scripts and begin to run the show.

Diva focused on blogs and Internet chat rooms where sexual abuse victims shared their experiences. Her task was to stir up energy toward violent retribution and recruit women who could be convinced to become willing assassins. Kali wrote a manifesto that was posted on the Nemesis website, titled "Dark Justice." It was full of fiery prose explaining why forgiveness was misguided and rehabilitation for men pointless. She wrote it in the voice of the Hindu Goddess: "Be my sword of justice; give these losers back to Me. I will smash them like clay pots that are misshapen and leaking. They will have another chance, in another life, but first their crimes must be stopped, their victims avenged. First they must feel the fire of My wrath." She told women they were liberators and some found it a heady message.

Women had been recruited and urged to take ordinary jobs with low-level access to the intended targets. Kali had learned quite a bit from Aurelia and the Cronation women — she just had a different emphasis: "Bad men must die." Not an especially poetic slogan but clear and to the point. The concept resonated with a lot of women, especially when couched in Goddess rhetoric that made it seem like it was like a second chance for men, a new lease on life through death. The women who had been badly hurt, raped by brothers, beaten by fathers, set on fire by husbands, denied tenure by college presidents, passed over by bosses — the list went on and on — had not found justice. Those like Kali, who had been misused and violated by religious leaders or others in positions of power felt especially righteous. There was no shortage of women inspired by Kali's message of empowerment, if emails to the Nemesis website was any gauge. Far fewer accepted the invitation to join the movement in person.

Kali claimed it was strictly ideological to her. Men like Rav Babka were essentially liars, spouting all sorts of "wisdom" but unable to act wisely or even decently in their daily lives. It was the cognitive dissonance that got to her the most; and violent means seemed a perfectly reasonable, even elegant, wake-up call.

Maybe it was having a plastic surgeon for a father. Reality can always be improved. Whatever offends, cut it off or straighten it out. Reality should conform to your will, to your vision. Where Aurelia, thanks to Phoebe's training and insights, had no illusions about men and didn't hold them to an elevated standard, Kali took a different approach: the more power a man has, the more responsible he is for whatever is fucked up. "They don't get it; they got to go."

Kali had no use for forgiveness. "I've seen too many men use forgiveness as foreplay and then keep playing the same games. The quickest way to reduce the rat population is shoot now, sweep up later." Or, as the Gulf War Vet she briefly took up with in high school — in a failed attempt to get her father's attention — described his mission: "I just kill 'em; let God sort 'em out." In this case, let Goddess …

Kali turned to Diva who was spinning herself around and around in the desk chair. "It's imperative that the crew comes back with this Eve woman without too much trouble. What did you see in your last fly over?"

"Well, they still have that sex colony on the south part of the property near the 'plant medicine' fields. All kinds of good looking young studs and older women getting it on in between playing pot farmers."

Diva's own sexual predilections tended toward the polymorphous perverse. She had no trouble with anything that got her hum button humming and, in her case, that included spinning in a desk chair with her heel firmly lodged against her crotch. She wasn't adverse to engaging with any animal, vegetable, or mineral, for that matter — as Kali discovered when the lingam stone from her altar to Kali went missing — as long as no male humans were involved.

Diva was especially adverse to sweaty older men whose pock-marked faces exuded the odor of stale cigarettes and cheap liquor, and whose hairy bellies spread out against her backside as they humped their way to the fifteen second heaven they thought was due them for "looking after" Diva — while her mother went to score drugs or was off crashing somewhere. There had been entirely too many of those men in her past, so many and from such an early age that they collaged themselves into one awful amalgamated monster molester, dried spittle at the corners of his mouth, stained wife beater, and tufts of wiry hair in his ears and nostrils.

It was through one of those nostrils, black hair resembling a thicket in the woods, that Diva escaped out of her body and into the imaginal realm one day when she was about ten. Nothing was ever the same again. She looked down from somewhere else on a small white girl under a man and realized it wasn't "her." How tiny that girl's wrists were! That girl, pressed against the faded green couch by the grunting man. Her eyes were black marbles dilated nearly completely, with just a faint line of gold iris surrounding. That girl didn't move or try to get away (how could she?) or make a sound. At the very moment the man grunted the loudest and then stopped, Diva had heard the cry of a raven outside and looked away from the girl on the couch. As she turned toward the sound, she felt a flash of pain.

Suddenly, she inhabited the raven's form. She felt the bird's soul wordlessly make way for her own and watched as the vinyl-sided house with the broken screen door became smaller and smaller. She was up above the houses, above the trees. She felt "herself" melting, spreading out inside the raven until her awareness was in the tips of the shiny black feathers and the sharp black beak. Her eyes adjusted to far sight and everything about the world of man shifted like the turn of a kaleidoscope, the center of the view was green and brown and gray. It felt like the time someone had slipped her part of a tab of acid at one of her mother's parties: she didn't feel afraid then, just relief as the kaleidoscope chopped up the man whose hand had reached down her pants after getting her to drink the cherry soda with the acid mixed in. He just got dismembered and rearranged into patches of color, his voice remixed into sounds without meaning, collaged into the music that was playing and the general noise in the room. Eventually she passed out and had no idea how many hands had touched her. When she woke up, everyone was gone, and she had wandered into the filthy kitchen to search for food.

Kali was the one who explained about shape shifting. Ever since they met at the Farm, Diva had been learning and practicing consciously shifting into the raven. Kali was the first person she'd ever told about it and she didn't think Diva was weird or crazy but incredibly gifted. And Kali had cried and cried when Diva told the story about how the raven took her into the sky and left that other little girl with the smelly man; it was the first and only time she'd ever seen Kali cry.

Diva tuned back in to Kali's voice. "'Tantra for Justice' is just an excuse to screw and chalk it up to a 'good cause.' What do they do to those men? Make them wear blindfolds? It's sick. The women are old enough to be their mothers, grandmothers even. I guess if they smoke enough weed… And really, Diva, is that the best use of your time? Watching middle-aged women practicing the *Joy of Sex*?" Kali shuddered.

"As for my mother, she is no danger to our plan. She continues to inhabit a realm of hell that Dante never imagined: one where women sit in salon chairs while highlights are eternally bleached into their hair, flipping through all the magazines looking for the next guru. The radio is just slightly off the station, and the stylist assures her she looks thirty. When she realizes how empty she feels, she just goes back for another one of Rav Babka's seminars. Anyway, if she had the attention span to read the manifesto she'd probably go for it just to get back at Dad — as long as she didn't have to mess up her manicure."

"Well anyway," Diva was spinning herself around and around in the chair with her eyes closed, "Aurelia was hanging out with that cute guy who ran over her mother. Talking, but no sex."

"You know, Diva, I'm not so sure the raven is such a brilliant shape shift for you. You never hear what anyone says and all you pay attention to is sex."

"And garbage," Diva said brightly coming to a stop. "Wow! That's a great head rush. Seriously, the compost pile behind their dining hall is like an awesome vegetarian buffet when I'm raven. I miss it."

"Yeah, well, you better find some rodents and road kill to chow down on next time, before you throw off your whole metabolism and your feathers turn white."

"Ha, ha. I'll become a dove and come back here with an olive branch in my teeth — that would really piss you off, wouldn't it?"

Kali punched Diva in the arm and in the blink of an eye she turned back into a raven and flew out the window.

"How am I supposed to overthrow the patriarchy with this kind of shit?" Kali fumed, "I need discipline and order."

Kali and Diva had discovered each other at a mother-daughter retreat they were both dragged to at Heartscape Farm. Miriam, Kali's mother, was recovering from a divorce from Kali's father, a celebrity plastic surgeon who had run off with one of his most successful boob jobs, a starlet just a few years older than Kali. But as a third generation Southern California fashionista, Miriam couldn't really get with the organic garden set at the Farm. When Kali, then Charity, showed an interest in the world of braless hairy armpits and social change, Miriam couldn't take it. She had already put Charity into and pulled her out of an art school for the gifted, a boarding school ranch where each student had her own horse, and a progressive Jewish day school. Every time Miriam found a new panacea, Charity paid the price.

Miriam's latest step on the road to nirvana and personal growth was Rav Wendell, a new age rabbi from Boca Raton who she heard about from another mom whose kid was in Charity's Bat Mitzvah class. While in Boca, she also learned about Heartscape — and when Charity split the yeshiva and threatened to kill herself if Miriam put her in one more place, it just so happened there was a mother-daughter retreat scheduled. A stint in the Midwest together, Miriam thought, might even things out.

Kali latched onto Diva when she realized they were the two youngest guests at Heartscape and easily had the two most dysfunctional moms. Diva's mom, who had kicked her drug habit but never brushed up on those parenting skills, left halfway through the retreat with one of the Tantra boys and never looked back.

Diva was used to being left places and wasn't alarmed. She was happy wherever she was fed, and it was a relief to be around only women, especially ones who were kind and motherly and uninterested in penetrating her bodily orifices. Kali noticed Diva's propensity to just space out in the workshops; she seemed to just leave her body.

Many of the women of Cronation experienced the kind of dissociation that Diva did but none had coped in such a creative way. Kali knew about shape shifting in theory but was too intellectual to master it herself. She found Diva rolling a joint behind the barn after a yoga session and took it upon herself to befriend and look out for the younger girl. After hearing her story, Kali convinced her to keep quiet about the raven, fearing the Crones would use the Story Alignment Chair to rob Diva of her gift.

When the retreat ended, Kali begged to stay at Heartscape, partly to keep an eye on Diva, who had more or less been adopted by the kitchen crew. Miriam was relieved to sign her daughter up for an internship of indeterminate length. The two girls studied texts on shape shifting in their spare time in the Cronation library.

After one of the Crone seminars Diva told Kali, "So I really should thank those assholes, huh? Aurelia is always talking about forgiveness. If it wasn't for them, I'd never have learned any of this shaman shit, right?"

Kali went nuts. "No, Diva! Thank the raven — but those filthy, disgusting scumbags were wronger than wrong. You did something amazing, like you transformed shit into gold — but don't you dare give those assholes any credit. They're evil and everyone of them deserves to die for what they did to you."

For days Kali fumed and paced around the Farm. There could be no redemption, she decided, for these men who had so violated Diva. She even tried to talk to Aurelia about it. "Some things are just wrong, right?" she'd said in a group session on forgiveness.

"Lots of things are wrong, every woman has been wronged, but it's what she does with it. How does she take that wrong and fashion it into a tool of truth that cuts through illusions so others need not suffer the way she did." Aurelia had made an offhand reference to the Hindu deity, Kali, and that stuck in Charity Greenberg's angry and fertile mind. She spent that evening in the Heartscape library reading about the warrior goddess, all red and black with her necklace of skulls, her sword of truth and her scythe to harvest what had reached the end of its usefulness. The image of fierce Kali, standing triumphant on prone Shiva with his tongue lolling out of the side of his mouth in ecstasy, captivated Charity.

She came back the next day to the forgiveness seminar on fire. "So let's bring some justice down on these men out there who've fucked everything up. We can't sit around here while all this shit keeps happening. You said it yourself: stop it before it happens again. Kali's sword."

The women who'd been at the Farm longer looked to Aurelia, waiting for her reply. Many of them came to the Farm in a state of anger; many had been abused like Diva; most were quite a bit older, used to not acting out, but instead to keeping their pain inside or turning it on themselves. Usually Aurelia was dealing with women who were out of touch with their own traumas and who needed encouragement to get in touch with their rage.

"Kali's sword is symbolic, Charity. It's about speaking the truth —the hard truth — about the world and about ourselves. Standing up to those who speak falsehood. It's a metaphor, not a call to violence."

"Why talk to them at all? They'll get another chance to try again in the next life…" Charity looked at Aurelia whose lips were drawn in a hard line. "Of course it's a call to violence! You know what, Aurelia? I think you're full of shit."

With that, Charity Greenberg stormed out of the forgiveness seminar. "So Aurelia turns out to be one more bullshitter," she fumed. "One more adult who talks one thing and does another. I was almost taken in, almost conned."

The truth was, Charity loved Aurelia. She had never seen truth and love embodied before. Like many of the women who came to Cronation, being in Aurelia's presence was both like a balm and a bomb at first. An unfortunate side effect of Charity's comparison of Aurelia to her own mother was that it focused and sharpened her rage — toward Miriam, her father, all the schools and teachers and heads of programs, and every inept adult she had ever had the misfortune to be in contact with, ending with Rav Babka and Miriam's clear preference for him and his abstractions of enlightenment over actually engaging with her own difficult daughter. Diva's story had tipped the scales for Charity. She couldn't bear the thought that this kid, who could've been her kid sister, had suffered so at the hands of men. Charity Greenberg had grown up in a privileged life. Of course she knew girls who'd been hurt, but not like Diva. And the love and other nonsense these women were spouting was too vague, too abstract, mostly just too much. She wasn't going to sit in that Story Alignment Chair and cry and wring her hands. She was going to do something.

"So the Goddess Kali is symbolic? Hell no!" Charity had a car, a credit card, and a mother who paid the bills without reading the fine print too closely. A mission was beginning to form in her head, and a new name: Kali, avenger of women. "I'm going to make her real. Diva gets into a raven? I'm getting into an ass-kicking, head-lopping, teeth-gnashing, sword-wielding Goddess of Truth!"

She found Diva trolling through the compost heap as raven. "Come on, we're blowing this pop stand!" She tossed the book with a version of the Goddess Kali on the cover she had filched from the Cronation library toward the bird who caught it in her beak. "What?!" Diva morphed back into her girl's body. "We're going to blow up the Farm?" Diva held the book away from her and took in the cover. "Oh boy!" She rolled her eyes. "You get into another fight with Aurelia?"

"Shut up. We're leaving, get in the car." They stopped at the gate of Heartscape and with the motor running, Kali tucked a cryptic note, addressed to Aurelia, into the gate: "The revolution is not an apple that falls when it is ripe. You must make it fall." Signed "Kali, (formerly Charity Greenberg)."

They drove off sending up a cloud of dust on the unpaved road that led out from Heartscape Farm to the highway. A plan to make the apple fall was already forming in "Kali's" head.

It had taken her a few years, but she had absorbed enough of the Cronation mission and methods to inspire her own streamlined and, in her eyes, more just and efficient movement. Now here she was, finally, on the verge of nudging the chaos into high gear in a twisted sort of valentine to Aurelia as much as a hate bomb to everyone who had ever caused her, or any woman, pain.

16 ———————

I was beginning to settle into the routine at Heartscape, no doubt a form of Stockholm syndrome. Once I'd seen and spent some time with Rae and my other friends, it was hard not to feel at home. Each day I spent with this community of women my life at Wentworth and Wentsouth seemed more remote. I got up every morning and went to meditation and yoga, often led by a woman in her seventies, like Audrey, who was as lithe as a teenager and kind to me and my stiff joints; her hand on my back could melt my muscles like butter and she had such kind eyes I could barely look at her without starting to blubber. I had breakfast with apples from trees that Harvey tended in the Heartscape orchards and no coffee, a first for me since high school. After breakfast there were study sessions, chores in the garden cultivating plants for food and for medicine. A light lunch was followed by singing. Afternoons were spent in different ways, depending on the needs and desires of the women. Working, learning, creating, and healing formed a healthy balanced life vastly different than any I had ever known.

In the large dining hall, as in most of the buildings at Heartscape, images of amazing women adorned the walls. Some were portraits in oil like the one of Septima Poinsette Clark, based on the famous photo of her regal profile that appeared on so many Black History Month calendars. I'd looked at that photograph many times before but always assumed that her beautiful face belonged to a dancer or an actress. I guess I'd never really seen it at all. I learned at the Farm that Septima Clark was considered the grandmother of the American Civil Rights Movement, working for many years for school equality long before what the history books report. She'd been a mentor to Rosa Parks, the one black woman I had ever heard of, and I still thought she just refused to get up that day on the bus in Montgomery because she was tired. These women had worked so methodically, so carefully, and with such dignity. Why hadn't I ever heard about them? Mrs. Clark taught at the Highlander Folk School in Tennessee and established the Citizenship Schools where poor people learned to read and write and master an understanding of the Constitution so they could pass the literacy tests that were in place to prevent them from claiming their right to vote.

Mattie said it was sad how little of the real history most people knew, especially about women. "We women have a legacy of revolution and reform that starts with Lilith and continues all the way to today, but all anybody wants to read about is celebrities."

I felt a little pathetic myself, thinking about my future plans for uplifting the downtrodden at the West Coast office of Wentworth and Wentsouth. When I read the quote under Septima Clark's portrait, I understood why she was practically a patron saint of the Farm. The plaque read: "I have a great belief in the fact that whenever there is chaos, it creates wonderful thinking. I consider chaos a gift. God created the whole world out of it." These women seemed to be comfortable with all sorts of chaos, while seeing the underlying order as well.

Mattie said Septima Clark was born too soon. "Chaos is just about the world's middle name right now. Can you imagine having a woman around who could say what she said and still look so dignified that she could get the biggest oaf to doff his cap, just by looking him in the eye?"

For my part, I spent a few hours each day in the SAC with either Mattie or Harvey monitoring the experience of my own brand of chaos. I had, for quite some time, apparently, been taking in every type of awful event the world offered up into what Mattie called my "etheric body." "It's like someone just pushed the record button when you were born but turned off the speakers," Mattie explained: "And the Source makes no mistakes. So this is important, we just don't know yet exactly why."

Could be seen as your basic cult indoctrination, I supposed. But, I had to admit, each time I finished a session in that chair I felt lighter somehow, stronger, although I had little memory of whatever they were roto-routing out of my brain. No, not my brain: my "cerebral-spinal fluid and cellular memory," as Mattie said.

I attended some Heartscape seminars and noticed that a lot of the information felt familiar, stuff I'd absorbed from Mom or the books and magazines she left in the bathroom when I was growing up. The plant medicine teas served in the afternoon probably helped open me up too. And the CBD hemp oil lotion in the massages, and the late afternoon tea served with Farm-grown apricots dipped in medicinally infused chocolate... I even heard something about the enclave on the west side of the Farm where young men were recruited for some kind of Tantric training that involved rites of passage for those women dealing with menopause. Rumor had it that the whole shebang at the Farm was financed by the proceeds of a proprietary formula Aurelia had developed that went well beyond "PinkViagra" for women, plant based, of course, that helped them transform their libido and activate it not only in body, but the mind, spirit, and soul.

The Crones were all about undermining the idea of "no pain, no gain" and replacing it with gentle relaxation into the holy arms of Creation where each woman could access her power, realize her gifts, and celebrate them

204   PAT B. ALLEN

freely. More radical than any violent revolutionaries, they had learned from watching the natural world, in the words of Joseph Campbell, "Revolution isn't smashing something; it is bringing something forth." A feminine metaphor if ever there was one.

I was feeling pretty mellow as I settled myself into a chair in the cozy seminar room alongside a couch where several other women sat, eyeing me nervously, with slight smiles and little waves. Maybe they had heard I'm the "One."

Mattie bounded into the room like a gazelle and just as quickly sat and settled herself into absolute stillness, bowing her head. Then she looked up, smiled, and began: "Okay, today we'll resume our discussion of the Holonic Shift in Consciousness. Humans are the aspect of the planet that brings self-reflective consciousness to the table," she announced.

"Self-involved navel-gazers," I muttered, apparently louder than I thought. Mattie looked at me quizzically. "That's what O'Malley used to call the worst of Mom's crew," I offered. I felt the couch dwellers move slightly away from me.

"Well, yes, sometimes consciousness raising got misused in narcissistic self involvement, navel gazing, if you like," Mattie admitted, "but every tool can be misused. We might not be able to personally gobble down and recycle PCBs like certain saprophytic mushrooms can — thereby reclaiming industrially polluted soil for future growing — but humans did figure out that Phanerochaete chrysosporium is the fungi for the future and then planted them in the right places. The shift to 'holonic' or 'whole' consciousness shows us not only the problem but also the solution. As long as we clear our auras and align ourselves to receive new information clearly, and cultivate right relationships with all our fellow beings — plants in particular — we can do our jobs as receivers and co-create a world in dynamic balance."

The other women were studiously taking notes in a variety of notebooks with collaged covers.

"Of course, recognizing that humans created the poisonous pollutants in the first place put lots of people on a long guilt trip that had just about killed the whole planet through the time wasted in handwringing and assigning blame. I'm fairly certain even Septima Clark might have been tempted to slap a few folks if she'd been around in the latter part of this century." Mattie had inherited a lot of Aurelia's flair for presenting ideas in lively ways.

"I heard," offered a blonde woman who sat across from me, "that there was a voluntary euthanasia movement whose members believed that if enough humans said mea culpa sincerely and then jumped on a pyre built inside a Hummer filled with flaming junk mail and empty Starbucks cups, Gaia might forgive us."

"One of my dad's sisters was involved in that mea culpa thing," I added, trying to be a good sport and a team player, or whatever the Crone equivalent of that was. "It appealed to a lot of really guilty Catholics for a while there. She didn't get into the immolation part. Mostly they just picked up trash and handed out coupons for aluminum travel mugs."

Mattie smiled, "There are those who say: 'what the hell? Might as well go down swilling java.' And, of course, there are those who think they have the answer and just needed you to sign up, as if the Goddess Herself would be impressed by a huge email list or hundreds of 'followers' on Twitter. But then as holonic awareness began to dawn and people woke up to the fact that the Earth is a sentient being, folks started to relate to Her with whatever relational skills they had, at whatever level of clarity, or lack thereof, they had achieved — so, guilty obsequiousness, outright terror, bargaining, efforts to control all came into play. Some, a few, were able to just listen patiently and learn that the Great She speaks in images, sensations, and signs."

I was beginning to feel distracted. I guess my "alpha male brainwaves" hadn't been reset completely yet. I cut in, apropos of nothing, and asked Mattie, "So how do most of the women get here? Surely not all of them are kidnapped the way I was?" That raised a few eyebrows.

"No, Eve," Mattie said patiently. "Word of mouth mostly. You know how women love to tell each other things, share resources. One hears about the Farm from a friend while she's getting her nails done — she tells her sister and so forth. You hardworking successful business types don't tend to pay as much attention to such things. Probably on the phone during your whole mani-pedi. And honestly, the culturally identified types like you haven't really been our focus up 'til now."

The other women looked at me sympathetically. "We're just glad you're here now, Eve. Isn't it great?" Blondie enthused.

"So," Mattie continued her talk, "there are infinite parallel truths. Reality is multiple, simultaneous, and not time bound..." At that point, I guess my latent guy consciousness took over completely and I'd started wondering what might be for lunch.

I gazed out the window. I had noticed lately that just spending time outside, walking in the woods and feeling the stillness of winter, was changing me. The bare limbs of the trees shaking slightly and the light on the pale landscape were beginning to speak to me. I was starting to see the trees as beings: there was an oak scarred by lightening, an elm that had been felled to a stump and now sent off hundreds of new shoots. It seemed spooky at first to think of trees as having personalities, histories that they might share with me. Trees were living, well, I guess "beings" is really the word, that I usually walked right by without even giving them a thought while I toiled full steam ahead in the business world. Of course, it's a lot easier to ignore the natural world in downtown Chicago where the only canyons are made up of glinting high-rises and trees are merely decorations placed in planters running down the center of the street, replaced when they begin to wilt. And it's not like I didn't walk right past plenty of human beings too, day in and day out.

Once, coming into the office early on a Saturday to go over some files, I saw workmen replacing the sizeable trees in some of the huge pots in the median. I asked why.

"Oh, yeah, with the car fumes, they only last a few months," the guy told me, "Then the trees go back to the nursery, like for rehab — you know, the way they rotate plants in them offices." He jerked his thumb toward Michigan Ave.

At the time I thought, "Gee, that's great. The trees get to go to a spa." Now that idea seemed insane. I'd always wanted to save the world, but had I ever really seen the world?

Heartscape itself was a parallel universe. Some of the women used it like the tree nursery: they went off into the world, did the best they could to "be the change they want to see," then when they ran really low on the love and compassion vibe, they came to the Farm to get recharged. Gina, Rae, and Marty had been doing this for years. Gina claims they invited me several times to join them, but I was always too busy with work.

But no doubt about it, lots of women were banding together now, all over the world — and these Crones? My own mom could have been one of them. She and Aurelia would have gotten on like family. But I guess that was the main point everyone at Heartscape was trying to make: family, familiar, we are all in this life together, that simple truth. Could it get any simpler?

I remembered a vision I'd had in church when one of O'Malley's sisters, my aunt Maureen, smuggled me off to Mass one Sunday morning. I was sitting, bored, listening to the priest babble on in the newly reinstated Latin Mass, when I saw a huge woman appear behind the altar; she was about twenty feet tall with a dark complexion. She had a man by the ear, a priest I think. He had a black cassock on, and she was dragging him off the altar for a time out. Or at least that's what it looked like to me. I was about six years old.

The vision came back to me after a SAC session where I saw my cousin Albert being led off into the sacristy by a priest. Aunt Maureen told me years later how bad she felt that she never took my vision as a clue about the priest scandals. Albert had socked the guy in the nose and quit being an altar boy, but plenty of other boys suffered terribly. "But you were a little Jewish girl, God forgive me. Who thought you could know such a thing?" Aunt Maureen had shared after a few drinks at O'Malley's wake.

Too bad, too, that my mother never let me stay overnight with my cousins ever again after she heard that Maureen had taken me to church. "What was I gonna do, Miriam, get a baby sitter on a Sunday morning, for Jesus' sake?" Aunt Maureen complained, "A little church won't hurt her." But Mom was firm.

I was startled out of my reverie by Mattie saying, "Alright then, see you all after lunch. Namaste, Sisters — Eve, can you stay around? Aurelia is speaking again at lunch."

In spite of all the detox work which, Mattie told me, was moving along at a record pace, I still couldn't sit any closer than the tenth row in any communal gathering where Aurelia was speaking. Her presence opened something in me that caused tears to flow in torrents, if I didn't just pass out in agony first.

"Aurelia taps into pure love," Mattie explained, "100% real. She sees you, sees each one of us. It's like she can see every level of you all at the same time. She sees your face, that little scar over your left eyebrow. She can tell you got that at camp when you fell out of a rowboat and almost drowned; she knows the other kids laughed at you but you were scared to death and cried yourself to sleep every night till camp was over. She sees all those memories that come up when you are in the chair, and all those walls your being has constructed to keep the pain out begin to fall away..."

"Guess you didn't get away with much as a teenager."

"Here's the amazing part," Mattie laughed, "I guess I just take it for granted mostly, I tested all this out, of course, like any child would. I stole something once, and I went in to see Momma, just to see what would happen. Would she get mad or what? I figured she would just know. I wanted to see if she got mad at me."

"So, what happened?"

"She looked at me and her eyes seemed flat," Mattie shuddered, "almost like coins were covering her eyeballs. It was as if I was seeing her from very far away. I felt so cold."

"So she gave you the silent treatment and you felt guilty. What's the big deal? My mother was great at that."

"No, that's not it," Mattie leaned forward. "Everything else about her was the same — hugs and kisses, her words. She asked me if I was feeling okay because I was being so quiet. I realized that I had shut down the flow between us, not her. It was funny. I was glad to know that I could do it, you know? Like, she's not all-powerful or something. But it feels so bad.

"Everybody needs that flow and that flow, Eve, well, that's just love. The thing about Momma and all the Crones is that they have practiced so long to always ask 'What is the loving thing here?' that they just do it, they just love. They are love, that's all.

"She didn't need to confront me about stealing, or lecture me," Mattie spoke quietly. "Feeling that force of love hit my closed self, I never felt anything so painful in all my life. Thinking that this is how most folks live their whole lives! Love feels like pain! It was like being locked away in an empty, soundless room, being smothered and beaten with nettles all at the same time. Momma saw I was shut down and she just kept sending love.

"They love us all, every one of us, and once you really feel that, well, you just want to pass that on and watch it grow and see what happens. It is like sunlight and rain on a dried-out plant. Love makes everything blossom and grow into its most true self. The thing is, many folks build up their walls from such an early age; they think it's natural to feel nothing. But everyone, Eve, feels love as pain when it comes knocking on a heart that's hidden behind a closed door."

I quickly wiped my eyes on my sleeve pretending to brush away a fly. Mattie looked at me expectantly. "Well, I've been loved in my life — by plenty of people. So why do I feel sick and pass out if I get too close to Aurelia, huh? Guess I'm just defective."

"No, girl," Mattie was looking straight into my eyes, and I couldn't keep them dry now, in spite of myself. "You just have stuck places, and when love comes in strong, it starts to shake them up. That hurts. But, isn't it something? Love breaks up all that stuck stuff, takes down walls. And, yes, it's our heartfelt tears that wash it all away."

"And you know what, Eve?" She ruffled my hair like I was a dumb but lovable sheepdog. Let me tell you a secret: Everyone who's been hurt, neglected, or unseen is waiting for someone to knock on her heart's door. Some, you can feel them, crouching behind the door, door's not even locked; they're holding onto the doorknob with all their might while praying that someone will bust their way in. Everyone wants that door to open. We all so need to be seen, and welcomed, loved and valued.

"The big lie that Cronation aims to overcome and set to rights is in all the ways the world makes it seem you have to pay for love, whether it's your performance review at work, wearing your hair some particular way for a lover, buying stuff that's supposed to make you happy. When you know that the love from the Source is there, unconditionally from the start, then you can see clearly and act joyfully. The line between work and play is erased. Everything becomes call and response. The Source loves every last one of us, and the way we know that is to have an open heart. Let the love flow in and wash away our disappointments and hurts. Once that happens to us, it's so much easier to admit our mistakes. Also to see what needs doing and to do it, in joyful service."

For once, I had no witty reply: I'm clutching Mattie and sobbing into her lap. For some reason an image of Candace shaking my hand outside Wentsouth's office comes into my mind.

"That's right, Eve. Forgive her. She doesn't have a clue and she never meant to hurt you. She's doing her part too. You'll see."

Through my sniffling, I snorted, "Damn, Mattie, quit reading my mind."

She just laughed and hugged me tighter. "This is a big day, Eve. You just got your ticket punched on the forgiveness train. Momma says that forgiveness is the greatest stumbling block for all humankind. But to really forgive and be forgiven means seeing all the fault. Understanding and accepting that we are all part of any painful reality and admitting our part, as well as seeing the faults of another, that's what turns love back on. Atonement, think of it as at-one-ment, its like attunement. Coming into that vibration, the direct flow of love, no strings attached, is the natural state of all being. Every time we feel hurt, we have a choice to deal with it and forgive — or put another brick in the wall.

"Everybody likes to think pain is caused by the other guy: 'He did this to me, so now I have to do this to him to fix things.' It sounds crazy, I know, but every act of revenge is a ham-handed way of trying to balance things and turn the love back on. It's just most people never get good instruction in the basic operating principles of being a human being. It can be so much easier than we make it."

Mattie's velvet voice just continued on. Suddenly entirely spent, I stretched out on one of the couches. I must have drifted off to sleep because I woke up covered in a hand crocheted afghan and saturated with an unfamiliar sense of peace. Which probably accounts for what happened next.

I heard the doorknob rattle. Harvey often came to get me after a seminar and walk me over to meals while Mattie made whatever reports of my sessions in the SAC were needed. I did notice I was never left alone for very long at that point and figured they thought I might still try to take off if I had the chance. Harvey always knocked and asked if I was ready to go.

I stretched from my fingertips to my toes and was feeling so warm and good I called out: "It's okay, Harvey, I was napping. Come on in."

Lately I'd noticed that Harvey was a very good-looking man and so sweet with Mattie. He seemed so at home at Heartscape, I wanted to get his take on all this. He seemed sane — although I'm not sure I could have reliably defined that term anymore. To be honest, the presence of an actual, living, breathing man was one of the things that helped me not go running for the highway.

I probably owe that to O'Malley, he was such a good guy, good and hard working and honest. I tended to extend the benefit of the doubt to men in general. I also guess I took in his judgment that Mom and her crowd were a bit daffy. I have to admit that deep down, I still believed in the Men in Charge. Not some particular man or men, just the concept.

I guess I still felt underneath that women don't really have what it takes to run the world. I mean really, do you think women would have built the interstate highway system? Thought up commercial aviation? The internal combustion engine?

When I had asked Mattie about all this she laughed and said these were all "dense matter solutions for a material era." No fault of men, she said. "Obviously those are all creative solutions appropriate to the aggregate level of consciousness of the age; and we needed to appreciate and give thanks for them, but not cling to them, like they are the be-all and end-all, as we have clearly done." Did I notice, she asked, that the things I mentioned were all forms of connecting human beings with one another? Now, she proclaimed, we are moving into another type of age, one where we will see energetic travel, communication and transport of goods and services, feminine and energetic solutions for an era of higher vibration. A kinder, gentler, lighter, and brighter sort of industrial revolution.

When Harvey didn't come in, I started to doze off again and found myself replaying conversations with Mattie in my head. "But we'll never get there," she said, as if it was plain as day, "if we keep thinking cars are the coolest way to get from one place to another." "One day, Eve, we'll look back and see how quaint and clunky even an electric car is. When we master shape-shifting, inter-neural message transmissions, and personal teleportation, you will laugh at your little dream of a hybrid sports car."

I'd seen plenty of science fiction movies myself, but Mattie said it's the "man-as-inventor" paradigm that has to loosen up. In the patriarchal paradigm, Man stands at the center of all things — which reminds me of Leonardo da Vinci's famous sketch of man as the measure of all things. I had that image on a poster in my office at Wentsouth.

"Leonardo discovered that the proportions of man were echoed in every part of nature," Mattie said when I told her, "But the Church took it over and made dogma out of it to support their authority, as if all of nature flowed from man. Instead of honoring the beautiful gifts that echo throughout the world, the Church fathers were fearful; they just wanted everything to come through them. They taught an ethos of control centered in men. Man thinks he caused all this. He thinks 'Whoa, this nature stuff is cool. What can I do with it?' Then he plays around for ages, drilling oil out of the earth to run his toys and then, 'Shit! I'm running out of this stuff. Where can I get some more?' Then he figures, 'Hey, that guy has some. How can I get it?' Finally, he says, 'I really fucked this up; the planet is doomed! He, Man, is still at the center of everything — the self-center."

This was the gist of what I got from Mattie's many enthusiastic lectures about the history of the human race and the various Cronation seminars I attended.

"Actually," Mattie had said, "the Source is shaking Her head. She could shrug us all off the planet at a moment's notice but She keeps on letting us figure it out. Now that we've begun to discover our limitations, we're at a very exciting place." She had picked up a book and read to me: "When we share our limitations with the limitations of others we complement our own and others' shortcomings, creating and recreating the golden mean thereby living in harmony, in the art of life. We can do this because nature's own golden proportions of reciprocal sharing are built into our own natures: into our bodies and minds," which are, of course, part of nature.

"That's what Leonardo saw, it just got misinterpreted. The basic pattern — forming processes of nature which have shaped the human heart and mind can continue to guide whatever the hand and mind are shaping when the hand and mind are true to nature."

"Up until now, humans have seen limitations as something shameful, something either to be overcome, hidden, or denied. Fact is, we can understand the golden mean, which is the natural unfolding of patterns in nature as the pathway of proportions, as shared limitations. We are on the verge of a new understanding of limits and how totally cool and necessary they are."

Mattie could get pretty worked up about this stuff, and I followed along as best I could.

The next era, Mattie proclaimed, would also usher in an unprecedented development of the intuitive function. I had issues with all this.

"So everyone will able to read minds like you?" I asked, exasperated. "I'm not sure that's so great."

"No," Mattie had replied, "Not 'read minds' but intuit: in - to - it, to see and feel your way into reality, past the first layer of appearances to the heart layer. Just imagine, Eve, if each one of us could see past the outside and into the heart, hear the truth behind what's being said and respond to that! Can you imagine? It's really possible. This will completely transform the feedback loop and boost us up as a species and get us running on the next highest developmental level."

Maybe Harvey and I could have a chat about this over a bowl of tabbouleh. My stomach was growling.

Just then the door began to open slowly. I instinctively ran my fingers through my hair. I wasn't sure if Harvey had advanced to the point of not being concerned about a woman's appearance and could look past the gray roots that were beginning to grow out in my sadly neglected mop of hair to see my inner beauty.

I looked up surprised to see two skinny women and one shorter, plumper one, all dressed in black leather, staring down at me. Let's just say I intuited that the light of love was not shining from their eyes, nor was it lurking underneath their dark sunglasses.

But when the plump one reached toward me in what I assumed to be a handshake, I tried to crank up the embers of one of Mattie's speech. "Hi, I'm Eve, you girls new to Heartscape? Did you happen to see a tall, dark man out there?"

The next thing I knew, a handkerchief smelling faintly of lavender was stuffed into my mouth and another held over my nose. I felt myself losing consciousness as the women brusquely rolled me up in the afghan and unceremoniously hauled me up onto their shoulders like an oriental rug being taken out for a cleaning.

17

The artwork created by the Crone Council was displayed in the barn for several days to allow the women to see and feel their way into the images. One large painting showed a flock of black-clad women and massive birds marching toward the right side of the paper, where a gathering of colorfully dressed women of all ages, shapes, and sizes seemed to be dancing. The space formed by the outline of their faces could be read as a heart, and behind the heart stood an image that resembled Aurelia, and behind her, swirls of dark and light. Some pieces were more abstract representations of dark and light in complex geometric patterns and others in simple forms and interlocking shapes. Lorelei's painting of the Pomeranian women provided a counterpoint of peace and tranquility, reminding Aurelia that multiple strands of reality always exist side by side. Another showed the profiles of two women who looked a lot like Eve and the former Charity Greenberg facing each other.

Aurelia felt a tightening in her heart as she gazed on the painting. "We bring into being that which we focus our energy on. Am I asking for trouble thinking dark thoughts about Kali?" Aurelia said to Elsie. "I can't deny she's on my mind, and whatever happens, it's not just up to me, is it? I suspect that child has some business with me too."

"There's no denying the energy there, Aurelia," Elsie replied gazing at the images. "What is most important is not to come to conclusions; we just have to trust the process and follow things as they unfold with clarity and love."

Women were milling about, looking, chatting; some were already seated, writing or sketching their responses. Aurelia and Elsie stood at the front of the room and began to focus on the women, allowing the energy to settle and things to come to order naturally. As the women quieted and took their seats, Aurelia began: "As you know from your own experience in the art space of the CIA studio, the Creative Source loves to speak to us in images. She sends us Her visions in myriad ways so that we can translate Her energy into form. That way we get to see that there is more than one way to understand what is taking place. We learn to delight in one another's unique translation. She teaches us to see from many vantage points and to honor one another's visions, to inquire collaboratively, in other words. Many in today's world see this as a waste of effort, but experience has shown that if we take our time and listen deeply, we do less harm than if we rush in."

"Measure twice; cut once," one of the women hollered out.

"That's right, Sistah: Some truths women have always known. So all of you, take your time. Let your knowing rise up from deep within. The Council of Elders worked together to receive these images to guide our next actions. Now we invite you all to join us in visioning and re-visioning to bring our guidance to wholeness. We ask every one of you, as you are so moved, to meditate and engage with these images: Make your own images; receive your words, music, dance steps — and we will build up and concentrate the energy of revelation together. We know a great step is near in the unfolding of the new era, the time of Cronation. We know the Source is waking and shaking Herself and we aim to serve Her as She does."

Elsie spoke next. "By honoring all the faces of the Creative Source in Her feminine Self we can raise the level of insight to a higher vibration. Each woman among us can connect to a reality greater than herself. So great that, while it will not wipe out your sense of self, it will show us the energy tendrils that connect you — each one to all the others — like squash vines in the garden or beans climbing on the trellis of corn stalks in a Three Sisters garden."

As Elsie spoke, tiny vortexes of light lit up in each woman and began to spin out threads of light towards others. Women in different work groups watched and felt as light lines intensified between co-workers, each groups' light reaching out and connecting to other groups, mixing subtly different shades of color together.

The elder Crone's connection to the Source was so clear, Elsie could manifest imagery as she spoke that others could see. The energy of some women generated pictures; some expressed themselves in words, some in movement, depending on the intention each one held and the gifts of her particular soul. The women were adept at alternating their roles at different visioning sessions so that the revelations became fuller and more complete.

"Remember," Elsie continued, "the Divine She has taught us to love both our gifts as well as our limitations, to see our limits as the way to make a space for another to manifest her wisdom, each bit a sacred and loving contribution, precious and unique. Each time one of us does so, as Aurelia did in letting the other Crones speak her story back to her, the light grows in power and force. As Phoebe liked to say, 'The Great She really does love each one of us completely and enjoys it when we do the same and play well together.'"

Vivian came forward next. "Children, let me tell you a story. Once, back some time ago, when the Akashic record readers, our astral librarians, learned that they needed codes to enter a complex set of records that hadn't been opened before, they invited the women who had been gardeners that season to vision with them. The presence of the gardeners activated new dream pathways for the librarians. Many of the women received images of seeds beginning to sprout in the dark ground and the librarians saw they did not need to 'crack the code' but rather to wait patiently, paying close attention, until the particular record opened on its own time cycle. Some had dreams where they saw Stonehenge-like formations with heel stones in certain places that guided them to the timing, Mid-winter moonset, to attend to the record. It was such a beautiful thing. So deep and so mysterious. It could only have been born of quiet and patient waiting and discerning."

The women, many of who had been a part of that learning, called back to Vivian, "Tell it, Mother, tell it!"

She smiled at them and continued, "From the growers, the librarians, who love order and efficiency so much, learned patience and that 'breaking,' even of a code, must be considered carefully and with discernment, for forcing it is a form of violence that harms the information and gives us a distorted reading, and hence leads us to wrong action. They learned that the information itself is just as alive in code form as it is in text and image, just like the seed is as alive as the fruit that eventually follows the blossoms. We all know that gaining knowledge and understanding by action, pushing, and doing has been the dominant strategy and been greatly overused as we watch the culture run down. As people begin to remember that 'time' as told by the clock is a made-up idea, first created to steal their labor, they grieve and get angry. 'Time is money' is practically engraved upon the closed hearts of many. Some folks can't imagine waiting as being anything other than a waste of time, perhaps the worst form of suffering — when to us, waiting is a form of prayer, of readying ourselves for the unfolding change that comes of its own accord."

"Amen, Mother," chorused the women.

For the women called to Cronation Vivian's words about time were gifts. Many of those present had gone from high school enslaved by a bell that shrilled every forty-five minutes to jobs where they punched a time clock and saw their life force drained out of them in five minute increments spent on assembly lines or washing toilets. No matter if your baby has a fever this morning, if you are five minutes late, that's a dollar off your check at the end of the week. So you need two extra dollars to pay for the baby's medicine? Should have thought of that before you came to work late. Time was a tyrant in the lives of so many and was one of the ideas Cronation was lovingly learning to soften and dissolve.

Aurelia herself had struggled with time and waiting all her life. As much as Riva had patiently instilled in her the ability to observe the natural world, how all things came in their own time, not necessarily on demand, Aurelia's restless mind often wanted to leap ahead to a solution to alleviate suffering, right a wrong, or correct an error. Now, of all times, she needed to feel Riva's presence, that Grandmother spirit, to breathe deeply and practice herself what she taught the women: "Trust the unfolding. Stay awake and hold on, because it will not, despite all your careful preparation, look exactly like what you expect." How many times had Riva spoken these words to Aurelia when she wept in frustration as a teenager!

Elsie stood again, walking slowly, leaning on a stick carved with the form of a voluptuous woman dancing with birds. Standing before the women she waited for silence, looking from face to eager face, most lined with age and years of hard work and sorrow: women, whose hands had scrubbed floors, emptied bedpans, and served fast food — all the while remaining unknown to those who employed them or who benefited from their labor. Who acknowledged the spark of the Divine in these women? Who gazed into their eyes and channeled the light of Divine love?

"Children, let us take a moment to thank one another, to praise one another and to welcome one another. Please, each one of you, turn to a woman near you and take her hands in yours. Look her in the eyes and take a deep breath. Let that breath out with a sigh. Now tell her, 'Thank

222   PAT B. ALLEN

you, Sister!' 'Thank you, mother!' Thank you for the labor of your hands, the wisdom of your heart. Thank you for being here, and you are beautiful!"

The women did as Elsie asked and fell into each other's arms and wept together, soaking up energy from one another that had so often been lacking in their lives.

"Now, Sisters, let us chant our praises to the Source in her ancient incarnations: 'Isis, Astarte, Rhiannon, Hecate, Demeter, Kali…Inanna." Elsie's creased face beamed in joy as the women's voices rose in the familiar chant, repeating the names of the ancient Goddesses, manifestations of the Divine Source at different times in history, showing up in the guise that was needed at that time, called forth from Her infinity by the imaginations of the people.

Next a group took up a chant of the women of the modern era that Cronation honored and claimed as saints, Septima Clark, Dorothy Tilly, Daisy Bates, Alice Norwood Spearman, Pauli Murray, Diane Nash, Dorothy Height and Jo Ann Robinson, Frances Freeborn Pauley, Ella Baker… over and over. Some chanting only first names, so well were these women's stories known to the women of Cronation.

Musicians took up flutes and hand drums to accompany and intensify the energy of the voices. The work of the chanting would continue for hours as the women raised their energy to whatever the challenge might be on a given day. It was always miraculous to see and feel the shift in vibration and recognize the power of the imagination when devoted in love toward one another.

All of a sudden, Aurelia noticed Harvey pacing at the back of the room looking extremely freaked out. Harvey rarely came near the hall when the women were chanting or singing. She swept from the front of the room and locked eyes with him as he gripped her arm and said, "Eve's gone."

"What do you mean Eve's gone?" Aurelia continued outside with her arm around Harvey.

"I went to get her. Mattie said that they had had a great seminar and a session together afterwards. She said Eve would probably be pretty tired, so we let her nap a little longer than usual. I just went to get her and the door is open. Eve and the afghan are gone. But I found this."

Harvey held up a black feather than gleamed with iridescence in the sunlight.

"Kali," Aurelia said and shook her head.

"Who?" Harvey asked, alarmed.

"Momma!" Mattie was out of breath and panicked. "I saw a strange car speeding away down the south road and there's fresh tire tracks leading away from the Research Building."

"Eve's gone," Harvey said to Mattie.

"What? She ran off? Why that little…"

"Mattie, get a hold of yourself!" Aurelia commanded. "She was taken by Kali's people, I'm sure of it."

"What should we do? Should we try to follow them?"

"No," Aurelia looked at Harvey. "Are you ready to go back into the dreamtime, Harvey? I'm pretty sure it was Kali who turned up in your dream. Maybe we can get an idea of what she's up to. The main thing is to trust that everything is unfolding perfectly and we must simply continue to look on it with eyes of love and an open heart. If we can all do that, we'll find the path of highest good. You two are the wise ones here. You've been working with Eve since she arrived. Look at the images from our session."

Aurelia turned and gestured toward the art work, "Kali's and Eve's forms show up in a number of the pieces. And Kali spoke to me in my witness to the image. She's definitely up to something dangerous. Get back to the SAC and go into the dream. I'll get with the council. I'm betting Phoebe will have something to add too. Mattie, what did you work on with Eve today? Harvey said it was big."

"Forgiveness."

Aurelia stopped in her tracks and turned to Mattie and Harvey, a beatific smile spreading slowly across her face. She hugged them both. "Oh, the Goddess is great! Well, I sure don't know how all this is going to turn out, but knowing that forgiveness is Eve's most recent lesson sure makes me feel better. Blessed be, blessings be...now go on and get to work. And, Harvey, take that feather and place it on the altar in the studio. We may be able to call the forces Kali is using if we invite them to join for a common good."

Harvey looked from Aurelia to Mattie and didn't move. "Don't you think it's about time you told me exactly what is going on here? I'm not just some big, dumb dray horse you can use to carry a load."

"Harvey!" Aurelia turned to him in surprise. "Where is all this coming from?"

"The dream, that little witch Kali!" Mattie snapped.

"Now let the man speak for himself, Mattie, please."

"She's right. The woman in the dream said I'm nothing but labor for you. A dray horse. I don't know what's going on here really, maybe I'm helping you do something awful, enslave all the men on the planet, I don't know...."

Aurelia felt Phoebe's presence, she heard her momma say, "I told you, girl, you owe this man more. Tell him what's going on. He's just as important as any woman here."

"Harvey," Aurelia began, but Mattie interrupted. "Momma, I can explain things to Harvey. You go on and find out what we need to do about Eve."

18

When I came to, the plump girl was sitting on my legs as I lay face down on the backseat of a vehicle that seemed to be proceeding at well above the speed limit. I was still rolled up in the afghan, which smelled vaguely of incense. I pushed the handkerchief out of my mouth with my tongue.

"I have to pee."

"Oh my God, she's awake! Where's the stun gun?"

"What? Look, you don't need a stun gun. Just tell me what's going on and where are you taking me? Is this some kind of Cronation stress test?" Besides a desperate need to pee, I had a splitting headache and my stomach was rumbling.

"Don't talk to her!" the driver commanded. "Really, Andrea, if you hadn't gotten us lost with your half-assed directions, we'd have had her back to Kali before the sedative wore off."

Kali! The one who had left Heartscape in a huff, bent on who knows what? I decided it was probably in my best interest to play dumb, not that it felt like a stretch. How had I gone from a highly paid corporate executive with a corner office to a sweat suit–wearing frump caught in the middle of a New Age catfight?

This was decidedly different than my car ride kidnap from Wentworth and Wentsouth in Mattie's taxi. These girls were mean and they weren't wearing pleather. The woman sitting on my back was definitely wearing cowhide and sweating in it, which amplified the raunchy scent in the car and reminded me of the locker room at St. Bernadette's High School.

"Yeah, well, I told you to use more drugs. She definitely weighs more than 110 pounds, and I said to soak the handkerchief longer," replied the woman sitting across my legs.

"It's that ditz bag Diva's fault. Just because she's so good at shape shifting, Kali sends her everywhere, but she's a flake and a rotten spy."

"Andrea?" I addressed the woman sitting on my legs, "I assume you're Andrea? Any chance I could get you to shift your weight a bit? I really have to pee and you're putting quite a bit of pressure on my bladder. You know, as we get older, the old bladder isn't quite as reliable, not so elastic as it is in you younger women." I was hoping to maybe activate a little latent respect-for-your-elders. These women seemed to be Mattie's age but I couldn't really tell from my vantage point.

"Don't move, Andrea!" the driver commanded.

"Look, I'd hate to pee all over the seat of your car."

"Let her up." The woman riding shotgun turned around, and Andrea shifted over so I could sit up.

"Well thanks, Andrea, I feel a lot better," I said, sitting up and rubbing my legs, which felt like logs. I'd read somewhere that if you could establish personal contact with a kidnapper, they often relented and freed you. I was a bit appalled to think that this was my second kidnapping in as many months. Why did they call it "kid" napping anyway? "Kid?" I was a middle-aged woman; there should be a different word.

"Shut up, bitch," the driver growled.

"Ouch! No need to yell." I did not like these women.

"She sure doesn't look like any Messiah to me," Shotgun sniffed.

Looking down at my maroon sweats, orange and green afghan, and bunny slippers I couldn't imagine what she was talking about. If anyone had Messiah energy, it was Aurelia and they couldn't have mistaken me for her no matter how bad their intelligence was.

"Thank God, we're here!" Andrea moaned, wringing her hands.

The driver lurched left and began driving down a long perimeter road towards what looked like an office park in the middle of nowhere. She pulled up in front of a collection of blockish buildings arranged around a manmade pond where a bunch, or I guess that would be a gaggle, of geese swam placidly.

I felt surprisingly calm. Perhaps the vegan diet at Heartscape, as Mattie kept assuring me, had rebalanced my body into a more mellow state. The cannabis tea and topical balm massages certainly didn't hurt. Of course the absence of coffee might be a factor. I wondered what they meant by "messiah." Could there be another meshugenah women's group operating out of the Great Plains plotting a different version of a new world order? Where were the weblogs exposing feminist conspiracy groups? Not that I would have checked them out, but I mean, where was Oprah? Shouldn't she or the gals on The View have been keeping tabs on such things? Bill O' freaking Reilly wasn't on top of this sort of thing? Who knew how many wacky women might be operating below the radar? This was the sort of thing O'Malley always joked about, "Give 'em an inch and, before you know it, they want to run the country instead of just everything else."

We didn't drive long enough to be in another state, I reasoned, and the terrain was still as flat as flat could be, so we couldn't be that far from the Farm. Of course, the role of reason was pretty unclear in the greater scheme of life, as I was coming to know it. And what on earth made me a magnet for these crazed women? I'm sure, if anything Mattie was telling me about the "Other Side" was true, that my mother probably had

228 PAT B. ALLEN

something to do with this. Maybe she nominated me as most likely to be easily kidnapped and brainwashed. Maybe there was some sort of bidding war going on for my services between revolutionary women's clubs. I was definitely lightheaded. The need to pee was becoming urgent. I crossed my legs.

The driver piloted the SUV into a parking spot close to the door. A sign at the head of the space said "Kaliendo Enterprises."

"Okay, don't try anything. Andrea, can you please at least get the stun gun out and cover her in case she tries to make a move? It would be nice to actually get her inside the building without screwing it up."

The driver and Shotgun both wore dark glasses, in spite of the fact that the sky was overcast and gray. Shotgun opened the door and I eased out of the seat.

I'm not sure what she thought I might try. I was wearing sweat pants that didn't even have pockets. I had nothing up my sleeve except some wadded up tissues from crying. I had a mutli-colored afghan over my shoulders and was scuffing along in a pair of old bunny slippers that Mattie had given me when I complained that my feet got cold in the SAC sessions. I suppose I might have flung the afghan over Andrea's head but where would I run in bunny slippers? Besides I really, really had to pee.

"My, you girls aren't very nice to each other…OW!" Andrea applied the stun gun to my thigh and I crumpled to the ground.

"Shut up," she said nervously and looked to the other two for approval. I decided to comply. Where the hell were all the oh-so-intuitive telepathic Crones now when I needed them?

I struggled to my feet and limped ahead of Andrea and behind Driver and Shotgun as we entered the building. It seemed like a fairly ordinary office building, but it was getting dark and I couldn't read the nameplates on the doors. We got into an elevator and stopped on the third floor. My thigh was throbbing but I was afraid to rub my leg and risk getting another shock. The women were silent. Although Andrea seemed to be sniffling back tears.

"Oh shit, we forgot to blindfold her," Shotgun said and untied her skull patterned neckerchief and tied it around my eyes. I'm sure this really completed my "messiah" look.

As the elevator opened Andrea gave me a nudge with the stun gun and we walked out and down a hallway. Just being in an office building felt kind of surreal to me, like any moment Wentsouth was going to burst out of a doorway, pull off the blindfold and say, "Practical joke! We couldn't send you to the West Coast without a little fun first, now could we?" And I'd go into a conference room for another Creative Change seminar followed by donuts and diet Coke.

"Okay, stop here." I heard a door open and Andrea pushed me through it into what could have been a meat locker, it was so cold. I still had the afghan draped over my shoulders and I pulled it tighter around me.

"This is the 'One'? Are you kidding? Diva, I'm going to kill you!"

I could have sworn I heard a crow caw as Andrea pushed me down into a chair and whispered, "Sorry about the shock. Diane really loves the 'special ops' part of this work. She was in the army in Iraq, I think, and I did get us lost."

Wow, what would a shot of Aurelia do to these women, I wondered. "It's okay, Andrea, really, I...I forgive you," I whispered. Where did that come from?

"Take the damn blindfold off, will you, please. Diane. This isn't Mission Impossible."

As my eyes adjusted to the dim light I saw across from me a very intense, dark woman with a flood of curly black hair and dark eyes. She looked pissed off and familiar. I recognized her from one of the group photos at the Farm. She looked older, thinner, and angrier.

"So, you're the 'One'? Doesn't seem like Aurelia is getting such good info from the 'Other Side' these days, does it, ladies?"

A half-hearted cackle answered this remark and the raven that I just noticed sitting on a perch near the table flapped its wings.

"Listen," I said, "With all due respect to whatever is going on here, which I am fairly sure is some sort of colossal misunderstanding, if I could just pee I'd be able to pay much more attention and maybe we could straighten things out."

The woman continued to stare at me but said, "Andrea, take her to the can and hurry up."

"Thank you so much," I said sincerely, bowing slightly as I backed toward the door.

"So, Andrea, what the hell is going on here?" I asked nonchalantly once we were out in the hall.

Andrea struggled with the key to the ladies room that was attached to a large plastic travel mug from someplace called Randy's Donuts. "Oh, please don't talk to me. I forgot the stun gun and I can't subdue you. I don't want to get in any more trouble. You can see how mad Kali is."

Inside the ladies' room, refuge of women in so many circumstances, I sat down and peed in blessed relief. Andrea did the same in the next stall. It struck me that somewhere embedded in this moment was the key to world peace: women needing to pee so often. If women were in charge, they'd never have time to plot war and other mayhem. The need to pee would keep breaking our train of thought and keep emotional storms from building to hurricane levels. Unfortunately, I couldn't follow that thought to a plan of any use in the moment and I didn't think Andrea would appreciate the insight so I kept it to myself.

"Look, don't worry, I promise I won't get you in any more trouble. Seriously, though, how are you connected to the Crones? I've seen that woman Kali. In a picture at Heartscape."

"I'm sure Kali will tell you everything you need to know. All I really know is you're supposed to be the one they've been waiting for and so Kali figured she had to get you out of the way so she could put her plan in play first. Oh my God, I have such a big mouth!"

"And by 'out of the way,' you mean…?" This was not sounding good at all.

"Well, she wants information and I've never seen her kill anyone yet."

"And by 'yet,' you mean…?"

"Kali's plan is for synchronized assassinations of men in key positions of power bringing on the necessary chaos for mass change. I don't think she plans on killing any women. Really!! I can't tell you this stuff, she'll kill me for sure."

"No one is going to kill anyone," I said in as soothing and Mattie-like a voice as I could muster. The flush of the toilets only slightly muffled Andrea's sniffling sobs.

When we got ourselves out of the stalls I said: "Now look, let's wash our hands and figure out what to do. For starters, you suck it up and get a mean look on. We're going back in there and you never said a word to me about anything, okay?"

"Okay." Andrea sniffed and blew her nose in a paper towel.

"Come on, mean face." I stood next to her, looking in the mirror at my own absurd reflection. "No giggling, I bet that really pisses Diane off."

I poked my thigh and winced. Nope, not a dream.

I closed my eyes and concentrated on Mattie's face, her holding me in her lap. Her words, "Once you feel that flow you just want to send it to everyone and see what happens." Come on, Mattie, tune in and help me out here!

19

You know her, this Kali?" Harvey asked as he and Mattie crossed the field to the main building.

"Yeah, she was at the Farm for awhile but she took off. She couldn't really handle it here. She and I didn't hit it off, I can tell you that!"

"Why not?'

"Charity Greenberg was her given name. She came to one of those mother-daughter retreats we had here awhile back. Then her momma left and she begged Aurelia to let her stay. She was always challenging Momma, had all these ideas about speeding things up. She spent hours in the library reading. Trying to find ways to trip up whoever was teaching, that's what I think. She's a rich white girl and…"

Harvey stopped walking and looked at Mattie.

"What? She is and she didn't like to work either, too good to mop a floor, never had to before. Then when she got into the detox work — well, you know, Harvey, it's not about theories. Your stuff rises up and sits you down in front of it. She didn't like that."

"Mattie, I've never heard you talk like this before. You're pretty worked up."

"Well, shit, Harvey, I watched this girl putting on airs like she's all that, disrespecting Momma, then she decides to call herself Kali? I wasn't sorry to see her go. She wasn't ready for Cronation. She didn't get it. She was one of those women who was all mannish in a really mean way. Not a manikin like Eve, poor thing, just got conned by the system. That happens to plenty of women.

"Kali knew exactly what she was doing. You know, Harvey, a woman acting a man is worse than any man. Thinks she's smarter than everyone, can't work with other women. Thinks she's smarter than everyone — and cold! That girl was like ice. She's all identified with the Warrior and that trip, without compassion, that makes her more dangerous than any man. She's an insult to the Great Goddess Kali if you ask me."

"Mattie, I don't know about this goddess stuff and all, but this girl seems to be under your skin. Seems like you have a personal beef with her," Harvey said.

"Well, maybe so. But now — if she's got Eve, she might cause some real damage to our work. So let's get to it."

Harvey was feeling a little queasy, "Wait a minute. What's with this Warrior thing? And if it's so bad, why is there a Warrior Goddess?"

"The Goddess Kali is part of the Triple Goddess energy. There's the Creator, the Preserver, and the Destroyer. Those three energies cycle through each person at all times and each is necessary. Kali carries two swords, one is like a scythe — it's curved and it represents the blade that harvests, that finishes things in their time, takes them when they're ripe. This can refer to an idea or to the fruits on those apple trees you tend. Then She also carries a straight sword, and that one is the Sword of Truth. She cuts through the bullshit. You know? She speaks the truth.

"Charity Greenberg thought she was born with the sword of truth in one hand and a silver spoon in the other," Mattie was on a roll.

"Here," Mattie took Harvey's hand. "This is important. Before we start on the dream, let's go into the Hall of Women. There's a painting of the goddess Kali and you can see what I mean."

Mattie touched the mezuzah on the door as they went inside. She lit the candle on the ledge under the painting of Kali. "Rabbi Leaf brought back this tanghka from India. Isn't it amazing?"

Harvey stared at the red figure with its multiple arms holding not only the swords Mattie had described but also a severed head, definitely male. She was wearing a belt of more male heads and stood on the body of a young man. A ghastly looking red tongue lolled out of her mouth as if she had just taken a big swig of blood from the bowl in one of her hands. Harvey stepped back and instinctively reached for his balls.

"Now men, in Warrior mode, being more action-oriented and concrete, they use real swords, or other weapons. The Crones say men just forget that there are other forms of transformation besides violent ones. The Warrior archetype has dominated human consciousness for thousands of years, and while that isn't men's fault either, exactly, they've gotten real stuck in it, but now it's running out of gas and the shift to the Crone era is happening and…"

By the time Mattie finished, Harvey was better informed about Hindu iconography but feeling really nervous.

"So, Mattie," Harvey began tentatively as they started walking back toward the SAC room, "what exactly do Aurelia and the others have planned for all the men once this big shift comes?"

"The men?" Mattie stopped for a minute and said, "Well, as the archetypal energy shifts away from the Warrior, men's combative tendencies will become less and less effective. They won't be as dangerous. The combative energy will drain out of them as their undeveloped feminine energy begins to rise and enter their consciousness."

"That's not what I mean." Harvey looked at Mattie imploringly. "I mean, what about men's feelings about all this stuff happening? This is a big deal, right? It's gonna be like a movie being played in slow motion, everything falling apart or something? It's already that way: wars, hurricanes, mudslides…"

Mattie looked at Harvey. "I don't exactly know. I guess I never thought about it too much. I suppose once the wave of energy gets moving, the men will all be sort of thrust out of their old ways of thinking, and, you know, just be so happy to see the light. I imagine it will be a relief."

"Uh huh."

The distressing vision that formed in Harvey's mind's eye was a cross between the Rapture as described by Tim La Haye and Jerry Jenkins in the *Left Behind* books — business suits and work uniforms just flying off men's bodies as they float heavenward toward a new woman-run planet — and the battle scene from Spartacus but in place of the gladiators with swords, was a horde of gray-haired women wielding brooms just sweeping the men into the gutter after Kali's dirty work was done. It was not a pretty sight.

"So what you're saying is that the entire male population, all of them, all over the world — CEOs, baseball players, car mechanics, drug dealers, accountants, and the guy who flips burgers at McDonald's — all at once are just gonna get zapped one morning with a love vibe and put down the bat or the wrench or the Blackberry and in unison drop to one knee and say to whatever woman is handy, 'Thanks, I see the light. You women are each and every one of you the embodiment of the Goddess, Source of all Life. I didn't see that before now, but now I do, and by gum, how can I serve you?' Is the Goddess gonna look like this Kali? 'Cause I can tell you right now, not too many guys could handle that." By now Harvey's voice was getting a little ragged.

"Well, you get it, you just said it yourself — women are the embodiment of the Goddess. She'll show up in exactly whatever form each man needs." Mattie reached up and put her arms around Harvey's neck, "I showed up in your life, didn't I? And I didn't need a sword." She smiled. "Feminine wisdom will guide the next era's unfolding — if you can understand that, I guess other men can too."

Harvey held Mattie away from him and looked in her eyes. "And the ones that don't? The ones who never met anyone like you or Aurelia? Who deep down are just scared shitless all the time, who feel so bad about not making enough money, are so tired of feeling like losers, who never felt good enough for their mothers or girlfriends or wives, or who think fighting is the only way to be a man? What about them? And let me tell you, there are plenty of them! You think the Crones are going to be greeted as liberators?" Harvey laughed bitterly. "It didn't work in Iraq or any other war. Why would it work for the Crones?"

Mattie stepped back and looked quizzically at Harvey, "Well, for one thing, we're not gonna blow up your towns! We aren't gonna come into the NY Stock Exchange or your corporate headquarters with guns blazing. We aren't gonna lob a grenade into your Sports Bar during Monday night football!"

"Great! That's what you're not gonna do. What are you gonna do to deal with the fear and the chaos? And what about this Kali woman? What if she shows up with real swords or something worse?"

"That's what the dream work is for, Harvey. Momma knows that, as a man you could be bringing in information that she's missing, a minority report if you will… She values that, all the Crones do. So we better get to work and see how the dream unfolds. I guess if Kali did kidnap Eve, she probably isn't sitting around lighting candles and meditating."

Harvey turned to Mattie and looked at her with determination, "OK, we better get into that dream. I might have more to offer than just heavy lifting. You know, Mattie, deep down, an awful lot of men just feel obsolete. We know women can do a whole lot of things as good or better than us. We see it every day. We just want to feel important or at least useful, and most of us don't know how to anymore."

Mattie took his hands in hers tenderly, "Well, I know you can't be feeling obsolete! And as for those men that do, well, 'obsolete' is just the moment before transformation, Harvey. Before being taken apart and put back together in a new way. Like you becoming a Cronation visionary." She grinned and tousled his hair, leaned in and kissed him lightly.

"Now let's go find out what those visions can teach us. It's all good. Really. You'll see."

20

Andrea was doing a pretty convincing job with the mean face. She shoved me into the room and I sat back down across the table from Kali and smiled.

"What are you laughing at?" she demanded and her leather-clad minions all moved towards me. Andrea fumbled with the stun gun. The raven flew up and turned into a mop-headed wraith who plopped herself into the empty seat next to Kali.

"So, you girls are going with the violence thing, huh?" I began. "How's that gonna work?"

"Why should we tell you?" the former raven asked as she spun herself around in the chair.

"Diva, cut that out!" Kali spit the words. "Before I use the stun gun on you."

"Goodness, guns are fun, aren't they?" I had no idea where that remark came from, but what the hell, I looked like the fool, I might as well play the fool. Anyway, Andrea wasn't close enough to zap me immediately.

"No, not fun, but efficient and necessary," Kali countered. "Guns make a clear statement."

"Oh, yeah, efficient if you don't mind the blood. And if by 'clear' you mean carnage. I've read that the blood spatter from gunfire entering human flesh is so wide that you can't ever clean it up. You know, 'out damn spot,' can't ever get it all." I was a bit lightheaded having missed lunch.

"What's the best thing about guns?" I continued, feeling a bit the way I once did years ago confronting a would-be mugger who accosted me on a dark street in Boston. He said he'd kill me if I didn't give him all my money. Problem was I only had a dime in my pocket. I was so pissed off at him for pointing out my miserable plight (college loans a week late, me too proud to call O'Malley and ask for some cash), I just started in on him about how mad I was, that I had exactly bupkis, that my loan check hadn't come in the mail that day as scheduled. He ended up feeling bad for me, apologizing for trying to mug me, walking me home and slipping me five bucks to tide me over.

Mattie told me later that I "brilliantly shifted the script" of Kali's story and undermined the whole thing. See, Mom, I can too be subversive! At the time I was noticing something that Mattie had been trying to get me to understand: We experience a situation like multi-track recording devices. Usually we are only aware of one track, what's being said in words. We have to make a decision to become aware of the other tracks. That's where mindfulness comes in. She kept telling me how many other tracks I had, more than average, I guess. The first step is to stay still long enough to let awareness make those visible.

As I sat with the Kali and her crowd, I noticed myself taking in not just Kali's tough words but also a dark sadness in her eyes, the sallow tone of her skin, the fact that the bones nearly showed through, the continual nervous movement of her long fingers. All of this broadcast a fragile quality that was really quite beautiful and undercut any fear I was feeling.

I heard Diva's flippant sidekick remarks but had a picture forming in my mind of a child dancing a frantic jig on the edge of a cliff, her eyes closed, daring herself not to fall. It used to be, Mattie had said, that only avatars could do this, but the Crones had learned how to move at will into a mindset that Mattie called "spaciousness," which allowed for more tracks to surface and play at the same time in awareness. It takes practice to get past hearing the multiple strands as noise. At first most people just shut back down. But when you instead keep breathing until all the strands sync up and then it's like a kind of human symphony in each person and becomes a grander and grander one as more people are together in a compatible space.

Mattie says that most people tune into these layers somewhat but they either think they're crazy or they can't decipher the music, so they just turn up the T.V. or plug in their headphones and listen to something else. I could now follow these internal riffs easily since being at the Farm. I thought it was sort of magical — until Marty pointed out I was no longer drinking coffee and wasn't at Wentworth and Wentsouth anymore with deals and spreadsheets and non-stop emails and phone calls engaging me in the continual task of translating the follies of old white men into reality. Whoa! Did I just think that? Who thought that?

Diva brought me back to the immediate moment by answering the question I had asked before I took a jaunt into spacious me.

"Pow, boom, you're gone! That's what guns are good for. Somebody fucks with you, somebody bigger, stronger, thinks they have the upper hand — Eliminato! Sayonara, sucker! What could be more fun than a little shit like me showing up as that fat fuck Rav Wendell Babka is holding forth, babbling his bullshit in a seminar under some tree in Boca. I fly up in my raven, light down right in front of him. I can hear him now, 'Blah, blah, look at this raven, who has arrived to show what a great teacher I am, blah, blah, the raven eats shit and transforms it by fertilizing the lotus' or some crap like that, congratulating himself for being all spontaneous. And all those stupid, love struck old ladies are taking notes and writing down his phony wisdom — until I morph back into little old me and blast the sucker

in the heart, or where one would be if he had one. Bam! Blam! Thank you,
Ma'am. Raven eats shit no more!"

"Who's Rav Babka? Sounds like this guy must have really hurt you,"
I was a little stunned by Diva's story. It felt like I was seeing a speeded up
reel of another movie in the background while she spoke. There was a lot
of story compressed in and under her words that I couldn't make out but
it was making me faintly nauseous. She was standing up in the chair now,
wobbling uneasily as the wheels slid back and forth.

"Oh great!" Kali stood up and pushed Diva back down into the chair.
"The 'one' is a half-assed psychotherapist?! 'That must have hurt — oh
here, punch the pillow, draw a picture, let's make a little sculpture and you
can stab the fucker with an exacto knife! Is this all Aurelia's got?"

"You too?" I offered.

"See, I told you," Diva taunted Kali and then turned to me.

"Kali won't admit it, but I'm pretty sure some guy fucked her up
too. If it wasn't Babka, maybe it was her dad or the headmaster at that art
school."

Kali had her hands on Diva's shoulders shoving her down into her
chair and was leaning over her shaggy head. Her mouth was twisted into
a sneer.

"This isn't about me," she hissed. "It's about all the women and children who have suffered. Look, men have had their chance. They fucked
it up every which way till Sunday and twice on Sunday. Priests fuck little
kids, holy men go straight for the bunghole, spiritual teachers fuck whatever stands still and then threaten her if she talks about it. Cops shoot anyone who looks at them cross-eyed and get a medal for it. Politicians fuck
the poor all over the world. Corporate morons piss and shit in the water
and then charge you five bucks to drink it. If I could push a button and
zap every last prick on earth, all at one time, I'd do it. Put a man in charge
and you can count on violence, stupidity, duplicity, and self-serving idiocy,

and you can't even count the ways. Child abuse, child soldiers, war, raping the planet. Is there anything they've touched that they haven't fucked with, wrecked, and ruined?"

By this time, Andrea was sobbing quietly. Driver and Shotgun just stood like statues with their arms crossed over their chests.

I was feeling kind of ill. This Kali woman conjured a lot power out of that pain. I wish she could spend some time with Mattie, but I noticed that she couldn't seem to maintain eye contact with me at all. I had to shift gears; I was definitely into multi-track overload. I just kept trying to keep Mattie's face in front of me. "Breathe, Eve, breathe into your back body, make space for what's there to come forward."

"You girls ever see those old cartoons where the cat and mouse are always fighting," the words just came to me. "The cat shoots the mouse and each drop of blood becomes another mouse and suddenly instead of one on one, there's hundreds, a whole army of mice and the mayhem just gets bigger and bigger, bloodier and bloodier."

Diva and Kali looked at each other and then at me.

"And your point is?" Kali asked.

"Violence begets violence?" I offered. "In your scenario aren't the men just going to come back and kill a lot of women? Don't they have more force at their disposal? Hasn't history kind of showed that is the pattern? Is that really a solution?" My head was beginning to hurt. "Let's say you could get rid of all the men, then what? No more children, no more human race?"

"There are plenty of sperm banks. We can start from scratch." This contribution from Diane only made Andrea sob harder. "Breed only females. Men are just defective females anyway, that Y chromosome is a broken X."

I tried another angle. "You've taken the name Kali, right? In the Hindu story of Kali, she goes after the demon, but every drop of his blood becomes a copy of him and so she just makes it worse by trying to kill him."

I was definitely stalling but I didn't know what else to do.

Kali looked at me, a patronizing smile playing on her angular face. "Actually, in Kali's most famous myth, it's Durga and her assistants, the Maktras, who wound the demon Raktabija in various ways and with a variety of weapons in an attempt to destroy him. They soon find that they have worsened the situation, as in every single drop of blood that is spilt from Raktabija, the demon reproduces himself. The battlefield becomes increasingly filled with his duplicates. Durga, in dire need of help, summons Kali to combat the demons. Kali destroys Raktabija by sucking the blood from his body and putting the many Raktabija duplicates into her gaping mouth. Pleased with her victory, Kali then dances on the field of battle, stepping on the corpses of the slain. Her consort Shiva lies among the dead beneath her feet, a representation of Kali commonly seen in iconography, the Daksinakali pose."

Touché, this girl knew her mythology. I was definitely out of my league.

"Wait a minute, Kali," Diva said, "you never said we'd have to eat these guys we kill, that's gross! Maybe I could do it as raven though."

"No, you don't have to eat them, little Diva." Kali laughed a thin, harsh laugh that reminded me of rusty metal. "We just dig a deep pit and drop them in; we just leave them there to rot and return to dust. Then we give old Mother Earth a break."

"You remember after Chernobyl," Kali said. "Nature righted itself pretty quickly as soon as humans butted out. Scientists were amazed, the simple absence of humans was all it took to restore order to nature."

I was beginning to see that the girl was stark raving mad and fueled by some bone-chilling rage. Kali didn't just want to do away with men, she was ready to torch the whole human race. Did her followers even realize this? Andrea looked at me expectantly, but Diva was clearly getting bored with the foray into intellectual brinksmanship.

"Look, Kali," Diva offered, "it doesn't even matter. If she's the 'one' then as long as we have her here, the Crones can't do whatever they plan, right? Like we have the missing part and they can't start an engine."

I began to breathe easier but then she continued. "We can just get to work and start Nemesis and as long as this one is in our hands, nothing should interfere, right? We could just tie her up until we're done."

Kali laughed, "Right you are, little Diva."

Just then I noticed a large painting on the wall. My eyes were finally adjusting to the dimness of the room. "Hey, isn't that 'Humeur Noctorne,' considered to be the Goddess Nemesis?" I was rusty but I did know a bit more about art history than I did about Eastern religion. "Is that a copy? It's beautiful."

"You know it?" I could have sworn I saw a glimmer of something soft in Kali's eyes.

"William-Adolphe Bouguereau, 1885?"

"It's 1882, actually. Nemesis, the Goddess of Vengeance and righteous retribution."

I got up and went over to the painting. The women all looked to Kali, but she didn't stop me.

"Holy shit! Is this the real thing? Where did you get it?"

The life size painting was exquisite: a tall, pale woman with a diaphanous black veil, a sliver of moon in the upper left corner. Bourguereau was a master who had gotten lumped in with the academic painters and got swept out of favor when the Impressionists became the next big thing. His style of Romantic realism was one of the multiple threads that just got edited out of most of the cultural discourse. He was rediscovered in the 1970s and by the '80s was appreciated, even if he never got his due in the mainstream. His paintings went for high six figures now at auction. Aversmith had consulted me once when a painting by Bouguereau came up for auction at Sotheby's. He recognized the beauty — and the fact that it was still cheap and would probably appreciate substantially didn't hurt.

Kali was standing next to me. I swear she gave off a chill. I shrugged the afghan up around my shoulders. "My mother bought it in the '70s. It's worth a lot of money. I promised it to a museum in Saudi Arabia who paid me a ton of money up front. They get it on loan for a few months a year now for their new Louvre outlet museum and for good when my mother croaks. I forged the papers. One thing at least that asshole Babka won't get his greedy hands on." Suddenly Kali seemed less like a terrorist and more like a pissed-off kid, a smart one, which made her volatile and dangerous.

The painting, though, the power of its idealized beauty, captivated me. I felt chills down my spine just looking at it. "Do you know anything about this artist?"

"She knows lots of art stuff, don't you, Kali? She's been to art school, art camp, art fuck, oh, not that one…" Diva was spinning again, obviously bored with this detour from guns and murder and enjoying her ability to needle Kali.

"I know this is real art," Kali pronounced, "not like the kindergarten crap that gets turned out by Aurelia and the hags at her stupid farm."

"Totally real art," I nodded. I was stalling again, trying to follow the thread. Was Kali another kid who'd been swindled out of her creativity by who-knows-who, or had something really awful happened to her that took her totally off track? It seemed like this man-hating and art were connected. She clearly had an emotional connection to Aurelia and the Farm, but I wasn't sure where to go with that.

"So doesn't it bother you to have this painting by a man up here on the wall?" I probed the inconsistency. "I mean, if this is Bouguereau's vision of Nemesis, where's her weapon? She's a pretty idealized version of revenge, isn't she?"

Diva stopped spinning and Andrea, Driver, and Shotgun all looked at Kali. I guessed deep discussions were not the strong suit of this particular revolutionary cell and they weren't used to seeing their leader challenged. I felt a trickle of sweat dampening each armpit. I took a deep breath and continued.

"Bougeureau was into justice. He made a lot of paintings that drew attention to the issues of the day, raised money to help house and feed less fortunate artists. And he championed women's admission to the art academies, including the prestigious Ecole de Beaux Artes. He genuinely honored the feminine in his work," I said and pushed on. "It may be an idealized, unreal version of the feminine, perhaps, but he clearly loved women.

"He also experienced a lot of tragedy in his life: four of his five kids and his first wife died before him. He channeled his grief into some of the most remarkable paintings of the late nineteenth century. His Pieta is a masterpiece. He really understood pain. I wonder what might have happened if his work hadn't fallen out of favor. I mean, look at how beautiful this figure is, moon, nature, not really so different from the art at the Farm, except in style. The message is the same: life is good, humankind is worthy of love and respect, human suffering can be transformed into meaning, into beauty...."

I was out of breath but so far Kali hadn't interrupted me. I was hoping to draw her out more about her experience at the Farm but, before she could speak, it became clear that Diva was fed up with me.

"Thanks for the art history lesson, Granny! Mr. Booger-roo sounds like a real nice old French guy, but he's already dead so why are we wasting time talking about him? There are lots of living, breathing assholes out there who need to get what's coming to them, right, Kali?"

I looked at Kali. She had been silent the whole time I was talking, like she was soaking up something she needed, but what would she do with it?

"Bourguereau may not be quite as post-modernistically politically correct as you are trying to imply," Kali replied slowly, "but he will continue to serve both justice and 'the feminine,' as you so quaintly call that stupid love fest of demented women." She pronounced the artists' name with a flawless French accent. "He's paid for a whole lot of Uzis. The other component of my deal with the Saudis."

She leveled her gaze at me and said, "Not that any of this matters. A painting by a man, a woman, or an elephant. It's just hard currency to me."

I knew she was lying about not caring about the painting, but her shell was harder than anything I could crack. I was feeling tired and angry. For one thing, I was famished; and I saw no evidence of food, nothing but crappy take out menus lying around the room and a microwave oven in the corner on the counter. I longed to be back at the Farm having Harvey massage my feet as I came out of the trance from the work in the SAC chair. I ignored Diva and looked straight at Kali.

"The Saudis? You'll take guns from the Saudis to kill men here while those guys don't let women in their country drive or even walk around the block without a male escort? Face it, Kali, you're a fraud. I'm no therapist, but it seems to me you're just acting out of your own anger and pain, just like any man would — unconsciously — and keeping the whole stupid cycle of violence going around and around. And telling yourself you're a revolutionary? This is a 'movement'? That's more full of shit than any man I've ever heard of. Well, no, not really, come to think of it; it's just a page out of their manual, isn't it? Using back channel means, duping the dumb and needy, getting others to do your bidding. A power trip."

I gestured at the other women. "Diva here is the future? A little video game come alive? Are you really going to play out some pseudo feminist version of *Natural Born Killers*?"

"I hate that movie." This from Andrea. Maybe she was hungry too. "And I hate what we're doing. I don't want to kill anyone, I just want to feel better and I want everyone else to feel better too, even the men."

"Try some dope. You'll feel better — and you'll really get off on shooting the guns," Diva offered.

Andrea turned toward Diva, "Diva, you're ridiculous. You're going to fly down to Boca and shoot Rav Babka? Where does a raven put her .357? Up her crazy ass? Kali, when I got involved in Nemesis, it was instead of killing myself. I was so depressed. Then I found your website and started emailing you. You seemed really smart and like you cared about me. I was able to get angry for the first time and not feel bad. I gave up everything to come here. I thought we were going to do something good, change the world. She's right — you are a fraud."

Diane pushed her sunglasses up onto her head. "Oh, yeah, Andrea? What are you going to do about it?" She turned her gun on Andrea, "you plus-size crybaby!"

Andrea turned back to Kali, brandishing the stun gun. "I'm sick of all this, Kali, and... And while you two were arguing I sent out an email to everyone in the network canceling Nemesis."

"You did what?!" Kali turned on Andrea in a rage.

"I've listened to everything Diva said every time she came back from her spy missions to the Farm and it sounded pretty cool to me. I've been on their website too. Then when we went out there to get Eve I realized something. The women at that Farm are happy, they love each other, and they're creating a vision, not just tearing one down. You are really angry and really hurt and I am too, but this isn't the way. The only person I feel like shooting is you, Kali. You don't appreciate anything we do. And I don't like feeling like that!"

"That's it! If we have to start with you Andrea, we can do that." Diva had a shiny black rifle poised on her shoulder, with Andrea's head in the sight. "Say the word, Kali, and I'll blast her to Kingdom Come, chunky bitch!" She was standing on the wheeled office chair and the rifle made her off balance.

"Are you crazy?" Kali shouted, and Diva swung around wildly and pointed the rifle at her.

Andrea lurched toward Diva and planted the stun gun firmly on her ass. The rifle jerked toward the ceiling and went off with a deafening sound. Diva fell to the ground. The debris from the blasted acoustic tiles fell like snow from the hole in the ceiling and covered Diva in a fine white dust. Andrea put down the stun gun, and we all watched as Kali dropped to the floor and pulled Diva onto her lap. Shotgun and Driver crowded around her, awkwardly offering comfort.

"Get the fuck away from me, you goddamn losers!" Kali hissed.

Andrea was shaking but she'd stopped crying. I was wishing Mattie had given me a few lessons in that mind-jujitsu stuff. This was getting way beyond crazy.

I felt for Diva's pulse, and it was thready and weak. "We have to get help."

21

"Momma, I need you to tune in here." Aurelia had left the work in progress in the barn and was sitting on the grassy hill that over-looked the main Heartscape buildings. The women were in the barn chanting, witnessing artwork by writing poems, dancing, and making music. The elders sat in a circle near the artwork, eyes closed, deep in silent communication with the Source; their concentrated pure intention of love held the space for the rest of the women to do their work. The Tantrikas were in bed with their consorts in their quarters near the stream at the lower edge of the property, prolonging intercourse in a variety of esoteric postures that hadn't been practiced since the Vedas were written. Mattie and Harvey were using the SAC technology to follow the thread of Harvey's dream and see if they could tune in on Kali and her gang. Lydia and the women who had arrived from Washington and around the country were monitoring the events in Pomerania and around the globe. And Eve was missing.

"Momma! Come on, it's all going to pieces. They've got Eve and I don't know what to do!"

"Aurelia, child, calm down," Phoebe answered. "It's all fine, it's all good. Everyone is doing her part. Trust me, from here I can see how beautiful it all is. Something beautiful is unfolding and you all are right at the center."

"Momma, how can that be? Eve was taken away right under our noses!"

"Exactly!" Phoebe laughed. "Honey, just stop a minute and appreciate how easy it is to lose your balance! You just finished telling all those women how you can never know ahead of time how change will look."

"But you said Eve has an important role to play and now she's gone." Aurelia was exasperated with Phoebe.

"What did you think that was going to be? Eve leading a march into The Hague and declare world peace? Hand you the formula for a chill pill you could pass out to all the men and have them swallow in unison like Holy Communion? Gracious, Aurelia, things are unfolding. If Jesus taught us anything, and Martin, too, for that matter, it's that being 'The One' in the sense of taking it all on your fragile human shoulders is not the way. Of course, neither one of them completely understood it until they got over to this side and could get the long view of the big picture, but really… No one soul can carry all the light, or all the dark for that matter, for the whole world. But each one can do her piece. Oh, I like that! 'Each one do her peace' — that's even better! I'm gonna send that to Medea Benjamin, I think she could put that on one of those pink tee shirts. That girl has such a fashion sense!"

"Momma, you aren't really helping here." Aurelia was feeling the connection to Phoebe fade.

"Trust, Darling! And keep the love flowing."

Aurelia punched the ground. "Damn it, Momma! You always leave when the going gets tough." Suddenly Aurelia found herself sobbing on the ground and she couldn't stop. Finally she exhausted herself. Feeling the Earth support her, Aurelia's breathing began to calm. She closed her eyes and saw an image of herself as a teenager kicking the wall in the barn, consumed with anger and grief after Phoebe left her with Riva.

"Why, you poor little thing!" she said to the image in her mind's eye. "I was such a feisty girl!"

She watched a comet-like flash of golden light enter the little girl Aurelia's heart as she thought those words. Then the scene shifted to Riva's barn, fully painted with signs and symbols, images of the changes to come, of beauty and love for the Source and the wonder of the natural world. She saw herself asleep on the barn floor, a paintbrush still in her hand. "My goodness, what wonders have I been blessed with? Thank you, Source," she whispered.

Aurelia gasped as the scene changed again. She was holding three month old Mattie in her arms, looking at a photograph of William, Mattie's dad, in his U.S. Army uniform. A captain in the endless war that finally knocked the skids out from under America's superiority complex, William died in Tikrit without ever seeing his daughter.

"What a sacrifice you made, William," Aurelia whispered, "taking your leave as you did and letting this work unfold. I sure hope you're on the other side getting tutored by my Daddy. According to Momma, he's got plenty to teach. I'm counting on that love fest we've all been working for finally coming into being when this Shift is done."

Aurelia watched as another comet of light, this time deep magenta, enveloped her young mother self and Mattie like the sacred flames around Our Lady of Guadalupe. She was draped in a cerulean robe embroidered with stars and both their faces shone with an almost blinding love. "Thank you, William. I miss you."

The next scene featured Phoebe, turning to leave Riva's. Standing in the dark before dawn, a look of anguish on her face as she and the other women left their children and all they knew, going off to have the visions that became Cronation. Aurelia silently wept as she saw how pained her mother had been to leave her.

"Bless you, Momma," she whispered and a comet of purple light entered the top of Phoebe's head and shot down her entire body lighting her from within with the fire of revelation.

The next scene showed Phoebe bending down to pick up the caterpillar off the road, her last act in that physical form, with the truck full of hunters bearing down on her. Now Aurelia was wracked with sobs. She heard the words: "If you save one life, it is as if you have saved the world."

Then she saw herself sitting by Harvey's hospital bed. This time a soft pink comet flew in a spiral from Aurelia's heart to Harvey's. She watched as Harvey's face dissolved in grief and tears and saw herself continue to radiate compassion and love to him.

"This is it?" Aurelia thought. Could it be that the change, the Shift is really the unfolding of simple moments of love in the hardest times? Passed between people in everyday acts of forgiveness and gratitude, each one lighting up a mandala until it is fully bright, glowing in a multi-hued pattern of complexity and wholeness, a pattern of energy that shifts like a kaleidoscope every time a new act of love or kindness takes place? Aurelia opened her eyes and saw the light pulsing in every tree, stone, and blade of grass. In the distance the Heartscape barn appeared as a multi-colored, swirling mandala. She felt her heart explode in her chest and looked down as her hands and then her entire body lit up from within with a soft, pulsing, golden light. An overwhelming sense of joy and peace filled her.

"Thank you, Source, Shekinah, Goddess, Momma, Riva," Aurelia shook herself and stood up. "Okay, Momma, I get it, it's all good, all happening. I guess I'll go down and see how Mattie and Harvey are doing. I never expected to be watching from the sidelines, but if that's my place, well, so be it."

Just then Aurelia noticed Sarah Leaf coming up the hill.

"Girl, am I glad to see you! I've been sitting here, feeling a little bit sorry for myself, then a whole bunch of little knots of regret and sadness just rose up in my mind and unraveled themselves. I feel better now but

I'm just about worn out."

Rabbi Leaf sat down and gave Aurelia a hug. "I could feel your energy coming up the hill. Tell me what's going on."

"Oh, I could see places in my past I hadn't grieved fully, still holding on — Momma, Riva, even William. I trust the Divine, but damn, I still get angry that so many of the people I love have been taken. Sometimes I'd just rather be with them, it feels so hard here. And what if it's for nothing? Even though Momma speaks to me plain as day, I sometimes lose faith."

"We all do," Rabbi Leaf said, "that's why we need each other. Aurelia, you teach us all so much, sometimes we forget that it's all the people we've lost that make that space in our hearts for the new to manifest. Some people just shrink and close up, but you just keep opening. That space in your heart is so big now, it holds all the women of Cronation instead of bitterness and regret."

"I know I'm blessed, Sarah, but sometimes I ache too."

"Sounds like the mikveh could help," Sarah replied.

"That's the ritual bath, isn't it?"

Rabbi Sarah nodded. "Traditionally Jews visit the mikveh after contact with something powerful like blood or death, anything that is in the realm of the awesome power of life and death — and you, Sister, you go to the place between worlds all the time. I'm sorry I never thought of it before. We immerse ourselves as a sign of dissolution, restore ourselves to life through a symbol of purified death."

"I like that. These memories and feelings were like little solid rocks I was holding onto, weighing me down. My tears dissolved them somewhat but to wash them away, give them back — I'd like that. I'd like to release as much grief as I can so I can be present in this moment when so much is shifting."

"Well, one thing this mild weather allows us could be a dip in the pond. Shall we?"

"You and me?" Aurelia asked.

Sarah grinned and nodded her head. "I'm game if you are. We can get some of Gina's cocoa when we're through."

"Why not? Come on, Sister, but let's get some towels and blankets first for when we get out."

22 ————————

Harvey was strapped into the SAC chair, set on dream scan. He began to breathe slowly and deeply and to defocus his eyes. He held the black feather in his hand, hoping it would help him tune back into the dream of Kali. Instead, an image of a beautiful little blonde girl appeared, sitting on the floor of a dark room, playing with some blocks. Shadowy adults moved about in the background. A woman with long, lank hair picks up the baby, who hugs her intensely. Then she hands the baby to a man, pulling the baby's arms away from her body and pushing the baby into the man's grasp. The baby cries and cries and reaches toward the woman. The man hands the woman a packet and she leaves, ignoring the baby's cries. Harvey felt nauseated and like he'd been pinned back in a wind tunnel. He dropped the feather and the image pixilated and then the screen turned to static.

"Mattie," he called out in a raspy voice. "I don't know what I'm getting here, but I feel really sick and this isn't the same dream."

Mattie sat slightly behind Harvey watching the images unfold. She massaged the back of his neck. "I feel it too, you're tuned into something really dark. Let's trust it's where we need to go. Are you willing to continue? Can you get it back? I'm right here with you. Remember, Eve is in danger."

Harvey clenched and relaxed his muscles in his face, arms, and shoulders and whispered, "Source, protect us from harm. Show us how to be of service. Let me do no harm; protect me from harm."

Mattie said, "Wow, Harvey, I'm so wound up, I completely forgot to set an intention and we're clearly into something dangerous. Let's add, 'Source, forgive our fears, forgive our confusion. Show us how to help bring the highest good for all.'"

Harvey clenched and unclenched his hands again and said "Mattie, hand me the feather. I dropped it and I think it's important. I know Aurelia said to put it on the altar, but I feel like I'm supposed to keep holding it."

Mattie smiled; intuition was an amazing thing! She picked up the feather and felt an electric shock in her fingers. "Oww! Are you sure, Harvey? This thing seems evil."

"Not evil, Mattie, just so full of pain. Maybe that's the same thing," he said as he took the shiny black feather from her.

An image began to form again on the screen as Harvey concentrated on slowing and deepening his breathing. This time the child was older, maybe two or three. She was skinny, dirty, playing outside in a patch of dirt in front of a rundown house.

"See if you can get any closer to the girl. Concentrate on the details of her hair, her clothes," Mattie whispered.

Harvey stared at her head, tangled blonde hair, matted like it hadn't seen a comb in a long time. Streaky smears on her face. She'd been crying and wiping her eyes with dirty hands. An old stretched-out brown sweater hung on her slight frame like a dress. She sat poking a twig over and over into a hole. Mattie noticed tears rolling down Harvey's cheeks. "Mattie, she's so alone. It's like her soul is just gone."

Harvey twirled the feather between his fingers and the scene faded. He kept his breathing steady and the girl returned. This time she was about twelve, standing in a filthy bathroom, in front of a dirty mirror, hair dye bottles askew on the sink. Harvey's vantage point was as if he were inside the mirror, looking back at the girl as she pulled up chunks of her wet, black hair and hacked them off with a scissors, dropping them into the sink.

"Oh Goddess! That's Diva!" Mattie whispered. "You're seeing Diva's story. She was Kali's friend. They ran away from Heartscape together."

"She was in the other dream too, I think," Harvey said. "She was the bird, the bird that turned into the girl and held up her finger like a gun."

Mattie and Harvey gazed at the scene on the screen for a while. Mattie had never seen something transmitted from the vantage point of a dreamer's absent soul. She was spellbound.

"Diva," Harvey called softly, but the girl kept cutting her hair and staring into the mirror. A heavyset older man, his belly bulging over his belt, stopped in the doorway and looked at the girl. Harvey started, forgetting that he couldn't be seen.

"Why'd ya do that? Now you look like a witch!" The man grunted and moved out of view.

The girl brought the scissors down against the crook of her arm and pushed the blade into her flesh until she drew blood. She winced and closed her eyes, a slight smile playing on her lips. Harvey moaned in pain and the screen faded to black.

Mattie watched as Harvey's body began to convulse. She adjusted the headset and straps across his chest and legs so he couldn't hurt himself and switched the dial to check his vital signs. "Harvey, it's a good thing you're strong and healthy," Mattie murmured as she watched the read out that showed his heart rate.

After some time Harvey's body began to settle into a quiet trance state. As Mattie turned the screen back to scan mode to watch where Harvey's soul was going, she found her own memories of Diva flooding back. She and Kali were troublemakers from the start at the Farm. The two were inseparable; laughing at their own private jokes, seeming to mock whatever Crone was speaking. Kali was a little older than Mattie and her competitiveness for Aurelia's attention had turned Mattie off. Growing up at the Farm, home schooled by Aurelia and the Crones, Mattie wasn't used to the edgy cynicism that Kali displayed. Mattie was already adept at monitoring the SAC process and was assigned to get Kali started. Aurelia hoped they might become friends, being close in age, and maybe Kali would soften up around Mattie. It quickly became clear that Kali couldn't handle the SAC detox work. She was used to relying on her intellect. The detox flooded her with emotions and images — about her father, about Rav Babka and her mother — and, while she bragged about talking circles around countless therapists, after the work in the SAC, she just shut down.

"Maybe I manipulated her time in the SAC a little to get her to go," Mattie thought. "Goddess, forgive me!"

Just then Aurelia knocked lightly and entered the room with Sarah Leaf, their hair still damp from the immersion in the pond.

"Oh, Momma, it's all my fault!" Mattie blurted out. "When Kali was here I think I overdid her in the SAC to get her to leave. I couldn't stand how she fought with you, and you let her! I was jealous of the attention you gave her and hated how she disrespected you and the other Crones."

Aurelia hugged Mattie to her and sighed, "Baby, not a one of us is perfect on this earth, and that is our biggest blessing. Everything we don't do right makes room for someone else to bring her gift, her light. Our limitations let us reach out for help to one another. And now Harvey has to help us find Eve."

"Oh, Momma, it looks like Harvey's been channeling Diva's story. So much pain, so much hurt, I didn't see any love at all. No one was there for her. I didn't know, I didn't know." Mattie sobbed.

Aurelia put her hands on Mattie's shoulders. "Now look here, none of us held those girls perfectly, not you and certainly not me, Goddess knows.

Lots of human pain can't be undone in just a few encounters, and different folks need different means. And sometimes love just magnifies the pain."

Aurelia thought back to how determined she had been to get to Kali.

"Sometimes, maybe most times, we just need to witness with a little distance and make a space for each one to unfold her own mystery. Do you agree, Rabbi Sarah?" Aurelia said to Sarah Leaf. "I do for sure," she nodded and handed Mattie and Aurelia each a cup of tea. "Now let's attend to Harvey and see what we can do to help his work."

The three women settled down behind Harvey's head. He was breathing lightly and peacefully. Mattie adjusted the dials to tune into Harvey's journey in the imaginal realm. As the image came into focus, they saw Harvey standing next to Diva in her present form.

"Oh my, what is he doing in her story?" Aurelia was alarmed. A cardinal rule of SAC work and dream scan was that the witness not change the content of the story in the dreamtime. Aurelia was firm in her belief that no one in a human body could know enough to presume to alter the dreamtime of another: change, forgiveness, and reparation had to be made in the body's present tense and only when initiated by the dreamer and with the dreamer's consent.

"Harvey knows better than to try and change the past, doesn't he, Mattie? Or is he being just like a man and assuming he knows what to do, just taking action without reflection?"

The women watched the images come into focus.

"Oh, Momma, look, he's okay. His soul is shadowing Diva like an angel or a spirit guide might do. She can't see him."

"Well, he doesn't know how to do that work!" Aurelia cried. "That's the work of a shaman, for Goddess sake! We need to bring him back here right now!"

Mattie looked steadily at her mother and said quietly, "No, I don't think so, Momma. You've said it yourself: We don't know exactly what the

Shift will look like or who will do what. Harvey had a clear and pure intention and invoked the protection of the Source when we started. He was way more focused than I was, let me tell you. Let's trust that and just hold the space for him to do his work. Isn't that the point of the whole thing?"

Mattie looked to Sarah Leaf, "Rabbi, what do you think? Can you give us your perspective?"

"Well, Jewish tradition holds that by witnessing from the outside, as we are doing for Harvey, one can never fully appreciate what goes on in any healing work. We must just hold the space and trust the bond between the person in the experience and the Source.

"I imagine, Aurelia, some people might have thought we'd lost our minds if they had seen us dip ourselves naked in the pond just now." Sarah smiled at the two women.

Aurelia gazed at her daughter. "My goodness, gal, you have claimed your power!" To herself she whispered "Ahimsa" for Harvey's sake.

As the women watched the screen, a translucent figure of Harvey knelt down next to Diva's limp body cradled in Kali's arms. As Harvey touched Diva's shoulder, the pair was enveloped in glowing light. Next, he placed one hand on Diva's forehead and the other on her solar plexus. Harvey's body in the SAC began to writhe and shake. The women looked from his body in the chair to the image of him on the screen and saw a stream of screaming dark images flying out of Diva's body, as up through Harvey's hands and out the top of his head, his eyes, his mouth streamed a pulse of golden light. Finally both streams began to ebb and fade and Harvey's body shaking in the chair began to quiet. The images on the screen faded to static. Harvey's vital signs were slow but steady.

Mattie looked at Aurelia and said, "Guess it's true: You don't know who will be called to do what!"

"May I say a prayer?" Sarah Leaf asked. "The Shehekianu blesses the moment, and this is an awesome moment!"

"Please, Sistah, do!" Aurelia said.

"Let's all stand around Harvey," Sarah instructed, "and just lightly touch our palms together. He is channeling healing energy and it can align all of us for the highest good. 'Shehekianu, vikiamanu, vihigianu, lazman hazeh. Let us acknowledge the presence of Shekinah in this moment and may She protect us as She is protecting Harvey, revealing mysteries, and holding us as witnesses to this Tikkun, this healing. Amen."

"Thank you, Sarah," Mattie hugged her. "You're like a big sister to me, I am so grateful for your presence here."

"All right, now," Aurelia refocused the women, "let's not forget that we don't know what Kali and Diva may be cooking up or what has befallen Eve. Can you get a GPS reading on where they are?"

"Of course!" Mattie replied as she punched some information into the SAC system via a keyboard and brought up a split screen: one side showed an aerial view, the other a near view of some buildings with map coordinates. "They must have Eve there, wherever they are. Harvey, you are something else!"

Mattie pushed a button that split the image on the screen into quadrants and brought the buildings into better focus. "It looks like some kind of factory or industrial park." There was a golden pulsing glow in one corner of the aerial view and Mattie sharpened the focus on it. "Okay, let's get a street map of this. It has to be the place."

"Do you want me to go with you?" Sarah asked Mattie and Aurelia. "Shouldn't Harvey have time to rest and recover?"

Aurelia looked at Mattie, "Your call, we're in new territory here."

Mattie put her hand on Harvey's head, "No, he's coming around and I think he'll want to go. Momma, you okay with this?"

Aurelia held out her arms to her daughter, "Source, protect you both, of course I am. Sarah and I will prepare things for your return."

23

Kali's energy seemed to create a sort of force field around her and Diva. The rest of us backed off. We watched as she cradled Diva's head and began to sob, "You stupid little shit, you fucked up little jerk, don't you dare die."

I looked at Andrea who sat with her knees pulled up but still holding firmly onto the stun gun. As Kali cradled Diva in her arms, I thought of Bourgeareau's Pieta. I wondered if Kali had ever seen that painting, and I wished there was some way to mirror Kali's compassion back to her. This crack in her diabolic façade was a great relief, but I was still convinced she was stark raving mad and worried about what she might do next.

"Andrea," I whispered, "did you really cancel Kali's plan? Is that what you were so nervous about?"

"Yes," Andrea smiled wanly, "but I don't know if all the women will take it seriously, I don't know if they got the message…"

"Can you get online and check?" I had the feeling there wasn't much time to waste. Andrea went over to a computer and sat down.

I heard a sharp click and turned to see Diane with a revolver pressed to the back of Andrea's head.

"Do we really have to go through this again?" Shotgun asked plaintively. "Look, Diane, so far no one's been killed, Diva's coming around and I'm starving. Put down the gun and let's order some Thai food." Diane blinked and dropped her hand.

Diva was sitting up and Kali was stroking her head, continuing to swear at her, but smiling now through her tears. Diva looked different somehow: maybe the fall had jostled her internal wiring a bit. "Yeah, I'm starved!" she said.

"Thai food is good," I said, "but it's vegan pizza night at the Farm. How long would it take to drive there? I couldn't really tell how long our drive was, being knocked out and all."

Andrea looked at me sympathetically. "Sorry about that. We did use a plant-based sedative. It shouldn't cause any lasting harm." I just started laughing and couldn't stop.

"I can fly there in half an hour," Diva piped up and Kali thumped her head. "You're not flying anywhere."

Andrea stood up, stun gun in hand. "Vegan pizza sounds really good to me. That's it. I'm driving.

"Kali, I've just sent a brief email to the Nemesis worldwide network in your name, telling them we've had an emergency and the website will be down for a while. I said you'd had a really important new revelation and you'd be sharing it soon, but in the meantime, you send your love to all."

Diva looked up at Kali, "You name is Charity, isn't it?"

"From the Latin, 'caritas,' love from the heart," I added. Diane rolled her eyes.

"What about the guns?" I asked, figuring someone would discover the shotgun blast to the ceiling and find out what Kaliendo Enterprises was all about.

"Let's take 'em down to the Farm," Diva suggested. "I bet those Crones can do some kind of spell with them or melt them down and make them into jewelry."

Kali had been silent during the light-hearted banter. "I can't go to the Farm," she said flatly.

"Why not?"

"Aurelia hates me."

I looked at Kali, Diva cuddled in her lap like one of those seagulls pulled out of an oil spill, disheveled and seeming very frail. The dust from the shotgun blast to the ceiling continued to sift down on them frosting Diva's spiky hair and Kali's black curls, seeming to age them before my eyes.

"She's got a pretty big heart," I began. "I'm no expert on Aurelia, I usually pass out when she comes into a room, but I really don't think 'hate' is in her repertoire."

"Reper-what?" Diva said, rubbing her head.

"Well, from everything I've learned about them so far, the women at the Farm have been building a movement based on love for a pretty long time. Since before we were born," Andrea seemed determined to shift things in favor of a trip to the Farm. "We can all get into the truck if we squeeze a little."

"I think Andrea's right, for a change," Diva looked up at Kali. "We would be okay there: the Crones are all into strays and outcasts. And take-out sucks."

The hate and all the energy seemed to have drained out of the rest of the group, but Kali just sat there staring off into space. The knock on the head seemed to have calmed Diva, or maybe just finally being held close by Kali did that. My annoyance and hunger had dissolved into a sadness so strong it was paralyzing.

No one spoke for a while. I just kept looking at Bourgeareau's painting, the sliver of moon in the dark sky, the graceful curve of the woman's body. Could he have imagined women like us, I wondered? Women who wanted to do the right thing in a complicated and messy world, trying to love each other and tripping over our rhetoric like men did, like anyone in power did, I guess? Just as it seemed we might all nod off like the last scene in some surreal version of *Babes in Toyland*, there was a knock on the door.

"Shit! The watchman?" Diane got up but Andrea was closer to the door. She smoothed back her hair, squared her shoulders and opened the door slightly.

"Hello? Oh! Come in."

It was Mattie and Harvey. Andrea stepped aside and they squinted as they entered the dim conference room.

"Eve, are you okay?" Harvey asked but then looked past me to Kali and Diva still entwined on the floor. "Wow! There you are! This is amazing. You were both in the dream... I, I saw your —"

Mattie interrupted, "Hello, Kali, Diva, blessings on you both. It's been a long time. Is that a rifle? Great Goddess! What have you all been up to?"

"We're busted," said Diva, trying to get up.

"Nobody's hurt?" Harvey looked at me hopefully.

"Not physically, no. Diva might have a concussion, but I think everyone is feeling a little bit wounded."

"And hungry." Diva was on her feet now, staring curiously at Harvey. "I know I've seen you when I flew around the Farm, but I think I might have seen you when I was passed out, too."

Mattie and Kali walked toward each other warily. Then Mattie just grabbed the other woman and started hugging. "Girl, I am so sorry! I know I wasn't your friend at the Farm before, but, Goddess, it's good to see you!"

"Can we go get pizza now?" Diva was tugging on Harvey's sleeve, like the man must be in charge.

He couldn't take his eyes off Diva and said, "Mattie, can we go now? We can figure all this out back at the Farm, don't you think?"

"What about the guns?" Andrea asked.

Mattie took a small pouch out of her jacket pocket and took a dousing stone out of the pouch. "Are there more than this one?"

Diane and Andrea nodded. "They're here," Andrea pointed to a large footlocker under the table. She and Diane pulled it out into the room.

Mattie held the end of the slender chain that had a teardrop-shaped piece of jasper on the end of it over the footlocker. We all watched as the stone rocked back and forth and then slowly began to circle clockwise. After a few seconds she said, "Yes, we can take them with us. Let's get the other one packed into the trunk and anything else that has a dangerous energy to it and get downstairs."

Andrea took charge and also got some computer files and notebooks. Kali just looked numb.

"What about the painting?" I asked.

"What?" Startled, Kali looked at me. "It's okay. Our rent is paid up and no one comes in here. The Saudis don't get it for a while."

"The Saudis?" Mattie looked at me quizzically.

"I'll explain later."

She rolled her eyes and gave me a hug. "I can't wait to hear all about it. Eve, I'm so glad you're okay!"

24

The next few days were hard. Kali, Diva, Andrea, Diane, and Susan moved into the Farm and the community began to find ways to accept them. It got easier once they stopped wearing their dark glasses indoors and exchanged their leather pants for sweats.

The weapons were brought into the barn and arranged on a table at the front of the room where the artwork was usually displayed. The guns — AK 47s, Uzis, handguns, even an antiquated shoulder-held grenade launcher — were laid out on velvet runners. Aurelia insisted that they be given a central place in order that the women could witness them properly.

"Nothing transforms like witness," she said.

Some of the women objected, terrified by the black steel objects that represented so much suffering all over the world. Especially those who were refugees from Columbia's drug wars and the gang violence of the inner cities. Some women felt compelled to touch the guns, hold them up, sight them. Guns were familiar in their lives and represented safety or sport; these women had grown up in rural areas and had fathers or brothers who were hunters, responsible and serious in their use of guns. The Crones held council for days about the weapons.

"We must be with What Is!" Elsie declared when some women suggested burying the guns or dismantling them right away.

"Beat the swords into plowshares," many insisted. It was the first big issue in some time that aroused so many different points of view.

"We can't just push them away. We must hear their stories first, honor them and all the many things they represent — before we try to change them," was Aurelia's firm declaration after listening to the many voices and conferring with the Council. She encouraged the women to touch the rifles, hold the pistols, and sift their hands through the baskets of ammunition that had been removed from each chamber — if they could bear to.

The women were gathered to begin the work of witness, learning and, eventually, transformation. Aurelia stood before them, as she had so many times. "Guns have punctuated my life," she began. "As most of you know, the police in Chicago killed my father in the '60s. My husband William was killed in Tikrit, Iraq, while serving as a captain in the U.S. Army. I am no stranger to gun violence yet I feel sure we must be brave enough to take our time and be guided by the Divine Source in how we approach the work that lies before us."

Some of the women grumbled that Kali and the others had upset the spirit of the Farm by bringing the guns and should be turned away.

Aurelia answered those charges: "Everything you see, yes, even these weapons, has been fashioned out of natural resources from Mother Earth herself, designed by human creativity and constructed by the hands of men and, yes, by women like ourselves. The stories contained in these objects are many-layered and dense. We must commune with them and understand the energy that has gone into their making.

"We seek their counsel just as we would consult the rivers and the trees to guide us in our actions. As the guns were made, so they can be unmade with new intentions. As we always do, we ask to be guided by compassion and discernment in our thoughts, words, and, especially, in our deeds." Aurelia noted that even the Crones of the Elder Council seemed subdued. "I know this is hard, Sisters, but the Source will guide us."

Rabbi Leaf asked to speak. "Trying to unravel the many strands of story and truth in weapons is an enormous healing for the whole world. Let's take our time and be patient. This is a Tikkun of the highest order, ahimsa, Sisters."

"Ahimsa," they replied and they set to work.

***

Kali became very ill almost immediately upon getting to the Farm. While everyone else was eating delicious vegetable pizzas served up by Gina, Kali asked for tea and just stared into space. She hadn't even seen Aurelia up close, but simply caught a glimpse of her across the field and fell into a fever, became delirious. She was moved to a hermitage, a tiny healing hut in a grove of trees some distance from the main buildings and was ministered to by women taking turns around the clock. Andrea volunteered to sit a vigil but the women encouraged her to take her own respite and sort through all she had experienced as part of Nemesis, to reflect on what had led her to Kali's movement and how that could inform Cronation, and to explore what she might want to do next.

Harvey asked to do more SAC work on Kali's behalf. He had entered Diva's reality, why not Kali's? He made his case before the Crone Council. "Look, it didn't harm me, did it? All I did was follow the images that showed up."

Mattie spoke on Harvey's behalf. "I was there — without the work that Harvey did we might never have found out where they took Eve. Who knows what might have happened?"

"But it is so classically heroic, so old-school shamanistic!" Aurelia had fumed to the Council after Mattie and Harvey left them to consider. "Aren't we falling into the old story? For Goddess sake! 'Harvey to the rescue,' man as hero, white man at that! We've spent decades building up our own women to claim their power and wisdom."

"And so you have, and so we have," answered Elsie. "From how I see it, Harvey didn't do one thing alone. You initiated him into Cronation yourself, Aurelia, when you forgave him for running over your Momma and allowed him the healing of restitution. He has worked here as a loyal member of the community, offering his skills and labor in the most humble way. Mattie taught him everything he knows about the SAC work."

"That's right, Aurelia," Rabbi Leaf added, "he and Mattie worked so closely together, they are equally responsible here for everything that took place. You heard Mattie: Harvey stated a clear intention to be in service to the Source."

Marty spoke next, saying gently, "Aurelia, can't you see the role your own daughter played here? How can you overlook Mattie?"

Aurelia had to concede that the others were right. Mattie and Harvey certainly worked together in concert.

"I hear you, Sisters, I do, but something bothers me. I just can't put my finger on it. There is some piece of this just outside my awareness that is telling me to be cautious, that we don't have the whole picture yet. I don't want to punish Harvey for happening to be in a man's body, Goddess knows, but something doesn't feel quite right."

"That's all right, Aurelia," Elsie touched her hand. "You rest and take your time, maybe get with Phoebe for a spell. We don't need to solve this today. Everyone is safe for now and we must remember to let things unfold. For one thing, Kali is still healing; with her presence here, we must respect her healing and not violate her energy field no matter how dire it seems. We must trust the guidance of the Source and maybe that's what Harvey needs to work with now. You certainly learned how pouring your love into little Kali before just caused her pain. She is not here to be rescued, that is an old trap."

Elsie's words calmed Aurelia.

"As always, dear mother, you bring us a perspective that we need.

How grateful we are for your wisdom." Aurelia bowed to the assembled women. "We must all spend some time reflecting and each be guided to right action. I'll take my leave for now."

Aurelia herself had yet to witness the weapons, though she knew she must. It still shocked her to realize the paramount role guns had played in her own life: her father murdered by police, her husband cut down by sniper fire. Her whole life was dedicated to peace and transformation, to the work of visioning a world without war. A world where men, women, and children would not be menaced by violence but free to create from love and wholeness.

She dropped into a chair and closed her eyes. "Show me, Source, what am I missing? Where am I blind?"

As she settled herself in the front room alone, "Gratitude" wrote itself in Aurelia's mind's eye like a finger tracing it on a steamy window. She heard laughter in the distance. Aurelia looked out the window and saw Andrea, Susan, and Diane coming up the path carrying something on a tray. They knocked on the door and came in.

"Gina helped us bake a cake this morning." Andrea put the tray down in front of Aurelia, white frosted, with the word "gratitude" in red letters. With Aurelia, the Source rarely wasted any time in answering her pleas for guidance.

"We are so glad to be here, it's like heaven, really. We are so grateful to you for taking us in, and especially for taking care of Kali, after what we did, kidnapping Eve and all. Do you think she'll be alright?"

"Oh, children! Come in and sit down. Let's have some of this delicious cake together. The Source always finds a way to send sweets to help us absorb difficult lessons. Diane, bring that teapot over here; I'm sure it's still warm from our Council meeting. Susan, will you fetch the cups?"

Once they were settled Aurelia looked from one face to the next. The three young women glanced down shyly at their teacups, but none of them passed out like Kali and Eve often had.

"You all know that Kali was here before?" They all nodded. "She was, and so was Diva. It was awhile back, and I'm afraid we didn't know how to meet their pain very well. Now, I take it from what I've heard, you say that each one of you have suffered some kind of pain in your lives and that's what led you to Kali, is that so?"

Andrea spoke up. "Yes, Mam. She has — had — a website where she spoke about women who had been harmed and exploited banding together for justice. There was this beautiful image of a woman on the site and she seemed to have a plan, or it seemed like it to me. She answered all my emails in such detail.

"When I first found Nemesis, I was in a bad relationship and when I read Kali's 'Steps to Freedom,' I got really excited. I left my boyfriend when she invited me to join; he used to beat me, but I never felt I could leave before. She said they were about to start actions to change the world and liberate women, and that sounded grand to me."

"What exactly was it that called you?" Aurelia asked.

"'Do you believe in justice?'" Diane spoke. "Those were the words above the image of the beautiful woman in the painting on her website. It was those two things together got me."

The other women nodded.

"She spoke to your intuitive self," Aurelia murmured. "She is so gifted, that girl. Such a way with words! You know the term 'justice,' the word to justify, means to bring things into alignment, and in ancient times the word 'just' signified a sacred formula."

The women nodded, thrilled just to be in Aurelia's presence and hear her speak.

"Well, except once we got there," Andrea continued the story, "she seemed different than in her messages. I thought there was a place, you know, some place to live and work — but there was just this office she rented in a half-vacant industrial park and we all stayed there, in sleeping bags. We got take-out food and reheated it in the microwave for days. Kali had a membership at the YWCA and we would take turns going there to shower. She taught us how to use the stun gun right away but mostly we listened to Kali talk. All of it sort of made sense and a lot of her ideas were, well, complicated — and she's so smart…. Then one day she told us about the Farm and how kidnapping Eve was the thing we needed to do because all of you here were standing in the way of justice."

"And 'justice'? What was that going to look like?" Aurelia was pretty sure she knew but she wanted to hear how Kali had explained her plan to these women and made it make sense. None of them seemed stupid, and they certainly seemed educated and probably more privileged than the average woman at the Farm.

"Well, she talked a lot about killing men. Sort of like it was a religious act, a sacrifice," Susan began.

"I had never heard of the Hindu Goddess, Kali, so when she explained the sword of Truth, it sort of made sense. She made it seem like we'd even be doing the men a favor, you know, releasing them from this harmful existence," Andrea explained.

"But then she and Diva would joke about it other times," Diane added.

"Kali kept a list of men — dictators, religious leaders like that Rav Babka — different men around the world who she felt were exploiting their power, men she read about in the news, I even think she had her own father on the list for a while but she crossed him off."

Andrea spoke, "I think once we got there and it wasn't just her and Diva and a website, it got too real. She had gotten the guns by then and I think kidnapping Eve was something to do, maybe instead of going on a shooting spree."

"Oh my Great Goddess, what is going on in that girl's mind? A shooting spree? You all must excuse me. Finish your cake and tea and relax here as long as you like. Thank you so much. You have given me a piece of the story that I need to meditate on. I have to go see about a few things but, you can be sure, it is gratitude we must be about."

"Then we can stay?" Andrea asked. "Here at the Farm, I mean."

"Stay? Of course you can stay! We are blessed to have you join us. The Source works in astonishing ways. Each of you brings something that all of us need to learn. I am deeply grateful for your presence, your honesty, and your compassion."

Aurelia stood up. "Blessings now," she said and smiling, fixed each woman in turn in her gaze and just lightly touched the pain that each one carried. "I must go now, but you all stay here as long as you like," Aurelia focused on her own breathing, noting how anxious she now felt. She wanted to find Harvey and figure out what the knot in her gut was all about.

"Aurelia," Andrea called after her, "when Kali is well, will you have her arrested?"

"Gracious, no! We will try to do better by her this time and help her heal her pain."

The three women smiled in relief, and Aurelia left to put her own thoughts to rest.

25

"I think we need to bring some more men here," Harvey was sitting next to Mattie on the hill leaning against the stone that marked Phoebe's grave.

"We? Why?" Mattie was pushing an acorn along the ground with a twig.

"Balance or something; men need to learn this stuff too."

"You just lonely for some male companionship? None of the Tantra boys like to drink beer?" Harvey looked into Mattie's eyes and she saw he was serious.

"I'm sorry, Harvey, I don't mean to make light of you."

"Make light of me! Mattie, don't you see, that's exactly what Aurelia's been doing — making me come into contact with my own light! When I was in the SAC chair and saw all the awful things that had happened to Diva..." He stopped as his voice cracked.

"I never knew," Harvey whispered softly, "what it could be like for a girl like Diva, no one to look after her. Those men who harmed her, they didn't know the damage they were doing to her."

"So you're letting them off the hook?" Mattie was incredulous.

"No, no, of course not, it's just that when I saw the men in each situation, it was like they were made of stone or cement. They were trying to get Diva's light into themselves. They were using her like a drug or something. They had so much darkness in themselves, so much pain, like in secret. Nobody saw it or could name it or show them what to do with it."

"And Diva learned to fly to get away from them. She just left them with her body while her soul took off in the form of the raven," Mattie said.

"And when they didn't get any light, just her empty shell, that stirred up the pain in them and they got pissed off. They tried to unload some of their darkness into her. In their frustration, they beat her up or looked for others to use. But Mattie, those men are like solid concrete. Can any amount of light break that up?"

"I don't know for sure, Harvey, but I don't believe the Source creates anything that can't be redeemed. That there are some that are irredeemable, that's what Kali believed, and that's why she wanted to just kill some men. Violence is always a low-level attempt at transformation. Sarah Leaf says there is a spark of the Divine in every person and nothing can destroy it."

Harvey was quiet, crying silently at all the pain in the world, suddenly beginning to see the connection: violence to try to get the light you crave, violence to defend your light from being stolen, violence to break that sense of being made of concrete…"Mattie, I don't think you really get it. What I mean is, men are in trouble. I just think of the men I know. None of them are such bad guys, but I recognize that quality of becoming like solid rock as they get older. None of us were like that as little boys. At least not in the beginning"

"Look, Harvey, I know that men are in trouble. The whole Cronation movement is about learning from the male misuse of power and learning how to do it differently."

"But is it different, really?" Harvey challenged "How can it be different? Without men involved, it's just another one-sided solution. You have all these advanced energetic ways of doing things, ancient wisdom and high tech and all. So if the Old Order falls like you say it will — okay, like it is falling — and you step in and take over with all your advanced stuff, how is that any different from the white man overpowering the Indians with rifles? Your power over our power — as a way of doing things, which is wearing out and not working so well anymore. Okay, it was always misguided... but you see what I mean?"

Mattie pushed herself up to her elbows. "We have advanced systems of thought, not just technology. We have conflict resolution, the ethic of care, understanding of interconnectedness, deep respect for all beings..."

"Except men. Who you treat like a retarded sub-species. Seriously, Mattie, what are the men going to do? How do they — I mean we — find meaning? We didn't set out to wreck the planet!"

Just then Aurelia came into view marching purposefully up the hill calling out, "Harvey, Mattie! Excuse me for interrupting. I need to get with both of you."

"Momma, Harvey thinks we need to have the men involved. Didn't Phoebe always say not to focus on the men, that that was an old trap and a distraction?"

"Well, Mattie, one thing we know for sure is something that might be right today doesn't mean it will be right forever! I suspect Harvey is having some insight on this, though the idea makes me want to lie down with a glass of gin and a cold rag on my forehead."

"Momma!"

Harvey looked at Mattie with just a tinge of "I told you so!"

"It came over me," Aurelia segued to what was on her mind, "when I was sitting with Andrea and those other women who'd been with Kali. They were attracted by Kali's message of justice in feminine form. That poor child had no notion of what that could become once it got beyond the idea stage. But the power to move people with your words is a strong tonic. It is very easy to get intoxicated by that drink! When those women showed up in the flesh, when it wasn't just her and Diva fantasizing, well, Kali's system just couldn't handle it. That place between imagination and action is where so many get tripped up!"

"Momma, I'm confused. What does Kali's breaking down have to do with bringing men to the Farm?"

"She's brought the 'men' with her. The 'men' are in her, as they are in all of us. All the things we call 'male' in our confusion about power and what it is, all that is alive in that girl with no critique, no examination through a lens of compassion. I believe if we can help her detox, her story will teach us volumes about what we need to know."

"So real men aren't needed after all," Harvey said mournfully.

Aurelia turned to Harvey. "Oh, dear brother, no. That's where you come in, Harvey. You've seen Diva's life and how the men fit into it, the harm they caused, and the pain they are in. You learned from it; you can translate from what you witnessed of male experience, and distill that knowing, adding it into the Crone wisdom. Eve has another piece. She understands some of the same things from a different angle. We're getting something here that has been just out of reach for so long, so, so long! Bless you, Harvey, for the courage to break the rules!"

"But I wasn't breaking the rules, Aurelia, I was following your greatest rule, 'Ask the Source for guidance and follow the signposts She sets up for you.'"

Aurelia looked at Harvey and Mattie. "How could I have missed it? You two have made the Hieros Gamos!"

Harvey looked puzzled.

"Hieros Gamos, the sacred marriage," Aurelia put a hand on each of their heads and stood between them. She saw figures of dark, male and female dancing together. They then changed to figures of light, pixelating and dissolving, flowing into one another, the passage of dark into light energy in constant flux. Aurelia whispered, "What you two have accomplished in your own bodies and souls together is what the wise have sought since the beginning of time." She lifted her hands from their heads to the sky: "Blessings and thanks, Source of All."

"Look, a rainbow!" Mattie pointed to the sky. The rainbow was circular and in motion. Within the circle they could see what looked like a party of light beings; they could hear silvery, far away laughter. They watched for a long time until the image faded.

"Women look at men and see power; men look in the mirror and see fear," Aurelia said.

"If they see anything at all," Harvey said quietly. "Many of us are so frozen our eyes don't see at all."

"And women," Aurelia added, "who are new to power look in the mirror and see justice, look at men and see mistakes and don't realize that just being in charge doesn't make you right. Or guarantee your actions won't cause more grief."

"But, Momma, what about all the wisdom you and the Crones have channeled? Are you saying it's wrong?"

"No, child, but I am saying it's incomplete. It would have been misguided of us to try and fix the men. Up until now, we haven't been really able to even see them clearly, see them as they see themselves, see them in ourselves. Harvey is right: without the men at the table we will end up imposing our will on them, just like they did to us when most of the power resided in their hands. Harvey — and to some degree Eve and Kali — can help us see men as they see themselves. New channels can open. This is a great breakthrough."

Aurelia heard the laughter again and smiled. It was Phoebe. "Girl, all of you get a gold star! Those of us up here have all been waiting for you to learn this lesson."

Aurelia could hear whoops and clapping. She arranged herself on the hill, her head near Phoebe's memorial stone, stretched out and closed her eyes.

"Come on, Harvey. Momma's tuning into Phoebe now, we can go see Kali."

Mattie bent down and kissed Aurelia's head.

Aurelia smiled, staring off in her trance state and said, "Bless you both. A woman in her power and a man in his true compassion."

26 ————————

It had been a weird few days. Andrea, Diane, and Susan were getting acclimated to the Farm. I could see myself in them as they melted in the love of the Crones, perked up with the fresh vegetarian food, and just relaxed in nature. Every time one of them saw me, I was in for hugs. They really felt bad about kidnapping me, but I kept saying, "All part of the plan, all part of the plan," as if I totally got what that meant.

I sat in with Mattie during Andrea's SAC session. She was ready for it and eager to get started. Mattie said it would help me integrate more of my own stuff if I witnessed someone else go through the process. Diane and Susan sat in too, but neither of them could stay the whole time without freaking out. Mattie wanted us to understand the procedure and wasn't rushing anybody. Andrea was more than ready and trusted Mattie completely after seeing how she embraced Kali at Nemesis headquarters.

Diva had declined detox so far because she figured she might lose her ability to shapeshift. No one pressured her to come and watch either. She hung out with Harvey, helping with the trees and, in raven form, played in the compost heap near the garden. Harvey was like a new big brother and she was really shining. No one was ready to explain all the ins and outs of Harvey's role in her healing yet. She often took a perch in one of the trees outside the hermitage, doing her own vigil for Kali in her soul's form as a bird.

"See how the screen goes gray when we get to a knot of pain?" Mattie was using a hand-held device to scan Andrea's body as she lay on a massage table. The screen showed areas of color as well as compressed gray space within the outline of her body that indicated where traumatic memories were held.

"Why is something like an elbow all gray?" Diane asked.

Mattie explained, "Suppose the perpetrator, in Andrea's case, her grandfather, sort of steered her toward the place in the basement where he abused her by guiding her by the elbow. First of all, her body records his touch and with it his intention — but secondly, her system compresses the memory into the tissue there. It's kind of like shoving something into the back of a closet or under the bed: it's not a place you use all the time so you don't notice and can forget what's there. That way it's easier to keep functioning and also not to freak out when she sees her grandfather in other situations, like Sunday dinner. Years later a woman might notice an ache or pain in a place in her body, usually when it's safe for memories to surface."

"How is that a good thing?" Diane wondered. "Maybe if she freaked out in the moment and said something someone would stop him."

"Not likely," Mattie replied. "Many children are punished if they try to draw attention to abuse; and sometimes their parent was abused as a child too, in many cases by the same perpetrator. The pressure to keep such knowledge at bay is often great. But it is also true that the silence adds to the grandfather's inner death; his light fades and fades and his body literally starts to calcify. With each generation, he keeps trying to get whatever he can from the girl children, to try to save himself. He has no real awareness of why he's doing this. But he can become like a dead weight that drags the whole family down without a word ever having been spoken."

Diane was angry. "That is so fucked up! This is why Kali thought killing men was a good idea. Just end the cycle."

Mattie looked at Diane and shook her head. "I know that seems sort of logical, but what if the grandfather was molested when he was a little boy? Would you feel the same way?"

Andrea spoke up from the table, "I don't think I would. I don't think it's so simple. What if his soul is just cut off there and then has to return to the same point and try again. Would anything be different?"

I wasn't really sure what I thought, it all seemed so complicated.

"Okay, that's enough for today," Mattie smiled at Andrea. "Rabbi Leaf will talk in her seminar later on today about the return of souls and what they need to heal and move on in their journeys. For now, let's all remember: none of us can see fully the experience of another so we strive for compassion in all our thoughts and actions."

I had Mattie's words echoing in my head as I left the session. I was assigned a shift to sit by Kali in the hermitage. I was a little nervous going to see Kali. Every time I remembered the gun going off at Nemesis, I still got chills. The women treated me like a hero when the story was told and retold around the Farm, but I didn't feel like one. After all, I had gotten to Nemesis by being drugged and rolled up in an afghan. Mattie said seeking out opportunities to be heroic isn't the point; it's what we do when we are thrust into circumstance that counts. According to Mattie, I'd done very well.

The Cronation initiatives were still going off as planned all over the world, according to the reports coming in, although it seemed to me that the date of December 21st was less and less likely for some major shift. But, what did I know? Well, I knew I felt strangely settled at the Farm. Lydia assured me she was in contact with Wentsouth and all had gone well for Candace in the Aversmith meeting. That seemed like news from Mars as far as I was concerned.

Now that she had shed her business attire, Lydia looked like a different person. She let her hair curl naturally with the dampness and didn't wear any makeup. She wore jeans and a sweater, but she still had that sense of calm that I was always drawn to at Wentworth and Wentsouth. And that scent of gardenia that I thought was perfume actually came from her close relationship with that flower, a member of the coffee family I learned. It seems the plant granted its perfume to Lydia to help counteract the energy of the coffee-jacked executives she worked with, myself included.

"I sent Candace some flowers from you and a note of congratulation as soon as you left. And I'm off on medical release, my usual cover," Lydia said. She laughed when I looked confused. "Oh, Honey, don't you worry; this will all make sense by and by." By and by, huh?

I got to the hermitage to relieve the morning shift; Gina and Rae were getting ready to leave. "How is she?" I asked.

"Oh, she's still in a deep trance state." Rae pushed Kali's dark curls off her forehead. "I got her to take some broth, but she didn't really come to full consciousness; her physical system is still unwinding. It will take a while."

"Oh, Eve!" Gina cooed. "Give me a hug! It's so good to have you here! All those years we couldn't get through to you about Cronation, and now you're finally here!"

"Yeah, well, I still don't exactly get it, but I guess I'm glad too." I was anxious about my duties and wanted to refocus my attention. "What am I supposed to do here?"

Rae handed me a small device as she stood up. "Oh, you can sit here by her bed or over on the couch. We are monitoring her vital signs and recording her dreams. You can draw or meditate, some women knit. The idea is to be a silent witness. Here's a journal — you just jot down anything that comes into your mind while you sit here."

"Why?"

"Well," Gina began, "as Kali's life experience becomes uncompressed, she is sending out energetic signals. Each one of us has different receptive frequencies that make us sensitive to different information. So, when you feel called to respond, you just write it down."

"Write it down." I felt extremely dubious.

"Yes," Rae continued, "her system receives your response. It's a form of mirroring, of mutual recognition that is vital to healing."

"What if I write the wrong thing? What if…"

"Don't worry, Eve. Just write your intention at the top of the page next to the date along with your name. You can read what some of the other women wrote to get the idea. The Source is guiding all of us. This is part of understanding our interconnectedness. Kali is actually functioning as a great teacher in this state."

Gina was straightening the tea things. I was a little bit miffed that Rae and Gina seemed to have as much command of this lingo as Mattie. Could I really have missed all the cues they had sent me over the years about this whole alternative universe that I was totally blind to?

"If you say so." I could feel I was stalling a bit. "Is somebody going to stay here with me and make sure I don't screw up?" I really did not want to be responsible for throwing a wrench into some cosmic healing process.

"No need, babe," Rae said. "After the Crones meditated on your role in everything that brought Kali here and derailed Nemesis, they agreed that she was calling out for you energetically, and they feel it's best if you're here alone with her, like you two have a similar vibration."

I must have looked upset because Rae added, "Of course, you aren't in a destructive spiral the way Kali was, Eve. You just have some insight into the male model and so does she. The Crones think if you just sit here and practice witnessing and become attuned to Kali's vibration, we'll learn something we need and it will help her heal as well."

"Yeah, well, where's the call button in case of emergency? My first encounter with this woman wasn't exactly a tea party." I was definitely into full stalling mode now.

"There's a phone to the main building. And here's a beeper direct to Mattie if you need her. Relax, Eve!" Rae said firmly. "It may not be a party but there's tea on the table. It's all good!" Gina kissed me on the cheek, and she and Rae left.

I sat down on the couch. I could see the late afternoon light on Kali's face, see her chest gently rising and falling. At least she's breathing.

27

S o, Momma, what about it?" Aurelia asked Phoebe. "I see now that Mattie and Harvey are working as a blessed team, but why do I worry about his taking over somehow? I have no reason for such a thought."

"Well, Aurelia, think about it — old story templates don't disappear, they remain contained within the organism which expands to open to new stories. They fade eventually from disuse, like paths not walked on, but there is always the potential to activate them by giving them energy — either through fear, when we tend to regress, or when we end up spending time with too many folks of a lower vibration for too long — if our own stage isn't well-fixed. But, child, it's not Harvey I'm worried about at all. It's the 'Harvey' in you! Let me make myself clear: the male or active energy in you — your own 'yang' — if you like. You are doing pretty well moving into your 'Moses Moment,'" Phoebe counseled, "but instead of worrying about leadership right now, you ought to be looking at your own loose ends."

"My 'Moses Moment'? My loose ends?"

"Moses didn't get it either until his father-in-law, Jethro, told him he needed to delegate more as governing the Israelites got more complex." Phoebe elucidated, "Now, I've spoken about this at some length with Moses. He says it's hard to break out of doing everything yourself, because the group is comfortable with the leader leading. So everyone conspires to keep things the same. Leaders lead; followers follow. Whether we say so or not, you are still the leader, the honcho, and the queen. And don't get me wrong, it's correct and all good and the women love you for it but… Harvey and Mattie have accomplished something historic and they need to be supported in taking leadership as a balanced team. This is a new story, and it needs to develop and have the details come through being actualized by their living out their shared truth."

"That I can do, Momma, I can support them. Besides, it feels like they're way ahead of me in some ways. But the loose ends… You mean the guns, don't you?"

"Uh huh! I sure do. Back to basics, girl. You have to do as you say. You told everyone else the truth — that was a lovely speech — about how all the raw materials that went into the guns come from the Earth Herself, and your own experiences with guns and all. But there is so much compressed in there, so much between the lines, stuff that is unconscious collectively, even for those of you at a pretty high level of awareness. You must do the work that needs doing, Aurelia, and your doing makes the space bigger for the rest to do theirs and so forth."

"Thank you, Momma, I still love to hear your praise and teachings."

"I know, I know," Phoebe's voice was tender. "Believe me, that never ends for any of us. We all love some loving. Why don't you go get with those guns and see what they can tell you?"

"Why don't I indeed?"

"It's a common trap of leadership, Aurelia, to think that saying something is the same as doing it. That's a god-complex. Thinking that speaking the words means you have it in your bones. But it is not the same. Till you do it, you don't know it. And it causes all sorts of damage to say one thing and do another, so keep a keen eye out for it. I can't think of a soul over on this side that didn't think he knew more than he did."

"Look at Einstein, poor man!" Phoebe was on a roll. "He thought his own commitment to the grandeur and beauty of the universe was enough. Never dreamed that something like the atom bomb could come out of his penetration of the Great Mystery. He and Moses spend hours arguing: Al says, 'Moses, how could you have let the Israelites call themselves the 'Chosen People'? A fourth grader could have predicted the tsuris that would cause down the line... Moses says back to him, 'Look, Albert, I'm not the one that made it easy for any meshuganahs to blow up the world.' Then Einstein says: 'No, but just to think it's a fine option and somehow justified by God.' Oh how they do go on! They can go for hours like that until someone reminds them both of all the good they did do.

"Believe me, Aurelia, not to pressure you, dear, but there are a lot of souls over here with their fingers crossed, counting on you and the Crones to free them in ways they can't free themselves. Why, Einstein hasn't been allowed back in a body again because everyone knows he'd try to fix things and probably make them worse. He's so sorry about how it went with the bomb and all, but he's not the one to undo it. Remember this, Aurelia: For all the wonders of your intellect, your experience, your wisdom, your compassion, and your beautiful energy, it is through our limitations that each of us ultimately serves the highest good. You all don't have to try so hard to do good if you can remember that you simply are good, Source-certified 100% G-O-O-D. Whether you do good, well that is truly up to you. Remember to open up, surrender, and allow the Source to work through you in co-creative process. All forms of life are energy with skin in the game"

"Okay, Momma, okay, I'll go down there and see what I can learn."

"That's it, Darling. Everyone just has to pull an oar to keep things moving. Ahimsa now and blessings."

With Phoebe's sign off, Aurelia opened her eyes. "I sure hope so. Ahimsa, Momma." Feeling a bit like she'd been on spin cycle in a washing machine, Aurelia got up to get to work on whatever it was she had to learn from the guns. "Limitations," she murmured, "that seems like a funny thing for Momma to say, but I guess she knows what she's talking about."

Aurelia stood up, shook herself fully awake, and made her way down the hill to the barn. As she entered the building, she noticed the cool breeze indoors and saw several windows open. She turned to a group of women sitting at a table with several guns in front of them. "Sisters, it's December here, solar panels or not. We need not heat the great outdoors!"

"Oh, Aurelia, dear," said one, "the energy is so powerful, we just need to breathe."

"I see. Forgive me, I'm about to do some witnessing of my own, and I must admit I am a little nervous."

"Well, do be sure to state your intention clearly, that should help," another counseled. "But these things do have so much power, Aurelia; it staggers the mind!"

"Thank you, Sisters, I will take care."

Aurelia settled herself at the large table and was immediately overcome with dizziness. The guns were laid out on a midnight blue velvet cloth against which the dark metal nearly blended in. Someone had arranged the guns and some of the ammunition into a mandala, the barrels of the guns pointed toward the center of the circle, seeming to spiral, with the triggers all facing in the same direction. Bullets, some of them brass colored and conical, others blunt and dull gray, circled the guns as accents. In the center of the circular pattern of hardware someone had placed a rose.

The image of a young woman with flowers in her hair placing a daisy into the barrel of a rifle held by a terrified National Guardsman, who was probably her same age, flashed in Aurelia's mind: Kent State. Images of events at Mississippi's Jackson State College that had occurred just days later floated up next. "Oh my!" thought Aurelia, remembering the deaths of two African American students and injuries to countless more in another tragedy yet to be redeemed through compassionate witness. Protests of all kinds, peaceful and violent, wracked so many campuses in the 1970s. The image that tied them together was the image of the gun. Police at Jackson State, National Guardsmen at Kent State, all had wielded guns and rifles. Was that the only way elders could deal with the desire for change, equality and justice that was rising up in the young?

Aurelia knew that fear was the unexamined energy behind those incidents and many more. Had things changed now? Could the Crones help usher in an era of peace and compassion? Back then, few elders believed that 'make love, not war' could be a valid and real path for transformation, and their fear had allowed guns to be fired, young people to be killed. Of course, few knew what it meant to deeply, truly make love, either. To construct a world from love is no small matter, Aurelia thought, as she closed her eyes and took a deep breath. She was finding it hard to focus. Enid, the woman who had opened the windows, came over.

"We've found that if we took one gun off to another table, we could bear it," Enid offered. "The lot of them together was just too loud, had too much to say. These things pack a wallop in more ways than one. Putting them into a mandala helped to quiet them somewhat — they felt honored by the attention — but boy, are they ready to speak!"

"Well, of course, that makes sense, Sister. Thank you for sharing your wisdom with me." Aurelia steadied herself by grasping the edge of the table.

"Can I really go where I am being asked to go?" she murmured. "Well, thank Goddess, I'm not the only one doing this work!" Aurelia muttered to herself. "Here I have told these women to do something without having done it first myself. But bless them, they figured it out. Maybe that's part of what Momma means about shifting the leader role."

Aurelia picked up one handgun, rearranging the guns so the mandala still had a symmetrical shape, and took it over to a table by the window. The breeze felt good. She placed the weapon in front of her and took a journal from her bag.

She gazed out the window. She recalled the etymology of the word "weapon." In Old English it meant "instrument of fighting and defense." And also "penis."

"What is my intention? What is my resistance? *Intention* she wrote, and beneath that, *I witness this gun. I learn about it and what it has to teach me. I do no harm; I am not harmed. I conduct this inquiry for the highest good of all and to honor the Source. Please make me an instrument of your peace. Oh, and if you have something to teach me about limits — preferably not by having me faint here — I'd appreciate it.*

As soon as she finished writing her intention, Aurelia felt her resistance rise up in her like bile. "But, Goddess, why am I witnessing these instruments of destruction? Why not just bury them in the ground as some of the women want to do? Is there really something here to learn? Is this necessary?"

She closely looked at the gun she had chosen, a Browning high power semi-automatic 9 mm handgun. Lying on its side it resembled a dog's head. She saw an elongated face, like the famished Doberman, Max, that several of the women had rescued from the highway. The hammer looked like his docked ear, even the colors — the warm brown of the wooden grip and the dark metal of the gun body itself recalled the colors of Max's markings. Aurelia picked up the gun. The wood on the handle was striated with cross-hatching that felt warm and homely in comparison with the silky smoothness of the metal that felt for all the world like skin in a surprising and most seductive way. Aurelia stroked the metal barrel of the gun. Yes, there was no doubt: Eros was present in this object.

A great deal of loving energy and attention had been invested in guns. No nonsense, no decorations, yet the Browning was an elegant object, she had to admit. The clip containing the bullets would fit into the grip, making it even heavier than it felt now. Heavy, almost dead weight —

the way a baby feels when it is deeply sleeping in your arms, or like a lover's back pressed up against yours in sound repose. Like a ripe pumpkin that you carry back from the field at harvest time. That kind of opulent heaviness, except that the Browning fit her hand exactly. This was the weight of intimacy and — like the baby, the pumpkin, and the lover — the gun also contained the weight of possibility concentrated into form.

She fingered the trigger, a delicate crescent moon, the only touch of lightness in the object, and the piece that discharges the deadly force. "The trigger, that which causes something to happen," Aurelia mused, "the one curved, distinctly feminine element of this gun."

She held the gun against her solar plexus and closed her eyes. As she slowed her breathing, a transmission of information began to filter into her consciousness as if she had always known it and was just bringing it to mind. She saw a boy in a homespun shirt at a rough table in a barn like the one she took refuge in at Riva's when she was a girl: She saw John Moses Browning creating his first gun at the age of thirteen from scrap metal from his father's gunsmith shop.

"How differently his creativity came to him than mine did to me!" Aurelia thought as she watched that scene and those that followed, unfolding in a series of frames from boyhood to young adulthood. John Moses was such a talented firearms designer that not a single one of his designs ever failed. He sold them to the Winchester Company and held more than one hundred patents before he died. Scenes speeded up in Aurelia's mind: She saw John Moses proudly sharing his handiwork with his father. She saw the first automatic pistol that Browning created in 1911, not much different from the one she held. She saw the bullet from just such a Browning automatic pierce the jugular vein of the Archduke Ferdinand as he was driven in a motorcade in Sarajevo in 1914, the event that effectively began World War I.

Behind her closed eyes images of World War I cascaded: men rendered otherworldly in gas masks, vibrating in unison with Howitzers as they pumped out bullets in a rain of destruction; bodies rotting in trenches; flame throwers painting the night sky with terror; submarines silently seeking targets under the seas; strategic bombers filling the sky; dropping poison gas and fragmentation shells on sleeping families below with only a fantasy of precision. Forty million dead, eight million prisoners of war, countless traumatized as twentieth century technology clashed with nineteenth century tactics. The pain was so widespread that for the first time — as war simultaneously penetrated the land, the seas, and the sky — even the aggressors saw themselves as victims. It was the dim beginning of a truth unfolding: Could a child make war on its Mother's body and survive? Didn't Browning ever stop to think?

"Please, Divine Source," Aurelia gasped, "must I continue?"

The others heard Aurelia gasp and looked up from their own work. Few had the breadth of consciousness to allow in so much collective imagery as Aurelia and the elder Crones did. Tears ran down Aurelia's cheeks as she saw the modern human history of war, speeded up, flashing through her mind. The Armenian genocide, a harbinger of the Shoah, the Shoah predicting Cambodia's killing fields, the deranged annihilation in Darfur and throughout Africa, the nameless war of international terrorism erupting in the cities worldwide. She shook with grief for a long time. The other women sent light to her and continued their own work.

"But John Moses Browning was no different than me," Aurelia muttered to herself. She wiped her eyes and sighed. "He was following the thread of his own creativity. How did it come to this?"

"Limitations," the word floated up into her mind. John Moses was engaging the limitations of each design and overcoming each one in turn. First the single shot, then the single chambered handgun, repeating rifles, and eventually, the machine gun. "Why he is the 'Father' of the automatic weapons in the hands of gang youth in the streets today!" She said aloud.

Aurelia felt wave after wave of nausea rise in her as she continued to breathe through them. Years of work with the detox process allowed her enormous capacity to see history in her mind's eye but this was nearly too much for her. "I understand his creativity was simply flowing down the channels that had been created for him by his Daddy and probably his before. What am I missing here?" In spite of the cool breeze coming into the room, Aurelia felt her body heating up.

She curled her finger around the curved trigger of the gun. The safety was on, blocking the ability of the gun to fire, despite the clip being empty. Guns didn't originally have safety locks. In fact, there are gun advocates who claim that safety locks are dangerous. Aurelia knew the favorite story of the pro-gun folks about the crazy man who broke into a family's house when the daddy was away on business: he began stabbing the children dead in their beds. One of the children, a girl of about ten, knew where her father's gun was kept, but the special safety lock prevented her from killing the assailant and saving her siblings. "Never mind that many more four year olds who got their hands on a loaded gun killed another child in play." Aurelia fumed at the thought.

The safety lock introduced a contradiction, an incomplete truth into the gun's reality, without challenging its basis for being. Aurelia sighed. "Why is it so hard for folks to simply hold alternative realities, to admit there are always multiple truths?" This is why, Aurelia thought, every story contains both truth and pain, and something deeper. Each story holds someone's best attempt to make sense of the world, to strive for meaning. No one ever set out knowingly to do the wrong thing, did they?

"I get that John Moses Browning wasn't an evil man. He was a creative, resourceful individual who was responding to needs around him. And now he's even celebrated as the Father of Homeland Security," she said out loud. "All right, Source," Aurelia muttered to herself, enough history. Let's see if the thing itself can help me see what I'm missing." She placed the gun on the table in front of her, took a deep breath, and began the dialogue, the heart of the witness process.

Well, Browning high power 9 mm, semi-automatic pistol," Aurelia wrote, "*what can you tell me?*

Gun: *Please, call me 'Brownie.' What do you want to know?*

Aurelia: *What on earth possessed men to create guns? Excuse me, I don't mean to sound so —*

Brownie: *Exasperated? You sound exasperated. You think if guns were never created, your world would be all perfect peace? Is that it?*

Aurelia: *No, of course not, but Goddess know, the pain and destruction you all wreak is a terrible thing.*

Brownie: *You're familiar with the saying, 'Guns don't kill people, people kill people?*

Aurelia: *Of course I am. Don't wear me out here! I'm going to get some tea. Excuse me, please, I'll be right back.*

"Dangerous and a smart aleck!" Aurelia fumed as she went over to the tea table. There were three pots of tea — black, green, and herbal — each labeled with the name of the tea of the day in each category. Some women needed a little jolt of caffeine from a strong black tea; others preferred a gentle herbal brew. The green tea of the day was Gunpowder, a Chinese tea where each leaf was hand-rolled into a tiny ball. Aurelia laughed — Gina had a sense of humor, bless her! Aurelia poured herself a mug of Gunpowder and went back to continue her conversation with Brownie.

Other women entered the room and Enid was advising them, as she had Aurelia, to take one gun at a time; each one had a lot to say. Although Aurelia knew the women as a group were no closer to perfect than men were, and that she herself was apt to take on a lot and even sometimes get a little bossy, she was proud of the group leadership model they had created at the Farm. Each woman's voice was valued, and while it slowed things down to work that way, the slowness itself usually seemed like a good thing in a world gone mad for speed and "efficiency" — to the point of losing all joy in the moment and making some stupid decisions about what mattered.

Why didn't anyone object to Browning's work? Aurelia asked when she was settled in her chair again and back to her witness writing.

Brownie: *Because the consciousness to foresee what could occur wasn't held by anyone in that time and place. Oh, I suppose if someone had gotten the idea to take the pistol up the mountain to a holy man in Tibet, he'd have had something to say, but no one in the American West could see anything but progress. Though please remember, worlds were evolving; this all occurred in the world where the developmental task was toward individualism, differentiating from the group, and, boy, a gun sure enhances the sense of being 'one,' if I do say so myself.*

Aurelia: *I don't know about that. With a gun you take away the one-ness of another person. They are reduced to a thing, a target.*

Brownie seemed to chuckle. *I believe you are missing the essence of oneness, my dear. The 'ultimate oneness' is the absence of all others.*

Aurelia shuddered as she let Brownie's comment sink in. *But that's so literal! So lacking in imagination!*

Brownie: *Au contraire, dear woman. Once a man saw what a gun could do, well, he realized he better do it to someone else before it got done to him. Where could those pictures come from if not the imagination?*

Aurelia: *So there must have been considerable fear involved with this individuating, after being mostly part of a group.*

Brownie: *You are so kind, and so insightful!*

Aurelia took a sip of her gunpowder tea and regarded Brownie warily. Was he mocking her? She saw what he was saying. Of course the imagination produces fear as well as joyous possibilities. A gun would seem like a pretty good answer to the fear of annihilation that must have been part of the first individuation. To pull away from others always feels like a death.

Aurelia: *I wonder if you are the type of gun that was used to kill my father.*

Brownie: *Not likely, police service revolvers are usually .38s. Of course, a throw-away might have been used.*

Aurelia: *So your purpose for being is to allow 'one' human being to send projectiles into the body of another at a rate and velocity that ensures serious damage and preferably death.* She winced, writing this.

Brownie: *My, how enlightened of you! Jumping to conclusions based on your closely held beliefs and all. I am a developmental necessity for the growth and unfoldment of the human race. You could say my purpose is to allow 'one' human being to enhance and strengthen his being-ness by protecting himself, his property, and his family from the damage that some other prick wants to inflict. An aspect of 'survival of the fittest.'*

Aurelia: *That old saw! Mutuality is the law of the ecosystem. We know that survival of the most cooperative is the real rule of nature.*

Brownie: *You'd be surprised how cooperative some folks become when a gun is pointed at their head.*

Aurelia: *You're just playing with me now. Maybe I should just go.*

Brownie: *Let's not get ahead of ourselves, there's more to the story!*

Aurelia: *Do tell!*

Brownie: *Well, there's a long story before the actual object, a gun, as we know it, appears on the scene. Before there were guns, there was gunpowder.*

Aurelia nodded to her tea mug. *I'm drinking a Chinese tea by that very name.*

Brownie: *Good, the Chinese, yes. They invented gunpowder. By accident, I might add. During the Song Dynasty there was a school of Taoist alchemy. The Chinese alchemists, like alchemists everywhere, were dabbling about seeking an elixir of immortality. Can you imagine? Isn't that a sublime joke? Ah, but more about that paradox later.*

Aurelia: *Well, our consultations in the Akashic records confirm that there were two strands of inquiry in alchemy. One certainly was material, but the other was about the transmutation of spirit, the evolution of consciousness, if you will.*

Brownie: *Very good, Aurelia. This is exactly the nub of the matter. Essentially the alchemists were those with a thirst for knowledge, a curiosity about how things work, how things change, about transformation, as you say. They often tried to keep the knowledge from the materialists who simply wanted to create gold in order to get wealth and power.*

Aurelia: *So the separation of matter and spirit is at fault?*

Brownie: *Not so fast. Don't just jump on that old chestnut. Let's look a little further, shall we?*

Aurelia: *Yes, let's. Long before the Song Dynasty, in the first century of the Common Era, I believe, we have the Axiom of Maria.*

Brownie: *Always digging for the female element! Can't help yourself, can you? The basis of the whole thing is as ancient as time, I suppose. Who knows how many women are rolled into 'Maria the Prophetess' or 'Mary the Jewess' or Mary Magdalene for that matter! Surely it must be common sense to see that before there was alchemy, which heated up elements in those funny looking vessels, there was cooking! Must we belabor the point that the feminine was present at every moment of unfolding, but the masculine was more into keeping records of what went on?*

Aurelia: *Every record keeper biases his own version, that's for sure. If I am not mistaken, the double boiler is still called the 'Bain Marie' in France in honor of Mary the Prophet who, as every woman, must have seen cooking as the basic act of transformative play.*

Brownie: *Sure thing! But let's get back to your Axiom of Maria. Do you remember how it goes?*

Aurelia: *Yes, 'Out of the one comes two, out of the two comes three, and out of the third comes the fourth.' That speaks to so many things, cell division, the human zygote becoming male or female, then in coitus coming together to produce the third, a child...*

Brownie: *Yes, and 'out of the third comes the fourth.' What do you Crones make of that?"*

Aurelia: *Back to Oneness but this time with consciousness. The Transcendent Function, the Divine on earth, the progressively smudge-free mirror in which we gaze at ourselves but see the Divine, the Fourth World…*

Brownie: *Remember who you're talking to here, or how you see me. I am that smudge-free mirror, the offspring of the man child, the energy of that union of mind and matter.*

Aurelia: *And?*

Brownie: *I am an instrument of transformation, as you say, on the material level. I may be the quintessential transformational instrument, as a matter of fact. What were the alchemists after?*

Aurelia rolled her eyes at Brownie's pedantic tone. *Eternal life, the creation of new life or the spiritual union with the Divine, depending I suppose, on the level of consciousness of the particular alchemist….*

Brownie: *So, failing the creation of new life…*

Aurelia: *The destruction of existing life!*

Brownie: *Bingo! Aren't you always telling people that creation can't occur without destruction? For something new to be made, something old must be dismantled? I am just the humble servant of transformation, Your Majesty.*

Why did you call me that? Aurelia asked, suspiciously.

Brownie chuckled. *Because with me at your side, you rise to a new level. No longer beholden to someone else, man or god. With me you dispatch obstacles, you, ah, transcend your limitations…*

Aurelia: *Limitations, there's that word again. What did Phoebe say? 'It is through our limitations that we serve the highest good.* Aurelia felt herself being led off track.

Brownie: *Highest good?* The weapon was gleaming now. *Who gets to say what the highest good is? Some guy? Some god you can't see? Stick with me, Baby,* Brownie's voice took on a smoky and intimate tone that sent shivers down Aurelia's spine, *and we get to decide what the highest good is! Maybe the highest good is the lowest good!*

She fingered his silky skin as the words sunk in, the invitation to power, the heady mix of power and no limitations, the ability to remove whoever or whatever was in the way.

Aurelia: *Force!* she exclaimed. *You materialize the element of force, which violates the basic natural law of things unfolding in their own time.*

In an excited voice: Brownie: *Don't you see how your mother is trying to control you? 'Highest good' my butt! Pardon the pun. She's just entertaining all those big shots on the other side, entertaining them with how she pulls your strings like a puppet. She wants you to have limitations because she has them now, big time. Those losers on the other side can't do anything without humans to act for them. She's jealous; she blew it and didn't complete the job. But with me in your hand, you can do anything, on your timetable. Who says you have to wait for things to unfold?*

Aurelia stared at the gun on the table in front of her. She could have sworn she saw Brownie wink at her as a ray of sun glinted off his surface.

Aurelia: *You're good, Brownie, you are really good! I get it. Your ability to transform material reality, aka human form, draws creative energy to you, you seduce humans...*

Brownie: *Aw shucks, whattaya say, Baby?*

Aurelia: *Oh my!* She put the gun back down and shook off the thrill of electric current that ran through her body and erupted in a sudden, brief but explosive orgasm.

Brownie: *Isn't your Tantra project founded on more or less the same idea? I mean, come on — sex, cooking, chemistry, shooting someone... you humans are always hankering to mix and match, come together, you know, 'do it,' aren't you? Steal a little fire from the gods? You women say it's all about timing, waiting, blah, blah. That little jolt felt good just now, didn't it?*

Aurelia: *All the havoc you and your brethren have wreaked through human history, the gun might really be the yang tour-de-force. Such economy of*

306 PAT B. ALLEN

means: You combine the promise of power, pleasure, transcendence, transmutation. Or, for those who won't submit to transmutation by more subtle means... okay, I'm getting this. The undeniable sensation of pleasure slowly ebbed away from her body.

Brownie: *Yep, nothing speeds up the 'fall of man' like a belly full of lead. Helps gravity along, if you know what I mean. If you think material reality is all there is, or the only place that exists — well, of course you'll work on that level for all you're worth! See? We're all working on the same side here. But old John Moses didn't care about that. He took a turn off the road long before the crossroads of 'truth or consequences;' he didn't know he was working on the Atman Project. He was just perfecting his creation.*

Aurelia: *What do you mean? He didn't think about the consequences?*

Brownie: *That wasn't his part of the picture. Don't you see? Somebody back in the Song Dynasty had already paved the road; he was simply improving it. Compartmentalization, 'only following orders,' 'doing your job,' — it all flows from the same impulse, that glorious level of human enterprise, 'man the inventor.' There was a ton of work to be done, things to create. It would have been counterproductive to have things slowed down by — what do you gals call it? Your 'ethic of care'?*

Aurelia: *I know it's time to shift the script, time for a new chapter in the story. The yang disease is exactly that addiction to perfecting the material at whatever level, without questioning the means themselves enough or the possibility of long term unintended consequences. Once the gun became possible, became an idea, no one questioned whether it was a good idea; it just became fascinating to see how it could be made and then improved. There was never a clear basic intention for the highest good, was there?*

Brownie began to recite: *Of course there was, in a manner of speaking. At that stage of human consciousness, the understanding of 'highest good' was limited. No one really knew that because they were at their own limits — like before Columbus discovered that you couldn't sail off the edge of the earth.*

Remember, Brownie continued, *the failure of one thing, through grace, brings in a better thing. Where sin abounds, grace yet more abounds. Thus, the short-sighted wisdom which would prevent falling, would by doing so prevent all progress to higher things; for each advancing form of life which God takes up springs out of the failure of that which preceded it.' That was Andrew John Jukes, a theological thinker, by the way, roughly a contemporary of John Moses Browning. Jukes had fewer adherents — it wasn't time yet. No center of gravity for humans about the sanctity of all life, that sort of thing.*

Aurelia: *So it may make sense that all the target shooters, marksmen, even real hunters who eat what they kill are really engaged in a spiritual discipline and that must be recognized and honored. Goddess know, there is a strangely sacred feeling when I pick up this object. So, Brownie, the dilemma you pose is never resolved is it? It unfolds minute by minute, again and again, like the breath.*

Brownie: *Ashes, ashes, you all fall down, one way or the other.*

Aurelia: *Down into matter, to learn what we must. But we don't have to resist it so, and we have learned to be more nimble in our ascent. It doesn't have to be a fight. It can be a dance. We need not cling to what has been. The Divine never left us. That's what women know and men need to find out. We aren't called upon to be God, but to evolve God-ness. Now I see what Kali needs.*

Brownie: *Hey, don't let 'em melt me down, I belong in a museum at least. Don't forget, 'those who don't remember the past, condemned to repeat it' and all that!*

Aurelia: *This is a lot to take in. I appreciate your wisdom, Brownie, now I must absorb it all.*

Aurelia stroked the gun but it was just an object, now that she withdrew her energy, and it remained silent as she replaced it on the table. She looked around the barn, women were each working out their own lessons, guns speaking different stories, all teaching different stories to each one.

She felt a sense of ease. Her own lesson learned, at least in this moment, she got up and carefully put Brownie back in the mandala where another woman could engage him to learn what she needed. The barn was suffused with light as she made her way out into the thin December day. It was time to rest, to absorb her truth, no bigger or smaller than any other, just hers. Aurelia gazed at all the women, some working together, some painting, some writing, some dancing. She looked forward to learning more from all the others. "Namaste, Sistahs," she whispered and bowed and left the barn.

28

The hermitage where Kali was recuperating — and where I was now sitting a vigil — was a tiny space, a hut really, with earthen walls, a stone fireplace, and willow stick furniture made comfortable with the addition of hand sewn and stuffed pillows. I imagined Heidi's grandfather might show up at any moment with an axe and an armload of firewood. Wait, better scratch that thought of the axe, with Kali's leaning toward violence and my not exactly understanding how all this mind morphing worked. I didn't want to plant any less-than-peaceful thoughts by mistake. I had finally traded in Mattie's bunny slippers for a well-broken-in pair of hiking boots after Elsie eyed my feet and pronounced my arches fallen.

"You need some good support, child," she declared while we were in the storeroom together one day. "Good support" seemed to be a theme from what I could glean leafing through the journal at Kali's bedside. Someone named Beatrice wrote: "Offered support by humming the Kalachakra mantra to ease our sister's healing journey." Another: "Held Kali's feet for two hours, felt much darkness release, directed it to the earth and sent supportive light energy in return." That one was signed "Wendy" in perfect Palmer Method handwriting.

I couldn't think of any relevant skills to offer: other's people's feet creeped me out and I didn't know any mantras beside "Om." There was a basket with some rattles, flutes, and a hand drum, but I didn't want to risk waking her up. Just as I was thinking about calling Mattie to check on when the next shift would be by so I could get the hell out of there, I saw Kali stir. Shit.

"Where am I?"

The hermitage was a bit dark and although my eyes had adjusted, I didn't think she could see me. "Ah, you're at the Farm, Heartscape. Land of the Crone and home of the brave?" I offered.

"I recognize you — the art history buff, the vaunted Eve. What happened? How did I get here? Oh wait," Kali pushed herself up to one elbow. "Mattie was there and Harvey. Shit." She flopped back down on the bed.

"What a fucking disaster!" Kali spoke with sudden energy. "I can't believe I'm back here with these Goddess worshipping idiots! Where's Diva?"

"Diva's fine," I said in what I hoped was a calm voice. "She's spending a lot of time in the compost pile. You've been more or less passed out since you got within fifty feet of Aurelia. Look, what's your deal? Women have been sitting here around the clock taking care of you. You were practically in a coma. And from what I can tell they saved you from doing a whole lot of damage."

"No way I passed out. I could always hold my own with Aurelia. Not like some of these wimps. What do you know? You're just a dupe." Kali rolled over and faced the wall.

"Actually, I'm an executive for a Fortune 500 company in Chicago, missy. I'll be moving out to the West Coast soon to head up a division there." She didn't tell me to fuck off so I kept talking. "Yeah, I had worked really hard. I was about to close a very big deal before moving out to the Coast. I was making a difference, I mentored scores of younger women, and I was well respected by the men I worked for."

"Stop right there, Ayn Rand!" Kali leapt out of the bed. Someone had gotten her into some sweat pants and an "I heart Milwaukee" tee shirt. "Don't tell me, at the last minute, some young chippy took over your gig and you got stiffed, right? Someone you slavishly mentored, no doubt."

"Well, she was one of my mentees. Actually, we had a fine collegial relationship, for your information. But how did you know that?" I was curious about why my story brought color to Kali's cheeks.

"When I was here before, Aurelia kept saying that was the script men were stuck in: Women were like battery packs; they'd use one up till she ran down and then get a newer model. Just like TVs or cars or phones. But women are morons. They think it's an actual relationship, and they actually think they're respected since no one is looking at their tits."

"Yes, well, that's a mean and reductive way of saying what happened to me, I suppose." I really didn't like this woman one bit. "Did Aurelia really say that? About the tits?"

"Not in so many words. But, well, weren't you angry? Didn't you want to kill the fuckers?" Kali was pacing around the tiny hermitage, hair flying.

I thought about J. Wendell Wentsouth that last morning, before Lydia shuttled me into Mattie's cab and started me on the magical mystery tour to Cronation.

"No, I guess not." I still couldn't really feel angry with Wentsouth, his jovial moon face, his back-slapping bon amie, his private bathroom that he needed due to whatever misguided pranks he'd suffered at boy scout camp. I had a soft spot for the guy. If anything, I'd admired how he'd overcome adversity and risen to the top without actually seeming all that bright.

"As a matter of fact," I confessed, "I'm embarrassed to say, my impulse was to strangle the other woman, now that you mention it. But then I got kidnapped and brought here before I had a chance to do anything except swill a little vodka and feel sorry for myself."

"Well you obviously belong here!" Kali had her hands on her hips and was staring at me. "You blamed the woman! That is so counterrevolutionary, so — well, just stupid! It's exactly what keeps men in power! You and all the other compassionate enablers. 'Poor Joe Blow, his daddy never hugged him!'"

"Oh, and excuse me! Buying arms from international terrorists and planning a campaign of mass murder. That's enlightened action is it? You whacked-out psycho!"

"At least I know who's at fault. It's men, first and foremost — but it's also women like you. You fuck things up so badly by going along with the status quo and then you want to hand it over to the next generation and pretend you're on some spiritual quest now. Like now that you're 'meditating' and eating vegan, the whole damn planet will just right itself, like that's what the whole things hinges on, you and your stupid guru." She crossed her arms and looked at me triumphantly.

I knew two things: I was obviously doing something right as support staff for the return of Kali's health and physical well being; she looked like she could run a marathon and her eyes were sparkling. However, the girl was just as obviously demented. I suspected she was angry with her mother and I seemed like a convenient punching bag, being roughly the right age and all. Since I was fairly sure she'd leap for my throat if I suggested such a thing, I refrained. I planned to suggest to Mattie that she hook the girl up to the detox machine at full throttle for the maximum time and in full leather restraints, if necessary, at her earliest possible convenience.

"You don't even know who I am and, may I remind you, I was brought here, apparently for some important purpose. And I have never had any sort of guru."

Fortunately there was a knock at the door before we began hair pulling and wrestling like fourth graders.

Aurelia entered the hermitage without waiting for our invitation. "What in Goddess' name is going on in here? I could hear you two shouting for half a mile! Kali, it's good to see you are feeling better. Eve, your support has clearly helped Kali regain her life force energy."

"Yeah, if by life force energy, you mean raging, male-bashing vituperation," I muttered.

"Aurelia, this one is a real loser!" Kali stormed. "I can't believe you're grooming her for anything. My God, she's pathetic."

Aurelia just laughed. "Alright. Settle down, both of you."

I noticed I hadn't fainted even though Aurelia was just a few feet away in this tiny room. But then, neither had Kali.

"Actually, Kali," Aurelia said breezily, "I'm so glad you've returned to consciousness with so much vigor. What I was coming by to say was I think it would be excellent if you two became roommates and shared both your strengths and your limitations. I think if you took turns listening to one another, you would both be able to help us with one of the vexing problems that only now is really coming into play. What I have just learned has made me understand something about the limitations of Cronation, and I feel the beginnings of where we might need to go next."

Kali and I looked at each other, and I'm pretty sure she was thinking some variation of what I was thinking: "Please, not her!" Maybe my telepathic powers were finally kicking in.

Aurelia continued: "Yes, you see, both of you understand some of what is missing from our plan to actualize Cronation. Kali, you are correct that men do present a certain, well, obstacle to the unfolding of the next era. Eve, you have long experience working within the male world and a highly activated male mind in yourself. Why, you have such empathy for the male mind and how it works, you seemed to thrive amidst your own oppression. And you both share a certain skepticism for the unfolding of the power of the Feminine through the Creative Source and that can be helpful, since there will be so many who feel lost in the coming time. It will be especially hard for those like you, Eve, and those like Kali's mother, Miriam, who think they know what's going on."

314   PAT B. ALLEN

"But —" I began to object, but when Aurelia turned directly towards me and smiled, I felt a little faint and had to grip the table to steady myself.

"Don't worry, Eve, you two won't be alone. I've asked Mattie and Harvey to work with both of you. You'll be a sort of 'Next Council,' you know, the next generation. Mattie and Harvey have achieved Hieros Gamos so they have a wonderful foundation, but they also need what you have to offer."

"But she isn't young," Kali whined. "She's gotta be at least fifty; she's my mother's age!"

"Fifty is not old, you little twit," I countered.

Aurelia laughed and put her hands on Kali's shoulders. "And sweet little sister, it was you, bringing the guns to us, that allowed this piece of our learning to surface and become clear." Aurelia hugged Kali to her and Kali stuck her tongue out at me over Aurelia's shoulder.

Great! I never had kids or siblings, and now I have to deal with a perpetual adolescent who makes the Bad Seed look like Eloise at the Plaza Hotel.

"Wait a minute!" I'll admit I was a little jealous of Kali in that moment. "I have a life, you know — a job? I appreciate all that you've got going on here, I really do, and I sincerely hope it helps the planet, and I seem to have played some weird role getting you two reunited. But, Aurelia, I think you're much more qualified to be a foster Mom to Valerie Solanas here. And besides, I have a contribution to make at Wentsouth West, you know, back in the 'real world'? I'm sure all that I've learned here will come in really handy when I get there."

"Oh, Eve, dear," Aurelia turned to face me now and, as soon as she touched my shoulder, I got a hit of that fresh gingerbread, warm bath, sun-on-the-shoulders-at-the-beach energy and I started to wobble. "I know you had your heart set on the West Coast, but Mr. Wentsouth's firm, along with most of the western edge of the greater Los Angeles area, slid into the ocean this morning at about 4 a.m. Pacific Standard Time. Lydia reported back from the weather watch Crones at the Council meeting this morning. Fortunately the Crones were able to organize a mass evacuation in time. But I'm afraid travel to the coast won't be possible for a while. A number of the expected major earth changes are moving into high gear all over so we'll all have our work cut out for us. Now come here, both of you."

Before I could even figure out my reaction to her nonchalant news about the demise of my future, Aurelia gathered both of us to either side of her and placed a hand on each of our heads. She closed her eyes and my hands and feet began to tingle and I felt a swirling sense at the top of my skull. I closed my eyes too. "Dear, dear, Divine Source, please fill these two with Your light, Your love, Your joy. Help them learn to lead us on Your path as we, all of your Crones, serve You in the Great Turning, the Great Falling, the lighting up of Your next phase, the fullness of Your moon, the roaring of Your ocean, the shifting of Your sands. Bless them in their strengths and limitations, and help us as we co-create this new and unknown path with You one step at a time."

Well, so much for hiking in the Santa Monica foothills, driving my red Hybrid sports car and planting a drought tolerant landscape.

29 —————— ⚬

So it happened that the Next Council was created and called to order, and I found myself sitting in a circle with Mattie and Harvey, Kali, Sarah Leaf, Aurelia, Elsie, Lorelei Winger, and Lydia, who no longer resembled in the least the efficient executive secretary. Her appearance in boots and jeans and wild hair served to further dismantle my precarious grasp on my past. If it wasn't for the gardenia scent I might have sworn I'd never known her before. Now that I knew how she had gained that perfume, I swear, I'd given up trying to discern "real" from "unreal."

We were gathered in a circle on chairs and cushions in the Wood Room, which had a sort of hunting lodge feeling but without any moose or deer heads staring down at us. As senior Crone and eldest Elder, Elsie began. She picked up a stone that sat on a small table in the center of the circle and addressed it.

"Welcome, Sister Stone, and thank you for giving up your place in the riverbed to guide our communication with one another and with the Source today. For you young ones new to the Council procedures, we use an object to help us regulate our talking. Whoever has the stone can speak; the rest of us remain silent, listening and witnessing, paying attention to what arises in us in response to the words spoken. Pay special attention to the feelings in your bodies; be curious and let the feelings lead you to the words you speak. We choose an object based on the quality of help we need, as intuited by whoever convenes the Council. Today I am honored to convene and I felt the need of Sister River Stone. She holds her place with ease amidst the rushing water. She is ancient and has witnessed many changes over the course of time, and she has been smoothed by centuries of experience. I ask her to ground us with her presence, to balance the quickness of your beautiful young energy that is so like the sparkling stream that splashes over her in her home place. When you all begin to meet on your own, you will decide on your own methods, but for today, Sister Stone will guide us. Shall we begin?"

We all sat silently in anticipation.

"Now, here is how it works: First we pass the stone around the circle and each one speaks of whatever is foremost in her mind. Or his," Elsie smiled and nodded to Harvey. "Once each one's energy has been opened in our circle, then whoever wishes to speak opens her, or his, hands like so," Elsie made a bowl with her two palms together. "This signifies your openness to receiving the words from the Source within you and also our intention to simply offer our words to one another as gifts. If the speaker finishes and no one is ready to speak next, place the stone back on the table. Sometimes we need a little silent time to let the words sink in."

I thought Kali seemed fidgety, but it may have only been my imagination. Since we'd started rooming together it was harder to tell where she left off and I began. I wondered if this was what parenting felt like.

Elsie continued, "Welcome to each of you," slowly turning her ancient gaze to each one of us. As always I felt a slightly electric thrill when her eyes met mine. I wasn't fainting or breaking into tears any longer in the presence of the elder Crones, but I just felt filled up and good.

"Dear Blessed Source, here we sit before You ready to convene another generation in Your service. Please open all of us to Your wisdom that lives in our hearts and is in us as we are in You. Let each one see their beauty. This is an historic event, a man joining in our Council. May each one present be an unfolding of peace, joy, truth, and compassion, to honor and delight You for the highest good of all that is. May all our ancestors and spirit guides rejoice together with us. Now, if each of you would state what is in your heart as we go around please." Elsie passed the stone to Aurelia.

"Thank you, Elsie, for that beautiful prayer and welcome. I remember when you and Momma and Riva and the others first called me into the circle of Cronation and what a joyous day that was. We are indeed here today to commence an historic development, one that flows from our foundations in the Source. We are here to allow new wisdom to come forth and to acknowledge the entry of the next generation to the forefront of Cronation. We welcome the Next Council. I tried to think of what those letters might stand for to see if NEXT was an acronym, but nothing came to me. So if anything comes to you all, just let us know. But perhaps the era of the catchy phrase is over, we shall see, we shall see.

"Now, I have to say, that although I never saw myself as the leader, the one in charge and all that, I have tried, I suppose, to fill Momma's shoes, both as a way to heal my own grief in missing her in my everyday life and also to serve the greater good. I must admit to a bit of nervousness in feeling like we're turning something over to all of you."

Aurelia passed the stone to Mattie, sitting on her left.

"'Turn it over,' Momma? I hope you mean allowing us to join you, to share the load, but surely with you still to guide us with your wisdom and love." Mattie looked around the circle and each one nodded in assent. I nodded madly, terrified, to tell the truth, by the prospect of Aurelia not being in charge; I realized that was certainly something I was clinging to. Kali just shrugged her shoulders and seemed impatient. Harvey opened his palms as Mattie passed the stone to him, bowing slightly.

"Elsie, Aurelia, all of you," Harvey looked around the circle, "I guess

I'm really honored to be included here and all, but I can't help it, the more I think about it, the more it really does seem to be the men's fault. We gotta do something to stop it, them, us, I mean..."

Harvey was starting to freak out. He was squeezing the stone between his hands like he might turn it into a diamond if he could just squeeze it hard enough. Kali snorted and folded her arms. I was next to Harvey and he passed me the stone.

I heard myself saying: "I'm new to all of this but I have a question: Are we really here to hear all the voices or only the ones that fit the vision we'd like to see?" Suddenly all eyes were on me. "I'm just saying, it's like the 'elephant in the living room.' Kali had the idea of killing lots of men in high places and I haven't heard it mentioned since she got here. I know you all have been witnessing the guns and I haven't done that yet, but just thinking about guns and all the suffering they cause, don't we have to do something to stop all the violence and craziness that men have created? I know from the business world — or at least I thought I knew — men as a group don't mean to do harm, but they do anyway, all the time. Not that women don't, but not as much.... All I'm saying is that shouldn't Kali's idea get a fair hearing if the world Cronation aims to create does honor the wisdom in all voices? I have to add that that vision scares me to death, but I don't have another one to propose."

Harvey looked worried, but he didn't speak and no one offered him any comfort. I passed the stone to Lorelei and noticed that Kali had uncrossed her arms.

"Well, Eve, if anyone in this room might have personal cause to share Kali's vision," Lorelie said, "it's probably me, living as I do in the seat of power in this country and seeing that power misused on a daily basis. Goddess knows, it's a good thing I didn't have a gun handy living in Washington all these years. Why, I might have murdered my own husband hundreds of times. Thank Goddess for the Secret Service!" She passed the stone to Kali.

Kali began to turn the stone over and over in her hands. I was mesmerized watching her long fingers.

"I...when I was here last time, I was pretty sure I knew what was wrong. I thought I knew a lot of things. I was sure I was smarter than all of you — not smarter than you, Elsie, I never though that. And, Aurelia, when you called me angry, I took that as a compliment. You all know I got to know Diva when I was here then. Hearing her story enraged me. What was going on here at the Farm seemed so slow, unreal, stupid, actually. A bunch of women sitting around thinking good thoughts while how many girls like Diva get hurt every day? Never mind the institutional violence, the gang violence, the police violence, the genocides. I guess it all became real to me because of Diva. I just couldn't stand it. I had to do something; that's how I was raised. You want something to change, you pick up the phone and call someone, light a fire somewhere, put things into action.

"Removing the men made sense to me, and one thing just led to another. The manifesto I wrote just sort of flowed out of my anger that no one, no so-called adult, was doing anything. Then I put up the website. And women started to respond to what I was putting up online. The women who wrote to me at Nemesis, they needed help and I wanted to help them." Kali stopped talking. Her face looked softer than I'd ever seen it, she really was speaking from her heart.

"But I want to talk about something else. I know I'm talking a long time." Kali looked at Elsie, who smiled and nodded for her to go on. "I witnessed one of the guns today in the barn. It was an old Uzi submachine gun. It's probably been passed around to hundreds of soldiers. It's rusty and old. As soon as I picked it up a movie started in my head." Kali's voice cracked and I could see she was fighting back tears.

"I saw all the firefights that weapon had ever been in, the hands that had held it — Jews, Palestinians, kids, a few women, but mostly men. It almost killed me, but I couldn't put it down. I could feel the heat, smell the dust, so many feelings rushed through me: terror, anger, power, deafening, maddening. Then I saw a man's face, smiling; he had a beard, just a guy.

"It was Uziel Gal, the man who invented the Uzi. He fled Nazi Germany, did you all know that? I didn't. I just felt him. Like a film almost, in a history class. As I held the gun, it was like his story was pulsing through me. He understood what the Nazis were up to; a lot of his contemporaries didn't get it and wouldn't listen to him. He got out to what would become Israel. Uziel Gal served in the 1948 War of Independence. After the state of Israel was established, he was made an officer and served in the Israeli Defense Forces.

"Holding that gun it seemed like I felt what he felt. I felt whole, complete. His design of the Uzi won a gun competition, but he never wanted it named after him. He was a modest man. He refused any royalties for his design; he felt it was just part of his service. I saw his face. He could have been my Uncle Saul; he could have been my father. If it wasn't for Uziel Gal, there might not be a Jewish people or a state of Israel. I might not exist. Wasn't he receiving something from the Source? He created that gun — Can that be wrong? I'm really confused. I don't know what to think or believe anymore." We all sat still, leaning towards Kali. She didn't pass the stone.

Tears were slowly falling from all the women's eyes. Kali's own tears were dropping onto the stone in her lap, darkening its surface. Harvey reached toward, Kali but she raised her hand to stop him. "That's the thing, isn't it?" She met his eyes. "You want to fix how I feel. That's what men do; it's what I wanted to do. It doesn't work that way, does it? There is no easy fix. Is there any fix at all?"

Harvey looked beseechingly from face to face, but none of the women spoke or tried to ease his discomfort or Kali's. They simply smiled through their tears.

Kali passed the stone to Lydia, who simply said "Ahimsa" and passed it to Sarah Leaf, the last woman to speak.

"Sister, you have touched on a deep mystery. People like to think about the Source as God, like someone they know. They like to think God is good; they pray for things. What I have learned from the teachings that Riva and Phoebe, of blessed memory, of Elsie and Aurelia, is that the Source, in truth, is boundless energy. She will give us whatever we ask for, limited only by our imagination. She can't prevent us from the consequences of what we choose. It is up to us to interpret what is good and adjust our actions accordingly.

"We are all learning as we witness these objects of great power and force, these guns, that you have brought into our midst. As Aurelia said to all of us before we began, these objects are made of elements from the Earth. Shekinah, our ever creating and loving mother, will co-create with us whatever we ask for. Can we understand that Uziel Gal put himself in service to the Creative Source in the best way he knew how? And at the same time, while we bless him for his intention to preserve the Jews, can we forgive him for believing that others must be killed? Because that was the limit of his vision, and the limit of the world's vision, at that time.

"But we can see further now, at least in our imaginations, the place where all things start. Can we also say we are ready to ask the Source to co-create a new reality with us, a different one, where we effect transformation in ways that do not involve us destroying these wonderful bodies She gave us? Are we ready to understand that She can guide us to the highest good for all, the Jews, the Palestinians, men and women, young and old, all people, all beings, all life on this blessed earth, Her earth? No one is outside of Her."

Rabbi Sarah lightly kissed the stone and passed it back to Elsie, who placed it back in the center of the table. Silence fell over us as we tried to take in all that had been exchanged.

I felt my head swimming as it dawned on me that I'd never really been in this kind of discussion before. Oh sure, I'd been in tons of executive trainings on "communication" and "breakthrough learning," enough workshops to last a lifetime. I'd emoted with the best of them, appreciatively inquired, and had files full of take-away lists of ways to do productive talking in a group. Something different was going on here; I wasn't sure exactly what it was. Maybe for all the corporate rhetoric, I'd never been in a circle of people who really, truly shared their deepest selves, with no hidden agendas to please the boss, or get a raise, to look like the sharpest knife in the drawer, to impress somebody from corporate. Underlying all we did in the work world was a belief in right and wrong, first and last, and if not good and bad, certainly good, better, and best. These are the sponsoring thoughts of the marketplace.

The women in this room had a desire to be in service to the truth with a capital "T" in all the meandering, uncomfortable, complicated ways Truth shows up. Oh sure, in business we all learned how to "think outside the box" but really — how far out of the box can you get if someone in the room signs your paycheck? Or even reports to someone who signs your check? How welcome would the Truth be that you'd really like to chuck the whole thing but not until you've used it as a stepping-stone to relocate to the West Coast, wherever that was these days. I felt like someone had blown the doors off every conference room in every high rise building I'd ever sat in; the walls were falling down like a cardboard box slashed with a box cutter to reveal a brand new reality, living, pulsing, enormously larger than what we ever thought possible. I could hear my mother, "That's why we took LSD, dear, only after we saw things as they are, we had no idea what to do next."

I was startled out of my reverie by Lorelei who had retrieved the stone. She addressed me as if what Sarah Leaf had just said was as plain as the nose on her face. "Eve, you raised an important question that has been simmering for me too. It came up in my witness to the guns: Why didn't I shoot Wright all those years? Goodness knows, I doubt if anyone would have blamed me all that much. Though, I know, dear, you may not have meant it so literally," she added in response to my look of horror.

"Kali, I ask myself," she continued, "why, with a seat so close to power, seeing all the jockeying for influence, the venal deals, didn't I try to bring it down? Especially with my involvement with Cronation. I've been a part of it since I met Aurelia in college. But perhaps that is exactly why. I learned early on to question the Source every day, to work at opening my heart as well as my mind. And, well, Source never answered my prayers by saying 'Shoot the bugger.'" She replaced the stone.

Harvey seemed about to jump out of his seat. Mattie swung her head toward the stone, gesturing for him to take it. He picked the stone up and said, "Mrs. Winger, if I may ask you, I'm not sure how to phrase this…" Mattie elbowed him and he blurted out "Ahimsa!! Right, I mean no harm and no offense here, but doesn't President Winger, I know he's done away with that title, but didn't he get the idea for that, among other things like the wars, from, uh, God? If you hear one thing and he heard another…." Harvey put the stone back like it was a hot potato but I was pretty impressed with his comment.

The elder Crones exchanged glances and let the silence sit a bit. I wonder what would have happened at Wentworth and Wentsouth if someone had asked old Wendell, "Hey, Mr. W., are we doing this merger for the good of the company or just because your yacht needs an overhaul?" Could Wentsouth even have imagined a difference? What was good for him was good for the company, what was good for the company was good for the economy, what was good for the economy — well, it got a little fuzzy after that but he had no doubt that it was good all around. A "God's in his heaven, all's right with the world" sort of thing.

Lorelei reached for the stone. "Thank you, Harvey. Believe it or not, you're the first person to ask me that question directly in all the time my husband and his family has been in power. Power — that's the key word here. The god-complex is an occupational hazard of any leader whether in business, politics, any place really. When one person is in charge in a hierarchy like that — or takes that much power and likes it — well, those around him begin to shut up. Every time there is no genuine, truthful feedback to adjust the course — as Sarah has just reminded us, those adjustments depend on every voice being heard — the path continues with the leader feeling righter and righter. No pun intended. I could never believe his mother named him 'Wright'!" Lorelei laughed, shaking her head.

I appreciated a moment of relief. This kind of discussion was harder work than anything I'd ever done in the corporate world.

Harvey held out his hands for the stone and Lorelei passed it around. "So what you're saying is: It isn't all one hundred per cent his fault. That theoretically, at least, anyone could have stepped in and offered him a different point of view?"

Lorelei nodded. "I certainly did at times."

Mattie put out her hands and received the stone from Harvey, saying, "Harvey, see this stone? We are using it to take turns. Can you think of another way a stone can be used in a communication process?" She handed the stone back to Harvey, who looked bewildered.

Kali cupped and raised her hands. Harvey got up to bring the stone to her, but Mattie caught him by the belt and gestured to the circle. He sat back down and passed the stone around. Kali was looking bright-eyed now.

"That was an awesome lesson just now." Kali beamed. "Thank you, all! First of all, another use of a stone for communication is: I could throw it at you, hit you in the head, to get your attention — especially if you aren't paying me any mind because you don't see me as important enough. Secondly, by sticking to a process that slows everything down — passing the stone instead of getting up — we give things time to settle. I never got that part before. I thought you were all just wasting time and I couldn't stand it. Since I was sure I had the right answer, slowing things down was just stupid."

Kali passed the stone around into Elsie's waiting hands. "We have a foundational belief in the wisdom of all voices," the old woman said, "that is the definition of community. Mr. Winger seems to believe that life is like that old television show, Father Knows Best. He still sees the world in a false hierarchy with him at the tippy top, hand extended to God the way Michelangelo painted it on the ceiling of the Sistine Chapel. Lorelei could have recited the Cronation manifesto from morning until night to her husband; he couldn't have heard it as any more than a fly buzzing in his ear. Or worse yet, if he had heard her, she might have been imprisoned and a wider crack down on women could have been started. It's hard when the Source tells us to wait, to work behind the scenes, to focus on receiving the vision and raising up young ones like Mattie and biding our time. Gracious, that is hard! But timing is as important as clarity."

Harvey slowly opened his palms again and Elsie passed the stone into his cupped hands. He held it for a long time, silently. Finally, he got up slowly and sat down in the center of the circle, holding the stone in his lap. He lifted it up and held it between his thumb and forefinger like an egg.

"Elsie introduced this stone at the beginning, thanked it and asked for its help. She treated the stone like another very important and esteemed member of the circle, a living being. If I can believe the stone is alive, it can be my ally, help guide me, I'd know to ask it to give me another point of view, the view of the ground, the view of the river. I'd have learned by now that the slow path has some wisdom to it, I'd at least know to ask! I'd never dream of misusing it as a weapon to hurt another person. Nobody teaches this to little boys. They just take the stone out of our hand and tell us we're bad the first time we throw it just to see how far it can go." With that he curled up in a fetal position with the stone against his belly and began to sob and wail.

We sat together in witness until Harvey's crying ceased. He wiped his face on his sleeve and returned to his seat. Once he was settled, Elsie opened her hands and, as the stone passed, slowly, reverently around the circle, I felt both peace and curiosity. What would happen next? I had no clue.

Elsie held the stone up with both hands, then she lowered it and kissed it, "Sister River Stone, thank you. Please take all our confusion and questions into you and return them to the river. May we continue to serve the Source in our confusion as well as in our clarity."

Elsie offered no answers, no bullet points, no to-do lists. We each had to sit with whatever we were feeling. I wasn't used to this. I always believed that action steps at the end of a meeting were a key to success.

Then Elsie began to hum a sound deep in her throat. A chant began as each of us added our sound. I tried to pull back the words of Sarah Leaf's teaching about the Source but it was too hard. I felt frantic for a moment: How would anyone know what to do? The chant rose up and I concentrated on adding my voice to it. I felt my confusion and my resistance melting.

As our voices rose and fell and eventually rested in silence, my eyes fell on the words carved over the mantle of the fireplace, a quote from Rachel Carson: "The more clearly we can focus our attention on the wonders and realities of the universe around us, the less taste we shall have for destruction."

30

Yang showed up late on a Friday afternoon and wandered through the woods surrounding Heartscape looking for his destination. He followed his sense of smell. "So many damn women in this place," he complained, "It's tough to get a reading," he groused as he sniffed the air.

Several of the women who had finished witnessing the guns were out harvesting potatoes and chard for dinner and thought they'd glimpsed a bear, but felt no alarm. The Crones had announced, based on a transmission from the dreaming cells both locally and internationally, that the time was drawing close and they should all be on the look out for signs. The women delivered the vegetables to Rae in the kitchen and went off to the Cronation library to consult books about the meaning of animals, the better to understand and welcome any spirits, helpers, and totems who would doubtlessly be showing up to help the arriving Shift. As a bona-fide shapeshifter, Diva was the go-to girl for animal sightings and they called her off the compost heap to go along.

"Did you sense a bear at all?" Andrea asked when Diva had resumed her human form. "We thought we might have seen one behind the garden."

"Nope," Diva shook her head. "But I was into some awesome rotting spinach, so I wasn't really paying attention."

Andrea led the way to the library, her favorite spot on the Heartscape farm, and pulled down some books and as the women settled into the armchairs, each supplied with a cozy afghan. Diva tagged along hoping for a chance to poke a little fun at Andrea, a favorite pastime.

"Hey, did you know the bear was sacred to the goddess Diana? She's a fertility Goddess. Also it's a symbol in alchemy for nigredo, the prime matter," Eden said.

"Yeah, well, nigredo means black, right? That's raven's middle name," Diva replied. "All things nasty and rotting. Me and Bear, we eat it up and shit it out. That's our contribution to this transformation stuff." She was looking at a picture book of birds.

Andrea made a face. "Look, it also says bears are omnivorous, they eat plants and meat, and it takes two years for their poop to decompose."

Diva punched Andrea's arm. "Yeah? Well, I bet they would even eat up a chubby Crone wannabe. Better watch out."

She and Andrea were still working out their post-Nemesis relationship. Diva was being given a pretty easy time of it at the Farm, it seemed to Andrea — no SAC sessions yet — but when she asked Aurelia about it, she had just said, "Each must heal in her own way and in her own time."

"Shouldn't bears be hibernating?" Eden asked. "Or is that another thing that climate change has screwed up? What if the bear is really crabby because he's tired and it's too warm for him to sleep? I can't sleep unless the room is really cold."

"That's a myth," Andrea said, looking up from a book on the subject. "Bears don't sleep all winter; they just don't need to eat. They stay in their dens a lot because they aren't out looking for food. But it says here that during their winter sleep, the black bear's kidneys shut down — and kidneys symbolize discernment. So if a bear shows up you should question your discernment." She looked meaningfully at Diva.

"Hey, I didn't 'sense' a bear. Question your own 'discernment,' Andrea." Diva was not easily drawn into self-reflection, Andrea thought with annoyance.

"Well, I think we should all thank Bear for showing up. Maybe we can get some honey from Rae and leave it out in a bowl for him."

Diva rolled her eyes. "Who are you waiting for? Winnie the fucking Pooh? Was the bear you saw wearing a red shirt, Andrea? That thing about questioning discernment was definitely meant for you. Now let's go for dinner, I'm starved." With that, Diva stepped to the doorway, shifted back into raven and took off towards the dining hall.

"I wish she'd teach us how to do that," Eden said wistfully.

"You're supposed to start with your imagination," Andrea suggested. "You know, visualizing your hands turning into paws or wings and stuff."

"Well, my imagination was stunted by a controlling mother and Catholic schools," Eden sighed. "Maybe the Shift will knock something loose in me, I'd love to be able to shapeshift like Diva."

"Be careful what you wish for," Andrea said with a shudder, recalling what little she knew about Diva's life. "I think for Diva it's more like a consolation prize. Come on, it's getting late."

* * *

The moon was shining in the bedroom window keeping Harvey from falling asleep. He wasn't sure about the Next Council, all that process stuff and the passing of the talking stone. It seemed like a lot of effort. Things were changing so fast, yet the Crones talked about biding their time, having patience, waiting for the right moment. Since his dream experience in Diva's story and finding Eve at Nemesis, the Crones were seeing him differently. Rabbi Leaf had convinced him to take a dip in the pond and said some prayers for his protection. Aurelia gave him a medicine bag and told him to start noticing things to collect and put in the bag, to start to cultivate his powers and honor his helpers.

So far, all he had was a little love note Mattie left him one morning when she was out for an early walk and an acorn that had hit him on the head — dropped perhaps by a squirrel who wanted to be his helper? All Harvey could think of were the Saturday morning cartoons where animals talked and wore pants and suspenders, so the helper thing still seemed a little hokey.

Elsie said the acorn was to remind him that the seed of everything that is to unfold is already inside him, just waiting for the right conditions. Then she told a story about certain pinecones that can only release their seeds after going through a raging forest fire because the fires are needed to create the right conditions for them to grow. At least that's what she said at the ceremony the Crones had to honor him and Mattie.

"I hope I can unfold without massive fires," he'd thought. As the Cronation arborist, all the Crones seemed to think an acorn was a fitting symbol for Harvey, and Mattie was knitting him a hat in the shape of an acorn cap.

"That's where women can get a little goofy," he thought. "What the hell would Wayne say if I showed up in an acorn cap?" Sometimes Harvey missed his brother and the other guys he knew. Once in a while he'd recruit a guy for a Tantra internship that he knew wouldn't work out, just so they could go out for a beer before the guy left to pick fruit in Chile or go work on a kibbutz. Harvey had convinced Al, who ran the local bar, to stock some organic beer — but most of those Tantra guys were strict vegans and couldn't bear a whiff of alcohol. The vibe in a bar or watching a football game would practically put them into a coma.

Aurelia assured Harvey that the male element of the human race was still necessary and valuable and that the Tantra guys were an extreme — like a type of sexual monk — performing a needed service to support the shift to the next era. But sometimes Harvey worried about the future. Such thoughts kept him awake at night. He could imagine that if more men got a chance to work the land and walk in the forest everyday like he did, TV sports might fade as a national pastime. But what if men were just obsolete?

He gazed out the window, watching the treetops sway. Suddenly the room darkened considerably. Harvey heard a loud sniffing sound and jumped, naked, out of bed. He grabbed the talking stick that Elsie had given him and Mattie to honor the Hieros Gamos and went to see what had suddenly happened to the moonlight. He stubbed his toe but kept himself from yelling. He looked over toward Mattie, who was snoring softly, her spiky hair forming a halo against the pillow, giving her the look of a hip saint.

Since the Hieros Gamos, he and Mattie had been sharing the small house Harvey had built on the edge of the Heartscape land. That part of "what was unfolding" he had no doubt about. Harvey adored Mattie and living together was the best thing that ever happened to him. The little house had a glowing energy now that made Harvey so happy. The elders had suggested that the two of them live together for thirty days while preparations were made for a true community celebration. By that time, from all available evidence coming in reports from all over the globe, the main Shift should have happened, the Crones believed, and there would be much cause to rejoice. "I hope I live that long," Harvey muttered.

There was something pressed against the window now, blocking the moonlight. When it blinked, Harvey jumped back and bolted downstairs. No one had mentioned that what they were waiting for might have large bloodshot eyes and be tall enough to peer into a second story window. Harvey hurried downstairs and out the back door. He crept around to the front and saw what looked to be a huge man wearing a ratty animal suit, maybe twenty feet tall and peering into the bedroom window.

He stared at the huge beast, then he looked down at the stick in his hand, carefully carved with two figures, male and female entwined in a loving embrace. "Shit."

The creature turned toward Harvey at the sound, waved, and began coming towards him, walking on two legs like an exceptionally scruffy man.

"Well, here goes. This is supposed to be a talking stick. So I guess I won't beat him senseless with it — although that seems like the logical thing to do." Harvey looked down at himself, wearing only his medicine bag, his member glowing in the soft moonlight. He hadn't thought to pull on any clothes. He was just concerned about Mattie's safety when he jumped out of bed and grabbed the stick.

"Well, if this thing kills me," Harvey swallowed hard, "I'm sure the Crones will work it into a good story. Maybe I'll become famous as the sacrificial transitional male, gave myself up to conquer the last vestiges of —"

"Yang." The beast extended a matted hand as it ambled toward Harvey. It had decreased in size as it moved closer, so it was now only a foot and a half or so taller than Harvey.

"Ah — greetings, Yang. I'm Harvey." He grasped the paw. "Welcome to the Farm?" Harvey slowly lowered the stick, which he realized he was still holding above his head in a menacing fashion.

Yang was rangy, covered with thick hair on most of his body and, Harvey couldn't help but notice, had a very long, dun-colored schlong. Harvey looked down at himself. He hadn't been around naked men since high school showers after gym class, but he was confident that adjusting for height, he measured up pretty well.

"Dude, you seem to be shrinking, your eyeball filled my whole bedroom window a minute ago."

"Don't rub it in. I don't have much time left," Yang spoke in a voice that sounded like Danny DeVito after a hard night in a New Jersey saloon. Up close he didn't seem scary to Harvey just really mangy, smelly, and very tired.

"Is there a place I can rest? I've got a lot to tell you since you seem to be the designated guy-of-the-next-age. It took awhile to find you. Not much to sniff." Yang wrinkled his dog-like nose. "In my heyday I could smell a real man for miles."

Harvey sniffed his own armpit reflexively. "Yeah, I've noticed that since I've been eating a vegetarian diet my sweat doesn't stink as much." He narrowed his eyes at the hairy visitor, who yawned, showing his rather long canine teeth in the moonlight.

"So, Harvey, is it? We've got a lot to go over, Harvey, my boy."

"Well, sure, but maybe I should wake Mattie up, or call Aurelia first."

Yang shot Harvey a look that said, "You're killing me here, wussy boy. Don't make me bitch-slap you." Then he sighed wearily and pulled something out of a flap under the fur of his left armpit.

Harvey waved his hand. "Man, that's ripe!"

"You try carrying around the instructions for your own funeral for two thousand years that were written on a goat skin parchment and probably soaked in goat piss to preserve them. So here, just leave this on the doorstep." Yang thrust the folded document towards Harvey. "The women will know what to do. This is just you and me now and we've got work to do. But first, is there some place we can crash? And is there anywhere to get a beer in this place?"

Harvey thought about loading Yang into the truck and driving to the roadhouse out on the highway, but the creature looked unsteady and he wasn't sure Yang would make it or how he'd explain his companion to the denizens of Al's Grill & Sports Bar. Harvey put the stinky missive on the doorstep, trusting that Mattie would somehow understand what was going on or the Crones would figure it out.

"Do you mind if I get some clothes? They're just inside the door on a hook. It is December after all, and I'm not as furry as you."

"Go ahead, Sally, but I don't have much time, and if we don't have this little chat, it could be a whole lot worse for the men." Harvey stopped in his tracks. "I told them they had to think about the men!" he crowed.

Then he ducked inside and grabbed his work shirt and jeans off the hook. Maybe he was finally going to have the chance to do something important, maybe save the day.

"Not 'them,' Kemosabe. The women can't do what needs to be done or they would have done it by now," Yang said, half to himself. "Don't take all night," he yelled after Harvey as he lifted his dick and peed against the side of the house.

"Guess I can do without clean underwear, I don't want to wake Mattie," Harvey thought looking longingly at the staircase that led to their bedroom. He had built the whole house harvesting by hand some trees from the property and scavenging most of the other materials.

"I guess all guys go through stuff for the woman they love." As he dressed hurriedly Harvey refocused. "Okay. 'Divine Source, protect Mattie and all the women. And whatever I have to do with this Yang guy, let it unfold for the common, no, the highest good of all.'" Just in case he picked up the talking stick and headed outside to rejoin Yang.

He decided they should go up to the hermitage. It was empty now that Kali had moved in with Eve. A pretty small space in which to spend time with a goat-smelling creature, maybe, but Harvey grew up sharing a room with two brothers and had survived all-night farting contests. And this was for the good of all mankind, after all.

As Harvey came out the door, with the talking stick under his arm and zipping his jeans, he noticed Yang folding the goatskin parchment into an origami crane, an amazing feat given his blunt, hairy fingers. "Women like artsy shit," he explained to Harvey. "This way they won't miss it. Although they usually have eyes like a hawk. You know, leave a mess after you eat and they go all ballistic."

"Can you walk a little ways? The place I want to take you is about a mile away. Did you piss on the house?" Harvey sniffed the rank odor.

"Don't you have a car?" Yang looked stricken. "If I have to go, shouldn't

I get one last ride in an SUV?" He folded his arms.

"The noise and the lights would attract a lot of attention and besides, there isn't a road to the hermitage, just a path."

"Okay, but I'm letting you know, I might not make it." Yang pulled himself up to his full remaining height, an inch or two shorter than Harvey now, clutched his chest and wheezed.

"Look, man, I know that kind of 'poor me' stuff works with women sometimes, but I am still a guy, and I know bullshit when I hear it."

Yang sulked a bit as they started walking, then he eyed Harvey slyly, "I was afraid you didn't have any balls at all."

By the time they reached the hermitage, Yang was panting a bit but hadn't gotten discernibly smaller. Harvey lit a candle and got an afghan off the bed for each of them and a bottle of Crone Nectar that was stored in the earthen cellar. He put two glasses on the small table. They settled down into two armchairs facing each other. Yang laughed a tinny laugh that segued into a coughing fit.

When he stopped, Harvey said "So?"

"Well, first of all, do you know who I am?"

"Well, judging from your name and appearance, I'd guess Asian? A yeti? Maybe a relative of the Abominable Snowman?"

Yang sighed. "Yang. As in yin/yang. Ring a bell? I'm sure you've heard about it from the Crones: One half of the whole, the essential male, the active principle, upward moving energy, sun, dominance…"

Harvey nodded, thinking, "If this shaggy flea-bitten bastard is the essential male principle —"

"I know what you're thinking, I've seen better days, I'm a far cry from Julius Caesar or Cesar Chavez, for that matter. The fact is, the male principle is on its way down, running out of juice, in need of a rest."

"That's what the Crones say! That's what this whole place is about," Harvey said excitedly.

"Thanks, Einstein. I really thought I was here for a pedicure, you know, or maybe a bikini wax." Yang started coughing again.

"Maybe some tea instead of the wine?" Harvey said as he got up and rummaged through the cabinets. "This Throat Coat stuff they use is great for coughs, has slippery elm bark in it or something."

"Stop, Kid, you're really killing me here," Yang rasped. "It's great that you're one of these new men, and it's great that you seem to have adjusted to all this Crone stuff, but I gotta tell you, the men out there are suffering." Yang jerked his thumb towards the door.

"Most of man-kind is not going down easy. It's making them act all stupid, shooting up people and places, and writing a lot of screaming doomsday books and movies that just mirror how it feels inside them. With me fading, they feel like the world is coming to an end."

"I know! That's what I've been saying to Mattie," Harvey agreed. "But I guess the Crones have been advised by all their counselors on the Other Side not to focus on the men." Harvey leaned forward and looked at Yang. "It isn't, is it? I mean, the world isn't ending?"

"That's where you and me come in." Yang slapped Harvey on the knee as he put a mug of tea on the table and then leaned back and pulled a huge hand-rolled cigarette from one of his pouches. He leaned forward toward the candle with the blunt held between his yellowed teeth.

"I'm not sure if smoking is allowed in the hut. This place is strictly for healing and stuff," Harvey said, turning his head from the pungent aroma Yang emitted from fumbling in his pouches.

"Well, this is strictly medicinal. Practically mainstream now, so don't worry — and if we don't smoke it, we can't get to where we need to go." Harvey looked skeptical but watched as Yang fired up a very healthy sized joint and took a drag then he handed it to Harvey. "You know this is bud from all female plants, that's one of the main ways the shift is happening. Enough of this weed and any man can make it through the Shift. Here, take it slow at first," Yang counseled, "it's probably gonna get you there quickly, what with all your space time travel and such."

Harvey took a tentative drag. He'd never smoked cigarettes, and the few times he'd tried pot he'd gotten headaches — but it was just some ditch weed his brother grew. Being more of a beer guy was fine with him. But this smoke didn't make him cough and smelled like cedar and leaves burning and just a hint of ripe jock strap. It did, however, bring tears to his eyes, almost immediately, though not from the smoke.

"How'd you know about my detox work?"

Yang snorted, "Where do you think I came from? The Salvation Army? What's with the tears, Mary?"

Harvey wiped his eyes. "I don't know. I just started thinking about my cousin, my brothers, the other guys that I was with when the truck hit Aurelia's mom. I haven't seen them much since I moved onto the Farm. They just think I'm on some guilt trip, they have no idea what I've learned or what I've gone through since I came here."

Yang nodded and took another hit. "Special hybrid: 'Rock the Shift,' perfect balance of CBD and THC. Whatever you're dealing with, this stuff will call it up. It's all about restoring a healthy homeostasis." When his coughing subsided he said, "Yeah, what do you think those guys would say if they knew what you've been up to here?"

Harvey sighed. "Stupid shits, all three of them. First they'd assume I'm getting laid all the time since it's all women here. Second, that I'm doing all the grunt work cause I'm mostly the only guy. And third, I'm an idiot because I recruit the Tantra guys and they do get laid all the time. Or they'd say I'm hypnotized or something, you know, being held captive, that the women are witches or something. I don't know. How could I explain what I saw when I dream traveled and saw Diva's soul getting so fucked over by so many men?"

Yang grunted and said, "Keep smoking."

"When I was still in the hospital after the accident, I tried to tell Wayne — my younger brother — about how Aurelia came to visit me every day. How she sat with me and listened and forgave me for running over Phoebe, and how that blew my mind. But Wayne just laughed and said he wanted some of whatever pain meds I was on." Yang seemed to be nodding off so Harvey poked him. "Look is this just some kind of male bonding bullshit? You said you were here for a reason."

Yang roused himself "No, no — here's the deal. The universe runs on a simple principle: The Great Tao, the Cosmic Unfolding, whatever you want to call it. Energy is constantly in motion, coming out of its oneness to separate and have something else to hang out with, so becoming two-ness, and going back and forth like that. Each of the two is a one and so it has its own two-ness, so things keep differentiating — it gets very complicated. But all things being One, they also contain the other thing that they are hanging out with. All things are constantly turning into their opposite, though with most things, not at a rate you can actually see. Constantly arising; constantly falling. It's all about a healthy homeostasis, like I said before. At the end of a cycle — like now — it gets pretty wonky, it seems things are really speeded up; but time is an illusion, so there you have it."

"But how is that possible?" Harvey was feeling a little fuzzy, and he was never much of a theory guy to begin with.

"Stay with me, man — it's because of the Ultimate Oneness. Everything is part of the big Oneness, but is also a little oneness, and everything in you is its own oneness. Like you've been mostly male, right? But you are obviously starting to manifest your pansy-assed side. And you aren't fighting it like a real man would."

Harvey lunged for Yang to punch his lights out, but Yang dodged and threw his head back and just laughed his tinny laugh, so out of character for such a hairy guy. "Sorry, man, this is sort of like the interview part. I just have to check you out to see which 'guy lights' you have switched on

— before we go."

"Well, if we're going somewhere, let's go. Wait. What's our intention?" Harvey was definitely in an altered state but clear enough to know that he didn't want to go off with Yang without the protection of the Source. Mattie would be proud of him, he thought.

"Our intention is simple: We're going to save mankind. Emphasis on the 'man.'"

31

Mattie stretched and rolled over. She had to admit she was pretty blissed out in this new arrangement with Harvey. Ah! Crone wisdom. She'd had her share of Tantra boys, a few crushes on women that took a physical turn, but this was something different.

"I wonder if he's up making breakfast," she thought, seeing his side of the bed empty. "That would be too good to be true!" She'd listened to stories about relationships from so many of the women over the years. So many had been treated badly by fathers, brothers, husbands and lovers, Mattie often wondered why anyone bothered at all. It wasn't until recently, with the return of Kali and Diva — women her age or younger — that she wondered about the future of relationships between men and women. Mostly it seemed theoretical, abstract. If the Crones could guide the Shift, would the balance of energy realign peacefully so that the men could joyfully see themselves as being in service to the feminine principle? Would humans see "male" and "female" in a more generous way, like a sliding scale of notes to be played on the wonderful instrument of the body? Would women accept the men graciously as they struggled with the changes to come, or attack them for past failings and what was bound to look like weakness at first? Sarah Leaf said the reason the Israelites wandered in the desert for forty years was so the generation who'd lived as slaves would die out and not pass on slave consciousness. Would something like that be necessary now? What kind of relationships would her generation have? Would transgender become the norm? Would a generation of men and women have to pass on before something really new could happen?

Mattie had so far lived the life of the eternal virgin in the true sense, a woman one-in-herself, like Artemis, the ancient Greek Goddess, living at one with the world, embracing life, immersed in nature and in the compassion and wisdom of the Crones. There wasn't anything she lacked that a man could provide; there just weren't any men as complete in themselves as Mattie was complete in herself. Before Phoebe died, and all was set in motion to bring Harvey to her, the Farm had seemed to Mattie like Eden, a place of beauty, simplicity, and awe. Life was marked by joy and service as women came there to be healed or to learn how to take healing into the world, and by the seasons that were celebrated with food and dancing and song. On her forays into mainstream culture she was always a curious visitor but one with no doubt about the illusory quality of the man-made world. She could shift her perception so deftly that even while driving a cab down Michigan Avenue in downtown Chicago, where she had retrieved Eve, she could blink and see the landscape as it had been before the skyscrapers formed the urban canyons of the city's downtown. With an intentional thought she could see the creatures that used to populate the lakeshore, or commune with the gulls and jays that still lived at the water's edge. She could see the mycelium filaments running for miles underground, surfacing as mushrooms in the forests beyond the city.

Most importantly, she could see the spark of the Divine in everything simply by choosing to focus on that aspect of reality. Sometimes the light Mattie saw in people on the city streets was like a flickering candle — and not always in the ones you'd think. She would always say a little prayer of encouragement to the light in the heart of someone who needed it, so often a man in a suit with expensive shoes looking important and carrying a briefcase. But until Harvey, her concern for men had been impersonal, detached, the kind of compassionate disinterest that would make the Buddha proud.

Watching Harvey's transformation into a shamanic light being as he entered Diva's dream and worked there to free her soul showed Mattie what was possible and gave her an inkling of another way the Shift might manifest. What else could they do together? She knew about the Indigo children out there raising the vibration and presumably reproducing. Maybe she and Harvey would have kids; maybe they'd have to build a nursery at the Farm. That was a funny thought! If humans weren't on their way out, maybe they'd find another way to continue, raise up a bunch of little full-spectrum light beings that could lead through love and celebration. Life was such a glorious mystery and Mattie loved to contemplate it. The Hieros Gamos between her and Harvey wouldn't be complete for a while. Things would unfold in their own time, she figured.

She surveyed the room from the comfort of the bed, under the cover of a duvet filled with feathers shed and gathered from the Farm's own ducks. A pretty bare space, this room, just waiting to come to life. After the ceremony, maybe they could decorate; choose some art from the barn. That made Mattie smile.

Then she noticed the talking stick was missing. It had been propped up under the window. Why would Harvey have taken the stick? It was to be blessed at the Hieros Gamos ceremony and dedicated before they used it together for speaking circles. Maybe he was out for a walk, getting the feel of it.

"Harvey, you here?" Mattie yelled as she got out of bed and pulled on her jeans. She padded downstairs in bare feet pulling a Dixie Chicks tee shirt over her head. "I better bring some other clothes over here. These are getting a little smelly." She went into the kitchen. "No tea made, no sign of breakfast made or eaten, no note. Whoa! 'No note'? Girl, watch yourself or you'll be writing to 'Dear Abby.' Are expectations like that encoded in the female DNA?" Mattie got herself a bowl of apples and chopped walnuts and sprinkled cinnamon and cardamom on top.

"Bless you, apples, bless you, nuts, for nourishing me with your life force energy. And my spice girls, thank you for favoring my body with your flavor. For the earth that nourished all of you, the rain that quenched your thirst, for the hands that tended you, I thank the Source of All for all of us. Ahimsa."

Even though it had been but a few weeks, it felt strange not to eat breakfast with Harvey. After a lifetime of communal meals with sometimes hundreds of women, Mattie found watching Harvey — the way he chopped the fruit just so, measured his ingredients before mixing, actually followed recipes — a source of endless fascination. He loved to place a carefully prepared bowl of food in front of her and watch her enjoy it. Harvey was shy about eating in the dining room. He said it made him realize what women must feel like to be looked at in public by men. Even though the women were loving and friendly, being singled out for attention made him feel like an object, a novelty.

As for Mattie, she often felt sorry for people who lived and ate with just one or two others rather than having a community. The things they miss! Singing for hours after meals, taking turns serving the food to each other, cooking in the huge gleaming pots that Rae kept in the spotless Farm kitchen. One of the Cronation principles was that all the jobs of service to the community were shared on a rotating basis. Not because they were a source of drudgery, as many of the women had been led to believe by the way such work was treated in the worlds they came from, but because of the blessings that flow from service that were so rich and varied. Every woman got the chance to serve the others by preparing and serving food, cleaning up, even scrubbing toilets, which although they were all one hundred percent composting, still needed some care.

Sometimes a rare new woman from a background where servants do all basic labor encountered Aurelia or one of the elders doing a menial task and would mistake her for hired help. One woman at her first dinner at the Farm fainted dead away when Aurelia was introduced and addressed the women. She actually stood up and said, "But that's the cleaning lady!" Then gasped and passed out when the assembled throng broke into laughter. It was all the Crones could do to talk her out of wandering the Farm in sackcloth and ashes afterwards. She apologized to Aurelia who looked her in the eye and said, kindly, "Sister, it isn't me you need forgiveness from. It's the Divine Mother whom you have been blind to in the eyes of all the women in your own life up until now. She was waiting for you in the one who cleaned your house, checked out your groceries, read your water meter, and served you that burger. From now on, just remember to greet Her each time you see Her, especially when you look in the mirror each day. That's all She asks."

Mattie had so many memories, stories, and experiences of her own. This new chapter with Harvey was an unexpected and sweet unfolding of their work together with the SAC chair, working with Eve, bringing Kali and Diva and the Nemesis women back to the Farm, and it was delightful so far. She was grateful to be called into service in the Hieros Gamos, the sacred partnership, and wondered what would come of that. But for now, where was the Dude? She put her scraps into the compost bucket under the sink and cleaned the dishes.

In the communal dining hall the women sometimes sang a long and complicated Hebrew prayer when they finished a meal that came from the Jewish tradition. "The Jews always took extra time after the meal to honor the miracle of their lives continuing, something that never felt guaranteed," Rabbi Sarah Leaf explained. "They wanted to prolong the time of embodiment that eating and singing provides because so much of the work they have been called to do is mental. It is easy to lose track of the blessing of being in a body. Plus we tend to eat heartily and need the time to digest our food," Rabbi Sarah Leaf explained.

She taught the women that the Jews had blessings for every possible occasion from peeing to building a house, from life to death. The women loved that they were blessing the things themselves as well as the Source of life, not a capricious father god who needed to be placated. They learned how to see and feel the energy increase in themselves as well as in what or who they blessed. Building these connections strengthens the flow of energy and created the "net of light" that holds all creation together, Sarah taught them. She also taught them as many traditional blessings as they liked, and urged them to make up their own, in their own words. Women posted versions they liked everywhere around the Farm, embellished with their artwork. To many of the women at the Farm, singing after meals was a highlight of every day. Raised to be "nice," or quiet, or seen and not heard, or to think that only "singers" can sing, the welcoming of every voice in song, in prayer and in discussion at the Farm was a revelation. Tears flowed regularly during those after-meal celebrations.

"How easy it is to forget to bless all the others who are part of creating each moment when you're alone!" Mattie thought. "Without a group to eat with and sing with, it's so easy to rush to the next task, to let your head lead instead of your heart." She gazed at her reflection in the window over the sink. Harvey had sited the cottage so that it looked out over a grape arbor that led to a small vegetable garden and then to the forest beyond. She washed her hands slowly and repeated a prayer that Sarah Leaf had taught them. "When I wash my hands, I remember the holiness of the body and I thank the Source for this particular body in which I travel." Just then a red-tailed hawk struck the earth and shot up again with a small black garter snake in its talons.

"Bless you, Harvey, for building this beautiful house and for the wisdom to nestle it so beautifully here on our Mother, the Earth. You know, if we just blessed every gift all day long, it would be hard to get into too much trouble!" She dried her hands and turned reluctantly from the window "Now where in Goddess' green earth is that man?"

Just then there was a knock at the door. Mattie ran to find Aurelia, smiling with a basket on her arm. She opened the door and fell into her mother's arms.

"Momma! Blessings, what have you got there? Come in!" Then she looked down — "Oh, what's this?" Mattie picked up the origami crane that Yang and Harvey had left on the doorstep.

"I brought you some apple cobbler that Rae made for breakfast. It was so delicious I couldn't bear the thought of not sharing it with you and Harvey. Where is that man?"

"I don't know. He wasn't here when I woke up. The talking stick is gone so I figured he went out walking with it."

"Maybe that's it. I didn't see him on my way here either. Some of the women thought they'd seen a bear last night," Aurelia said. "Did you hear anything? Maybe Harvey heard something." Aurelia looked alarmed, not a countenance Mattie had often seen on her mother.

"Momma, do you really think a bear ate Harvey?" Mattie had her hands on her hips, her head cocked at her mother. "Come on! He grew up around here, remember? I think he'd know how to stay out of a bear's way."

Aurelia sat down. "Oh my! You never know where the Source will challenge you next! I just flashed on Phoebe losing my daddy, and me losing yours, Riva losing my grandpa Walter." There were tears in Aurelia's eyes. "I'm just a mother here in this moment, plain and simple, Baby. I want my girl to be happy and to have some babies of her own! Forgive me for all my fears and wishes. Ahimsa!"

Mattie hugged her mother tight and the two of them cried tears of grief for all the mothers, wives, daughters who'd ever lost the men they loved. Then Mattie placed her hands on her mother's shoulders and looked into her eyes. "Each of those men was killed by men, for men's folly, Great Grandpa Walter by the slave traders, Grandpa by the police, and Daddy by soldiers in a misguided war. The Source has guided Harvey here to us to help heal all that. I'm sure of that much, Momma."

Aurelia embraced Mattie and the two of them rocked and cried for a long while.

"All right, Momma, let's have some of that cobbler. I'll warm up the tea. Bring over that thing you found on the step, too, will you?" The two women settled down at the kitchen table and Aurelia placed the crane between them.

"It looks like origami, a peace crane, but it's made out of hide of some kind. It's stiff from the cold. Let's let it warm up while we enjoy this blessed food. Maybe Harvey will show up to share it with us."

Once they had settled at the table, Mattie asked, "Momma, what do you think about Kali? And that story about her mother running off to that Rav Babka man when she left Kali at the Farm before. I know she and Eve are starting to balance each other, but do you think that stuff about murdering men to set things right, do you think she's over that?"

"Oh my, she's getting there," Aurelia assured her. "You heard her vision about Uziel Gal and the machine gun; she's learning how complex things are. As long as she saw herself as an outsider she could fall into trying to be a hero, seeing herself as rescuing Diva. That's a powerful tonic against her own pain. That's how we come to seek community. We feel our own limitations and realize we need others. It is such a gift that she brought us those guns! Who could have imagined?"

Aurelia finished her last spoonful of apple cobbler. "Bless that Rae, the girl can bake! Look, Mattie, we are getting into unknown territory here. That's both the blessing and the challenge of this moment in the unfolding of the Shift. I've been thinking a lot about this, believe me, and

I'm beginning to see it a little bit more clearly. You know that Phoebe has been able to guide me quite a bit since she left us but lately she either hasn't been showing up or just giving me brief and cryptic messages."

Mattie nodded, feeling a little rush of energy. What if she lost Aurelia? How would she handle that?

"And while up until now we were guided not to focus on the men, it's also clear from the work that you and Harvey have done, that the issues with the men are now coming into play — and we don't know yet what all that will mean. I can only imagine how angry Kali was when her mother left her here to go off after that guru man. Her father left her too, for a version of herself, for a young woman. It must be even harder to lose someone when you see it's their choice to leave you, that they prefer someone else."

"But, Momma, you taught me that the way we see the Divine Source, how we come to truly know Her is through others. And no one of us can do it all for another, so sometimes people they have to leave, don't they? We rail and suffer in our losses until we see that She is still there for us and that each human houses a blessed spark of Her, but only a spark. You said it's how we learn to love everyone as a manifestation of Her."

Aurelia gazed at her daughter whom she loved more than anything. "Mattie, you've been raised here and loved by so many people who have worked their whole lives until much of their shadow has blown off their souls like so much dust. When more shadow shows up, well, they work some more, and they do it every day. You have had so many worthy, beautiful embodiments of the Divine to love and teach you. Think of how many varieties of the spark of the Divine have mothered you. You know in your bones and soul that I may be your mother but I'm not the be-all and the end-all. You have Elsie; you had Phoebe; rest her soul, you have Rae and Lorelei. You have never been at risk for thinking that one little old human being, male or female, has all the answers or is always right or should be able to fill all your needs. And I've been blessed with knowing that it is an unnecessary illusion to think that, as your mother, I am all there is, the ultimate authority. I ask in every breath to be guided in how to love and nurture you and, even so, I could only do the best I could, not be perfect."

Mattie nodded. Indeed she was blessed with teachers and mothers in abundance.

Aurelia continued, "I don't know much about this Rav Babka man, but there aren't many men who know how to handle lots of women hanging on their every word. Still, when he tells them they are holy embodiments of the divine when they feel more like worn out old shoes that is powerful. They are calling down a lot of energy between them — but they may not know what to do with it. And some women imagine that receiving the attention of such a man is the same as doing their own work. It's like taking all the credit for your beautiful home when it's cleaned by a maid, decorated by a designer, and your meals are prepared by a cook."

The Divine had gifted the women of Cronation with the deep knowledge that many steps are needed for anything to ripen to its fullness or to reveal itself in completion. Haste and efficiency are not of value before the time of harvest. Presenting beauty while hiding effort was a sham that provoked envy and shame in others. Hiding the steps of any task and pretending to have streamlined things was a way to get followers but not a way to pass on wisdom.

"Let the seams show,' Phoebe always told me. If you are teaching others, you must let them see how the thing is made; telling folks about how you came to your understanding is just as important as the understanding itself. Otherwise they just have to take your word for it. That is how fake gurus are made: they hide the seams and often they hide the scissors, so no one can make any alterations to what they have created. When you hide the seams, then needy people can mistake you for the Divine Herself. Everyone must sew their own garment of wisdom, Mattie, and give credit to all the threads and patches. You take the cloth you were given, but you take it apart and remake it into something new, something that is your own."

"I see, Momma. In a way, that is what Kali was doing, isn't it? She took that painting her Momma had and she turned it into guns."

Aurelia laughed, "She took a thing of beauty and traded it for the means to create her own vision, yes, I guess you're right, employing the law of 'Kind Inference' to quite an extreme. But think about it, Mattie — my first reaction was horror. Her vision was centered on killing that Rav Babka and maybe her own daddy but she is smart enough to see that plan as murder, plain and simple — so she mixed in what she had learned here at the Farm."

"Now hold on, Momma," Mattie was shocked. "She didn't learn anything here like that!"

"She got the idea of being a part of something larger than herself, Mattie, that's a fact. How she interpreted it, well, that's another matter. And look at her Nemesis plan — she spoke to women about their abuse and their pain and they responded. Why, she was on the path of becoming a guru herself. If she hadn't had those women come back here and snatch Eve, well, who knows what could have happened? And if you and Harvey hadn't seen a path…"

"You've always taught me that everything that happens is the sum of the moments that went before, Momma. Right action flows from the daily effort to correct our course in love and gratitude, and to turn honestly to our community to verify what we think we know."

"It's a humble path," Aurelia added, "one that seems tedious at times, but it works. Community is something humans are still learning about. It's not created just by collecting people who agree with us, although that's a step. It's about being open to the unexpected, like the guns. It's also about widening our vision to include more and more of life, people and all beings, into what we see as our family. Not picking a guru but seeing everything and everyone as a teacher. We share not just our strengths but our limitations as well. I am so grateful that those Nemesis girls are here. And Harvey too. Let's save him that last piece of cobbler."

32

The embers of the joint were burning out in a clay vessel shaped like two cupped hands. If any of the Crones had happened by and looked in the window of the hermitage, they would have seen Harvey, head thrown back, legs splayed, asleep in an armchair. On the chair opposite him, curled up and sawing logs, there appeared to be a fairly large, and rather mangy, coyote. Their spirit bodies were standing outside and above, in the velvet night sky, gazing down at the Farm.

"So let's start out simple," Yang said. "Let's check out your brother."

"Wow! This is awesome!" Instantly, Harvey's vantage point was about a foot away from where his brother Wayne was sitting on the couch in the family room of the house where Harvey and his brothers grew up swearing, fighting, and playing Grand Theft Auto IV. Wayne was the only one of the brothers still living at home. He had a part-time job as a janitor at the local junior high school and, though he swore that the accident hadn't affected him, Harvey saw an unmistakable dullness in Wayne's eyes. He watched as Wayne threw down the controls of the game and got up to get a beer; popped the top and sat down on the couch again, staring into space.

"Jeez, he seems really lonely," Harvey said.

"Yeah, well, that's because he is."

Harvey's mom came into the room, looked at Wayne and shook her head. She went upstairs to bed.

"She doesn't see it," Yang said.

"See what?"

"See that open space in his chest?"

Harvey squinted and saw an almond-shaped opening in Wayne's chest. He jumped back. "What the hell is that?"

"That's a mandorla." Yang was sitting on the kitchen table scratching his ass and eating whatever verminous lice or critters he found lurking in his three thousand year old hide. "The vesica pescis. When two circles overlap they form this space; in this case the circles are the male and female principles. The space is only open for a little while every few thousand years or so. But while it is open, big stuff can happen. It needs to be activated, you have to go in there and flip the switch, so to speak."

"What the hell are you talking about? Flip what switch?" Suddenly Harvey found himself inches away from Wayne, peering into this strange little opening in his chest. He could see that the mandorla held a little shrine. There were tiny lights outlining its edges, one side in red and one side in blue, with a white light at each point of the almond shape. Inside there were garlands of flowers strung, pots of incense burning and a small table covered with a golden cloth.

"What is this shit doing inside my brother?"

"Look more closely. What do you see?" Yang replied.

"There's a table with a little red cushion on it, flowers and stuff, oh, and a little doll, it looks like a baby doll that a kid would play with."

"Pick it up," Yang instructed. "Kiss it like it was a real baby and place it on the cushion."

Harvey sighed, "This is why I never did drugs," but he did as Yang told him to, even if he felt stupid kissing a half-inch-long plastic doll.

"Okay, it's on the table? Great, now repeat after me: 'Abracadabra.'"

"Abracadabra," Harvey said solemnly.

Yang cracked up, laughing his tinny laugh. "Just fuckin' with you, man! You should see your face. That is a power word but not the one we need. Here, say this...." He handed Harvey a small scroll made of goatskin that he pulled out of the pouch under his left arm. Harvey braced himself for the smell of old cheese and sweat socks but instead the room was filled with the scent of roses. Wayne looked up quizzically.

"Can he smell that?" Harvey asked as he loosened the red string that bound the tiny scroll.

"It's probably really faint for him, but if he can smell it even a little bit, that's a good sign," Yang replied.

Harvey looked at the scroll, black lettering in a fine hand, but he had no idea what it was. He thrust the scroll toward Yang, "This is in some language I don't understand."

"It's written in Hebrew, actually some of the words are ancient Aramaic," Yang said, "Look again."

When Harvey looked back at the scroll he saw the words were slowly transforming into English — but not in words he could comprehend.

"Cool. But I still can't make it out."

"Just read it the way it looks, Dickweed. It's a transliteration of a prayer for the return of the Feminine. And don't take all night, we've got more work to do." Yang was picking his teeth with a serrated steak knife he'd found in a drawer.

"Nahazir et ha Shekinah limkomah bet Zion uva tayval culam," Harvey intoned and then watched, mesmerized, as the tiny doll inside of Wayne's mandorla began to move its arms and legs and cry. He backed away and looked at Wayne and saw tears rolling down his brother's cheeks as well. He looked at Yang for an explanation, but none was forthcoming.

"Okay, cool, let's go. Don't worry, he'll be okay."

Yang put a hand on Harvey's shoulder and they were suddenly walking down Michigan Avenue in downtown Chicago. Harvey realized they were still invisible to everyone else when a power-walking woman passed right through him. Thanks to all the climate irregularities, Chicago's winters were practically balmy these days — when they weren't having a record-breaking blizzard. They sat down at an outdoor table in front of a Starbucks and watched the early morning commuters rush in and out, talking on cell phones and clutching their half-skim double-caf lattes.

"What do you see?" Yang asked.

"Lots of folks too busy to live?"

Yang nodded. "Check it out."

When Harvey looked again he noticed that every woman he saw wore a sword in a scabbard that banged against her leg. Some were in power suits, some in impossibly high stiletto heels and stylish coats, some in jeans and sweaters. They all seemed oblivious to the hardware they sported.

"Some kind of a women's pirate convention in town or something?" Harvey asked, bewildered.

Yang snorted, "Look at the men."

Harvey blinked and this time he could see beneath the suits and the starched shirts, beneath the parkas and trench coats that the men wore, past the work shirts embroidered with a guy's name over the pocket. Each one had a mandorla in his chest, like Wayne did. Some of them had carved walnut doors with intricately engraved locks; others were boarded up like broken storefronts after a riot. Some were surfaced with metal plates that appeared seamless, and some were covered with rusty, much-patched tin.

"None of them are open like Wayne's was," Harvey marveled.

"Nice call, Professor. So what can we do?" Yang was finishing the dregs of a double Americano with extra sugar that some guy had put down on their table and forgotten about while yelling into his blue tooth head set, and jumping into a cab, apparently on his way to "murder some prick."

"Say the prayer?" Harvey offered.

"Not enough. Won't penetrate. Plus there are way too many to do each one."

"I wish Mattie were here. She'd know what to do!" Harvey groused.

"Listen to yourself, Harvey, you fucking wuss bag! 'Ask the woman, ask the woman.' If the women could fix this, don't you think they'd already have done it? This is men's work to free men! The rest will come after this."

"Listen, Yang, Mattie is the smartest, most amazing person I've ever met."

"That's not saying much, douche bag." Yang was getting agitated. "You've never even been out of the state. This is probably your first time in Chicago, isn't it?"

"No, I was here on a class trip to the Sear's Tower in the sixth grade. What's going on, Yang? This shit was actually starting to make sense for a minute. You shouldn't have drunk that coffee; you're all jacked up now."

Yang leapt to his feet, dukes up, complete piloerection bristling down his back. He looked twice his size, which was now several inches shorter than Harvey. He reminded Harvey of a dog his dad once had to put down — a 'fear biter' the vet had called it.

"Calm down, man, you said we had more work to do."

When Harvey stood up, he noticed he had a scabbard strapped to his leg, hanging from an elaborate jeweled belt. The gold handle of a sword protruded from the top. He placed his hand on it and it rose out of the scabbard, seemingly on its own. He was now facing Yang, coffeed up and swearing, his paws balled up into fists, dancing back and forth in front of the Starbucks like a manic carnival plush toy boxer.

That's when Harvey noticed the mandorla in Yang's chest. The matted chest hair had parted and sculpted itself into a yellowish grotto that framed the almond shaped space. Time seemed to stop as Harvey peered inside.

Harpies, harridans, and bats flew around an enormous black stone cave with dripping stalactites. Further inside, Spartan mothers, sending sons off to war, were repeating the mantra, 'Come back with your shield or upon it.' There were nuns with rulers bent over boys seated at grammar school desks, repeatedly whacking their knuckles and calling down the wrath of Jesus upon them. The cave was like an echo chamber where these and countless distressing messages endlessly rose and fell. Mothers shaking their heads, sadly holding report cards in front of shame-faced boys, angry, tight-lipped women hanging sheets from wet beds out the window for the whole neighborhood to see, while small boys hung their heads and cried. Prim kindergarten teachers waiting endlessly for fidgety boys to sit still before they'd begin to read the story. Mothers in aprons, bruises on their own faces, hitting boys with wooden spoons, taunting them, "Don't cry, don't cry, you sissy." Women taking endless objects — rocks, toys, scissors, food out of little boys' hands, intoning "No! No! No!" He saw mothers in fur coats with scarlet lips holding a manicured finger to their lips at the symphony, shushing little boys in tiny suits.

He saw mothers standing by as fathers beat sons with belts. He saw priests fucking altar boys in the sacristies of a thousand churches, counselors at endless camps and Boy Scout leaders at jamborees sodomizing children in the woods. He saw black men's lifeless bodies, ropes around their necks, swinging from branches, black men shot in the streets of cities, fields of skulls in Cambodia, a Nazi soldier bending to kiss his son and then shooting the son of a Jewish mother in Auschwitz in the next second.

He saw men in yellow bulldozers pushing off the tops of mountains to make way for luxury condos with swimming pools in Arizona where there isn't any water. He saw men constructing endless bridges, tunnels, highways, golf courses, skyscrapers, hospitals and schools; he saw laboratories, factories, industrial parks, expanding and growing larger and larger until they blotted out the earth beneath them. He saw residue from fertilizers, excrement, and factory waste flowing into streams and rivers like poison into a junkie's vein.

He saw pages and pages and pages of books, turning at a speed that prevented any of the words from being seen. Silicon-enhanced strippers slid up and down poles in bars in front of bald-headed men in cheap suits with expense accounts and bad breath. He saw men in sunglasses, pants at their ankles as young girls sucked their cocks and spit the rancid cum on the ground. He saw politicians down on all fours wearing just their blue blazers and socks while a woman in black stood over them with a cat o' nine tails, raising red welts on their backsides. He saw the atom bomb exploding, raining down hundred dollar bills from the mushroom cloud of toxic smoke and fire. It was a movie screen of horror in Yang's mandorla, an endless reel of naked pain, unacknowledged, denied, and disowned.

"Come on, you son of a bitch! Do it, you bastard!" Yang screamed, and Harvey blinked and looked at his hand grasping the jeweled weapon. He felt calm. He stepped back, raised his arm, and plunged the sword up to the hilt into the mandorla in Yang's chest. They were face to face. He could smell Yang's fetid breath. Harvey held him up, still impaled and looked into the creature's eyes. "I get it, man, I get it! I'm so sorry. And thank you."

Yang closed his eyes, a slight smile played on his lips. "I was afraid you might not have the balls."

Harvey pulled the sword out of Yang's chest — and all the images he had witnessed flew out in a screaming, stinking, red and black spiral. The city scene of cars and streets, buildings and people around him turned grayish and smoky and dreamlike. Harvey watched as an enormous mandorla appeared between Lake Michigan and the street; it was horizontal and blinked at him like an eye. Then it opened wide and with a terrible howling sucked the stream of images into its black maw, blinked again, and was gone. Yang was limp in Harvey's arms.

33

I was a little nervous about Aurelia's prediction that it was my destiny to work and room with Kali. She was the kind of woman that I always avoided — smart but dark, ambitious and a little mean. I never recruited her type for Wentworth and Wentsouth. Too edgy, I'd say. I imagined she was how I might have turned out if Mom had married O'Malley's rival for her affections, a smart guy from Harvard.

He came to her funeral and caused a little stir, good looking, dramatic. "So, you're Eve? I was a friend of your mother's in college. She was quite the firebrand. Sorry for your loss, a loss to the world as well." He asked me what I did with a flattering level of intensity and less than thirty seconds into my answer cut me off and moved on. I remember once when he called Mom after O'Malley died. "He's like a shark, never sleeps and always feeding," Mom had confided. "No heart, no real concern for other human beings except how they can serve his ends. But when he turns on the charm, look out!"

He was famous, written twenty books on politics, always on the talk shows. "He couldn't hold your father's jock strap," was Mom's answer when I asked if they'd been seriously involved. I learned from Mom to avoid the ambitious ones and in my line of work that pretty much ensured I'd be alone.

When I told Aurelia I had some "issues" about Kali, she just laughed and said "Why, Eve, Kali's just your shadow and you are hers, no doubt. The teacher shows up when the class is in session! There are no accidents in this sweet life."

My roomie and I were supposed to meet Harvey and have him run me through a SAC session so Kali could watch and see if she was comfortable resuming the work of clearing some of her pain in this way. She had at least gotten to the point of admitting that her anger at both her parents was possibly the source of wanting to kill men. Since she'd witnessed the guns and received the information about Uziel Gal she seemed to have softened and relaxed quite a bit.

But when I entered the room where all the SAC equipment was kept, it was dark. I knew Mattie and Harvey were sharing the cottage that Harvey had built. Maybe they were just lingering over a romantic breakfast. I waved to Kali as she came down the path, her hair still wet from the shower. She looked younger and less scary in her sweats. I stifled the urge to tell her she should have worn a hat and would catch pneumonia in the cool December air.

"Hi. Harvey isn't here," I offered, hoping she'd decide to take off. She looked relieved.

"Look, I'm not really sure I want to get involved in this stuff again, but I had some pretty freaky dreams when I was laid out there in the hermitage. They've been on my mind. Can I just tell you? Without the contraption and stuff?"

"Sure, I don't know how to hook up the equipment anyway," I admitted. "Do you want to just talk here, in case Harvey shows up?"

"No, I'd rather walk. It's always been easier for me to talk about weird stuff if I'm moving."

So, that's how I spent three hours with Kali, wandering all the back paths of the Farm as she more or less morphed back into Charity Greenberg, or maybe I just "withdrew my projections" as Mattie would have explained it to me.

"You know how I got to the hermitage in the first place, right? Can we go over that?" She began, her words causing puffs of mist in the cold air.

"Sure, after the stuff at your, er, office, after Mattie and Harvey showed up..."

"Look, Eve, I'm really sorry about kidnapping you. I know now how insane that was. I really can't believe how far Nemesis got. I'm actually starting to feel some compassion for that flake Rav Babka. Honestly, if you give people a grain of truth or a crumb of hope they'll pretty much follow you anywhere and do whatever you say. It's freaky." Kali looked genuinely amazed.

I felt a definite opening to trust and said, "For the moment, for the purpose of argument at least, can we both agree to suspend our doubts and take a ride on our faith in Aurelia and the other Crones? A few of them are my best friends from college, Rae, Gina, and Marty, and I trust them more than anyone on earth. Let's suppose there really is some kind of thing — a 'Shift' — going on, and we're a part of it. Don't we want to be kind to each other, be generous with ourselves? Like Mattie is always saying, do it for the highest good? So let's, for the moment, let's say it's all good, okay? No hard feelings. After all, it was more or less a kidnapping by Mattie that got me here in the first place. Believe me, making sense of all this is hard for me too."

Kali smiled and suddenly I saw a lovely young woman before me; maybe she could have been one of the women I mentored at Wentsouth. She hugged me and took a deep breath. "Okay, here goes. So I'm dreaming. I see myself and I've got this huge sword, but it's really heavy. I can't lift it so I'm sort of dragging it along the ground. Do you know what a tallit is? A prayer shawl?"

"Yeah," I nodded. "My mother was Jewish, New Age-y Jewish, but I know some of the basics."

Kali rolled her eyes, "Mine too! We'll have to talk about that some-day! But in the meantime, I think it will help you get the dream. Okay, so I have this heavy sword and I have a tallit over my shoulder and I'm walking into this black, smoky fog. It looks like the wildfires in California when I was growing up. Just this awful, roaring force. But I'm not coughing or anything, which seems weird, since I have asthma. And I'm going into this blackness. The whole time it's like I'm in slow motion, dragging the sword and struggling to put one foot in front of the other, but I know I have to keep going. I feel horrible. I'm scared, I'm tired. I feel really hopeless, like the world is ending.

"Just when I think I can't go any further, the smoke starts to clear — and I see I'm in a grove of trees. It's night. The sky is inky black — no, inky blue, almost black, because I can see the outlines of the trees. The trees are black and barren and I can see them against the sky. A woman comes to-wards me from out of the grove. She takes the tallit — which, by the way, has stayed pure white, which is insane. I wear black all the time because I always spill stuff on myself. I'm a total slob — anyway, she takes the tal-lit and she drapes it over my head. She thanks me for coming. Then she touches the sword. Suddenly it's really light, almost weightless, I can lift it easily. Then she looks into my eyes and I feel myself getting lighter and lighter, not my weight but like I'm being filled with light. But the strange thing is, she's made of darkness. She's like a black and white movie, she's shades of gray but with some blood-red parts. Her lips are this dull red, and parts of her dress are red. She seems sort of like she's made of smoke. Or a veil. She's not solid, is what I mean. Then she takes the tallit off my head. I look down and see she has the Earth in her hand. Well, not in her hand, it's floating above her hand, the size of a tennis ball. It's so beautiful and it's turning slowly. And it seems like she's offering it to me.

Kali had a faraway look in her eyes as she related the dream. "Then I raise the sword; actually, the sword raises itself. She's looking deeply into my eyes and smiling and I feel really peaceful but also energized. Not like coffee energy, just calm but powerful, I guess. Like everything is okay, I'm okay, the world is okay. Like there really is someone or something in charge, or there's a force that isn't random, that is power but also love. Oh, yeah, and one more thing — I saw an hourglass and it turned itself over or was turning itself over." She took a deep breath and sighed.

"Wow, Kali. That's intense!"

"Oh, yeah, and one more thing. She gave me a new name. Ashera."

I was fascinated by the dream. Spellbound, really, and so honored that Kali was willing to share it with me. Lots of possible meanings flooded into my head, but I heard Aurelia's voice in my head saying, "Just hold the space, just hold it." So all I said was: "I think this is something for the Next Council. Maybe we're all supposed to work with your dream together."

By that time we were near the hermitage, "Oh, I tried to scribble down as much of this as I could in the journal," Kali remembered. "Let's see if the door is unlocked and I'll get it."

"Yeah, and maybe we can warm up." I was freezing and Kali's hair formed stiff, icy ringlets around her face.

As Charity/Kali/Ashera rattled the doorknob, we were greeted by a low menacing growl. We looked at each other, shrieked, and ran all the way back to the compound.

We skidded to a stop in front of the dining hall where Mattie and Aurelia were talking excitedly with Rae and Elsie. "So this parchment," Mattie was holding something that looked like a dirty handkerchief, "was on the front step this morning, folded into an origami peace crane. We let it warm up and unfolded it and there's writing in Hebrew on it and it looks really ancient."

Aurelia looked more serious than I had ever seen her. "Does anyone know where Rabbi Sarah is? We must convene the Council right after lunch."

368 PAT B. ALLEN

When she spotted Kali and me it was like someone turned up a three-way bulb to high; she beamed at us and then looked wide-eyed. "Kali, Eve, why you two look as if you've seen a ghost! You're all out of breath!" Kali got her wind back sooner, "Aurelia, I think there's an animal or something in the hermitage." I was leaning on the fence still panting.

"Momma!" Mattie was clearly alarmed, "Do you think a bear got Harvey after all and dragged him off to the hermitage?" But there was something else about her. She seemed positively daffy — I mean, a bear would just eat a guy where he mauled him, right? I'm no naturalist — maybe he'd drag a meal off the main road and into the woods — but hike to a remote cabin, unlatch a door, go inside, and lock the door behind him?

Mattie's hair was flattened down on one side, she was wearing an old tee shirt and jeans and a flannel shirt of Harvey's. I realized I'd never seen her unhinged before. Not when I was freaking out in her cab, not when we saw the cache of guns at Nemesis. Mattie was like equanimity incarnate. Then it hit me: she's in love! Mattie and Harvey! I knew that, I knew about the Hieros Gamos, or at least I'd heard the Crones talking about it but I realized I was a little bit jealous. Good thing I was still recovering from our little run which could account for my red cheeks.

"Eve, did you girls see a bear?" Aurelia asked. "And did you see Harvey?"

"No, we heard a really fierce growl, coming from inside the hermitage, and we took off. Kali had been telling me about some of her dreams, and I think we might have been in a slightly altered state. You know," I glanced at Mattie, "maybe we overreacted."

Kali snorted. "It was a really fierce sound. And the door was definitely locked. I tried the knob. So whoever or whatever was in there locked the door behind."

Elsie had been silent throughout this drama. Finally the rest of us calmed down to sync in with her energy. This was one of the amazing things I noticed about the elder Crones. While Aurelia raised the energy just by looking at someone, Elsie could enter a noisy, crowded room and do absolutely nothing, and it would calm to silence in seconds. She could also sound just one or two words of a hymn and the rest of the women would have song flowing out of them like a waterfall. Wish I'd had that skill at Wentworth and Wentsouth: Some joker was always asking his buddy a totally irrelevant question when I was in the middle of a presentation. I never wanted to set them off and risk channeling the old nuns or some waspish schoolteacher in their minds, so I always just gritted my teeth and answered them, no matter how inane.

"We must call all the women to Council," Elsie pronounced. "We are entering a state of unknowing. I've never seen you, Aurelia, nor you, Mattie, quite so beside your dear selves." She smiled warmly at them. "This is an important moment, precisely the moment when so many good-hearted endeavors veer off the path and hitchhike straight to hell. Something is happening. Here. Right now." She raised a finger to the sky.

"Listen."

There was absolute silence, not a tree stirred. It felt for all the world like a storm was about to hit but the sky was clear and bright. I noticed we had arranged ourselves around Elsie in a circle, like filings around a magnet. She looked at each one of us —Aurelia, Mattie, Rae, Kali, me — and smiled into each one of us. And it felt, to me at least, like a tonic or a transfusion of hope and faith and strength, like what Kali had described getting from the woman in her dream.

"The moment we have been working towards for so long is about to commence. Let's gather together to hold the space. After lunch, of course." Elsie grinned. "You don't want to be serving the Divine on an empty stomach now, do you?" We all laughed at that.

"And, Aurelia, pass that note to Rabbi Sarah at lunch. I have a feeling it will explain a great deal," Elsie instructed.

And so, with no more fanfare than that, Rae went off to ring the lunch bell a little bit early, and all the members of the Cronation Community gathered in the dining hall and shared a healthy lunch in preparation to, as Elsie put it, "commence to sit."

"Shouldn't the Crones be painting or something?" I whispered to Mattie. "You know, isn't that how they figure things out? Maybe they can see where Harvey is? Or a dream scan — shouldn't somebody be doing a dream scan? Or organizing a search party?"

I was never that good at sitting still or waiting. Probably got that from O'Malley's side of the family: "idle hands are the devil's workshop" and all that Catholic business.

"You saw the look in Elsie's eyes, Eve." Mattie was clear. "She was as sure as sunup. I felt her words go straight to my heart, and all my fears about what's happened to Harvey just melted away. She just hooked us all up to the Source through her own faith. Can you imagine how thin the veil is for Elsie? We may not have her with us in body for much longer. Her wisdom is so powerful, I wonder if the world would be in such a state if people hadn't forgot how to honor the elder women! Listen, the Crones know a lot, Eve, an awful lot — but the most important thing they know is that they don't know everything."

Meanwhile, next to us at the table, Kali was musing to Aurelia, "You know, there was a time when if you said you were going to all go sit in the hall and wait for something, it would have driven me wild. Why do I feel so calm now?"

"Oh, Baby, praise the Goddess!" Aurelia answered. "This part is such a sore spot for most women! Watching men build the world for the past three thousand years, we forgot the importance of receptivity. We blame things on the men a lot, but we ourselves have come to devalue the capacity to receive, the very work of the prophet. So many think it's all about woman running things, but it isn't that exactly. Walking that so-called walk can be downright destructive: just burn a woman up to cinder, if most of your time isn't spent listening carefully — every single day — for your map. What you say just shows how much healing is needed. Why, how can the Great She return, if everybody is too busy — men and women — to answer Her knock on the door? 'Listen more and act less,' that is Her message. 'Let Me work through you.' 'Allow,' She says. Don't go off and try to fix it all on your own."

"Do you think She could have come sooner if we had gotten quiet sooner?" Kali wondered.

"Time is not a construct in the dimension where this is all coming from, Kali," Aurelia reminded her kindly. "I think you know that. And we aren't talking about some kind of lethargy or woe-is-me passivity, 'What the hell, it's hopeless anyway so do anything or do nothing.' No. We are talking about active listening and awakened discerning, right action that grows out of fertile stillness.

"Our choice is, as it always is: Do we experience change as a prayerful unfolding or a violent reordering? For Her, it is just a waking from Her nap, same as you did in the hermitage. Which reminds me — Eve mentioned dreams? Were you two able to work on that?"

"There's a lot, Aurelia." Kali grinned at me. "I took some notes in the bedside journal right after I woke up. I hope the bear or whatever it is doesn't eat it! But the main thing, or one of them, is that a dark woman appeared and called me by the name Ashera."

Aurelia's eyes widened, "Blessed She! That's wonderful! Do you know what that name means?"

Kali shook her head no, so Aurelia continued. "The asherot were the sacred trees that created the groves where the women worshipped thousands of years ago. You'll need to get with Rabbi Sarah; she can fill you in on the details. Your people have been front and center for every big Shift on Earth, Kali. You should be proud. Was there anything else?"

"Yeah, I had a really heavy, clunky sword and she touched it and it became really light and easy to handle." Tears streamed down Aurelia's face and I watched her take Kali's hands in hers. "You must share this dream with Rabbi Leaf when she arrives. It is really happening!"

Just then a powerful shaft of lightening lit up the sky outside the windows, followed by the loudest crack of thunder I ever heard. A few of the women gasped. Elsie calmly stood up and said: "The time is now, Sisters. Place your attention on your crown chakra, at the place where the top of your head touches the air: Picture the top of your head opening like you were unscrewing a mason jar full of Rae's delicious pickles. Now place your two feet firmly on the ground and picture roots just shooting down into the good sweet Earth. As you breathe, see clear light streaming down from above — see it streaming into you, clearing and cleansing every organ, blood vessel, muscle fiber, and bone. See that light carrying away all that is outworn: ideas, identities, cells, attachments, fears. Give all that debris back to the sweet Earth to nourish Her; She needs all She can get in the way of material to recast and remake the world. And She needs each of us to be as clear and empty as we can be in order to send Her love through us. Now, through those soles, the souls of your feet, feel the pulsing heartbeat of the Earth. Let your own heartbeat follow that rhythm. Relax into Her heartbeat as we become one to withstand, and hold, and welcome Her great return."

As Elsie's voice faded, I heard a flapping sound. I cracked my eyes to see that the room was now dark and just in time to see Diva slip out of raven and into the seat next to Kali.

We all breathed together like that as thunder and lightening rolled and crackled in the sky. It seemed like an eternity — and like one split second.

34 ———————

Harvey blinked and looked around the hermitage, a blinding headache making him feel as if his eyes were traveling a second or two slower than his skull. A pungent odor challenged his deep breath. "Yang? How long have we been here? What was in that joint? My head is killing me! Yang? I know you're here, Dude, I can smell you." Harvey wobbled to his feet. Yang wasn't in the armchair though tufts of his smelly fur permanently coated the seat and a trail of it led to the bed. "There you are! You sly devil, leave me to sleep in the chair while you slink off to the bed. Yang?" There was a slight rattling sound coming from the bed. Harvey looked down to see what he imagined Yang's great grandfather would look like if there were such a creature.

Yang's abundant hair had turned white. His jawbones seemed about to protrude through his skin. He opened his eyes and regarded Harvey with a wan smile, "This is it, pardner, the end of the trail, Yang is sinking and Yin is rising. The next three thousand years will be guided by the broads, for better or for worse. You did it. I guess you aren't a complete pantywaist sugar-sucking girly-boy after all," Yang wheezed and coughed and fell back against the pillow.

"Should I call a doctor?" Even as he spoke, Harvey realized all he could do was sit down and shut up. He was a small part of a much bigger production — hell, he might be nothing more than a stagehand in all this. His eyes filled with tears.

"I never imagined I'd go down like this," Yang rasped, "I was sure the guys would figure it out, admit to all the stuff they had really fucked up, take charge, give me a big send off, you know? Maybe halftime at Super Bowl Sunday. Hell, that's the biggest holiday on a real man's calendar, isn't it? Build a big bonfire out on the field. Free beer. All you guys could put something up there to burn up, signify your enlightenment — your iPhone, your rifle, your old jockstrap from college. There'd be free beer, did I mention that? Maybe the networks would allow bare-breasted dancing girls, you know, just this once, since football would probably be outlawed the day after the women took over, what with all the player brain damage and stuff. Or maybe they wouldn't televise that part.

"It could be like that Burning Man deal: you know, that nut job thing they do out in the desert? That's what they've been trying to do out there, you know, burn up 'Ol Yang, the assholes. Wussy boys already so yinned up in their wigs and dresses that they can't get their dicks up…. trying to push me off before I'm good and ready to go.

"So, Harvey," Yang struggled to focus. "Listen, if we're gonna get this show on the road, you gotta do one more thing. Reach in here, under my arm and get this last parchment out, will you?"

"OK, but you're not gonna make fart noises with your armpit like Wayne always does, are you?" Harvey asked as he gently pulled back the covers and let Yang guide his hand under his left arm — it felt to Harvey like he was reaching into endless space. A rolled up parchment found its way into Harvey's hand and he withdrew it and pulled the covers back up over Yang's skeletal form.

"Okay, first get some candles," Yang instructed, his voice almost a whisper. "I'm sure they have more candles here, and place them around the bed and light them. Then start reading, real slowly. When you finish, go back down to the women; they'll know what to do next." Yang looked directly into Harvey's eyes and grinned, "You are one lucky son of a bitch. I hope you know that." Then he closed his eyes and waited for Harvey to begin.

After he had the candles lit, Harvey unrolled the parchment and, as his eyes adjusted to the candlelight, he saw that the script was in a different foreign language like the other parchment, equally inscrutable — but like the first one, it slowly turned to English as he moved his eyes across it. This time it formed words he could read.

"Say 'Welcome Traveler' using the subject's name," Harvey solemnly intoned.

"You idiot!" Yang wheezed. "Some of that is instructions for you. Try to read what it says without reading the damn instructions!"

"Sorry, man, I see now. I've never been at a Shift of eras before." Harvey noted the directions appeared in slightly bolder script. Would anyone else see it this way or was he getting the remedial version?

Harvey cleared his throat and began again: "Welcome, traveler — ah, Welcome, Yang, and listen carefully. There are six stops on this road you are to travel and I will accompany you to each one. You have been yearning to stay and continue in this life as the head honcho, commander-in-chief, the decider of every decision, but it's time to go. It is time to yield your power. If you can go peacefully, you will begin a great liberation for all who are left, both men and women, to continue.

"Now, it is your nature to say, 'Fuck those sons of bitches, who cares about their liberation?' Such thoughts are likely to come into your mind along this journey and characters that are dressed in three-piece suits may speak such words along the way. These men will resemble those you have held in high esteem and, likewise, who have revered you. Do not call out to them. Even if they look so familiar as to be confused with high officials with whom you have gone hunting. Or even if they seem to be major league sports stars. Instead, recognize them as projections of your own wishes and fears. They are illusions. If you go with them, or even if you are tempted to take their words to heart and give them your energy at this crucial moment, your journey to the light will be derailed; you will return to a life in a body and in a station much like the illusion you have embraced. Humankind will miss the chance to bring in more light, to seat the Shift at the highest possible level, for the good of all — pressure's on, Dude," Harvey ad libbed for a moment.

Harvey continued reading along as the words on the parchment magically transformed from ancient Sanskrit to English. "To prepare for these certain challenges, before we travel far, in your heart say these words: 'I abandon all revenge, all desire to get even, all fantasy of eternal gamesmanship, all desire to die with the most toys or else fuck them up so badly no one else gets to play with them. I recognize and relinquish the selfish notion that my demise must also mean the demise of all else. I reconcile with the fact that the end of my domination need not be the end of the world, nor the end of men. I will neither fear nor embrace the peaceful nor the wrathful deities that I encounter, as I recognize that they are my own projections.

"Know that if you can accomplish this, your name will be revered for all the time of the next era, plaques and monuments will be raised to all the good things you have actually done through all the men who have lived, and all the not-so-good stuff will be understood in its deepest intention, forgiven, and washed away. And you will attain the Divine Light, instead of having to come back to this existence for another round of suffering. You will have your most deserved rest — until the time comes again for Yang to rise again.

"If you accomplish this transit, once mighty Yang, you will become strong and refreshed, developing in complexity and beauty for the next round, whenever that is. You will be honored by all who live. Songs will be written about you and maybe even a movie will also be made. You will be beloved of the Great Divine from whom all things flow, and you will finally know that this has always been true."

Harvey noticed he was sweating profusely when the word "relax" appeared on the parchment. Definitely the remedial version. He took a deep breath and looked over at Yang who seemed to be sleeping peacefully, his chest barely rising and falling.

Mattie's face came into Harvey's mind. "I know I can do a better job of this if I ask for help," he thought. Closing his eyes he focused on Mattie's face and whispered, "May everything I do here be for peace, love, and the highest good of those I love — no, wait. May everything I do here be for peace and the highest good of all. Ahimsa." He smiled to himself. Mattie would be proud of him.

"Quit congratulating yourself, asshole. We've got a long way to go," Yang opened one watery eye and wordlessly shot that thought into Harvey's mind.

"Okay, okay." He shifted himself in the seat and resumed. "Dude, you see a light in front of you…" The parchment here said, "Insert image that will make sense to the dying person." Harvey racked his brain and then continued. "You see a light brighter than the ones that light up the field each week for Monday Night Football. The thundering sound you hear is like the teams rushing out of the locker rooms onto the field with the sounds of the fans roaring in the stands. The players are huge, hulking guys who could easily crush your head like a melon. You are standing in the middle of the field and they are hurtling towards you — but do not fear them. They will not crush you; they are apparitions of your own ambitions, chimeras of your own fear of annihilation."

Just as Harvey was beginning to get the hang of the way the text on the parchment unfolded, these words appeared: "narrate a particular struggle that will evoke for the dying a monumental and significant clash."

"Shit. Guess I better go with the Super Bowl, that was Yang's own choice. But which one? Source, give me the words." Harvey closed his eyes, and images began to rise in his mind as if he was tuning into a T.V. newscast.

"Okay, Yang, it's January 21, 1979, Super Bowl XIII, at the Orange Bowl, in Miami, the Pittsburgh Steelers versus the Dallas Cowboys, a monumental match up of titans..." Harvey went on to narrate the game, even though it had taken place before he was born. He made up some commercials and a halftime show cobbled together from stuff he remembered and stuff he thought Yang would appreciate, including some topless dancing girls in white boots and a topless all-girls high school marching band in blue pleated skirts with nothing on underneath.

"Yang, these are your desires, and they are illusions. If you are able to refrain from embracing them, you are ready to enter the blissful realm of joy, eh — as soon as you run the gauntlet of avengers of your karma. You will see ways that seem to promise escape from these avengers. Do not be fooled. In life all the wily escapades you tried to pull to evade responsibility ultimately fucked things up more in the long run. Now is your chance to right all that. Instead, face each one in the fullness of your Yang-ness. Do this for yourself and on behalf of all beings that have inhabited male bodies. Do this for all those who used those bodies to overpower others, to cheat, to evade responsibility and to honor all those who respected and curbed their power."

Now, in addition to reading the words on the parchment, Harvey, too, was beginning to see in detail the visions he was describing to Yang. His own breathing became labored and he realized that this was what Aurelia and the Crones meant by doing "work on behalf of the world." Saving mankind was not a piece of cake.

"Do not turn away or try to explain. Simply meet the eyes of each one and offer from your heart your regrets for her or his suffering." An endless column of weeping mothers, bent over their dead sons, some still with guns in hand, appeared. Some wearing gang colors, others in army and marine uniforms, police officers and the victims of police violence, Vietnamese women, women in black burkas showing only their eyes, African women with bare, slack breasts holding starving babies. Mothers holding babies with misshapen limbs, malformed faces, others with defects caused by chemical waste, lead poisoning, and oil spills, or by drugs meant to help some illness. Little boys imprisoned in gray lines of energy appear, entangled with inept parents, teachers, and venal authority figures. Then a line of animals — cows, chickens, lambs, dogs — each making a desperate grieving sound. Images of the Pacific Garbage Patch, deadened coral reefs, and river deltas appeared as if projected into the room.

Yang was restless on the bed, as if he wished to turn away from the horrible visions. Harvey put a hand on his forehead. "This is really hard, Dude. You're seeing and feeling and making reparations for every guy who ever cheated on his wife and lied about it, every jerk politician who decided that sending guys to war was a legit foreign policy. Hell, even for guys who ate a burger without thinking about where it came from; every scientist who made a drug formula that turned out to have terrible unintended consequences, every developer only in it for the bucks. Look into the blameless eyes of these animals, your fellow creatures, the eyes of each one sacrificed at the hand of ambition to create a product, a process, or a belief. Ask for forgiveness from every animal, every being — human or otherwise — needlessly harmed by man's pride.

Notice, Yang, how explanations and excuses, strategies for getting off the hook, rise in your mind: 'It isn't my fault.' 'That's what people wanted.' 'It's all the politicians' doing.' 'War is heroic.' Notice these thoughts — and see them for the shreds of cowardice, the blind spots, the self-delusion and indifference that they are. Let them rise up and fade away like steam from

your piss on a cold day. Know that for millennia real harm and terrible suffering has been done in your name and fueled by your unchecked energy
coursing through humans."

Tears were streaming down Harvey's face now. "Bless those who have
been harmed by your strategic planning, your pyramid schemes and get
rich quick ventures, your dishonest wars, and your simple lust and greed.
Bless those who tried to offer a different perspective and were mocked,
shut down, or eliminated. Do not sneak away to the figures lining the
streets of your vision, handing out money and contracts with loopholes and
ad campaigns that say it's all right. Know that catchy slogans are of no use."
In Harvey's mind, he saw those figures pop like balloons.

"You're doing great, Yang. Not too much further to go — now you
see women with angry faces offering you guns to kill yourself. Resist. This,
too, is an illusion; it will not cause healing but only more pain. Now you see
beautiful women with big hair and big breasts reaching out to console you,
chanting, 'It's not your fault.' Do not go to them, they are hungry ghosts."

"Pop" went image after image, "Pop, pop."

"Keep walking, noble Yang. See the doors held open inviting you into
clubs and fancy restaurants — do not enter. See the valets holding open
the doors of beautiful cars, and walk on by. Keep walking, Yang. Now there
are people with signs bearing your name, T.V. screens with your image,
billboards extolling you in a thousand forms. Ignore all this. 'Pop, pop.'"
Harvey watched as the images vanished.

"You are not here to save the world through your inventions. You did
not know all you thought you knew. You did not set out to cause suffering,
but cause it you did, and then you closed your eyes to it. You are called to
be in the world and to be awake to it. You are called to open your eyes, see
what is, to ask for help and consultation, to make the corrections called for,
Yang. If you have recognized yourself in every face — the suffering and the
duplicitous, the huckster and the wicked, the tender and the bereft — if

you have done all this, Yang, you will see before you a light. It will not be the klieg lights of a stadium or the spotlight of a stage, but a warm and welcoming light."

When no image of light appeared in his mind's eye, Harvey stopped reading and closed his eyes. "Come on, man, what is it? What are you holding onto?" As he said those words, Harvey saw a skeletal man, parched skin wrapped in a threadbare blanket, under a highway viaduct. "Yes, Yang, him too, perhaps the most betrayed of all.

"For all those who loved you and honored you and were abandoned to fend for themselves, for the suffering you took on in your form as soldier returned from war — he too is welcome, is forgiven, is loved. For every man who followed you down the path of the strong silent type, the hero, the leader. For every man whose devotion to you led to suffering and betrayal. Release them all, Yang, from the bondage to the impossible ideal of 'Man' as it has come to be viewed at this moment in history — and humbly ask their forgiveness."

A single tear escaped under Yang's eyelid and Harvey saw and felt a warm, deep golden light fill the hermitage.

"All those who dwelt in you — mostly men but many women — who followed your lead to the exclusion of the still small voice that had always been there, that began to grow in every soul, to call for correction, to call for the beginning of the next era. All can be redeemed now as this new era begins. To admit this truth is to free the next era to learn from you, to honor you in the best way even as a new configuration takes shape. Now I feel it, I see that light, so I know you do too!" Harvey was improvising a little bit here, but what the hell, it felt right. He looked back at the parchment.

"You will see the welcoming light. You will hear musical bells and, if you look down, you will see that you too are made of this wonderful light. You will see within your being a small round object, dark and shriveled like an old piece of fruit. That is the Yang that was, the energy that drove so much invention; that tried and succeeded in fulfilling the mandate of the Source in the best ways it knew how, that understood that mandate as one to go forth and subdue creation, that interpreted Her willingness to allow as a license to plunder and in the end ran amok, stayed too long, and needs now to be returned and redeemed, to be made new before you enter the light. In this way, your return is in alignment with what must come next, the evolving truth.

"So while part of you fears this next moment, and part of you wants to take down the whole shebang with you, release these thoughts, these ungenerous emotions. They do not befit your highest self, noble Yang. For without you, Yang, the world is not complete, cannot turn, the sunrise nor the moonset. There would be no crops grown and no babies born without you. Know, Yang, that you save the women from repeating your errors if you release the old; they, too, will be freed to find sacred balance that the Source has always offered.

"Know now, once and for all, that the Divine never abandoned you. You have always been loved. Know that the universe is not and never has been a cold, unfeeling place but, out of ignorance and fear, you gave men coins to cover their eyes, to block them from the terror of belief in the endless void of Nothingness. For without that, your promise of invention, the dignity of standing tall in nature could not have unfolded. Return, Yang, from your exile. Know that you have been loved in your entire painful and joyous journey.

"Now, Yang, turn for one last moment from the light and toss the dark ball, saying these words: 'For the good of all beings, for the next unfolding of the joy of creation, for the delight of the Source, I, Yang, return to the wheel of life — to come into balance with Yin, to swirl and turn and nurture and balance the wheel in a new configuration, to serve in justice and beauty, colorful and elegant, joyous and generous — in holy partnership in the hearts and souls of all who welcome me.'

"Enter the light, noble Yang." Then there were no more words on the parchment.

The light in the hermitage began to swirl and pulse and become even brighter until it filled the room and was all that Harvey could see. And he saw the now compressed black ball of Yang energy, no larger than a rotten apple, disappear into the light, released at last, to land where? Harvey did not know. He stood over the fragile remains of his friend and stroked his forehead. "I love you, man," he said. "We've had a good run."

35 ────────

At some point during the storms, the power went out and the dining hall was plunged into darkness. I bet most of the women didn't even notice. But, like I said, sitting still was never a strong suit for me. Still, something about sitting peacefully in the dark with a bunch of women while lightening cracked and wind whipped across the landscape felt oddly thrilling. I could believe that some sort of cosmic housekeeping was going on. It struck me that by sitting, we were doing something — not doing nothing, as I had thought when I was bugging Mattie about why the Crones weren't painting. Not that I could tell you even now exactly what it was we were doing.

When the lights suddenly returned there was a collective gasp as we looked up to see snow falling outside, already a few inches deep. The sky seemed so close, like a quilt pulled up over our heads. It reminded me of Christmas morning at one of my aunt's houses. Mom never went along, but O'Malley always took me on the rounds to each of his sisters' homes; I never told Mom how much I loved the piney smell of the tree festooned with tinsel and colored balls, my little cousins running around in their nightgowns. I'd eat a piece of buttery cinnamon toast and drink milky, sweet Irish tea.

We always left while my aunts were getting their broods dressed in their best for Mass. O'Malley and I would kick through the snow, him whistling and me holding his hand, "As much a blessing as anything that could be had in a church," he'd say, grinning down at me.

There was murmuring as the dining hall came to life, then clapping and laughter. Mattie was next to me, stretching and rubbing her eyes when Diva shouted, "Hey, there's Harvey!"

Sure enough, Harvey stood framed in the doorway against the blizzard, carrying something wrapped in a blanket like a sleeping child. Mattie was up like a shot and Harvey placed the bundle down and hugged her. The place exploded in cheers and whistles that somehow then organized into a very up-tempo hallelujah chorus. This place was really something. I wish Mom could have been here for this, all these women working out some answers and having a high old time in the process; and if it was nothing more than the joy and celebration in the moment, that was a lot. O'Malley would be rolling his eyes, but he'd get it too, I bet.

Aurelia went up and hugged the couple and, after a brief conference with Harvey, turned to all of us. "All right now, let's settle down. As you can feel, Sisters, in your bodies and souls, remarkable things have been happening in the world. Each of us here helped to hold the space for such a momentous event as the Shift, well, as it is shifting! We may well be called upon to do more of the same as things unfold.

"Those of us who've given birth know that the contractions come, then they subside and let us rest in between. Our Divine Source is so wise! So, do not underestimate the power of what you all have been doing here. Please check in with yourselves and see if you need to rest, to reflect, or maybe just go out and play in this blessed snow!"

Everyone laughed at this and Rae stood up, "Anyone for dining tray sledding? I know our hills aren't very much, but even a gentle slope can be fun. Be my guest — just bring the trays back by dinner time." The women roared and applauded. Aurelia nodded to me and to Kali, and when the ruckus subsided, said, "The Councils will have to delay that treat, Rae, thank you. I trust we will all have cocoa with marshmallows afterward? Now if the Elders and the Next Council members would come to the Wood Room, I'd be deeply grateful."

Diva gave Kali a big hug and went off to join the sledders. Kali and I made our way over to the Wood Room.

"Eve, do you think something awful happened while we were in the dark? I had some pretty scary visions, and I really thought the world might have ended. When I saw the snow falling, I was sure that it was ash from some cataclysmic fire or possibly fallout from a bomb."

Being Jewish and Irish usually squares the expectation of doom, but this time I felt a deep peace. "No," I said, "I guess I trust Aurelia. And I bet this meeting will clear up a lot of things." That was the truth, but I'd mostly hoped to reassure Kali. She looked really pale and uncomfortable, and I did wonder — I hadn't thought much about Aurelia's news of Los Angeles sliding into the Pacific — were there more of those sorts of events we hadn't heard about yet?

Mattie was already on the porch when we trudged up the steps and stamped the snow from our feet. "Leave your wet things on the hooks in the hall. There are slippers and pajama bottoms in baskets by the door."

We each took a pair of hand-felted bootees, slipped off our wet clothes and pulled on colorful flannel pants. Mine had a moon and star pattern in white on a dark blue background. Kali's were covered with ducks. A fire was already crackling in the Wood Room, and the bundle Harvey had been carrying was now set down in front of the hearth. Harvey was setting up chairs in a circle.

Once we settled ourselves, Aurelia began, "First, everyone just take hands and let us give thanks for the energy that flows through us all and that is the Divine Source Herself. We are so blessed to be in these bodies at this time. There is so much to hear about. Let's just quiet ourselves and pray as always to be used for the highest good of all, to be suffused with light, and to be guided to right action." We all murmured our responses.

I looked around the circle. Everyone was wearing pajama bottoms and all sorts of slippers, many hand knitted and felted by the women at the Farm. We looked like a motley collection of children staying up late for a bedtime story. Harvey was holding the carved talking stick making me think of him as a shepherd of dream sheep, the ones O'Malley used to count with me when I couldn't fall asleep.

After a few moments of silence, Aurelia said, "Harvey, dear, since you're holding that talking stick, would you like to begin our speaking?"

Harvey shifted in his seat and leaned forward on the talking stick, his hands covering the entwined figures. He took a deep breath. "Sure, well, I guess you could say I went on a journey. It was a lot like seeing the men in Diva's life when I was in the SAC, except I saw all the stuff that..." He choked back a sob and fell silent. Then he rose slowly, placing the stick next to his chair, and went over to the hearth.

He picked up the bundle and laid it on the floor in the center of the circle. Harvey looked at Mattie, "Did you find something on the ground this morning, a note on parchment?" He passed Mattie the stick.

"Why, yes, the writing was in Hebrew so we gave it to Rabbi Leaf. Sarah, what can you tell us?"

Mattie passed the stick along, but when it came to Elsie, she said, "Children, using the stick feels cumbersome today. Does anyone else feel that way? I propose we just rest it down and speak our minds without it. Something makes me feel as though we don't need its service today."

I had been thinking the same thing, and it startled me to hear Elsie voice the thought. I noticed Kali seemed transfixed by the shrouded form in the center of the circle.

"I held the parchment during our time together in the storm this morning," Rabbi Leaf related. "It describes a part of the Tikkun, the repair of Creation that we have all been a part of here at the Farm and that you, Harvey, have helped to bring to a stage of completion. It's a text from an ancient mystical work. The words say, 'When Israel is no longer in exile, the gates can open and Shekinah can return.'"

Harvey looked bewildered.

"I know, that sounds cryptic, doesn't it?" Rabbi Leaf continued, "This text has been interpreted in a very literal way by lots of people to mean that if the Jews would just return to the physical place of Israel, then the Messiah, in their minds, Jesus, would return to walk the earth and make everything okay."

Harvey looked confused and Kali looked impatient. "They just can't seem to give sweet Jesus His rest!" Elsie fussed, shaking her head.

Sarah chuckled and continued, "Consider this: Israel means one who wrestles with God. I take that to mean one who engages with the Creative Source, one who understands that the Source is all-potential, that it is through our own bodies, hearts, and minds, our words and deeds that 'God' — or more accurately — the Creative Source, becomes manifest. In other words, we wrestle meaning from all the potential meanings. We create reality."

Harvey brightened. "So you mean if we let the part of us that creates new meaning and new ideas to be in charge, we can save the world? Shekinah means all of you, right? The women, the Feminine, Mother Earth? It's time for men to stop holding onto their — our — view of the world and let the new ideas you all have been 'wrestling' with come to be." Everyone laughed, except Kali.

"That's right, Harvey," Sarah nodded, "except it isn't only about women. The spark of the new is in everyone, everything, waiting to be invited to ignite. It's about each one letting go of the past, releasing our fixed ideas, sacrificing our sureness that we know what's what and welcoming Shekinah, the Feminine face of the Divine, as a state of receptivity in ourselves. We all need to open to new ideas on every level. Like Elsie saying we didn't need the stick to speak right now."

I remembered a book Sarah Leaf had been carrying earlier, *The Magic of the Ordinary*; the title alone went against everything I'd ever learned in business. Being sure of yourself was how you got things done. Being extra-ordinary was a prerequisite for everything in a competitive world. If you could put on an aura of sureness, most people would get with your program. Yet, while I had no idea what Sarah and Harvey were actually talking about, I knew when I looked at Elsie and Aurelia, at Mattie and Harvey, at Kali and the others, that I was in that place that everyone seeks — that businessmen, gurus, leaders of every stripe, maybe every human being in different ways, some spectacularly misguided ones, were aiming for. I didn't know what to call it.

"Teshuvah," Sarah Leaf said quietly, smiling at me from across the circle. "What we are all experiencing here in this moment is Teshuvah, a turning from what has caused harm, and a return to what is essential."

"But what is essential?" Kali blurted out, "And how do you know? Look at those women, playing out there in the snow like children," she gestured to the window. "Is that essential?" Her voice was harsh and dark.

"Essential means essence," Sarah said gently. "Same root as the verb 'to be.'"

Elsie nodded. "Playing like children? Oh indeed, child, that is it in a nutshell! We are Her children, every one of us; every single thing we do is play to Her. Imagine She's been napping, and we've gotten into a truckload of mischief while She rested. It is the time in the cosmic cycle for Her return — and She needs us, desires us, to turn up our light as high as we know how, to call Her back into our midst.

"There is great fear and turmoil in the world. We are called to be in it, to be a witness in our essence, to remember that our light is what is essential to banish the dark of old ways. The Divine She is calling out to us to remember Her, to stop all our doing and make way for Her return, to hold up the lanterns of our hearts. As we all know the string of busy progress has played out for so long in one direction; it must roll naturally back now, even if for many it snaps back and hurts like a taut rubber band breaking under strain. It seems like forever to us in our mortal view, but for Her it is just a short time. Our task, what we have been called to do, is to witness that process in joy and in peace. Each one of us here has an important role to play."

As Elsie spoke, I looked again out the window at the snowball fights and listened to the hoots of the women. Diva was flying in raven and dropping snowballs on Andrea's head. I had to smile; I could see the light filaments in each of them, between and among and around them all, in the trees. The snow itself was simply light, laughing, joyous light, vibrating with beauty.

When I turned back to the circle, I felt a sharp pain. Kali's fear was visible; when I looked at her, she seemed encased in lead. I could not see her light. A second skin like Kevlar was visible to me just below her surface. Seeing it took my breath away. I looked back at the women outside and listened.

"Elsie, with all respect, I hear what you are saying — but what about evil?" Kali looked pleadingly around the circle. "What about all the bastards out there? Do you think they're all out playing in the snow? Planning a party for the Great She? No, they're lying and cheating and hurting people, making bombs. Is that going to magically stop because we're 'full of joy'?" Kali made air quotes around the last words and I realized I was holding my breath. When I looked down, I saw my own chest was encased in the same darkness I saw in Kali. I glanced at the window; I couldn't see the filaments of light any longer.

"We're just playthings to your Great She," Kali raged, "is that it?

When She feels like coming back, She can stop the mayhem? Clean up the playroom? Where was She when Diva's life was being wrecked?"

A charged silence filled the room. "Kali dear," Aurelia gestured to the window, "look at Diva. She is able to accept and celebrate the gift of shape-shifting, which was her refuge from her pain. Why? Because you loved her. You saw her pain and her wounds, and you reflected back her gifts. You are 'She' just as each of us is when we act from love. There is no 'She' out there lounging around, filing Her nails watching us mess up, anymore than there was ever an old man with a white beard shaking an angry, fatherly fist at us. Consciousness is what we are talking about. We are Her consciousness; it just makes it more fun to tell it this way, in stories."

Kali was crying silently, and when Aurelia held out her arms, she went to her and let herself dissolve in Aurelia's embrace. "Each time your mother or father chose someone or something over you," she murmured to Kali, "and told you some half-baked story, it was like they handed you a brick and said, 'Here, build a wall around your heart.' You protected your essence as best you could by locking it away. We must tell stories to experiment with consciousness, and — as Elsie said — that is play, Divine play. You were doing it with Nemesis, but maybe we can all help it get a little lighter!" Aurelia held Kali away from her so that she could look into the younger woman's eyes. I suddenly realized why Kali didn't faint when she was at the Farm before: her wall was that strong.

As Aurelia rocked Kali in her arms, I felt a humming begin to grow. Though I couldn't tell the source of the sound it comforted me and I felt myself relax. My mind had been my refuge, too — maybe not as unshakable as Kali's, but I know I was always skeptical of women, women's circles, all the things Mom was into with her women friends. I couldn't see it then but they were preparing the ground for this time, for what Rabbi Sarah called the Teshuvah, the Tikkun. I felt something dissolving, ebbing away, being replaced by a feeling of strength and a kind of power that the ocean or a really old oak tree or a hummingbird has, wordless but undeniable, happy and calm.

I looked down and saw that my hands were glowing again. I could see the filaments of light traveling up my arms and down my legs. I looked around the circle and saw the light emanating from Elsie's heart, and Aurelia's, Lydia's, and Mattie's, all pulsing toward Kali. I looked down at my chest and said, 'Me too!' and saw the light shoot like a comet to join the aureole that surrounded Kali in Aurelia's arms.

"Kali, may I speak?" Sarah Leaf asked. Kali nodded and sniffled, and Sarah smiled at her. "I believe that the reason the great Goddess Kali came to you is so that you can use Her sword of Truth to cut through the wall and free your own heart. Show yourself the compassion and love that you showed to Diva. It seems like time to receive your other gifts, besides the gift of your fine intellect."

I wondered if Kali would share the dream of being given a new name, but suddenly Harvey raised his hand. "I think I have something to offer here —

"Those men who hurt Diva tried to steal her light. I don't mean that as an excuse, but they felt empty and tried to steal what she had. I saw what happened to Diva when I traveled into the dreamtime. I saw man after man who was empty try to fill himself up and dump some of his own pain. I'm going out on a limb here —" Harvey looked to Elsie and then to Aurelia. When both women nodded, he continued, "What I see is that men have had more power but less understanding of the light. I totally get why you wanted to kill men, Kali, I really do. But as much pain as you suffered, your light and Diva's light were never harmed." As Harvey spoke I saw a blue light that flowed and wove its way under and around the circle of women. In places it mixed with the golden yellow of the women's light and created beautiful shades of green. It was as if a basket was being created to hold all of us together. "I am so sorry for everything that happened to you and, on behalf of the deranged Yang in every man, I apologize — to you, Kali, and to all of you." Harvey looked around the circle at each of us in turn.

I looked up and noticed, as she nodded to Harvey, that I could see Kali's light again; she looked relieved, like a little girl and a beautiful woman all at the same time.

"Harvey, you have been somewhere, on behalf of the Great She, it sounds like. Can you tell us?" Aurelia asked gently. "Kali, would that be all right?"

My vision of the beautiful basket of light ebbed away slowly but the feelings of being held and protected seeped into me like a tonic.

Elsie spoke next: "We are all sitting here in our pajamas — which usually means a story is ready to be told. So, Harvey, why don't you begin, son, and tell us where you've been. What task has the Divine sent you on?"

"Well, it all started when Yang showed up…" No sooner did Harvey have these words out than tears began to stream down his face. I never minded seeing a man cry: O'Malley was a fountain anytime there was a sappy movie or babies around, which, in our extended family, thanks to his clan, was pretty much always.

Kali returned to her seat and the Crones all sat patiently waiting for Harvey to continue. He pointed to the bundle on the floor in front of the fireplace.

"Yang? Like yin/yang?" Kali asked.

"Exactly!" said Harvey, wiping his nose on his sleeve. "He was like all the guys I ever knew, combined with all the politicians and T.V. talk guys, and some mangy coyote out of the swamps of Jersey all rolled up into one scruffy dude. But what can I say? He showed me stuff that was amazing. I really liked the guy. But he said it was time for him to go. Well, time for his energy, this Yang-ness, to be sort of shut off — wait, no — limited, curbed, I guess, so the Yin could flow, and stuff would become more balanced after that. Yin wouldn't have to be so violent like in extreme storms and floods and fires. He took me to see my brother Wayne, and I could see into Wayne and there was this mandorla thing and women with swords, and then I had a sword I had to stick into Yang and all this awful rotten stuff flew out, and Yang said you all would know what to do next...." he finished his tale breathlessly and he looked hopefully to Mattie and smiled wanly.

"Did Yang leave the parchment on the doorstep this morning?" Mattie marveled. "Goddess, was it only this morning? It was folded into the shape of an origami peace crane, but so stiff from the cold we had to wait for it to warm up before we could unfold it."

"Yeah," Harvey nodded, "Yang said if he made it into a crane, you'd be sure to notice it and wouldn't miss it because it would be beautiful and all."

Elsie laughed out loud, "Well, that is charming, yes, indeed, Yin is about beauty. What's the word in Hebrew, Sarah? Tiferet, isn't that it?"

"That's right. When love and discernment are both awakened, the heart opens and a transforming beauty is possible. Unless the two work together, the flowing of energy and the limitation of boundaries, right action isn't really possible. Each tempers the other.

"As Mattie said," Sarah elaborated, "the parchment is ancient. Actually, Yang has been keeping it safe all these many years until this moment. Kali, you asked about evil; and, Elsie, you mentioned Tiferet, which is beauty. For the world to function in beauty, it requires judgment or limitation as well as compassion or love. These two elements joining together create Tiferet."

"Look, Rabbi, with all due respect, you've lost me." This discussion was making my head hurt. "Can you bring this down from the cosmic realm? I get the light part. I can see that the women playing outside are creating the light, and I see it in each of our hearts here in this room. But what do we do?"

"Yeah," Kali echoed. "What do we do?"

"Let it be," Aurelia said quietly. "We let what is taking place be and we let ourselves be with it. We just hold the frequency of love and light as best we can as we go about our work and lives."

"She's right," Elsie picked up the thread. "All the doing has been done for the moment. Riva and Phoebe, bless them, are on the Other Side helping to send what is to come. Our task is to receive it here for this while. Each one of you, in your own way, has been part of flipping all the switches to let the new flow commence. Harvey, you helped Yang wind down; Eve and Kali, you two have opened yourselves to Yin. Soon Harvey and Mattie will celebrate the Hieros Gamos, the marriage of the two energies."

The two looked at each other bashfully.

"And then maybe I can go to my well deserved rest, along with Yang!" Elsie let out a hearty laugh. "Sarah, can you continue explaining a bit more about the meaning of that parchment?"

Sarah nodded, "As many of you know, it is said that the ancient sacred texts were written 'in black fire on white fire' and were composed without vowels. This custom continues to this day. There are no vowels written in a Torah scroll and there are no vowels in this parchment. Now for the Torah, there are generally accepted vowels to create the meaning of the words, which over the centuries the rabbis have agreed upon; you would see these in a modern printed book version of the Torah. But, because in the scroll the vowels are absent, we understand that all possible meanings exist — and it depends on how we read the text as to what we learn from it. Changing one vowel in one word can alter the meaning of everything else."

Kali was squirming in her seat. My head was starting to hurt again; this sort of thing was why I steered clear of religion as much as I had.

Finally, Kali couldn't contain herself and raised her hand. Rabbi Sarah nodded to her. "So anyone can twist the text to his own meaning, can't they? Especially if he's learned?"

"That's a great question." Sarah smiled. "That is why community is so important: No one person can come to truth alone. This truth is at the core of Cronation as well. Now, what is also important is to understand that all possibilities exist in every moment. The impulse for good and the impulse for evil, each exists in every moment. In fact, the stronger the light, the more it draws in the dark impulse in its wish to be redeemed. It is our choices as human agents of the Divine that determine what will happen. That's why both love and judgment are needed, flow and restriction, energy and direction. The consonants represent that which is unchanging, a sort of structure, like the laws of Nature; and the vowels are like the energy that fill in the particular details and determine what will manifest."

"You make it sound like adding spices to a vegetable soup to make it taste Mexican with chilies or Indian with curry," Rae said. She had just entered the room with a carafe of cocoa and a bowl of homemade marsh-mallows.

"That's a great analogy," Sara laughed. "But the vowels are limited by both your intention and how wide your understanding is. If you only have chilies, well, then it's always going to taste like Mexican soup."

"And if you were raised eating only soup flavored with chilies," Aure-lia added, "you might believe that chilies make the One True Soup!"

We all laughed and the atmosphere lightened a bit. Rae passed around steaming mugs of cocoa and pulled up a chair to the circle.

"Girl, we can always count on you to ground us with your cooking when things get heady!" Mattie declared.

Elsie nodded to Sarah, "Now, child, tell us if you know — why has this parchment found its way here to us?"

"That's so exciting." Sarah grinned and nodded. "As I said, the parch-ment has only consonants and so it is waiting for the vowels to be filled in. We have actually been preparing for this task for three thousand years. As Aurelia has told me, you and Phoebe and the other Crones knew way back in the 1960s that a new age was dawning and that all the old ways would be challenged."

"That's right, dear," Elsie agreed, "we knew what didn't work, that's for sure. But it wasn't until we went into — well, I guess you could say we went into exile, which the Divine Source taught us what we needed to get things started to get on track. It wasn't so fancy, really. She revealed that it was about not trying so hard, not so much the 'sweat of the brow' sort of thing. She was thrilled with all the amazing things humans had created — you know, cures for diseases, the Internet, and such — but She realized we'd let it go to our heads a bit, we'd got a little carried away. When we began causing as many diseases as we were curing, causing some with our 'cures' in fact, She saw we were losing track of some of the basics, well, that upset Her.

"We Crones were so dismayed about the guns; for us that was the last straw. When our men took them up in the Black Panthers Party, we knew we had to look for a different way. She gave us to understand that guns were just a try at instant transformation. Didn't that nice boy John Lennon write a song about it? Instant Karma, I think it was. He understood it so much better than most. Of course, we all go back to Her one way or another, so it makes sense that She wasn't as bothered by 'how' we get there as we were. In the men's playbook, war and fighting seems to be the only means they know to clear the way for something new. All that bloody carnage, we were sure there must be a more elegant way, a more artful way, to create large-scale transformation besides war. She let us know in so many ways that it was time for Her to return, for the balance to shift once more, and that we were to prepare the way."

Harvey was getting restless, and Elsie seeing this nodded to him.

"This parchment came from Yang," Harvey spoke slowly pointing to the disheveled pile on the hearth. "This was a very strange experience for me. But Yang took me to places — and I saw some awful stuff. Yang said it was time for his energy to shrink back into the dot thing." Harvey gestured toward a silk yin/yang banner that hung on the wall of the Wood Room. "I saw that men were suffering and also causing women and children to suffer, but I feel like there is something more that has to happen. Did it say anything in that parchment about a funeral for Yang?"

Sarah Leaf continued Elsie's thought, "At the moment when the Source began to shift to the era we are now bringing to a close, words became the most important currency. She knew that this would be both wonderful and terrible, both astonishing and diabolic. It was the moment when the simple circle of life leapt to the next level, manifesting as the unfolding spiral of complexity for humans. Remember, this isn't time as we know it. The Shekinah, the feminine aspect of the Divine, is now ascending. As you all know, we have been preparing for Her in everything we do here at the Farm. It is a time of breaking down and of reintegration at a higher level. The previous phase was one of separating things, differentiating one thing from another, so that each could be seen in its own right."

"That's what Yang was telling me," Harvey added excitedly. "That it was all about specialization. That's how the masculine and feminine got so divided, right?"

Sarah nodded. "The next development that is unfolding will be integration of each of us internally — as well as groups and communities, at a more harmonious and complex level. That is, if enough people can release the past forms that no longer serve us and tolerate the chaos and confusion that follows letting go. It will take sitting still for a while. Then we can have a new model, a partnership of love and respect for all energies, for both masculine and feminine and all shades on the spectrum from light to dark; this is what the Hieros Gamos that Harvey and Mattie have experienced is all about. It is also what each of us can experience within our own being."

"Maybe we could have a ceremony without words for Yang," Aurelia suggested, "one where we honor all the things that were created by that active energy that no longer really serve the highest good of all."

Aurelia looked around the circle and noticed that Kali seemed a million miles away. "Kali dear, what's on your mind?" Aurelia asked kindly.

As I sipped my cocoa and felt myself drifting like I did as a child when the adults were talking about stuff I didn't totally get, I wondered what was going on in the world outside of the Farm.

36

Day was dawning in Boca Raton. Miriam Greenberg awoke to the
alarm clock function of her cell phone. Rav Babka was scheduled
to lead a morning meditation and then speak about "Inner Peace, World
Peace, and Your Piece of the Pie" at the rustic Babka Knish Retreat Center.
Miriam was in charge of making sure the pavilion was set up with pillows
and fresh coffee and, of course, slices of the babka of the day. There were
a number of women corporate executives attending the center this week,
and the Rav was tailoring his message to their particular spiritual needs —
only partly to ensure that funding for his enterprise would fall under the
category of corporate social responsibility.

Miriam's roommate, Shoshana, was snoring lightly and the early sunlight illuminated her face against the pillow. Like Miriam, she began seeking spiritual solace after a bitter divorce some years ago; Rav Babka had
developed a very big following among women scorned. In addition to his
many more ethereal teachings, he encouraged the women to seize as many
assets from their failed marriages as possible — as a proactive step in their
healing. He had several good tax attorneys on his staff and made no secret
of the fact that the very existence of the retreat center was the result of
grateful devotees who had made use of these consultants as part of their

healing and spiritual unfolding.

"I never noticed how pretty Shosh is," Miriam thought, gazing at her roommate while pulling on her yoga tights and sports bra. She tiptoed into the tiny bathroom that the two women shared, lifted a brush to her curly hair, looked into the mirror and let out a terrified, bleating scream. Shoshana sat bolt upright.

"Miriam? What's the matter? Is it the cockroaches? They're as big as hamsters in Florida. I told you, always close your eyes and count to ten when you turn on the light in there!"

When Miriam didn't stop screaming, Shoshana jumped up and went to the door of the bathroom. "Oh, hello…I thought it was… Miriam?"

"Look at me!" Miriam wailed, "What the hell happened?" Miriam's hair, a mass of tangly curls like her daughter Kali's, had been a coppery red, a shade her hairdresser called 'spitfire.' Instead, she now sported locks in shades of gray, maybe 'smoke' or 'cloud mist.' Seeing Shoshana behind her reflected in the mirror she screamed again. "Look! You too!"

Shoshana rolled her eyes. "Miriam, I don't dye my hair. I've looked this way since I was forty-five." She and Miriam had roomed together before at Rav Babka's retreats. "Actually, I think you look a lot better this way."

Miriam was leaning on the sink and staring at her reflection. "Shosh! My boobs are gone too!" She clutched her noticeably slack sports bra. Miriam's boob job was a souvenir from her marriage to the plastic surgeon. "This is insane. What's going on? I'm going to be late!" She ran back into the room, pulled on a sweatshirt to hide her diminished bosom and grabbed a baseball cap. "Rav Babka better have an explanation for this!" she muttered as she stalked off to the outdoor pavilion where the Rav held court in the morning.

When she got there, the pavilion was empty. She spied a note on the seat of the throne-like chair where the Rav should have been seated.

"Morning sessions cancelled. Please see the bulletin board in Reception for further information." Miriam threw down the missive and sprinted over to the office/lounge area where coffee was usually served, along with the daily babka — a filled pastry in honor of the Rav, who was enamored of the communion service of the Catholics and also liked a bit of sweets in the morning.

The smell of burnt coffee assaulted Miriam's nose, and a fly buzzed lazily over leftovers of yesterday's offering, a poppy seed babka. She switched off the burner under the coffee pot and squinted at the message board. From what she could tell, Rav Babka, his lawyers, the center executives, and senior staff had all left the retreat for an offshore location. Retreatants were urged to pray for guidance — according to a hastily scribbled note on the bulletin board — as it appeared that the end of the world might possibly be imminent. Babka wished them well and suggested they trust their "inner Rav" as they contemplated their next step.

Miriam switched on the T.V. in the lounge — normally only used to show DVDs of the Rav's teachings, in a never-ending loop, to new arrivals and occasional curious wildlife. It barely got reception from a local station, but, through the static, Miriam could make out a newscaster describing computer anomalies worldwide.

"Fractal images, nature scenes, and, in some cases, old sitcoms such as *The Brady Bunch*, are being broadcast over networks that previously served up everything from the financial market news to major pornography sites." A young woman reporter was showing a grainy video feed of men staring at computer screens full of flickering, kaleidoscopic mandalas.

"Without the continual mediation of the expected electronic content," the reporter continued, "men were befuddled and, in some cases, plunged cold turkey into acute awareness of their bodies. For some, this was apparently such an overload of sensory data that they ran screaming into the streets. Others were filled with a sense of overwhelming love, breaking into song and dance in subways, delicatessens, and factories. There seems to be an inversely proportional trauma response to culturally defined success, but experts have yet to weigh in on that topic.

"Many wives, girlfriends, and daughters awoke this morning to find the men in their lives curled into fetal position, some catatonic, many sobbing quietly. Men with long-term animal companions, i.e. pets, seemed to fare a bit better, according to an animal psychic we consulted for this story. Cats and dogs were found positioned close to the bodies of their suffering masters. 'Stay at home Dads' also seemed to fare quite a bit better than most.

"We spoke briefly with Joe Cassidy, out with his one year old son, Trevor, in a jogging stroller: Mr. Cassidy, what did you experience this morning when you and Trevor went out for your daily jog?"

"The sky seemed unusually bright and little Trevor, here, was just babbling away like usual. But my wife called from the office and said that things were pretty crazy there. Her boss and the other executives were all in a conference room singing camp songs in rounds."

The reporter, a young woman with an all-woman camera crew, running their equipment off solar-powered backpack generators, switched feeds to a high rise office building and continued: "In board rooms and locker rooms, classrooms and consulting rooms, men have reported experiencing a feeling of their knees buckling, sudden profuse sweating, and many even began to cry for no apparent reason. Starting at about 4:20 p.m., Eastern Standard Time yesterday, what some are calling an 'emotional tsunami or tidal wave,' flowed in a wave pattern, originating somewhere in the Midwest, outward in all directions to the East Coast and to the West, and North and South to the poles. There have been reports of a similar, sometimes milder, version of what's being called by pundits, ME-OWS, or 'Male End of the World Syndrome,' affecting some women, as well, especially corporate executives.

"In a related story, no one has been reported injured as what has been described as a tornado — or something like 'a cosmic washing machine set on the delicate cycle'— careened through rural Louisiana. However, some inmates in various state and county facilities, veterans' hospitals, and old age homes were affected; some sort of fine mist was reported dousing staff as well as inmates and patients with golden light.

"Scientists conjectured that beings from outer space may be playing havoc with the molecular makeup of our infrastructure, but no one knows for sure. Here with me, via our reporting team in Louisiana, is Mr. Elroy James, until yesterday an inmate of the Ascension Parish Sheriff's Prison, Mr. James, what did you see?"

"Why, I didn't see nothin' but I felt like I was being given a good scrubbing by my Grandma, that's what. I never felt better in my life, I can tell you that, Miss!'

"What do you make of reports of extraterrestrials possibly being behind this, Mr. James? Do you think the tornadoes came from outer space?"

"I thought maybe they just got a new contract for the cleaning, maybe something like that," Mr. James replied, waving to the camera. "Hello, Grandma, you have something to do with this? I sure feel good!"

"There you have it. As a result of what might be 'a cleansing wave of light,' a powerful anomalous weather pattern originating in the upper stratosphere, or, possibly, an intergalactic terrorist attack, men and some women in almost every strata of power are suddenly overcome with tender emotions, while the many of our most unfortunate citizens seem to have been granted a new lease on life filled with joy and celebration.

"Up next: A yacht carrying about a dozen people towards Grand Cayman Island was apparently sucked into a vortex at sea. The sloop, Rav Knish, reportedly registered to a Rav Wendell Babka, was last seen before dawn by a Coast Guard vessel after it sent out an S.O.S.

"In another weather-related story, standing by with me is Jean Von

Ellzey. She is part of a team of women who spent last night's storm drumming and dancing on the beach behind me. Far less damage was reported on this coastal stretch, and Jean and her cadre may be the reason. Jean, can you tell our viewers the meaning of your activities and the name of your group?"

"Why certainly, dear. We are all from one of the weather cells of the Cronation Movement. Since we are all well past menopause, our energy calms the storms somewhat by balancing and absorbing the vibrations of the excessive estrogen concentrated in this part of the country — you know, from hormone shots, eating feedlot beef, that sort of thing."

"The Weather Underground, in Croatia, did you say?"

"No, no, dear. Cronation Weather Cells. We're Crones, dear, wise women elders. You can Google that when you get back to your office; the computer systems ought to have righted themselves by then."

Miriam froze in front of the wavy T.V. picture. Cronation? That's the group running the Heartscape Farm, where she'd left her daughter, Charity. Miriam had been so immersed in her consults with Rav Babka's lawyers that she hadn't spoken to Charity in ages.

The reporter was breaking up, "More on the disappearance of Rav Wendell Babka, an often controversial spiritual leader who has recently come under investigation by the IRS — after a word from our sponsors. This is Ashley Coker, reporting for WBRZ, Channel Two, Baton Rouge News."

Just then Shoshana appeared. "Look, Miriam, I have just about enough gas in the rental car to get to the airport. This place seems to be history. I heard from the gardener that all the Keys and most of South Florida might be under water in awhile, there are some aftershocks sending high waves. Part of some kind of planetary cleansing. He said he heard on the news."

"Damn Rav Babka! Did you know the IRS caught up with him? He assured me everything was on the up and up. Just like every other man, he's left us to fend for ourselves!"

Shoshana looked at Miriam, "Now or never, Toots — we were fools to count so much on a guy named after a sweet roll. Come on, let's go."

And so Miriam and Shoshana drove towards the Jacksonville airport — only to run out of gas in the tangle of cars trying to flee the area. They abandoned the rental and began to walk. "If we can get away from the access roads," Miriam suggested, "maybe we can hitchhike. I've got to get back to that Farm and see if Charity is okay. I never meant to leave her indefinitely. I hope she's okay."

"Right." Shoshana took two apples from her bag. "Here, there wasn't much in the kitchen."

"My God, Shosh, what was I thinking? What's going on? Where did my boobs go?"

"Good riddance, Honey," Shoshana started to laugh, "they never fooled a soul."

Miriam stuck out her tongue, "Hey, look, those are the women I just saw on the TV!"

Up a ways on the side of the road, they saw a group of women in yellow slickers, standing at a table handing out cups of water.

"We don't use plastic bottles, no, dear. That's so bad for the environment. These cups are biodegradable, made out of cornstarch. Just bury them under some leaves when you're done and they'll be recycled by nature in a jiffy!" Jean was handing a cup of water to a woman with a golden retriever in tow. They shared the water; the pooch happily taking messy slurps in turns.

"If you'd like to join us, we'll be returning to Heartscape, the Cronation Headquarters, tomorrow morning."

"Shosh, did you hear that?" Miriam elbowed her way to the front of the table. "I need to get to Cronation!"

"You'll have to wait until tomorrow like all of us," Jean said cheerfully. "But really, dear, you needn't push and shove." Jean kept on ladling out water as Miriam stomped her foot.

"You don't understand, you silly hag. My daughter is there and I have to see her as soon as possible."

Shoshana watched in amazement as Miriam slid to the ground as the elderly woman calmly reached over and placed two fingers on her neck. The women waiting for water gasped and took a step back. "Don't worry, dears. It just put her into a light trance, no permanent harm. We'll help her get to her daughter tomorrow. And she'll remember her manners once she's had a nice rest too! Everyone at Heartscape is somebody's daughter!"

Then, to Shoshana she said, "Why don't you take your friend over to that tent? She can have a nice nap. She'll be fresh as a daisy by morning when we're ready to leave. Millie and Jane, can you girls bring the stretcher here and help this nice woman get her friend settled?"

The next day a compressed air-powered bus was parked outside the collection of a half dozen tents off to the side of the empty interstate.

"Why, with the roads as empty as they are, we should be back at the Farm tonight," Jean chirped cheerfully. She was standing behind the same table, handing out circular cakes of compressed granola. A blue enamel pot of tea was boiling on a small camp stove and the women were helping themselves, politely taking turns.

Shoshana and Miriam approached the table, and Jean handed each of them a cake. "It doesn't look like much but it's chock full of grainy goodness."

Miriam hung back a bit, but Jean gestured with the cake, "Now, dear, eat up. You must keep up your strength. We have a long ride ahead of us, but you'll see your daughter before you know it."

"Thanks," Miriam said sheepishly. "I'm sorry I was so rude yesterday; I'm just worried about my daughter. And whatever you did to me gave me the best night's sleep I've had in some time."

"Why, that was just a little energy adjustment. Your system was overheating. Have you been eating a lot of refined sugar lately? And don't worry, dear, if your daughter is with Aurelia and the Crones, I'm sure she's just fine."

As they sat under a tree in the breaking dawn, Miriam looked at Shoshana. "I feel like I'm waking up from a dream. This is the first morning I can remember not having aches, pains, and postnasal drip — and we slept in a tent! That woman, that bus, what's going on?"

A woman holding a clipboard came by and squatted down next to them. "G'morning ladies." She flipped up the cover to what turned out to be a wafer-thin laptop.

"What's that?" Miriam asked as the woman positioned a tiny solar panel to catch the sun.

"Isn't this cool? Cronation Science Cells perfected these portable solar cells to work with all sorts of small appliances. I'm Beatrice, by the way. I just want to get some information from you. You want to be dropped off somewhere along the way? You weren't part of one of the Weather Cells, were you?"

"No, we were at a retreat center in Boca. There was a lot of storm damage, and the director took off," Shosh explained.

"A man?"

The two women nodded.

"Did you take a good look around before you left? Lots of men have been found under beds, locked in bathrooms, that sort of thing. The ones who weren't prepared really took it hard, had the skids just knocked out from under them." Beatrice was booting up the laptop. "Names?"

"Miriam Greenberg and Shoshana Stern."

"Thanks."

"What do you mean, 'men are under beds'? Do you know what's

going on?"

"Sure. The Shift." Beatrice smiled at Shosh and Miriam. "The women of Cronation have been working for decades to help effect a planetary realignment as the Feminine principle comes back into ascendancy. The energetic balance of the earth is in a process of reconfiguration, so that the power that has been concentrated in the male principle is being released and the dormant energy in the Feminine principle that has been recharging for the last several millennia is unfolding." Beatrice explained all this as if it was plain as day.

"I remember something like that from the workshop at Heartscape," Miriam said to Shoshana. "That's the Farm they're talking about. I really thought they were talking, you know, symbolically."

"Nope. The era of the Crone, the wise woman, is here, full tilt boogie," Beatrice assured them, "We are now living in Cronation, the nation of the Crone. Everything from the cellular level to the galactic expanse has been reformed. Each of us in a female body has a role to play and, of course, everyone else along the bio-gender spectrum does too. But it's us older gals that have to step forth now and take the lead." Beatrice winked at the two women.

"Well, maybe that explains your boobs," Shosh said, laughing and nodding toward Miriam's boyish chest. "You need to be all real if you're going to go Crone."

Beatrice looked up quizzically.

"My hair turned gray overnight, and my, ah, surgical enhancement seems to have disappeared," Miriam explained.

"Right. That sometimes happens. During earlier stages of the Shift, we learned that women who had advanced their consciousness could spontaneously recover from prior interventions that no longer matched their higher vibration. Not only emotional healing integrates at new levels, but also manifestations of higher consciousness cause physical changes. I'm betting you must have gained a deeper sense of acceptance of your latent Crone self. You no longer felt the need to adhere to a stereotype of female beauty by being young and bouncy anymore.

"Maybe old Rav Babka did you some good after all, Miriam," Shosh mused.

Miriam looked at Shosh, "You know what? I don't think the Rav had anything to do with it. I think it's our friendship." The two women embraced and tousled each other's gray hair like kids.

"The Shift is a natural evolution," Beatrice continued. "There have been energetic nets of support woven throughout the universe for years. Like for you two: friendships developed that gave you each more than you realized. There is a wave of gratitude that is vibrating through the world, like the secondary seismic waves after an earthquake. Lots of people are going to suddenly realize how grateful they really are for a whole host of things that have escaped their notice.

"Still, lots of men — well and to be fair, women too — just couldn't feel this coming or couldn't open up to it. Must be hard living in a male body, so used to being in charge and thinking you know what's what. When men began to become brittle and unstable on the molecular level, well, it just scared them shitless. They never realized that their sense of things as normal had been held in place by mind programs that are just gone now, obsolete. They could feel fine about waging wars, hoarding corporate profits, mining all the planet's resources, because it was the tail end of the archetypal pattern of the Hero, the rugged individual, the separation of the one from the many. That mindset has been dissolving for ages. Think of it as a vast computer sweep, deleting all the 'cookies,' all the increments of energy holding a particular idea in place. Women too, of course: any areas of our own blind acquiescence to the Warrior/Hero model — finally, poof!" Beatrice snapped her fingers.

"In your case, you must have been a believer in being an assistant to the 'Great Man,' am I right? The hair and the boobs — you've been in denial about who you really are. Welcome to your lightbody." Beatrice proclaimed this cheerfully, as Miriam rolled her eyes. "No, really, you're doing great, not everyone has handled the restoration of their essence so well."

"What do you mean?" asked Shosh.

"Well, women who were more completely male-identified are having extreme MEOWS symptoms — you know, Male End of the World Syndrome. Like the men, they are freaking out — but really, for the most part, as the energy shifted through this most recent wave, anyone who has done the slightest preparation seems pretty much okay. I think the really grounded energy of the Crones and the others who are so clear is helping you hold the new frequency. The shift from metaphor to manifestation! It's really grand, isn't it?"

"Well, I'd like to get to the Farm, if that's okay. My daughter Charity is there," Miriam said. "Shoshana, what about you?"

"If this Farm is the headquarters of this manifestation of the Feminine principle, count me in," she playfully saluted Beatrice and hugged Miriam. "This sounds way better than listening to another lecture by the Rav's lawyers on how to get more alimony."

"Well, great! We'll be leaving in about an hour. Maybe you two can help break down the camp and pack the gear onto the bus," Beatrice suggested. "We're going to have a drum circle before we leave to fix the energy at an optimal level for recovery of the ecosystem. You know, to thank the mycelium who will call up the saprophytic mushrooms to do their thing in digesting and removing toxic waste, to ask the ocean to be as gentle as possible in restoring homeostasis, and to provide the greatest amount of emotional support by singing to activate and charge the energy grid for the population in the area." Miriam and Shoshana looked at each other and grinned.

"Then it's onward! Into the new age, as citizens of Cronation, let the Age of the Wise Woman unfold!"

37

"The waves of love have been flowing outward from our little haven in the heartland, our Heartscape, our home for women weary of a world in which profit replaced people and politicians replaced prophets." So, here I am, back in the barn, listening to Aurelia channel the collective wisdom that has been distilled over years and years of women's witness, into truths for the present moment. "Here we have answered the call to hold the truth of the cycles of our Great Goddess, our dear Mother Earth, our Divine Source, against the lie of endless unchecked growth, the monocultural mania of self-replication, and murder of diversity, of science without a silence that we can enter to hear Her guidance and respectfully seek Her blessing as we make plans to co-create with Her, rather than to exploit Her rapaciously to our own blind ends, without respect.

"Because here, in this land, the land of the loving and the home of the brave, we, the women of Cronation, have gone within ourselves, again and again, together and in solitude, but always, always holding and being held by the community, the compassion of our beloved community, as we seek Her Truth, as we listen for Her guidance, as we untie our knots and give ourselves back to Her again and again. Where we give thanks for Her abundance and Her capacity for renewal...."

We are seated in an enormous circle, and in the center are two empty chairs, placed back to back. As I look around the circle, I see faces shining with joy, wet with tears, serene and grinning.

This ceremony was cooked up by the Crones and the Next Council to mark the culmination of this stage of the work, and to officially unveil the Crone Era, to make public and to celebrate, the declaration of Cronation. It was also to give ourselves a chance to integrate and prepare for the work ahead, when we would, in various groups, leave Cronation to minister to a world that we knew was in a state of disarray and suffering.

"So now, Sistahs and Brothers — for I welcome our Tantra brothers today as well as our dear brother and son to me, Harvey, to our circle — to commence the celebration that will call on Her, our Divine Source and our Eternal Mother, to accelerate and to modulate the flow of Her feminine energy back into the world. We pray for ease for the many who will experience this flow as terrifying. We pledge to hold the frequency of love as the flow dislodges, dismantles, and discombobulates all that is untrue, unjust, and unnecessary. As stories realign for kindness, as illusion is illuminated, may we remember we are all blessed. It is all good. All voices are needed and honored. And now I ask our dear elder, Elsie, to initiate our first ceremony, the Chairs of Reunion."

Clapping and cheering, whistling and stamping, the ululation of the women brought back the memory of the first time I saw Aurelia speak. This time I felt a little dizzy, until I realized I wasn't making a sound. As soon as I began to clap and cheer and let the energy move through me, I felt fine.

Elsie rose to her feet and waited for the crowd to grow quiet again, broadcasting her love just by being still. When finally even the hounds had settled down, Elsie began, in her usual matter-of-fact way. "Actually, Aurelia, if you don't mind, I'd like to ask Rabbi Sarah to tell the story of the Source first. It's such a beautiful story and it will get us all ready and in the right mood."

Rabbi Sarah stepped up and hugged Elsie as we all sighed and hummed. Elsie never failed by her own simple acts to teach us all the deepest lessons of sharing the light, recognizing the gifts in others, all the many ways there are in each moment to show our love and appreciation of one another.

"Thank you, Elsie, I accept this blessing, and I am honored to tell the story that you have told to me so many, many times. Well, here it goes," Sarah began. "The Divine Creative Source came upon the idea of calling human beings into existence. Some say Source was lonely and wanted more company; some say the evolutionary moment of self-reflection was at hand and that humans developed as the organs of self-awareness of the Source. In any case, humans would then be able to reflect back the infinite possibility contained in the Source. Now, some say the angels lobbied against this idea, knowing that even without a body, beings couldn't always be counted on to perform as expected; they had learned this from one of their own, Lucifer. The angel Raphael was forceful as he made the point that being ensconced in bodies would be a great and messy distraction from the task of praising creation. How could these 'humans' concentrate on praising Source, when they had bodies complete with organs of pleasure and reproduction, the need to eat and eliminate waste?"

Elsie laughed at this point. "Folks like to blame it on poor Lucifer, but it's the Source who wants more out of existence than all praise all the time from all creation, although She does love it when we sing and such!"

"That's right," Sarah continued. "So the angel Raphael said, 'let's divide them in two so they have to find each other and learn from each other to complete themselves —and let's send them out that way. That will give them something to do.'

Then Source was heard to say something like, 'I know perfection perfectly well and I'm a little tired of being praised for it. I long to explore imperfection.' She liked Raphael's idea. She recognized that perfect replicas of Source would be lonely in their wholeness, having no motivation to connect with each other. Searching for their other half would be fun to watch.

"And so, right before we are born, the angel Raphael touches each one of us, right here," Sarah gently touched her upper lip, "above the lip and to make us forget our Divine origin. Source has given us the gift of finding our own way to Her via the path of imperfection and the treasure hunt of discovering completion together with one another!"

More applause and laughter as the women touched their mouths and looked and commented on the uniqueness of the tiny furrow each of us has above our lips. We laughed and shouted and clapped our hands. Many of us had known imperfection, failure, and other negative attributions to be just a code word for 'woman.' A part of me wondered what men would make of this story — but I realized they had actually written it themselves, casting all things feminine into the shadows. And of course, a man could always grow a mustache to cover up the furrow of forgetfulness and pretend it wasn't there.

"And gracious sakes! We have forgotten plenty!" Elsie exclaimed, as she stood thanking Sarah and hugging her. "Thank you, dear. Now, these chairs, back to back, symbolize a state of unknowing, with the possibility of reconciliation, a kind of completion. For this ceremony, we sit back to back and each one states her truth, facing away from the other. Then the group, beloved community, hears and witnesses both of us in our individual and incomplete truth; as we continue to take turns speaking until we come into a shared vibration and discover what actions are needed. As we listen with open hearts to the one story and then listen to that of another, we discover how to connect the strands of our truths together. We allow a vow to arise that we both can take together. As we do this, the community weaves a net of light, love, truth, and support around us through the energy of their witness. Once we feel ready, we turn the chairs to face one another and say our vows with the community to witness them and hold us in them. Now I'd like to ask Aurelia to continue."

"Thank you, Elsie. Many of you have been performing your own reconciliations in these past days, and many of you have helped one another to reconcile with a person who has passed on by acting as a surrogate. Blessings on all of you for these gifts that strengthen our community. Today, our sister Charity Greenberg, whom some of you know as Kali, and who soon will take yet another name, will be acting on behalf of the Shift by engaging in a public enactment of this rite with her mother, Miriam, who has recently rejoined our community. For now we will return to her name given at birth, Charity, as she is in a profound transition with her mother."

Charity/Kali was seated next to me, and I squeezed her hand as she got up. She and Miriam came forward and took the seats.

"Now Charity and Miriam, daughter and mother, have chosen to be our actors today because they embody the one exact configuration that represents what needs healing in our world." Aurelia slowly circled the chairs, gazing at all of us in the larger circle, intensifying the energy. Beyond the circle, there were Tantra guys seated in the corners of the barn, enclosing the circle in a square. They began softly playing marimbas, hand drums, and flutes. Each corner had two musicians, one guy doing slow, tai chi-like movements and another one making marks on a sheet of paper affixed to the wall. The four young men in each corner, all wearing a color to mark one of the four directions, moved in beautiful synchronicity.

"I speak my truth: I was born Charity Greenberg, to parents of wealth and privilege. I could not accept and appreciate those gifts because underneath them was a lie." The music rose a bit in volume as if to underscore her words but the drum held a slow, steady rhythm, like a heartbeat.

Then Miriam spoke: "I speak my truth: I was born Miriam Weiss, the child of immigrants, who came to this country to flee persecution. I was never told the details of their story, but I sometimes heard my mother crying at night."

Charity spoke again: "I took the name Kali because she is the Dark Mother who wields the Sword of Truth that cuts through lies." The Tantra musicians answered with some sharp tones on the flutes and the ones drawing created varied images of Kali, tongue lolling, wearing her skirt of skulls.

Miriam: "I continued to look to men for a strong father figure to keep me safe from the violence in the world. I was taught that everyone wanted to kill the Jews." Miriam's voice caught on these words, and I saw Kali's lips press in a thin hard line.

Charity: "I felt abandoned by you." The drumbeats slowed.

Miriam: "I did abandon you when I searched for God in the form of a man, instead of taking care of you." The drumbeat quickened and the flutes played a soft counterpoint, a yearning sad sound.

I saw Kali's shoulders drop, and then she buried her head in her cupped hands. She was sobbing, and I wondered if we would be able to hold the space for her without anyone rushing in to offer comfort. The music seemed to provide the support all of us needed to keep breathing.

Slowly Kali stood and turned her chair to face Miriam's back. She sat down and spoke in a strong voice: "I would like to return to you, Mother."

Miriam half stood and turned her chair: "I am here to receive you, my child." The room was silent as Miriam whispered the words.

The two sat facing one another until one thin note from the flute began to play music of a different tempo. Elsie stood and placed a hand on each of their heads. They were sitting, knees touching. Now Rabbi Sarah joined them and recited:

"So today, Charity, daughter of Miriam, daughter of Kali, let us acknowledge the next era and the next name the Divine has called out for you: Ashera, the sacred tree of the sacred grove of ages past. And Miriam, let us witness that your name means 'water,' the loving water of nourishment that will replenish the sacred in Ashera and in the world."

Elsie lifted her hands and stepped back, and mother and daughter — Mother and Daughter — embraced on behalf of all mothers and all children everywhere and for all times. The music grew louder and more intense, the tempo increased, and soon the women in the circle began a spontaneous snake dance around the room, undulating around Miriam and Ashera, around the musicians and movers and artists, dancing their way outside into the field next to the barn where the next rite was to take place.

Of course, Rae and her helpers had set up beautiful buffet tables that would be filled with food once the rituals were completed. O'Malley would have appreciated how the Crones always knew when to come down to earth for a hearty bite to eat.

Once we reconstituted the circle in the field outside, where snow had melted and a soft breeze blew, Aurelia spoke, "Thank you, Ashera. Thank you, Miriam. I feel lighter already. How about you all? We roared back our delight. "We have a bit more to do before we complete our celebration with the wonderful food prepared by Rae and Gina and their helpers is presented."

Miriam and Ashera were arm in arm. I could see a resemblance now between them that I hadn't seen before. Their two curly heads — one light, one dark — and an exuberant playfulness that had been frozen in them both, was now freed.

"Let's settle ourselves here on the ground," Aurelia proposed.

Colored blankets and quilts defined the circle, and we all settled down and got comfortable. Diva swooped down as raven and transformed into her girl self next to Aurelia, like a happy child.

"Elsie? Will you start us off with the next story?"

"Surely, dear. Well, some say that the Divine Source, in order to get to know Herself fully, She needed to divide Her oneness into parts; so one part could see the other and learn more, especially if She was to keep up with and understand the high jinks of these clever human beings She had made. So, separating into king and queen, male and female, moon and sun, light and dark, Source did all this to learn about the experience she had offered to these human folks."

"Did the angels object to this?" Diva interjected?

"Oh, my! Yes, they did! This time all the angels protested; they made a terrible fuss! But, no matter, Source was determined to learn. What wasn't apparent at first was that these humans had the same capacity as Source to manifest appearance and reality, and Source couldn't control their thoughts."

"Just like the angels predicted!" Diva affirmed.

"That's right! Well, the humans were intrigued by this male-female, mother-father thing and the differences they could see and they thought about it a lot. After all, they saw the moon and the sun, the sky and the earth, not to mention all the animals. But they discovered something else. They discovered that when they came together, loneliness went away and so did pain.

"Now the King part of Source got angry because He felt very lonely. His Queen was off all fascinated with the humans, they were all fascinated with one another, and He was, well — He just felt left out. I think we all know how that feels! 'Isn't that why You created these pesky things, to stop this terrible loneliness?' He grumped to the Queen.

"But as I said, She was fascinated, because She saw that when the humans got together She felt also something else. Not loneliness at all but joy, awe, and reverence for Her King, for Herself, for all They could together evoke into being. In that split-second She understood the essence of transformation, the alternation of coming together and separating; it wasn't a once and for all thing in either state! It was a constant process. She was very excited and ran to tell the King, because She knew He was unhappy with the present arrangement. But when She reached Him, She found He had built a fortress and locked Himself in the turret of the uppermost tower. And he had huge gleaming weapons he had conjured trained on the humans.

"'Let them abandon me! Those ungrateful pests,'" He roared.

"The Queen screamed, 'Stop! They aren't leaving us forever! They are just trying to learn about transformation!'

"'Transformation? I'll teach them about transformation!' He thundered back. And with that, He opened fire full force, sending wave after wave of his anger, pain, and hopelessness into the humans."

We all gasped, even the Tantra guys stopped playing. Elsie let the silence hang for a bit.

"But," she smiled. "The Queen threw Herself in front of the humans who at that moment were sleeping, cradled in each other's arms. She absorbed so much of the blow that She was grievously hurt. Still, she chose her children and crept away to join them.

"'I'll be back,' She cried, 'When you figure out what you've done, you silly King.' And so our dear Queen, our Mother, has been recuperating, resting, ever since."

"But what about the humans?" Diva asked.

"The energy that the King propelled into them filled their dreams and has lasted a long, long time. Until now. When enough of us awakened to see we still have the power that was given to us originally. We never lost the power to create our dreams, to create the world, to heal the King in ourselves and in the world, and let Him reunite with his Queen and then get some rest."

At this point Mattie and Harvey, both dressed in white, came walking toward the circle from the barn. Harvey was carrying the bundle that held the scant remains of Yang. The Tantra guys set up two cushions in the circle facing each other and carried a nest-like structure of twigs and brush and placed it in the center between the two cushions. Harvey and Mattie took their places on the cushions and the guys resumed the music.

After a bit, Harvey got up and circled the nest-like pyre three times, in a clock-wise direction.

"Thanks to the father, the king, to all fathers and all kings, who taught us so much about making and doing. For all they created and all the good in what they did, we say, 'Thank you.'" All of us repeated: "Thank you." "And in their quest for perfection, we call them to account for their failure to give full measure of respect to the mothers and the queens and, especially, to the Crones who have taught us that the great value of imperfection is that it opens us to one another, reminds us of our incompleteness and offers us a way to be whole by coming together in community."

Harvey sat down and Mattie rose. She was wearing a white tee shirt with a pale pink lotus flower silk screened on the front and a long white flowing skirt. I'd never seen her looking so, well, queenly and so beautiful. She walked around the nest of twigs in the opposite direction, counter-clockwise.

"To all our fathers and to all our mothers, we dedicate ourselves to balancing and re-balancing the active and receptive, the doing and the being, the work and the play in joy, awe, and reverence. We ask the blessing and witness of this community, of our elders, of our sisters, our brothers, our friends. We ask the blessings of the birds, animals, the sky and the earth, the galaxies and all that exists that we can scarcely imagine. And we offer ourselves in service to the Hieros Gamos, the sacred marriage of all opposites, with our gratitude."

Harvey rose again, was handed a small torch by one of the musicians, stepped forward and lit the pyre. "Goodbye for now, Yang, I'll never forget you."

The flames leaped, the twigs crackled, and the Tantra guys stepped up the music.

We all sighed as Harvey and Mattie embraced. The Hieros Gamos was complete; signifying a new era of peace, harmony and abundance had begun. The women began to sing, clap, and dance, while I went over to the tables to help Rae serve the food.

ACKNOWLEDGEMENTS

The title of the book came when a dear friend asked, when I turned forty, and was hardly thinking of such things, "How is your Cronation coming along?" Becoming a Crone, a wise older woman, is a vocation that many more women are choosing to embrace these days, thank Goddess. Whether a Crone in age or in wisdom alone, there are so many women who have added to and supported this book, more than can be named. First and foremost, to my ancestors, relatives, many dear women friends and authors who now reside on the other side of the veil sending guidance and wisdom, I am grateful for your help. I especially honor Laurie Neustadt, Ruth Wardlaw, Margaret Naumburg and Florence Cane.

My deep gratitude goes to Wendy Lauter, with whom I have played on a regular basis for many years in the seams between the worlds to glean meaning to understand how our inner and outer worlds connect. To Karla Rindal, whose eagle eye edited for grammar and flow but also for story. Her reflection of pleasure in reading the story gave it the midwife's support to be born, to begin that last push, after what seemed an endless time incubating.

Thanks to the talented professionals and pioneers in the new world of publishing, Amy Schneider and Dave Reeser, I have learned about the exciting and creative alternatives to traditional publishing. Thanks to proofreader extraordinaire Kimberly Gooden, for being one of the professionals that make this world possible. And thanks to Shea Cadrin for designing and creating the Cronation website and graphic presence so that we have a place to create our virtual Crone community.

My deep love flows to my daughter, Adina Allen, mother of Remez, and Rabbi of the new era and her partner in life and creative endeavors, Jeff Kasowitz, son-in-law to me and father of Remez. They are doing the work to bring a world of joy and celebration into being right now. And, finally to my partner in life and all things, John Allen, who perpetually wrestles with Yang while acknowledging the power of the Feminine as he holds the space for all the many things a man can be.

www.ingramcontent.com/pod-product-compliance
Lightning Source LLC
Chambersburg PA
CBHW060242030726

47493CB00024B/1533